SHE'S POSITIVE
BY
DELORES FOSSEN

AND

AN UNEXPECTED CLUE
BY
ELLE JAMES

**A terrible secret sparks two
undeniable passions…**

Hot-shot hostage negotiator Colin never expected to
have to work with his ex, Danielle, again or to realise
that he still wanted her…whilst pregnant Ava never
thought she'd see gorgeous Ben again after he
was presumed dead!

More shocking surprises are revealed as the
Kenner County Crime Unit mini-series continues…

KENNER COUNTY CRIME UNIT:

*A dangerous connection hidden in Colorado binds
them together, but could the desire they share
be even more powerful?*

SHE'S POSITIVE

BY
DELORES FOSSEN

All the characters in this book have no existence outside the imagination of
the author, and have no relation whatsoever to anyone bearing the same name
or names. They are not even distantly inspired by any individual known or
unknown to the author, and all the incidents are pure invention.

First published in Great Britain 2010
Harlequin Mills & Boon Limited,
Eton House, 18-24 Paradise Road, Richmond, Surrey TW9 1SR

© Harlequin Books SA 2009

Special thanks and acknowledgement to Delores Fossen for her contribution
to the Kenner County Crime Unit mini-series.

ISBN: 978 0 263 88270 4

46-1110

Harlequin Mills & Boon policy is to use papers that are natural, renewable
and recyclable products and made from wood grown in sustainable forests.
The logging and manufacturing processes conform to the legal environmental
regulations of the country of origin.

Printed and bound in Spain
by Litografia Rosés S.A., Barcelona

Imagine a family tree that includes Texas cowboys, Choctaw and Cherokee Indians, a Louisiana pirate and a Scottish rebel who battled side by side with William Wallace. With ancestors like that, it's easy to understand why Texas author and former air force captain **Delores Fossen** feels as if she were genetically predisposed to writing romances. Along the way to fulfilling her DNA destiny, Delores married an air force top gun who just happens to be of Viking descent. With all those romantic bases covered, she doesn't have to look too far for inspiration.

To all the wonderful folks at the Hudspeth Center.

Chapter One

"The hostage is Luke Vaughn, a three-year-old boy," Colin Forester heard the tech explain.

Colin didn't react. Not on the outside anyway. Inside, however, there was a firestorm of emotions. Colin had been an FBI hostage negotiator for seven years, and he'd seen the worst of the worst.

A kid hostage was the worst.

This one was hardly more than a baby. And the boy was in big trouble because this wasn't an ordinary hostage situation.

According to the preliminary info Colin had gotten from his director at the Durango FBI office, the hostage taker wasn't the usual perp for this sort of crime. He was a professional hit man. That's the reason Colin had left Durango as soon as he got word of the kidnapping, so he could get to Kenner City and try to put a stop to this.

"Tell me about the hit man," Colin said to Rusty Cepeda, the young Kenner County Crime Unit lab tech who was driving him to the estate. Rusty was obviously a rookie tech since he wasn't on scene but rather playing chauffeur to Colin.

"His name is Boyd Perkins. Age forty-one. His rap sheet goes back nearly two decades, and he works for Nicky Wayne, a Vegas crime boss."

So, not just a hit man but a career criminal.

Rusty continued to maneuver the four-wheel drive up the rain-slicked steep mountain road toward the Vaughn estate where the child was being held. It was a fifteen-minute trek from Kenner City to the estate, Rusty had told Colin when he'd picked him up in town. Colin wanted to use every second of that time to learn whatever he could about the persons involved.

"Boyd Perkins," Colin repeated under his breath. When he made contact with him, he would call him by his first name. He'd try to establish a rapport while he diffused a situation that could turn deadly. "And Boyd's ties to the Wayne crime family have been verified?"

"Oh, yeah," Rusty confirmed. "And I guess you heard Boyd murdered an FBI agent?"

"I heard." Colin had to take a deep breath. That alone made him want to take Boyd down, but arresting him for murder would have to wait. "Go over the details of the kidnapping again." And Colin shut out the summer wind and the rain that were assaulting the vehicle. He shut out everything so he could focus.

"About ten hours ago, the boy's father, Griffin Vaughn, reported that his son had been taken hostage inside the estate. The sheriff then called the Kenner County Crime Unit and the FBI, and we all hurried out to the scene. The estate has a gate, and it was locked up tight. Boyd's controlling the gate from the inside. One of the FBI agents, Tom Ryan, was able to make phone contact with Boyd, but Boyd wouldn't negotiate."

Not yet anyway. Colin would have to change the hit man's mind. "What about demands? Has Boyd made any?"

"Only that he wants us to move away from the house. We figured you could help with getting him to tell us what he's after."

It was near the top of the list, and then Colin could start to work on a compromise. "Did Boyd say if the child was okay?"

"He says he is. But Boyd warned us if Luke's parents and the officers didn't stay far away from the place, the boy would pay the consequences."

That clenched Colin's gut into a tight knot. The threat of violence. God knew how the kid was reacting to that. He didn't know much about three-year-olds, but Luke probably realized he was in danger.

The Jeep crawled up the last leg of the road, and Colin spotted the house next to a lake that reflected the iron-gray sky. The place deserved to be labeled an estate because it sprawled out in front of them, seemingly taking up most of the mountain top. It'd be a bear to secure a place that size, but on the upside, the lake and the rugged terrain surrounding it might make it impossible for Boyd to escape.

"Any idea where Boyd's holding the hostage?" Colin asked.

"We're not sure, but he seems to be using the security system to monitor what we're doing, and that system has cameras. Lots of them. He knows when we get too close to the fence, for instance. That's why we set up operations on the east side of the property. The owner, Griffin Vaughn, said that's a blind spot for surveillance. We've been bringing in the team that way so Boyd won't know we're putting agents in place in case we have to rush in for a rescue."

A rescue. That was being optimistic. Because if it came down to the point where agents had to storm the house, Luke Vaughn's chances of survival were slim.

"I heard you saved a kid over in Mesa Ridge about a year ago," Rusty commented.

Colin settled for a "Yeah." But that hadn't been one of his success stories. Yes, he'd gotten the child out of the domestic violence situation. But he'd lost an adult hostage in a murder-suicide. Colin hadn't been able to talk the twenty-eight-year-old man out of putting a bullet in the child's mother.

He always remembered the failures.

Those were the ones that ate away at him and made him want to work ten times harder so that it wouldn't happen again.

Rusty stopped about thirty yards from the estate fence and right at the edge of the activity. Even though everyone was dressed in rain gear, Colin spotted two fellow FBI agents and a man with a Kenner City sheriff's hat. In addition, there were two Kenner County Crime Unit members carrying field kits.

Rusty opened the driver's-side door but then turned and snared Colin's gaze. "You'll get this boy out of there?"

"I will." With that promise he wasn't sure he could keep, Colin threw open his own door. The rain came right at him, like razors whipping through the air.

"Colin?" someone called out.

Colin recognized the man walking toward him. Tom Ryan, FBI, and the commander for this particular crime scene. The lanky, somber-faced agent made his way to Colin, and they shook hands. "Damn glad you're here."

Colin nodded. "What's the latest situation report?"

"Hell in a hand basket probably isn't what I'd put in an official statement, but things aren't good. There are no injuries, but the kid's three years old, Colin."

"Yes, I heard." And Colin couldn't let the emotion in Tom's voice get to him. *Focus. Shut out everything but the job.* Because emotion wasn't worth spit right now. The job, his training, his experience—those were the things that would free little Luke.

"My wife, Callie, is over there with Luke's parents. She's trying to keep them calm." Tom whipped his thumb toward the woman carrying a field kit. She had dripping wet blond hair and was looking around on the ground. Trailing behind her, with their gazes fixed on the estate, were no doubt the Vaughns. "Callie's the head forensic scientist at the crime unit, and she's looking for any trace evidence so we can try to verify that Perkins is working alone." He paused. "We're supposed to be on a romantic getaway," he added in a mumble.

Tough timing, but Colin wanted all of them there. Anything at this point could be valuable in dealing with Boyd Perkins, and maybe Callie or her team would find something that would help him with this negotiation.

Rusty left them to join two others who were hovered under umbrellas outside a police cruiser and a black four-door FBI standard-issue vehicle.

Tom led Colin toward an older-model white van. "We've set up a command post in here out of Boyd's line of sight, barely. We wanted to get as close as possible in case he tried to escape through the front," the agent explained. "Boyd's using a prepaid cell phone to communicate. No way to trace it. And so far he's refused to answer the house phones."

The prepaid cell phone could indicate this was premeditated, but then a man with Boyd's record probably used phones like that all the time. "You said we could see the front, but what about other escape routes?"

"All covered, and that's no easy task. We have an agent at the back of the estate, but there are miles of tunnels beneath this place. Boyd has the tunnel entrances on his end blocked off so we can't get to him that way. But I've put barricades at the end of each one, so he can't use them for escape. And Boyd knows that."

Good. Colin didn't want the man to have any options other than dealing with him. The job started now. And Colin took a deep breath, cleared his mind and stepped up into the van.

His clear mind suddenly got very cloudy.

Right there in front of him perched on the dull brown leather van seat was the last person on earth he wanted to see right now.

"Colin," she said as if she'd been expecting him.

Well, he sure as hell hadn't been expecting her. "Danielle," he greeted once he got his teeth unclenched.

"You two know each other?" Tom asked, apparently not realizing that was the mother of all loaded questions.

"Oh, we know each other," Colin snarled. "Danielle is my ex-wife. Or at least she will be…" He checked the date on his watch. Not that he needed to. It was for show. He knew exactly when the divorce would be final. "In three more days." He stared at her. "What are you doing here, Danielle?"

She spared him a glance with those cool green eyes. Eyes the color of an Irish four-leaf clover, he used to say, adding that she was his lucky charm. But that was the old days. He wasn't feeling nearly as generous with the sappy compliments since she'd walked out on him three months earlier.

"Callie and I are old college roommates," Danielle volunteered. "She thought it'd be good to have a child psychologist on the scene, so she called and asked me to come out and help." Danielle held out her hands, palms up. "And here I am. I take it you're the negotiator they called in."

There went the clenched teeth again. "They wanted the best." Colin made sure he sounded as cocky as he could.

Since she was seated across from a narrow table that held phones and other communication equipment, Colin plopped down next to her, bumping his hip against hers to nudge her over. It wasn't the brightest idea he'd ever had. Danielle and he might want to claw out each other's eyes, but his body still reacted to her. Probably always would. Because even though their marriage had been a disaster, the sex had been the best ever.

His body obviously wasn't going to let him forget that.

The hip-to-hip contact earned him a little glare, but Danielle didn't budge. Colin gave her another nudge. This time, a verbal one. "I don't need a child psychologist. I can handle this myself. And you'd only be in the way."

Those green eyes suddenly weren't so cool. She mumbled something under her breath and shoved some wet wisps of hair from her face. Then he noticed her left hand.

No wedding or engagement ring.

Just the faint imprint where they'd once been.

Colin kept his own left hand hidden away. No need for her to see that he hadn't gotten around to taking off his ring yet. But he would now. He slipped it off and put it in his pocket.

He tossed her another stony glance. Got one from her in return. The glances turned to glares, and they sat there, staring at each other.

The rain had obviously gotten to her mop of shoulder-length caramel-brown curls. Not in an unattractive way, either. Much to his disgust. She looked as if she'd just stepped from a warm shower. Her face was all dewy, and her cheeks were flushed with color. She looked healthy and content and probably hadn't lost a minute of sleep over their breakup.

"Any time you guys are ready, I'd like to get started," Tom said. He was standing outside the van volleying glances at both of them. And probably questioning if they were real professionals. They certainly weren't acting like it, and that was Colin's cue to get to work. Later, after he'd established contact, he'd figure out a way to give the boot to his soon-to-be ex-wife, and she could take her dewy fresh look and get the heck out of there.

"Do we have any long-range eavesdropping equipment so we can monitor what Boyd's doing?" Colin asked Tom.

"Equipment's on the way. Should be here any time now. We've requested an infrared thermal scanner, too."

Good. Because they'd need both. The estate was a big place, and they'd have to pinpoint Boyd and Luke's exact location if the worst happened and negotiations didn't work. Then, they might have no choice but to move in.

Colin picked up the cell phone from the table and

looked at what was written on the manila notepad. "Is that Boyd's number?"

Tom nodded. "I've tried to keep him talking, but he always hangs up."

Well, Colin would see if he could fix that. "Make sure the parents stay at a distance. I don't want them in on this conversation." He turned on the recorder, punched in the numbers and put the phone on speaker to free his hands so he could take notes and start creating the hostage taker's profile.

The first ring seemed to take several minutes. Waiting was the hardest part. Colin slowed his breathing to keep himself calm. Took another deep breath.

Boyd Perkins answered on the fourth ring.

"Boyd?" Colin didn't wait for the man to confirm it was him. He also jotted down the start time of the call. "I'm Special Agent Colin Forester."

"What do you want?" Boyd growled. But it wasn't overly emotional. More the tone of a man who'd been inconvenienced than one who was angry.

"I just want to talk. And I want to know how Luke's doing."

"The kid's fine. *For now.*"

Colin wasn't immune to that threat, but he eased it aside. "Good. That's good, Boyd. Now, I need to know how we can keep it that way. You must have demands, but so far you haven't let anybody know what those are."

"I want time to finish up some things in here."

"Time?" Luke repeated. That sent an uneasy feeling through him. "For what?"

"Nothing to do with the kid," Boyd readily answered. "I'm looking for something. When I find it, I'll let you know. But for now, I want all you badges to back off and go back down the mountain."

"We have backed off." What they couldn't do, however, was leave the area. "But Luke's parents are worried about him, and I'm sure Luke misses them. He's a good kid and has no part in this. Why don't you let him go and then we can talk about giving you that time you want?"

Boyd made a sarcastic grunt. "If I let him go, you'll just storm in here and kill me. Not gonna happen. As soon as I find what I'm looking for, I'll get back to you."

"Wait," Colin said, since it sounded as if Boyd were about to hang up. "I want to talk to Luke. I want to make sure he's okay. Before you say no, think about it this way. We *badges* will be a lot more cooperative if we know the boy hasn't been harmed."

Silence.

The moments crawled by.

Oh, yeah. Waiting was the hardest part.

"I'll get back to you on that, too," Boyd snapped, and he hung up.

Colin turned off the recorder, jotted down the end time of the call. Just a little under two minutes. It was a start, even though he doubted Boyd would call back any time soon.

"Any idea what Boyd's looking for?" Colin asked Tom.

"We think he's after fifty million dollars. The previous owner might have hidden the money in the estate or in those tunnels I told you about."

Fifty million? Whoa. So, this was a crime of greed, not passion. In some ways that made it easier. Boyd likely wouldn't harm Luke because the child was the very thing that would give him the time to search for all that money. But Colin had to wonder—what would happen if Boyd got his hands on the cash? That, however, was an issue for later.

First, he had to settle another concern before it went any further.

He turned to Danielle. "This isn't going to work," he let her know.

Her chin came up. "I can help."

Maybe she could. She was a darn good psychologist, but Colin couldn't do his job if he had to sit side by side with her. Too bad he couldn't just tell her that, but that would mean admitting that she'd slashed his heart to bits. No way did he want her to know that. Better to let her believe that the only thing left between them was the bitterness.

And not this ridiculous attraction.

"Danielle," he started. It was his negotiator's voice. Calm, friendly, but with just a hint of detachment. "This standoff could go on for days. Weeks, even. You don't want to be here with me for that length of time, do you?"

She opened her mouth. Closed it. Repeated the process, adding a defeated sigh, before she shook her head and prepared to exit the van. "I need to talk to Callie."

Colin scowled. She was giving up with hardly a fight. Yep, she didn't want to be there. It was really over between them.

He gave a crisp nod and was about to tell Tom to locate another psychologist, but the phone interrupted him. On the caller ID screen, he saw that it was Boyd.

"Boyd," Colin answered, turning the recorder back

on. "You'll let me speak to Luke." He tried not to make it sound like a question.

Boyd didn't answer. There was a shuffle of movement on the other end of the line. Colin listened, trying to make sense of every sound. After several seconds, Colin realized the person now on the phone had a different breathing pattern than Boyd's.

"Luke?" Colin said. "Are you there, buddy?"

"I'm here," the boy answered.

God, he sounded so little.

And scared.

Colin's pen snapped under the pressure of his grip, and he grabbed another so he'd be ready to write. "Luke, are you okay?"

"I guess. But I wanta see my daddy and my mom. *Please.*"

Danielle pressed her fingertips to her lips, and Colin saw her blink back tears. He'd never seen her break on the job. *Never.* But the little boy's plea would have gotten to anyone.

Well, anyone except Boyd.

There were more muffled sounds, and Boyd returned to the line. "He's still whimpering," Boyd complained.

"I'll talk to him," Colin insisted. "I'll calm him down."

"No. You're done talking to him. I want somebody else. Somebody that knows how to handle kids, and I don't mean his parents. Don't want to talk to them. Put Dr. Danielle Connolly on the phone."

Colin's heart went to his knees. Apparently so did Danielle's. She froze, and her eyes widened.

"Dr. Connolly," Colin repeated. "What makes you think she's here?"

But Boyd ignored that. "Dr. Connolly?" Boyd said in a much louder voice. "I know you're in that white van. Get on the phone now."

Danielle stared at Colin. Waiting. Her eyes pleaded with him to do something. And since he had no choice, he gave her the nod to go ahead.

"I'm here, Boyd," Danielle immediately said. "How can I help?"

"You can calm down this kid for me, that's what you can do. You can make him understand that his whining is making me crazy."

"Of course, I'll talk to him. Please put him on the line." Danielle swallowed hard, and the waiting began again.

Colin mentally groaned and cursed a blue streak.

This shouldn't be happening. They were in a blind spot. Boyd shouldn't be able to see them or monitor what they were doing, though Tom had said *barely*.

His gaze fired toward Tom. "How did he know she was here?" Colin mouthed.

Tom shook his head, grabbed a pair of binoculars and aimed them at the estate. After several moments, he shook his head again. "Boyd hasn't reangled the security camera."

"What about the police scanner?" Colin whispered. "Did anyone say a thing about her coming here?"

Another shake of his head. "She drove straight up without going into town. No one other than those of us on the scene should have known that she'd arrived."

Oh, hell.

Not good. Because either Boyd had found a way around the blind spot, or they had a leak, and someone was a traitor.

Chapter Two

Danielle was aware of the possible security breach, also aware that a leak could compromise everything, but all of those concerns faded when she heard Luke's voice.

"I don't like doctors," he told her. It wasn't said in a bossy way. The boy was frightened.

"Don't worry. I'm not that kind of doctor. I don't give shots."

"Good. 'Cause I don't like shots, neither."

Colin was whispering something to Tom, but Danielle shut that out. "What do you like, Luke? Do you like to watch TV?"

"Yeah. I like Spider-Man, too."

Danielle smiled in spite of the situation. "Why is he your favorite?"

"He kinda gets to fly. That'd be fun. I could fly up high with the birds and not fall."

Danielle was relieved that he seemed to be relaxing a bit. "I'll bet it would be fun. Do you play video games, too?"

"Sure. I got lots of 'em, but the funnest is Safari Explorer. I play with my daddy." He paused. "Can my daddy come and get me?"

"Soon," she assured him. She heard the tremble in his voice and knew she had to pull him away from that reaction. Judging from Boyd's comments, the tone could set him off. Danielle wanted them both calm. "Luke, have you found the lost baby giraffe in Safari Explorer?"

"Not yet. The purple hippos knock my boat over."

She mentally went through the levels of the game. "Ah, there's a trick to that. Want me to tell you what it is?" Danielle glanced out of the corner of her eye. Colin was staring at her now.

"Yes, please," Luke said. She'd found her connection, and now she had to make the most of it.

"How about I just give you a hint about how to get to the baby giraffe? That way, it'll still be your game, and I won't really be helping you too much."

"Okay."

The hopeful little voice cut her to the bone. She wanted to get him out of there. But she couldn't. Creating a distraction and keeping the situation calm was the only thing she could do right now. "Here's the hint, Luke. When you cross the river, don't go in a straight line. Do you know what that means, not to go in a straight line?"

"Sure, I do. I'm smart, and I can do it. This time, I bet I get away from those hippos."

"I'll bet you do, too. You'll get to the other side, and you'll be one step closer to finding the baby giraffe." She took a moment and thought out her next move. "Luke, why don't you put Mr. Perkins back on the phone?"

That earned her a raised eyebrow from Colin. "What are you doing?" he mouthed.

"What I need to do," she mouthed back.

Oh, yes. There it was. The inevitable tension. When

Callie had called her and asked her to come to the Vaughn estate, Danielle hadn't known that Colin would be there. But if she had, it still wouldn't have stopped her. She wanted to help this child, even if she had to go through the emotional roadblock that Colin would create.

Besides, she needed to talk to Colin.

At least Danielle thought she did. She was in her element talking to Luke, but her soon-to-be ex was a different story. Communication had never been their strong suit. Ironic, considering their jobs both hinged on excellent verbal interaction.

"Yeah?" Boyd snapped when he came back on the line.

"I need a favor," Danielle calmly explained. "This is something that'll help all of us, you especially. A three-year-old child gets bored easily, and if Luke's bored, he'll keep thinking about what's going on. He'll keep *whining*." She nearly choked on the word. It wasn't whining when a child was being held hostage. It was a natural human reaction.

"So how do I keep him from not being bored?" Boyd wanted to know.

"Let Luke play his video games. No matter where you are in the house, the system shouldn't be that hard for you to set up. In fact, he'll probably be able to help you with that because Luke's very smart." She needed to remind this monster that he was dealing with a precious life. "While you're at it, give him some books, crayons—"

"And that'll keep him quiet?"

Danielle decided to push a little. "Well, the only sure way to keep him quiet is to release him so he can be with his family."

"You're wasting your breath, Doc."

Fine. That was Colin's area anyway. She'd leave that to him. "Just please give Luke the activities to do. And make sure he's eating right. Not too many sweets, or it might make him hyper or irritable. Do you have a good supply of food at the estate? If not, we can have some brought in—"

"I'll give the kid his video games. That's all you need to be concerned with."

"How do you know me?" Danielle asked before he could end the call. "Have we met before?"

Boyd laughed. Not from humor, though. It seemed as if he was taunting her. And then he hung up.

Colin reached over, turned off the recorder and made some notes. "I think he has a visual on the van. Maybe some hidden camera that the owner didn't know about." He seemed to be talking to himself. "If he saw us get inside here, he could have used a laptop to do a computer search."

Yes, but that wouldn't explain how he knew her name so he could do such a search. And that only added to all the other questions and concerns.

Danielle tried to control her reaction. She tried to tamp down her breathing and her racing heart. But she failed. Her breath shattered, and she got up, despite the sudden dizzy spell. She had to get out of there. She couldn't come unglued, not in front of Colin.

"Are you…okay?" Colin asked.

"Fine," she lied.

Danielle knew she couldn't go far in case Boyd called right back, but she maneuvered herself around Colin. No easy task in the converted van. She had to squeeze herself between him and the table while she was hunkered down so her head wouldn't hit the ceiling.

It put them face-to-face.

So close, she took in his scent. The clean smell of the rain. His musky aftershave. The wet leather of his black jacket and Lucchese boots. Unfortunately, even with the slight scowl he was sporting, Colin was as hot as ever. He had a face that women noticed, with those classic good looks, midnight-black hair and sizzling blue eyes.

Well, *she* noticed anyway.

Always had. For better or worse. Colin Forester knew how to make her body beg. But at thirty-eight she was old enough to know that she needed more than great sex. She needed a husband. A family. And while Colin was a pro at his job and in the bedroom, they hadn't seen eye to eye in other facets of their lives.

And that was the very reason Danielle quickly moved away from him.

That scent, those eyes, could pull her back in, and she couldn't go there. He obviously didn't want to do that, either.

The rain had turned to a light mist so Danielle didn't bother getting an umbrella. Besides, she was already damp from the earlier trek from her car to the van. She stepped onto the soggy ground, the mud squeezing over her heels—again. She'd made the mistake of dressing for work in a skirt suit, but this obviously wasn't a normal work situation.

That was true on many levels.

Luke's parents came rushing toward the van. Her friend, Callie, was right behind them, trying to stop them, but it was a losing battle.

"Stay back," Colin warned. "We think Boyd might have a visual on the van."

That stopped the parents, and Colin got out so he could go over to them.

"You talked to Luke?" Griffin Vaughn asked her. She felt the concern in both Griffin and his wife, and the worry was etched on their rain-soaked faces. They wanted their boy back.

"I did. Your son is okay. He's a very brave little boy, and he's holding up well." Because Danielle had to catch her breath, she tipped her head to Colin. "Special Agent Forester will give you the details of the conversation."

Danielle stepped away, leaving them with Colin. She needed just a minute. But she didn't get it. Callie stepped right in front of her.

"Okay. What's wrong?" Callie demanded.

Since Callie and she were nearly the same height, it was impossible to avoid eye contact. Her old friend might be a forensic scientist who preferred to deal with facts and evidence, but Callie was no dummy in the emotional arena. Plus, Danielle doubted she was being very secretive. Talk about wearing her heart on her sleeve.

"It's always emotional when a child's involved," Danielle said, figuring Callie would see that it was a ploy to change the subject. "And it doesn't help that I'm in the van with Colin. Before the last call, I was about to get out and ask you to scrounge me up another vehicle."

Callie caught on to her arm and moved her to the end of the van. "Never met a shrink who could dodge the truth. Must have something to do with all that empathy and connection to other people." She shook her head.

"Look, I didn't know the FBI was sending in Colin, and if this is too much for you, then I'll get someone else."

"I've already established a rapport with Luke. And maybe with Boyd, too. It'd be a setback to replace me at this point."

Callie took in a weary breath. "Colin, then—"

"No." God. Danielle hated that she had to say this, but she had no choice. "Colin's the best, and Luke needs the best right now."

"I don't doubt that Colin and you are both good at what you do. But I can't have you two at each other's throats. That won't help Luke. That won't help any of us."

The dizziness hit her again, and Danielle had to grope behind her to catch on to the van. "Trust me, Colin won't let anything personal get in the way of doing this job. Especially not anything personal that has to do with me."

But she was talking to the wind because Callie was just staring at her. "What's wrong with you? Are you sick?"

"No," Danielle answered as quickly as she could.

Callie just kept staring. "You're not doing fertility treatments again, are you?" She didn't wait for Danielle to deny it. "Because I figured after all this time, you'd given up on having a child."

"I did give up." Danielle hadn't meant for that to sound like the start of a confession, but it was. "Callie, I'm pregnant."

The words rushed out of her before Danielle could stop them. Mercy. She needed to tell someone this secret.

"Pregnant?" Callie's mouth dropped open.

She looked at Danielle's stomach. There was a slight baby bump there, probably not even noticeable to anyone else, but even so it was concealed behind the sapphire-blue business jacket. However, she couldn't conceal her swollen fingers. She was retaining water like crazy, and just the day before her fingers had reached the point where she'd had to use soap and then oil to remove her wedding and engagement rings. Of course, with her divorce looming, the rings would have had to come off anyway.

That didn't explain why she was wearing them on a chain around her neck.

"The doctor said it's a miracle baby," Danielle told Callie. "That there was only a one in a million shot I'd ever conceive." But she had. And she was carrying that miracle inside her. "I'm nearly four months along," she added. And held her breath. Because Callie could and would do the math.

It didn't take her friend long. "Colin and you split three months ago. It's his child." And there was no doubt in her tone or expression.

Danielle didn't even try to lie. "Yes."

Callie grabbed on to her shoulder as if she were about to whoop for joy, but the joy went south in a hurry. "You haven't told him."

"No. I meant to. I mean, I tried. I phoned him right after I found out, but he was away on assignment. Days later, when he finally got around to calling me back, the divorce papers had just arrived, and he was in the worst of moods."

"Oh, damn." Callie groaned. She glanced around, probably to make sure their conversation was still as private as it could be, considering their location. Callie moved her even farther behind the van. "How do you think Colin will take the news?"

That was the million dollar question. There were

times when he'd seemed indifferent during the fertility treatments. Times when he'd asked her flat out to stop. Coupled with his long hours and intense assignments, Danielle wondered if he had truly ever wanted a child.

"I don't know how Colin will feel," Danielle admitted. And she certainly didn't know how he'd feel about her being his baby's mother. He was finished with her. He hadn't made one attempt to stop the divorce. So, he might see the baby as some kind of trap that would keep him connected to her.

Danielle didn't want this baby to ever feel that kind of resentment. Like she had. Before her parents' divorce, how many times had she heard her father say that her mother had trapped him into marriage? She wanted better for her child, even if that meant having only one parent.

Callie touched her arm, rubbed lightly. "Look, I'm your friend, Danielle, but I have to think of Luke first. He has to be the priority here."

"I understand." Danielle had already had this argument with herself and knew what she had to do. "Now isn't the time to tell Colin I'm carrying his baby. Best to wait, until all of this is resolved." And even then she wasn't sure she'd go through with it. Maybe it was better if Colin never knew.

Callie nodded. "You can do that? You can work with Colin and keep this secret to yourself?"

"What secret?" someone asked.

Danielle was glad that Callie caught on to her or she might have fallen on her face. Because the someone was Colin, and she didn't know how he'd gotten so close without Callie or her noticing, but he'd managed it. He was only a few feet away.

Close enough to have heard everything.

"What secret?" he repeated, putting his hands on his hips.

"Just girl talk," Callie volunteered.

Colin looked at Callie. Then, at Danielle. He wasn't buying it, and that would make this assignment even more uncomfortable. Colin was like a bulldog with a bone when he thought he was on to something.

Callie excused herself and headed toward one of the vehicles. Danielle sprang into action, too.

"Did you calm down Luke's parents?" Danielle asked, forcing herself to move. She should return to the van. To the job. She had to be more like Colin now and concentrate only on what had to be done.

But Colin caught on to her when she tried to walk past him. The eye contact came, and he examined her face with those intense blue eyes. "What secret?"

Best to try to keep it light. "It wouldn't be a secret now if I told you, would it?"

He still didn't let go of her, and it seemed as if he changed his mind a dozen times about saying anything. "Are you seeing someone else?"

"God, no." She saw the surprise go through his eyes, and she wanted to smack herself. The denial had come much too adamantly and quickly. She should have let him think that he was right, and he wouldn't have pressed about the secret.

But she didn't want to hurt him.

Or maybe that was wishful thinking on her part—that Colin would be hurt or jealous if she had another man in her life. It wasn't logical, but even though their marriage was over, the thought of him with another woman would hurt her to the core. That was something she'd have to work out eventually, because if he hadn't already, Colin would find someone else. Someone not obsessed with having a baby. Someone more sympathetic to the ever-increasing dangerous assignments that he volunteered to do.

She glanced at his left hand.

No wedding ring. He'd already removed it, and he didn't have the same swollen-finger excuse that she did. Colin had removed the ring because for him this divorce was a done deal. No more negotiations. Just the cleanup.

So that there wouldn't be any more questions, Danielle eased out of his grip and headed toward the Vaughns, who were about thirty feet from the van. Griffin, the father, was trying to talk Tom into calling Boyd again so he could speak to him. Which wouldn't be a good idea. It was best to keep Boyd calm, and a conversation with a terrified, angry father definitely wouldn't help.

"Boyd has agreed to set up some video games for Luke," Danielle told them. They stared at her and hung on to each word. "As I build a rapport with Boyd, I'll try to make the conversations longer with Luke, while Colin works for your son's release."

"But I have to talk to Boyd. I'll pay whatever he's asking."

"Right now, he's not asking for money."

"Then offer it," Griffin insisted. "And I want to talk to Luke. I have to hear my son."

Even though her child wasn't born yet, Danielle understood that. "I'll see what I can do."

Both Colin and Tom looked at her as if she'd lost her

mind. And maybe she had. Unless Griffin could totally keep the fear out of his voice, the call might upset Luke. It might make things worse. But Danielle couldn't stop herself from seeing this as a parent. If their situations were reversed, she wouldn't take no for an answer.

She would do anything to talk to her child.

Tom led the couple away, back toward the fence. Danielle climbed into the van. Colin was right behind her and dropped down on the seat next to her. Not by choice. It was the only place for him to sit so he'd be right next to the phone.

"You shouldn't have given the father that kind of hope," Colin grumbled.

"Hope is about all he has right now. And us. Colin, we have to get this little boy back to his parents."

"Us?" he repeated. "Does that mean you're staying?"

"I'm staying." But the real question was, could she get through this without having a total meltdown? She was already a hormonal mess.

Danielle tried to change the subject again. "Any word on how Boyd knew I was here?"

He stared at her so long she didn't think he would drop the subject. Finally, though, he did. "Tom thinks he might have some kind of equipment that allows him to tap into the on-site communications system. Or the van might be in his line of sight after all. Griffin Vaughn insists this is a blind spot, but that doesn't mean Boyd couldn't have found a way around it."

"Either of those possibilities is better than having a mole among us."

Colin lifted his shoulder. "We can't rule that out yet."

The relief was obviously short-lived. "You really

think someone out here could be a traitor and feeding Boyd information?"

Another shrug. "Boyd works for a powerful criminal, Nicky Wayne. Wayne has a lot of money, and money can corrupt people. Even people who wear a badge."

She looked around and prayed he was wrong. They had enough on their plates without worrying if someone was aiding and abetting the enemy. "So, what do we do—move the van farther back?"

"Too late for that. If Boyd's manipulated the security camera, then he knows we're here."

Yes. That included Tom and Callie, too, since they had stood close to the van.

"Plus, I want to stay in the immediate area so that when the eavesdropping equipment arrives we'll have a chance of hearing what's going on inside," Colin added.

It was a good plan. One that would likely cause extreme stress. She didn't know if she could hold her tongue if she heard Boyd yelling at the already frightened child.

"So, how'd you know about that video game?" Colin asked.

It took a moment to switch gears. "Part of the job. I use games sometimes in therapy, to help a child relax. If we can get Luke to concentrate on the game, he'll be less likely to get on Boyd's nerves. A calmer Boyd is what we all want, right?"

Colin looked at her. Full eye contact. She felt the muscles tense in his right arm, which was pressed against her left one. "Right," he grumbled.

But he wasn't talking about Boyd. They were back to the secret.

Danielle braced herself for more questions and was in such a high state of anticipation that she jumped when the ringing sound shot through the van. Because she was so close to Colin and therefore close to the phone, she saw it was the same number as before. Boyd's number.

Round two was about to start.

Colin flicked on the recorder and answered the call on speaker. "Boyd, it's me, Colin."

"Yeah, I know who it is, *Colin.*" It sounded as if he were mocking the friendliness that Colin was trying to establish.

Still, Colin stayed calm. "What can I do for you, Boyd?"

"You can tell me what the hell you think you're doing."

"What do you mean?" Colin still sounded calm, but she felt him tense again.

"I said no badges and no parents near the fence or the gate. You didn't listen. You didn't obey. Now, somebody's gonna pay for that."

"Boyd, just calm down. I'll get them out of here."

"Not just the parents," Boyd barked. "Everybody but the doc and you."

That sent a chill through Danielle.

"I want you two nearby, just in case I need some, uh, what do you call it? Yeah, leverage," Boyd joked. "That's what you two can be—my leverage in case your friends are stupid enough to try to storm the place."

Colin glanced at her. "Are you asking Dr. Connolly and me to trade places with Luke?"

"No. I'm thinking I got the best leverage of all with the kid. You and the doc will be my backup of sorts."

Colin was shaking his head before Boyd even

finished. "I'm a federal agent. You can't get better leverage than that. Dr. Connolly doesn't need to stay."

"Yeah. She does. Grab your binoculars, Colin, and have a good look at the west side of the house. Not the house itself. I'm in the garden."

Oh, God. Outside. Not where they'd expected a hostage taker to be. The usual pattern was for the perp to remain concealed.

"That's where I am right now," Boyd continued. "Watching you. Oh, and save your bullets because the kid is right here with me, and you wouldn't want the little fellow to get hurt, now would you?"

Danielle heard Luke then. He was asking for his father again. Mercy. This could turn very ugly fast.

Colin did look through the binoculars and cursed under his breath. "He's watching us," he scribbled on the notepad. "And he has a rifle."

"Tell them to leave," Boyd insisted. "And no tricks, no dragging their feet. They got five minutes to clear out."

"Evacuate now!" Colin called out to Tom. "The situation's escalated. Boyd's not in the house. He went onto the grounds, and he can see us."

Tom cursed. So did Colin under his breath. And the place turned to chaos. Everyone began to scramble toward their vehicles. Except Tom. He raced to the van, took the notepad and wrote, "We'll go to the other side of the mountain, out of his sight but not too far."

However, it would be far enough so that Colin and she wouldn't have immediate backup.

"I don't want Dr. Connolly here," Colin said. It took her a moment to realize he was talking to Boyd again. "I want her to leave with the others."

"No way, Colin. I'm calling the shots."

"I know you are, but it'll be easier if you only have Luke and me to watch—"

"Oh, the doc won't give me any trouble, and since she's your wife and all, I'm thinking she'll be able to keep you in line. Because, after all, you being the do-gooder Boy Scout kind of man that you are, you'll do anything to keep the little woman safe, won't you?"

The muscles in Colin's jaw turned to iron. "Boyd—"

"Enough of this!" Boyd yelled. "I'm opening the front gate. Now, here's what I want you to do. No guns. No equipment or bags of any kind, except for the cell phone you're using right now. Leave your wallet and the doc's purse in the van. Both of you put your hands in the air and start walking toward the estate."

Colin and she glanced at each other, both trying to figure out how to handle this. But their time for decision making was cut very short.

"Just come, Doctor," Luke said. His voice was shaky, and he sounded scared again. "Mr. Perkins wants you to come really, really bad."

"You want me inside the estate?" Colin asked. He fished out his wallet and personal cell phone and dropped them onto the table.

"No. See the guesthouse just inside the fence?"

Danielle had already noticed the small building that had a similar facade to the estate itself. But the guesthouse wasn't the problem. It was getting there. Colin and she would be out in the open.

"You can wait here," Colin told her. He climbed behind the seat and took off his shoulder holster. What he didn't do was remove the backup pistol that Danielle knew he always carried in an ankle holster. "I'll talk to Boyd. I'll make him see there's no reason for you to be on scene."

But there was a reason. A huge one. Even if Colin figured out a way to keep Boyd calm and get him to back off his demand that she be there, it would mean she wouldn't be around for Luke. He needed her, and she wasn't going to abandon him.

"Please come now," she heard Luke say. His voice filled the van and seemingly the entire mountain. He hadn't shouted, but he might as well have because his words slammed through her. *"Please."*

"I'm coming," she let him know. "Just think about your video game. About those hippos. Think about saving the baby giraffe." Danielle got out of the van and lifted her hands into the air.

"What the hell do you think you're doing?" Colin mumbled in a gruff whisper.

"We're doing the only thing we can do. We're saving a child," she reminded him.

And she started for the guesthouse. Still cursing, Colin hurried to maneuver himself in front of her.

Danielle could feel Boyd's rifle trained right on them.

Chapter Three

This nightmare had just taken a bad turn.

Colin knew letting Boyd dictate the situation was a mistake. He had to figure out a way to stop this from spiraling out of control.

"Stay behind me," he warned Danielle.

And by God she'd better listen. She should have stayed in the van and let him talk to Boyd. Not that it likely would have helped. Boyd seemed hell-bent on getting them out of that vehicle and into the open. But he might have been able to convince Boyd to allow anyone other than Danielle to walk into what could essentially be a trap.

"We didn't have a choice," she whispered.

Colin cursed because he knew she was right.

He lifted his left hand, a show of surrender, but he kept the cell phone in his right. If necessary, he could get to his backup weapon that he'd moved from his ankle holster to the back waist of his pants, but he might not be able to get to it in time if Boyd starting shooting. If that happened, Danielle and Luke could be hurt. Or worse.

"Boyd, I'm asking you man-to-man to send Dr. Connolly back," Colin insisted. Danielle and he slowed when they approached the high metal gates. "If you do, it'll prove to me that you want to work toward a peaceful resolution. You don't need two more hostages."

"Well, you won't exactly be hostages. You'll just be staying in the guesthouse. Nearby but not underfoot. I've got a camera fixed on the place, and I'll know if you try to leave or if you try to bring in any badges."

The explanation sounded almost logical, but Colin immediately found the weak spot in Boyd's argument. "But why risk having us so close at all? You can obviously watch us in the van, too."

But Colin knew the answer before Boyd even spoke.

"True. I can see the van, if I stand outside. I'd prefer not to do that. Plus, you wouldn't be in rifle range there, now would you? I want you close by. Because soon, very soon, I'll have some…chores for you two to do."

Since the phone was on speaker, Danielle obviously heard that, and her sharp intake of breath caused her lips to tremble. Colin didn't want to think of what a hit man would consider *chores*.

The only thing good in all of it was that perhaps this meant there was no mole. Boyd seemed to have found a way around the blind spot by going outside. That still didn't explain how the man had figured out who Danielle was. She wasn't exactly a public figure. But maybe Boyd had access to profiler or facial recognition software. If so, he could have spotted her when she arrived and gotten a picture of her to feed through the software. Colin hoped that's what had happened.

Because the alternative made him damn uneasy.

"This is a waste of time," Colin tried again. "Just give us your demands, and we can end all of this."

"Demands can wait," Boyd said, causing Colin to mentally curse. Colin couldn't offer up all of Griffin's bankroll, not on his first try of negotiations anyway, but he needed to get something on the table that he could use to bargain with. Once Danielle and he had some cover, he could do that.

"Luke?" Danielle said, aiming her voice toward the phone. "You doing okay? Are you still thinking about the hippos?"

"No."

Oh, man. That little voice had a way of cutting to the bone.

"Well, you should think about them," Danielle continued. "Because Agent Forester and I are here. We're on the grounds. We're walking through the gate right now. And we'll do whatever Mr. Perkins tells us so that he won't be upset. How does that sound?"

"Okay, I guess. Is Agent For-ster good or bad?"

"Oh, he's very good. His job is to help little boys like you, and he's the best." Her mouth was still trembling, but she said that with a boatload of confidence.

Confidence that Colin wasn't sure he deserved. He should have gotten her out of this before it even started. He thought of the other woman, the one he hadn't been able to save. That couldn't happen again.

It. Couldn't. Happen.

"Stop right there," Boyd ordered, his voice slicing through the silence.

They were still a good twenty feet from the guesthouse. Literally with no place to hide or duck for shelter if Boyd started shooting.

"Take off your jackets," Boyd demanded.

Colin had anticipated the demand, but Danielle obviously hadn't. She gasped and mumbled something. Colin wasn't happy with the demand, either, but Boyd wasn't stupid. This was a weapons check. Colin only hoped it didn't extend to the gun he was trying to keep hidden.

Danielle slowly unbuttoned her jacket. Like her lips, her hands were shaking now. That only made him curse more because she shouldn't have to be going through this.

Colin dropped his jacket onto the ground in front of him. Danielle did the same. And she stared down at it, completely dodging his gaze.

"Now take off your shirts," Boyd added.

This time, Danielle's gasp was a little louder.

"Rethink that," Colin insisted, aware it wasn't his negotiator's voice. But hey, he wasn't speaking as an agent now, but a man defending his wife's, well, whatever. Honor and modesty seemed insignificant compared to the hostage situation, but he didn't want Danielle to have to strip down in front of a hit man.

Colin unbuttoned his shirt, popping a few buttons in the process, and he threw the garment onto the ground with his jacket.

"Prove to me that neither of you are armed," Boyd countered.

Colin's hands went to his hips. "I don't mind taking off all my clothes, but think of your young hostage."

"He's not watching. Strip!"

Hell. Boyd wasn't going to give them any breaks. "Keep your clothes on," he mumbled to Danielle, and he passed her the phone so his hands would be free. He needed to do some maneuvering.

Colin pulled off his boots, socks and empty ankle

holster, and he put them on the growing heap of clothes. Next came the pants. This was the tricky part. He slipped the snub-nosed .38 into the back pocket and eased off his pants so the gun would stay in place. His wedding ring was in that pocket, too, and he didn't want either falling out. He dropped the pants onto the heap, as well.

Leaving him to stand there in his boxers.

With Danielle staring at him.

Since he'd been married to her for over three years, she'd obviously seen him buck naked, but for some reason, it felt damn uncomfortable. And even more uncomfortable that she'd probably have to strip, as well.

"Satisfied?" Colin said, turning toward the phone that Danielle still held.

"Yeah. Now, it's the doc's turn."

"She doesn't even know how to fire a gun," Colin protested. To diffuse this, he needed to go on the offensive.

Too bad Danielle wasn't going to like it.

But it was better than a strip-down.

Colin stepped slightly away from her so that he was still partly shielding her, and he met her concerned gaze. Concerned being a massive understatement.

"I'm going to lift your top a little just so he can see you're not carrying concealed."

She blinked. "Turn around. I'll do it."

Colin blinked, too. "Jeez. I've seen everything you have beneath those clothes."

"Turn around," she insisted. And she dodged his gaze again.

Great. Was she hiding some kind of body hickey that she'd received from a lover she'd adamantly denied having. He'd gotten a *God, no* from her when he'd suggested that she had found someone else. Still, it wasn't his business anymore.

Even if it felt as if it were.

Danielle didn't budge until he turned his back. Colin faced the direction where he thought Boyd was still standing, and he heard Danielle's movements behind him. A moment later, her shirt dropped into her clothes pile. Followed by her shoes.

Then, her skirt.

Which meant she was standing there in her bra and panties. He hoped it wasn't the skimpy underwear she preferred to wear. The woman certainly had stimulating taste in undergarments. His favorite was a devil-red set, with the bra barely covering her nipples and panties that left nothing to the imagination.

Unlike now.

He was imagining.

And cursing himself.

"No gun," Danielle announced. "And I'm getting dressed now."

"Take your things into the guesthouse," Boyd insisted. "Dress there. I'll call you after you've had time to get settled."

"Get Luke those video games," Danielle added, but Boyd had already hung up. She scooped up her clothes and held them in front of her like a shield.

She hurried toward the guesthouse, and even though Colin moved to her side after he gathered up his own clothes, he still caught a glimpse of the underwear.

It was the devil-red set.

Thankfully, the door to the guesthouse was unlocked, and she started to dress the moment they got inside. Not slowly, either. She was breaking some kind of speed record. Colin dressed, too, as he looked around to see what potential security hazards the place might have.

Windows for one thing. Two of them faced the estate, which meant Boyd could use them for surveillance. Colin went to them and shut the plantation-style blinds. He also locked both the front and back doors.

He strapped on the ankle holster and put the gun back inside, and after he put on his pants, he checked out the rest of the guesthouse. There wasn't much to it. The main area had a sofa, two chairs and a small kitchen off to the right. On the left was a large bedroom suite with a bath. The decor was crisp and clean, the kind of place he would expect for the guests of a multi-millionaire like Griffin Vaughn.

"You think he has the place bugged?" Danielle asked.

"Maybe. But I doubt it." He took the phone from her and made sure the end call button had been pressed so it would save the battery. Colin didn't want to think what would happen if they lost use of the cell. The guesthouse had phones, but he couldn't rely on those since Boyd had so far refused to use any of the estate phones.

"Check and see if we have food and water," he instructed.

She finished buttoning her blouse but not before he caught a glimpse of her breasts. Yeah. That bra really didn't hide much.

Danielle went to the kitchenette while Colin searched the place for bugs. Not that an eavesdropping device would be easy to find, but he looked in the obvious places. Under the phones. On the lamp bases. Beneath the coffee table and bed. He was just getting up from the floor of the bedroom when Danielle came in.

"There's plenty of bottled water and canned goods."

So, they wouldn't starve. Of course, that was the least of their worries.

Danielle made a sweeping glance around the room, and her eyes landed on the bed. "Uh, how long do you think we'll have to be here?"

"Your guess is as good as mine." But he understood her hesitation about the bed. "If we're still here tonight, I can take the sofa."

"Oh. Sure." She didn't sound relieved, exactly, but he didn't know what that tone meant. His ex was certainly acting funny. "Maybe when Boyd calls back with his chore list, he'll give his demands and you can continue with the negotiations."

Yeah. And Colin was betting that eventually those demands would include lots and lots of money, especially if Boyd didn't find those millions he was searching for. Griffin Vaughn was probably already gathering together as much cash as he could manage.

He looked at the way Danielle was gripping the door, and he tipped his head toward the sofa. "Why don't you sit down? It might be hours before Boyd calls back."

She didn't argue, but what she did do was stagger a bit when she turned around. Colin went after and caught up with her before she reached the sofa.

"You okay?" he asked. He turned her toward him so he could study her face.

"Sure," she said in the same tone and speed as *God, no*.

And that made Colin suspicious. "You and Callie were talking about your secret." He knew there'd be fallout from this question, but he rationalized that since they were now a team to save Luke, then he had a right to know her mental and physical state. "Are you taking those fertility drugs again?"

"No." Yet another quick response. But then, she shook her head. "I'm just a little dizzy, that's all. I saw some crackers in the cabinet, and I think I'll have one."

She stepped away from him and walked across the room. Oh, yes. She was unsteady. But maybe it was just nerves. He hoped so because he knew those fertility drugs were hell on wheels when it came to Danielle's health. They made her raw and jumpy. She didn't need either with all the other stress.

She opened the pack of crackers and nibbled on one while she rested her back against the countertop. The silence came. Closing in around them. Making the situation more awkward than it already was. They didn't dare talk about anything important or anything that would help Boyd because even though Colin had looked the place over, it didn't mean the hit man couldn't hear their every word.

Danielle finished off the cracker, had another one and then made her way back to the sofa. Toward him. But she didn't sit. She stopped only a few inches away, came up on her toes, and put her mouth to his ear.

"Did you manage to keep your gun?" she whispered.

He nodded. Tried not to react to her warm breath and the closeness. He failed and reacted anyway.

Colin switched positions and put his mouth to her ear. "The next step is to negotiate you out of here."

She shook her head. Probably because she didn't realize it would send his mouth brushing across her cheek. Like a kiss. She stepped back. Continued to shake her head. "I can help," she mouthed.

"So you've said." Because their eyes were now locked and they were still very close, he debated whether he should just tell her the truth. Or at least part of it. He went for a partial. "You distract me."

"What?" she said with a little whispered outrage.

"You still have that red underwear." And he added a smile to ease the tension between them.

The corner of her mouth lifted, too. Almost a smile. Before she waved it off, as well. "Colin, I can't."

He didn't want that clarified, but he had to wonder—was she talking about sex or something else? Since the best part of their marriage had been sex, he figured he had his answer.

The phone rang, and Colin actually welcomed the intrusion. Especially since it was Boyd. "This is Colin," he answered.

"All settled in?"

"As much as we can be settled in. Now, it's time for action, from you. We've cooperated with everything you've asked. I need your cooperation in return. What will it take to get you to release Luke?"

Boyd hesitated so long that Colin wasn't sure he'd answer. "I want a helicopter when it comes time for me to leave."

"A helicopter," Colin repeated. He went to the other side of the room where there was a desk and wrote that down, hoping there'd be more details. "When and where?"

Again, he hesitated. "Noon tomorrow, I guess."

"Don't guess. Let's nail down a time because I've got

to run this past my boss." It was a standard ploy not to give in too quickly. Always leave room for negotiation.

"All right, noon. You can have the pilot land in the open space at the back of the garden. No one else other than the pilot will be in the chopper, understand?"

"I understand." Though the pilot would have some kind of backup. Colin didn't know whom or what just yet. That was an issue to be worked out with the FBI office.

"I'm not finished," Boyd let him know. "I also want fifty million dollars wired to an offshore account in the Caymans."

"Fifty million." The same amount that was supposedly hidden somewhere in the estate. Did that mean Boyd was giving up his quest to find it and settling for Vaughn's money instead?

"When I confirm the money's been transferred and the helicopter's here," Boyd continued, "I'll tell you where and how you can find the kid."

"I don't know if Griffin Vaughn has access to that kind of money," Colin bargained. Though he probably did. Thankfully, the man was rich and was willing to pay to get his son back. Once they had Luke safely out of there, they could work on apprehending Boyd and retrieving the ransom money.

"Then he'd better find access," Boyd barked.

"I'll let him know what you said. But before any funds are transferred, I'll want proof that Luke is all right."

"Oh, you'll get proof. And remember, don't do anything stupid. Because you might not be in that van, but it doesn't mean I don't know exactly what you're doing. Got that?"

Boyd hung up before Colin could even respond.

Danielle checked her watch. "Will the Vaughns be able to come up with that much money so soon?" she whispered.

"Probably." Heck, they might even have it ready.

And Boyd would have known that.

So, why the delay? Why not request the helicopter and the money immediately? Maybe because he hadn't given up his search after all.

Because Colin wanted to save the cell battery, he used the house phone to make the next call. He didn't have Agent Tom Ryan's number, but he called the Durango office and had them do the transfer.

Tom answered on the first ring. "What happened?"

"Danielle and I are in the guesthouse, on the grounds. Boyd says he has visual, and who knows—he might even be listening. But we finally got some demands. Fifty million in an offshore account and a helicopter. He wants them by tomorrow at noon."

Tom made a sound to indicate he was thinking about that. Colin understood that sound. Tom was wondering about the delay, as well. "Talk to Griffin Vaughn and work out the details," Colin suggested. "See if this is even possible and get back to me."

"I will. Are you and Danielle safe there?"

Colin glanced around, and his attention landed on Danielle. She looked pale and uneasy. "Yes, we're safe." But that was for her benefit. He had no idea if that was even true.

Colin hung up and made a note of the time of the call because when this was all said and done, he'd need to do a thorough report.

Danielle stood, her hand gripping the sofa. "I need to go to the bathroom. I won't be long."

"Wait. Let me check the place first." He'd done a cursory, but if she was going in there, he wanted to be as sure as he could be.

Colin stepped in ahead of her. He looked in the medicine cabinet, the linen closet and around the toilet area. The shower was massive, built for two, and he examined the sprayer head and the knobs. Nothing dangerous there. It all looked clean.

Danielle was still in the doorway, but he didn't miss it when her grip tightened on the frame. He also didn't miss that she'd gotten even paler.

"What's wrong?" And by God, this time he would get an answer.

He walked toward her but only made it one step. Before he heard the sound.

A thump.

Colin stopped. Listened. Danielle listened, too, turning in the direction of the sound. It'd come from the living area, and Colin brushed past her to see if he could find the source.

Another thump.

This one, louder than the first.

Even though it was a risk if Boyd had visual access, Colin drew his gun and positioned himself in front of Danielle.

The third thump was more of a bashing sound.

And that's when Colin knew.

Someone was breaking in.

Chapter Four

Despite her sudden dizzy spell, Danielle looked around for something—anything—she could use as a weapon. Of course, Colin had his gun, but she didn't want just to stand there while he had the responsibility of protecting both of them.

Mercy, was Boyd trying to get inside?

Or maybe this was someone who was helping Boyd. Someone already on the grounds of the estate that the FBI didn't know about. It made sense, especially considering Boyd was looking for that hidden money and might have brought help with him.

But why would Boyd come after them now?

Colin and she had followed his rules to a T. Well, except for Colin's gun. Perhaps Boyd had the place bugged and knew about the weapon. If so, there was no telling what the man would do.

Danielle grabbed a heavy onyx candlestick from the dresser, and she followed right behind Colin as he made his way into the living room. At first, she'd thought the sound had come from the front door, but she realized she was wrong. It was coming from the closet next to the door.

There were more sounds of someone shuffling around. A bash of what she thought might be something slamming against the wall.

Colin took aim at the closet, and because she was so close she was touching him, she felt the muscles in his body turn to iron.

"Who's there?" he called out.

"Special Agent Dylan Acevedo," someone whispered. "We came through the tunnels."

Colin glanced at her, and she could see the surprise and questions that were no doubt mirrored in her own eyes.

The closet door opened, and there indeed was Agent Acevedo. And he wasn't alone. He stepped from the closet and following him were two other men. One was middle-aged with a blond buzz cut and stocky build. The other was much younger, with dark hair and eyes. All the men carried equipment bags and had small flashlights clipped to their collars.

"Are you being monitored?" Dylan mouthed. He set two bags on the floor and turned off his flashlight. The others did the same.

Colin shrugged. "We're not sure," he answered in a barely audible whisper.

The young dark-haired man took out a piece of equipment from one of his bags, turned it on and walked around the room, pointing the wallet-size device in every direction.

"No bugs," he announced several moments later.

All of them let out breaths of relief. Colin holstered his gun so he could shake hands with Dylan.

"This is Special Agent Jerry Ortiz," Dylan said, pointing to the older man. "He's the senior agent for FBI operations at the Kenner County Crime Lab." He then tipped his head to the other man. "And that's Bobby O'Shea, a forensic analyst. We were on our way to deliver supplies to you when Boyd ordered everyone but you two off the mountain."

"How did you find your way through the tunnels?" Colin asked.

"We used some thermal equipment and literally followed the heat source—you two."

Colin glanced at her. "Then, you'll be able to use the tunnels to get Danielle out of here."

Dylan nodded. "Sure."

"Wait a minute." Danielle put the candlestick aside and stepped between Colin and the other agent. "I'm not leaving until we get Luke away from Boyd. What if Boyd calls and asks to speak to me again?"

"We can have the call transferred to you," Colin readily answered.

Danielle slapped her hand on his chest when Colin started to move around her. He was acting as if this were a done deal. And it wasn't. "At any minute Boyd could come down here to the guesthouse and demand to see me," she reminded him. "Or there could be a problem with a call transfer. If I'm not here or if he can't speak to me right away, he could take it out on Luke. Or you."

She hated that she sounded so emotional, especially with that *or you* part. Worse, her chest slap suddenly seemed a little intimate so she drew back her hand.

"I'm not leaving," she insisted. And she repeated that to Dylan, Bobby and Jerry.

"She has a point," Dylan agreed. Bobby and Jerry mumbled an agreement, too.

Colin scowled at all of them.

Probably because the mood suddenly seemed more than just awkward, Dylan cleared his throat and turned to Bobby. "Go ahead and set up the long-range eaves-dropping equipment."

"You brought the equipment with you?" Danielle asked at the same moment Colin asked a variation of the same question.

Dylan nodded. "We figured you'd want to hear what Boyd's saying and doing."

Of course. This way, they could possibly pinpoint their location, and Danielle would be able to listen and make sure Luke was okay.

"We need to monitor Boyd, too," Dylan added. Bobby got to work setting up the equipment on the coffee table. "We know Boyd's trying to find the fifty million dollars that was probably hidden by the former owner, Vincent Del Gardo."

"So I've heard. Del Gardo, another mob guy," Colin added. "Well, he certainly had fifty million and probably a lot more to hide, but Boyd probably hasn't found it yet. Just a little while ago, he demanded a helicopter and fifty million in an offshore account. Does that mean Boyd's giving up the search for the cash?"

"Maybe." This time, it was Jerry who answered. The older agent propped his hands on his hips and watched Bobby put on some headphones and adjust the controls on the equipment. "Or Boyd could be planning to collect both the Del Gardo money and the ransom for Luke."

Danielle hoped not because if Boyd were still looking for that money, it could delay Luke's release.

"I'm in," Bobby announced.

That sent all of them in the young agent's direction. There was no visual feed, but Danielle could hear something. Beeps and sounds of a video game. But not just any video game. She recognized a familiar lion's roar. Good. Boyd was letting Luke play Safari Explorer.

"I want you to record everything," Dylan instructed Bobby.

"And report anything suspicious you hear back to me," Jerry added. Though Jerry was a senior agent, that earned him a bit of raised eyebrow from Dylan, and Danielle wondered if there was some kind of power struggle going on here. She hoped not. "Remember, Boyd's a killer and a liar. We can't take anything he says as gospel."

"What's going on?" Colin demanded, taking the question right out of her mouth.

Dylan glanced at Jerry who nodded before Dylan explained, "We think Boyd might know something about Ben Parrish." Since Colin started to bob his head as if he suddenly knew what this was all about, Dylan looked at her to deliver the rest of the details. "Ben is an FBI agent, and he's missing."

"Probably dead," Jerry interjected.

Dylan shrugged, though the shrug didn't convey the emotion in his eyes. "If not dead, he could be hurt and unable to contact us. We need to find him. In addition to needing lots of answers, his wife, Ava, is a forensic scientist, and she's pregnant. She's scared, and she wants to know what happened to her husband."

Danielle felt instant empathy. Other than being pregnant and scared, she didn't have anything in common with this woman, but she wanted to help. Maybe this was another side effect of pregnancy hormones.

"We don't want to take anything away from your primary mission," Jerry continued, talking to Colin. "We want you to negotiate the boy away from Boyd, but we can't just let this opportunity go, either. Finding Ben is critical."

Colin glanced at the equipment. "Will the audio feed go directly to the crime lab?"

"No." Jerry didn't seem pleased about that, either. "Transmission is spotty out here at best and will have to be sent to us via disks. Once the disks are in the lab, I'll analyze them and try to enhance them so we can get every word of conversation." Jerry hitched his thumb toward Bobby. "So, the plan is we'll leave Bobby here to monitor Boyd, while Dylan and I go out and try to find this missing agent."

Danielle immediately thought of a concern. "What if Boyd figures out Bobby is here?"

"Bobby will have to avoid that at all cost," Dylan explained. "If Boyd comes down here, Bobby will just have to use the tunnels to hide. In fact, that's where we'll put the extra supplies just so there aren't equipment bags lying around."

"Maybe Boyd won't go into the tunnels and find the bags," Jerry mumbled.

Mercy. She hoped this didn't come back to haunt them, but on the upside, she could hear Luke playing the video game. He wasn't whining, and Boyd wasn't fussing. Maybe it would stay that way, and maybe Boyd would stay out of the tunnels.

"What about the helicopter Boyd requested?" Colin wanted to know.

"We already have someone working on that," Jerry

confirmed. "And from what I understand, Luke's father is gathering funds as we speak. He wants to give Boyd the money."

Of course he did. He wanted his son back.

Danielle automatically slid her hand over her belly. Just for reassurance that her own child was safe and well. But it was a mistake. She realized that Colin was looking at her. Probably because he thought she was cramping from yet another round of fertility drugs.

"Has anyone said anything about Boyd maybe having a mole in the FBI or maybe at the crime lab?" Colin asked.

Dylan and Jerry exchanged glances again. "We're looking into it," Jerry finally said.

Danielle didn't intend to let that go. "But you think there might be one?"

Jerry shook his head, but it wasn't a very convincing denial. "We have a new lab assistant. Rusty Cepeda. He just started work a couple of days ago."

"Rusty?" Colin questioned. "The kid who drove me up to the estate this morning?"

"Yeah," Dylan verified. "We didn't know there was an issue about a possible mole."

"And Rusty might not have anything to do with this," Jerry quickly added. "But because he's new, Callie wants us to take a hard look at his background."

"Please do," Danielle insisted. They had enough issues without adding a mole to the mix.

"We brought you a cell phone charger, an extra phone, a laptop and a weapon," Jerry continued, pointing to the equipment bags. "If you need anything else, give us a call, and I'll get it to you." He turned back to Dylan. "We should get out of here."

"You might want to wait a minute," Bobby said. He turned up the volume on the eavesdropping device.

Danielle heard Boyd's voice, though there was some static that made it difficult to understand exactly what he was saying.

"He's talking to his boss, Nicky Wayne," Bobby supplied.

That got everyone's attention. It was a long shot, but she hoped that the notorious Nicky Wayne would insist that Boyd release Luke immediately.

"Still no money," Boyd said. And whatever else he added was lost because of the static.

"Can you make the reception better?" Colin asked.

Bobby shook his head. "This is the best I can do."

Boyd said something else that wasn't clear, and Danielle could barely hear the beeps of Luke's game. It sounded as if Boyd was moving farther away from the boy. Maybe so Luke wouldn't overhear the conversation.

"You're sure you want me out tomorrow?" Boyd asked. He paused. "All right. Consider it done." Another pause and Boyd ended the call.

Well, that certainly didn't give them any revelations, but it was a start.

"If I could get closer to Boyd, that might help," Bobby said, turning down the device. The young analyst looked at Jerry. "Sir, what if I move the equipment deeper into the tunnels toward the estate?"

Jerry pulled back his shoulders, perhaps because he figured this could be dangerous if Boyd detected what was happening. It certainly sounded risky.

"I think it's worth a try," Dylan spoke up.

Jerry didn't look as if he wanted to agree, but he

finally nodded. "Just be careful and remember to report back to me everything Boyd says." Jerry shook his head. "This guy is bad news, and I want him put away."

Colin and the men shook hands, and Jerry and Dylan grabbed the equipment bags. They left the two others sitting on the floor but those would have to be tucked out of sight. The men made their way back through the closet and into the tunnels. Bobby picked up his eavesdropping device, as well, and turned on his flashlight.

"If I get better reception in the tunnels, I'll move all of my stuff down there," Bobby told them, and he disappeared down the steps behind the other men.

Colin and Danielle stood there. In silence. Both of them staring at the closet.

"If Boyd finds out about this…" she mumbled. She couldn't finish. She didn't want to think of what might happen.

"Yeah," Colin verified. He stayed quiet for several moments before he looked at her. "You don't owe me an explanation, but I'd like one."

Danielle didn't intend to jump into an answer. Any answer. But the request certainly caused her to swallow hard. "An explanation about what?"

His gaze landed on her stomach.

Oh, God. Colin knew about the baby.

She tried not to panic, though inside that's exactly what she was doing. "I'm fine, really," she lied, hoping the lie would be enough. Now was not the time to tell him that he was going to be a father.

Danielle tried to move away from him, but he caught on to her arm. "What's going on with you?" he demanded. "Why the *secret* comment to Callie? Why the strange behavior?"

She forced her chin up. It was time to go on the offensive. "Strange behavior? Maybe because a boy's well-being is at stake, and I'm having to work next to my estranged husband. That's worth a moment or two of strange behavior, don't you think?"

Apparently not. Because his gaze drifted back to her stomach again, and the only thing Danielle could do was brace herself for *the* question. If Colin did indeed ask if she was pregnant, she wouldn't be able to tell him a direct lie. Not about that.

But there was no question from him. Just his glare, which started to soften. There was still plenty of fire in those blue eyes. Plenty of emotion, too. But it started to change. Slowly. Subtly, at first. However, she recognized that look.

The fire wasn't all from his anger over the lack of answers.

Just like that, her body started to soften, too. Actually, it started to insist that she move closer. She didn't.

But Colin did.

He leaned in. Until he was close. So close that his shirt brushed against her breasts and sent a warm tingle through her. His gaze dropped from her eyes.

To her mouth.

His breath touched her lips. Not a kiss exactly, but it was just as intoxicating as the real thing. And that's why she couldn't stay put.

Danielle tried to get away from him, but Colin held on to her. Of course, she wasn't trying that hard to move. Her feet seemed anchored in place, and her body was screaming for that kiss to happen. Probably because her body knew a kiss from Colin was a prelude to hot sex.

"Okay," she said, just to be saying something. "So, we're still attracted to each other. So what? We always have been, and we both know where that got us, right?"

She'd meant it as a stinging jab to get him to back off, but because her voice was still reacting to the near kiss, it came out steamy and more like an invitation for him to continue.

And that's what he did.

Colin leaned in even closer. Danielle still didn't move. She just stood there waiting for the inevitable. She wasn't any better at resisting him now than she had been months earlier.

He took his hand from her arm and slipped it around her waist. It was gentle. Coaxing. Something that Colin was especially good at doing. And just when Danielle thought—finally!—the kiss would happen…

It didn't.

That's because a deafening sound blasted through the room.

Chapter Five

What the hell was happening?

That was Colin's first reaction, and it was quickly followed by the realization that he needed to protect Danielle. He pushed her behind him and drew his weapon, but his gun wouldn't be much defense against this.

There'd been an explosion.

The blast shook the guesthouse and sent pictures and other items crashing to the floor. Colin moved Danielle aside before a heavy framed oil painting came crashing down on her. He got them to the center of the room, away from the falling debris and out of the path of an overhead light fixture that was swaying and looked ready to drop.

Colin looked around to see if he could identify the source and origin of the explosion, but there was nothing to indicate that the blast had occurred in the guesthouse itself. However, there was dust rising from the tunnel opening where Bobby and the others had exited only minutes earlier.

"The tunnel," Danielle said on a gasp, and she headed straight toward it.

Colin caught on to her again. "Wait. Don't go any closer. There could be a secondary explosion."

Or the tunnel could be damaged to the point that it was ready to collapse. He didn't want to speculate on what'd happened to Bobby, Jerry and Dylan, but Colin had to consider that the men had been hurt or even killed.

He waited several moments, to make sure everything had stopped shaking, and then Colin began to inch his way toward the closet opening that led to the tunnel. He didn't get far because the cell phone rang. He checked the caller ID screen and saw it was Boyd.

Colin cursed. Took a deep breath to steady himself. And he answered it.

"I didn't figure you for a stupid man, Colin," Boyd greeted. "Maybe I should have made it clear about staying put. Maybe I should have also let you know that I set explosives in the tunnels."

Oh, man. So, that's what had happened.

"There's no good reason for you or Dr. Connolly to be in the tunnels," Boyd continued. "So, tell me? Is she hurt?"

Colin debated his answer. Boyd obviously didn't know who'd been in that tunnel, which meant he didn't have visual surveillance and he had assumed that Danielle had been the one to trip the explosive. It sickened Colin to think that could have happened. After all, he'd tried to force her to leave via those very tunnels, and they could have become a death trap for her.

"I should check on her," Colin finally said.

"Right. And if she's alive and well, tell her not to go down there again. Got it?"

Colin had to bite his tongue over Boyd's flippant attitude. "I'll tell her."

"Oh, and Colin? No ambulance if she's hurt. You'll just have to deal with the consequences yourself. Consider it her punishment for acting like a fool."

"I'm sure she's sorry." Colin somehow kept his voice calm. He looked at Danielle. To see how she was holding up, and he could have sworn she was paler than she had been just minutes earlier. "How's Luke?" he asked Boyd.

"Those video games work like a charm. The kid hasn't made a peep since he started playing them."

"And you can thank Danielle for that." Colin needed to do a little damage control because he didn't want Boyd to sever communication between Danielle and Luke.

"Thank her for me," Boyd barked. "And tell her next time I might not be in such a generous mood and forgive her for disobeying my orders to stay put. Don't forget I'm holding all the cards here, Colin."

"I won't forget. Neither will Danielle. We both just want Luke back safe."

"Yeah, yeah." And with that taunting farewell, Boyd hung up.

Colin clicked the end call button so he could try to get in touch with Dylan. However, the phone rang again before he could do that.

It was Jerry Ortiz.

"What happened?" Jerry frantically asked the moment that Colin answered.

"An explosion. Are you okay?"

"Dylan and I are fine. We'd just made it out when we heard the blast. What about Bobby?"

"I was about to check on him." And God knew what he'd find.

Colin made his way to the opening and looked down into the dark hole. There were stairs leading down, and Colin could see just a glimmer of light. "Bobby?" he called out.

"I'm here," the young man said. His voice was shaky. No surprise there. He'd likely just come very close to being killed.

"Are you hurt?"

Bobby didn't answer right away, causing Colin some uneasy moments. "I'm fine. Just shaken up a little. I was still a good twenty yards away from the explosive device when it went off."

"He's fine," Colin relayed to Jerry. "I'll check him out and call you back if he needs help." Though with Boyd's no-ambulance rule, it might be hard to get Bobby away from the estate.

Colin ended the call and handed Danielle the phone so he could help Bobby up the stairs. The young man was covered with a fine powdery dust, but Colin didn't see any cuts or gashes. Thank God. Bobby had gotten lucky.

Bobby clicked off his flashlight and brushed off some of the dust. "I'm guessing Boyd did this?"

"Yeah. And there might be more explosives."

With his breath gusting, Bobby carried his equipment back to the coffee table. "Guess I'll have to settle for poor reception up here."

Now that he was certain that Bobby was okay, Colin turned his attention to Danielle. Yep. She was still pale. Still trembling. And he didn't think it was because of their near kiss. Either this stress was getting to her, or she was sick.

Colin took the phone from her. She had the cell clutched in a death grip. "Why don't you get some rest? It could end up being a long day, and night."

Danielle's chin came up, a sign that she was about to argue with him. But she didn't. She wearily pushed her hair away from her face. "I'll pick up the things that the explosion knocked down."

"I'll do that later. Rest," he insisted.

She looked around as if deciding what she should do. Rest obviously wasn't something she planned to consider. "Jerry said they brought us a laptop. I think I'll use it to see if I can figure out a way to contact Luke through the video game."

"You can do that?" Colin asked.

"Maybe, if he's playing online. But it's a long shot. Most kids his age only play with their game system, but I know some parents who set up the game online so they can play with their kids even when they go away on trips. Besides, I doubt Boyd would let him go on the Internet, though." She took the laptop from one of the equipment bags. "Still, I have to try."

Danielle carried the laptop into the bedroom. She didn't shut the door, and instead of sitting on the bed, where she might be able to take a nap, she took the straight-backed chair in the corner of the room.

"Nothing's going on inside the estate," Bobby relayed to Colin. "It sounds as if the boy's still playing his video game."

Good. So, Boyd hadn't taken his anger out on Luke. That was something, at least. Colin sank down onto the sofa next to Bobby and called Jerry back. However, it wasn't Jerry who answered. It was Dylan.

"Everything okay?" Colin asked.

"Maybe not. Jerry and I just checked the tunnel, and the one leading to the road is fine, but the others, well, it's probably best if we don't go back down for a while. I'm pretty sure some of the support beams are cracked. Plus, there was another trip wire leading off one of the side tunnels. There's no telling how many explosives Boyd has set down here."

Great. Just great. That tunnel could have been an escape route, and Colin was very much afraid he would need one for Danielle before this was over.

"I don't think Boyd wants to blow up the place," Dylan continued. "But he's definitely trying to deter anyone from coming down here."

Then that meant Colin had to do everything to make sure this standoff ended with the arrival of that helicopter tomorrow.

"We're headed back to town now," Dylan added. "But we'll get an expert up here to check out the tunnels."

"Thanks." Colin hung up and made another call to Agent Tom Ryan for an update.

Tom answered right away. "Jerry Ortiz just called about the explosion. Is everyone okay?"

"For now." He'd try to keep it that way. Colin considered mentioning that Danielle wasn't feeling well, but he knew that would only rile her. Besides, he couldn't get her out until the tunnels were checked, and that might take a while. "What's the latest on the helicopter and ransom money?"

"The helicopter is firm, and we have an agent who can pilot it. Griffin Vaughn will have all the money together by tonight." Tom paused, and Colin knew what that pause was all about. Just because Boyd might get his demands, it didn't mean this would result in a smooth transfer.

"I'll do whatever I need to do," Colin promised. Paused. "Talk to me about Dylan and Jerry. Are they men you both trust?"

"I'd trust Dylan with my life."

Well, that was a start. "And Jerry?"

Tom cleared his throat. "He used to be the best, but he's had a tough time recently with a bad divorce."

Ah, something Colin knew a little about. A divorce could certainly affect a man's concentration. "Thanks for the info. And call me if there's a hitch with either of Boyd's demands." Colin hung up in case Boyd phoned back. He had call-waiting on the cell, but he didn't want any delays when it came to Luke.

Colin slipped the cell into his pocket and got up so he could pick up the pictures and other items that had fallen during the explosion. He started with the broken glasses and worked his way around the room. He had his hands full when he glanced in the bedroom at Danielle.

She was in the chair, computer on her lap. She'd unbuttoned her jacket. The top of her blouse, too. And she was asleep. Man, she looked exhausted.

He put the broken items into the trash and went back to the bedroom, quietly closing the door so that the transmission from Bobby's equipment wouldn't wake her. He eased the laptop aside and put it on the dresser. She didn't wake up. Didn't even flinch. So, he picked her up to move her to the bed.

Colin only made it one step.

Her eyes fluttered open, slowly, and her gaze drifted

to him. She shook her head as if trying to fight off the effects of sleep. Wait. Not sleep. Her eyes widened. Her breath went thin. And because he was holding her, he felt her body go soft and warm.

She was fighting it, he could feel that, but she slid her arm around his neck. Her mouth came to his. Not willingly. This seemed to be the last thing on earth she wanted to do, but she didn't stop.

That kiss jolted through him.

She made a sound of utter frustration and deepened the kiss. She tasted as good as she always had. Maybe better. Because Colin suddenly felt starved for her.

And that meant this had to stop.

"Danielle," he warned.

She made another of those frustrated sounds and turned slightly so that her left breast was pressed right against him.

"Colin," she warned back.

But then, her eyes widened. And widened some more before she groaned and forced herself to move away from him.

"Don't read too much into that," she said, as if that explained everything. She wiggled out of his arms, and in doing so wiggled against him.

He was toast.

She stood, fixed her clothes that in no way needed fixing. Fixed her hair, too. And tried to look indignant and unaffected by that kiss.

"I'm sorry," she added, turning.

But because he was aroused and apparently stupid, he caught on to her and stopped her from putting any distance between them. "I'm not sorry." Though he should be. Obviously, being aroused made him say dumb things in addition to doing them.

She drew in a shallow breath. "Colin…"

Uh-oh. He felt another lecture coming on, and since that wasn't going to make him want to kiss her less, he decided to nip the lecture in the bud. "I know you don't want to be married to me, but that doesn't kill the attraction. You've already admitted it's still there."

She didn't say anything, but she did concede he was right with a shrug. Still, that didn't stop her from turning away and starting for the bathroom.

Colin saw it then.

Because her jacket was open and the top three buttons of her blouse were undone, he saw the gold chain. And the wedding and engagement rings that hung on the chain.

She followed his gaze, and her hand flew to cover the rings. It was too late.

He reached out and caught on to the rings. Despite the gold and diamonds, they were warm because they'd been next to her skin.

"Don't read too much into this, either," Danielle said. She pushed his hand away and went into the bathroom.

But he did read a lot into it. Why was Danielle wearing her rings around her neck? Did that mean she hadn't given up on their marriage?

Colin intended to find out.

He went after her and grabbed her by the shoulder and spun her back around so she was facing him. Yeah, it was stupid. But he didn't care. He had to know why she was still wearing the rings he'd given her. Rings that symbolized their marriage.

"Why?" But that was as far as he got with his question.

Their eyes met. The fire that was always there between them went off like a powder keg. Colin shoved
his hand into her hair, hauled her to him.

And he kissed her.

There was nothing dreamy and sleepy about this one.
It was hot, hungry and filled with months of longing and
need. His need. And hers. Danielle proved that need when
her arms went around him, and she kissed him back.

Just like every other kiss they'd shared, this one
quickly got out of control. Her hands were on him.
Touching his chest. Something that couldn't happen
because her touches made him crazy, so he grabbed
both of her wrists in one hand and pinned them against
the doorframe.

That didn't stop her. She fought to get closer and
played dirty. She ground against him. Her sex against
his. While they played that crazy erotic dance with their
mouths. It didn't take long before Colin knew he was
out of control.

Did that stop him?

No.

He caught her leg, lifting it so that it slid along the
outside of his thigh. The sliding created some interesting sensations, but they were paltry compared to the
hard contact that happened with her sex against his.
That's because, with their new sex-against-the-door-
frame stance, her skirt hiked up.

Nearly all the way up her thigh.

And those silky red panties skimmed right against
his zipper.

Oh, man. He wanted her bad. And that couldn't
happen. He repeated that to himself several times.

Managed to regain a little control. But that control went south when Danielle shifted her body. He reacted to that shift and his hand went from her leg to her thigh.

His fingers curved along the inside of her thigh.

So close to those red panties that he stood no chance of resisting. He touched her. Barely. His fingers skimmed over that warm, damp silk, and he felt her respond. She responded in other ways, too. Her breath raced. Her hips arched forward and his skimming fingers turned into a full-fledged touch.

He couldn't have sex with her. His brain knew that, though this was such familiar ground for his body that he had a hard time convincing certain parts of himself. Well, one part anyway. No sex. But he could give her a little relief from this pressure cooker that their kisses had created.

Colin adjusted and slid his hand up, so he could move his finger down her stomach and into her panties. But she stopped with his fingertips nearly touching her skin.

Actually, she froze.

And she latched on to his wrist and pushed his hand away.

"I can't," Danielle said through rough gusts of breath.

She drew down her leg, as well, and shoved her skirt back in place.

He mentally skidded to a halt, and Colin stared at her. It took him a moment to gather his thoughts. More moments before he managed to speak. "You're right."

And she was. They had to stop, but what he couldn't figure out was why it'd come at that exact moment. She'd been fine—translation: she'd been on fire—until the kiss had turned to more intimate touching.

"I'm sorry," she mumbled. She looked away. Frowned. Sighed. And generally looked as uncomfortable as she could possibly look. "We need to talk. After Luke is rescued."

He studied her puzzling expression and nodded. "Okay. About what?" And he hoped to hell this wasn't a confession that she'd found someone else.

But she didn't answer. Danielle just stared at him with her mouth poised to say something apparently pretty darn important.

The knock cut off anything she'd been about to confess.

"Colin, you need to come out and listen to this," Bobby said from the other side of the door.

Since Bobby's request seemed more than a little urgent, Colin turned and went right away. Danielle was right behind him. Good thing, too, since this might involve her trying to keep Luke calm. However, it wasn't Luke's voice that Colin heard when he went back into the living room and walked closer to the eavesdropping device.

Boyd was talking to someone.

"You should have warned me that somebody was going into the tunnels," Boyd said.

That got Colin's full attention. "Who's he talking to?" he asked Bobby.

"I don't know. And we can't hear the other side of the conversation. So far, Boyd hasn't mentioned anyone's name."

No, but it was clear he was talking to someone who should have insider knowledge of the tunnels. And therefore, the estate.

Hell.

This meant they might have a mole after all. Or else

Boyd had someone positioned near the estate. Someone he was relying on to do surveillance.

Colin really hoped it was the latter.

"That's not an excuse," Boyd snarled to the person on the other end of the line. "We pay you to help, and you're not helping if you can't or won't tell me what's going on."

Colin moved even closer to the device. Danielle, too. And with her attention pinned to the conversation, she sank down onto the arm of the sofa.

"What about the helicopter?" Boyd snapped.

Colin wished he could hear what'd prompted that question. And what caused Boyd to pause. Maybe when the disk was sent to the lab and enhanced, they'd be able to figure out who this person was. One thing was for sure, Colin didn't want the new lab assistant, Rusty Cepeda, to have anything to do with the disks.

And he wanted to make sure Jerry was on the up-and-up. From everything he'd heard about Dylan, the man was trustworthy, but he wasn't so sure about Jerry.

"No," Boyd said, his voice slightly calmer now. "Don't worry about the negotiator and the doc. I've got plans to take care of them."

Danielle raked her fingers over her eyebrow and shifted slightly. Colin had a slightly stronger reaction. Every muscle in his body knotted. Boyd's comment sounded like a threat.

"I said I'd take care of them," Boyd repeated. He paused. "No. I need them alive, for now, so they can do a few chores for me."

And with that, Boyd laughed. "I hope they get a good night's sleep because tomorrow…well, let me just say there'll be hell to pay."

"HELL TO PAY," he repeated under his breath. He slapped the phone shut and cursed.

He hated to admit it but Boyd was on some kind of power trip. Or else he'd gone crazy. Maybe both. But it was clear that Boyd was working his own agenda.

Which could be dangerous.

He couldn't afford for Boyd to start blabbing, and the man seemed way too close to doing just that.

The game plan had been simple. Find the fifty million dollars that Del Gardo had hidden, get out, and the two of them could split the generous "finder's fee" that Nicky Wayne would give them. But had Boyd done that?

No.

Instead, Boyd had gotten himself into a half-assed situation where he had to take a kid hostage. Nothing like having agents and crime lab workers combing the estate and finding that money.

Yeah, Boyd had really screwed things up.

And he could do worse than that.

Boyd could give away the identity of the so-called "mole."

He cursed again. That couldn't happen. Because he was the mole, and one way or another, he had to stop Colin, Danielle and anyone else from finding out. And if he had to kill them, so be it. He would.

Hell to pay, indeed.

He took a moment to compose himself, wiped the concern off his face and went into the Kenner County Crime Unit so he could get to work.

Chapter Six

Hell to pay.

Boyd's words went through Colin's head as he poured Danielle and himself cups of coffee. So did the other part of that conversation.

I need them alive, for now…

That had kept Colin up for most of the night.

From the moment Boyd had ordered them from the van to the guesthouse, Colin had feared for Danielle's safety. For her life. And Boyd had made it crystal clear that Danielle and he were mere pawns in this. Boyd would kill them—or at least try—if and when he decided they were expendable.

Colin grabbed the two mugs of black coffee and walked past Bobby, who was essentially monitoring silence. Luke had gone to bed around nine, and other than Boyd rattling around in the estate, there'd been no other sounds. Definitely no other phone conversations. It'd made for a quiet night. Too bad none of them had managed to get much sleep despite the uneventful hours.

Bobby had stayed in the living room, with the monitoring equipment on so he wouldn't miss anything.

Danielle had taken the bed, and Colin had ended up on the floor. He didn't mind the discomfort, because he knew he would just toss and turn anyway. And besides, it hadn't seemed a smart idea to climb onto that king-size bed with her. His brain was on autopilot when it came to Danielle.

The kiss had proven that.

Colin went back into the bedroom where Danielle was sitting with the laptop. She'd showered earlier, and even though she'd had no choice but to put back on the same clothes, she now smelled like strawberry shampoo.

"No luck with the video game," she told him. "Luke didn't play any of it online."

"Well, it was a long shot anyway."

She still looked frustrated that she hadn't been able to make the online connection. "What about the arrangements for the helicopter and the money?"

"All done," Colin assured her. He checked the clock on the nightstand. "If all goes well, in about five hours, we'll have Luke out of there."

"If all goes well," she mumbled.

Yeah. Boyd was still calling the shots, and Colin didn't trust the man. Still, Boyd couldn't stay holed up on the estate forever, despite his threat that there'd be hell to pay.

He set the mug on the table next to her. "I thought you could use this."

Danielle looked at the brew, slightly turned up her nose and eased it aside. "Thanks, but I gave up coffee."

"You what?" Because he was sure he'd misheard her. Danielle could empty an entire coffeepot by herself.

She gave him a forced smile. "I decided I could live without caffeine."

He silently groaned, because she had given up coffee in the past, during those frantic attempts to get pregnant. The caffeine combined with her fertility meds had made her too jittery.

Danielle studied his expression. "No, at the risk of my repeating myself, again, I'm not on fertility drugs," she said as if reading his mind.

The woman knew him too well.

"Good." Except he should have given that answer some thought because her mouth tightened a bit. "Sorry. I didn't mean it like that."

She shrugged and stared at her computer screen, though he was certain she wasn't seeing anything there. He'd hit a very big raw nerve.

"It's okay," she shot back at him. "I never felt as if you were that committed to fatherhood anyway."

Okay. This was an old argument, and it wouldn't lead to anything but a new argument. In the past, he'd just let the argument blow up so it would end and they could get on with their lives. But this morning, Colin just wanted to erase that tension he saw on her face. Danielle already had enough tension with the Boyd situation without their personal stuff being involved in this.

"I never had any objections to fatherhood," Colin clarified.

That caused her head to whip up. "Really?" she said with total disbelief.

"*Really.* It was the treatments that I had issues with. They were painful for you."

Danielle put her focus back on the computer and mumbled, "Sometimes. But I knew a baby would be worth all of that and more."

Yes, it would have been *if* Danielle had gotten pregnant. She hadn't. And that had made all the pain and discomfort seem pointless. Heck, he could say the same for these discussions about the treatments. Nothing good had ever come of them.

"About that kiss," he said so he could change the subject. Though he certainly hadn't picked one that was less volatile. "Want to talk about it?"

"Do you?" she countered. Now, she turned those cool green eyes on him.

Except they weren't so cool.

The heat was still there, and she must have realized that, because the corner of her mouth lifted. "Hormonally speaking, I've always had a weak spot when it came to you."

"Hormones, huh?" He shared a smile with her. "But at least you stopped when the kiss got too hot. If you'd left it to me, we would have had sex. And I think both of us know the timing would have sucked."

She made a small sound of agreement. Barely an agreement at all. And that got Colin to thinking. If the attraction was still there and that strong, was that enough for them to try again? But he shoved that question aside.

The timing still sucked.

"Anything else about our possible mole?" she asked. Obviously, he wasn't the only one who wanted to change the subject.

"Nothing. I'd worried that maybe the mole had told Boyd that Bobby was here. But so far, Boyd hasn't mentioned anything about it."

Danielle made that agreement sound again. "Maybe that means the mole didn't know about Bobby."

Maybe. That was the most logical explanation, and if so, then maybe Dylan and Jerry hadn't mentioned to anyone that they'd brought the young man with them. Of course, there was another possibility.

Maybe Boyd did know.

Unfortunately, Colin couldn't think of any good scenarios as to why Boyd would stay quiet about that.

"Luke's awake," Bobby called out from the other room. "Boyd's having him phone Dr. Connolly now."

That caused Danielle to spring to her feet, and she practically tossed the laptop onto the bed. Colin put his coffee aside and grabbed pen and paper from the nightstand so he could take notes.

"Is Luke okay?" she asked Bobby.

But Bobby's answer was drowned out by the ringing of the cell. "I'm about to pick up," Colin told Bobby so that he'd stay quiet. And then Colin answered. "Good morning, Boyd." Best not to let the man know that Bobby had relayed that it would be Luke calling.

"Agent For-ster," Luke said, his voice small and sleepy. "Can I speak to Dr. Connolly?"

"Of course." Colin put the phone on speaker and passed it to her.

"Hello, Luke. How are you this morning?"

"Okay. I guess. I played Safari Explorer a long, long time last night, and I found the baby giraffe. He was lost in the jungle, and I took him back to his mom."

"That's great, Luke. I knew you'd be able to find him."

"Well, it wasn't easy, and I'm still real sleepy. But Mr. Boyd woke me up 'cause he said I had to call you and then eat breakfast. Not a sugar breakfast, either. He said you said it had to be good for me so I'm gonna eat oatmeal with raisins that he's making in the microwave."

"Good. Oatmeal's healthy. But what were you supposed to call me about?" Danielle's voice was friendly and calm, but Colin could see the tension in her face.

"He didn't say it in a mad way or anything, but Mr. Boyd wants you and Agent For-ster to do something for him. Chores, he said. I have to do chores, too, like picking up my toys, but he said these chores were bigger than that."

Chores. Something Boyd had mentioned in the same context with there'd be *hell to pay*. Colin hoped like the devil that this wouldn't delay Luke's release.

"What are the chores he wants us to do?" Danielle asked.

"I gotta put him on the phone so he can tell, but I'm supposed to tell you something else. I'm supposed to say that you need to do just like he says or else he won't let me play Safari Explorer." Luke paused. "Please do like he says, Dr. Connolly."

Danielle's bottom lip trembled a bit. "I will."

Colin only hoped that they could follow through on that assurance. Both Danielle and he waited. Breaths held. And finally Boyd came on the line.

"Just wanted to let you know how important it is for you two to cooperate," he said. "I figured it'd sink in better if you heard it from Luke's own mouth."

"We know how important this is," Colin assured him. He moved closer to the phone. "Now, what's this about chores?"

"I need both of you to go into town for me. You can use the van that the crime scene folks left behind."

"Town?" Colin questioned. And he got yet another bad feeling about this. "For what?"

"Get a pen and paper because you'll want to write this down."

"I'm ready."

"I need some more peanut butter, the crunchy kind. The kid eats a lot of it. I also want a metal detector—a good one that the crime lab should have. Not some piece of junk you can get from a discount store. And Luke wants Safari Explorer Two because he finished all the levels of the first game."

Colin guessed that maybe the metal detector was to find the money. Maybe Del Gardo had hidden it in chests or some other containers that the device could detect. But the other two items confused him.

"Luke will be going home in about five hours," Colin reminded him. "He won't have a lot of time to eat peanut butter or play another video game."

"Five hours is a long time for a kid."

True, but Colin prayed this didn't mean that Boyd intended to delay the release just so he could continue to search for that money.

"It's seven-fifteen right now," Boyd continued. "Get going and be back here no later than ten-fifteen."

Three hours. That was plenty of time to make the trip and collect the supplies, but that wasn't Colin's concern. "How about I send Dr. Connolly to get the things, and I stay here just in case Luke or you need something?"

"Nice try, but then I figure you'll say she's had an accident or something, anything that'll keep her in town and away from here. No. You're both going, and you'll both be making the return trip. Call me when you get back."

Danielle shook her head. He knew her objection, and it was different from Colin's. He merely wanted her away from the danger, but she didn't want to be that far from Luke in case something went wrong.

"But what if Luke wants to talk to me while I'm gone?" she asked.

"Simple," Boyd answered. "If you've done exactly as I say, without bringing in any badges or anything, then I'll let him call you. Even if you're in town. See? No more reasons or excuses for you not to go."

Colin didn't like the whole idea of this trip, but apparently Boyd wasn't giving Danielle and him a choice, especially since two of the three items on the list were for Luke.

"Oh, and Colin?" The smugness in Boyd's voice caused every nerve in Colin's body to go on full alert. "One last thing. You leave now. I'm timing you, and you gotta be in that van in exactly one minute."

"Or what?" Colin challenged.

"You don't want to know *or what*," Boyd challenged back.

Colin cursed because he wasn't sure he did want to know. Besides, this wasn't the time to push Boyd into doing something that none of them wanted.

Danielle put on her shoes and hurried for the door. Colin was right behind her, and he held the cell phone so both of them could hear anything else Boyd had to say.

Apparently, the man wasn't finished.

"Don't lock the front door," Boyd said the moment they were outside. "Remember that one-minute rule about getting out of there," he added. "Don't stop. Get to the van."

Colin glanced back at the door. And at Danielle. She motioned for him to hurry, and that's what he did. Jogging, they went through the gates and to the van.

"By the way, while you two are gone, I'm gonna do a little inspection of the guesthouse."

Hell. That put a tighter knot in Colin's stomach and nearly caused him to turn around and go back.

"I'm heading down there right now," Boyd added. His smugness was still there, and it came through as a threat.

Danielle looked at him, and she saw the concern and the fear in her eyes. Colin had that same fear and concern. The only silver lining in this was that Bobby was almost certainly eavesdropping on this conversation.

"Why an inspection?" Colin asked Boyd as calmly as he could manage. He handed Danielle the phone, they buckled up and he got the van started, though he didn't want to leave. He wanted to warn Bobby. But he couldn't. Because disobeying the "rules" might cause Boyd to take Luke and run. Or worse.

"I just want to check and make sure you're not hiding anybody in there," Boyd said. "Nothing to worry about, right? Because I know you wouldn't risk something like that."

Colin had a split-second debate with himself and knew he had to leave. He couldn't risk Boyd nixing the deal.

Was this a bluff? Or did Boyd know that Bobby was inside? Either way, this could be a dangerous turn. Colin prayed that Bobby could get himself and all the equipment down into the tunnel before Boyd reached the guesthouse.

"Now, get the van moving or the whole deal is off," Boyd threatened. "The helicopter, the ransom. Everything will be off, and I take Luke and run."

"Run?" Danielle and Colin said in unison.

"You heard me right. Despite what you might think, there's another way out of here. And if you don't play nice, the Vaughns will blame you for never being able to see their kid again."

Chapter Seven

With the cell phone now clutched in her hand, Danielle waited for Bobby to call. She didn't dare risk calling him for fear that Boyd would hear the sound of the incoming call and put his crazy backup plan into motion.

"You really think Boyd can escape with Luke?" she asked.

Colin had stopped on the side of the road, just out of sight of the estate but close enough that they could respond if Bobby needed them. "It's possible."

Even though she already knew that was the answer, it still sickened her. They had to get the child back to his family. She couldn't fail at this.

Colin grabbed another cell phone from the van's glove compartment and keyed in some numbers. To the Kenner County Crime Lab, she soon realized. He explained what was going on and asked them to gather the three items that Boyd had requested. Good. That would save them some time. Except time was the one thing they seemed to have a lot of. After all, Boyd had given them three hours, and even if they hurried, it would take at least an hour of that. An hour was more than enough for Boyd to be able to go through the entire guesthouse and comb the place for any sign of Bobby.

The phone in her hand rang, and the caller ID indicated it was from the Kenner County Crime Unit. Since Colin was on the line with the lab itself, she prayed this was from Bobby.

"Yes?" she answered cautiously, just in case it was Boyd who was making the call.

"It's me, Bobby." He not only sounded safe, he sounded calm. "I grabbed everything I could and went into the tunnel. Just in case Boyd comes down here looking for me, I'm going out to the exit on the road and will hide there. Let me know when and if it's okay to go back."

Danielle blew out a long breath of relief. "We will. Just be careful in case there are any more explosives hidden down there."

"I will," Bobby assured her. As soon as he hung up, Danielle let Colin know what was going on.

"Bobby's okay," Colin relayed to the crime unit, and he ended the call with them and started the drive toward town.

That was one bullet they'd dodged.

Heaven knew how many were ahead.

"Remember," Colin reminded her, "there might be a mole at the lab. Rusty Cepeda. Or maybe even someone else. Don't say anything important in front of anyone that you don't trust completely."

She nodded and wondered who that would be. Other than Callie and Colin, she didn't have anyone on her trust list.

Danielle replayed Bobby's words in her head. He'd definitely been calm. Not the tone of a man who'd barely escaped possible death. Of course, she didn't know him well at all and maybe this was normal for him. Still, it wouldn't hurt to check and make sure he didn't have any skeletons that would make him become a mole.

For that matter, it wouldn't hurt to do the same to Dylan and Jerry. Sometimes people who volunteered to be close to the crime scene were part of the crime. But Danielle didn't know how Colin would react to having his fellow agents investigated.

Even though they had plenty of time, Colin didn't waste any of it. He drove down the mountain on the winding road and went straight to the crime lab. Callie was outside waiting for them, and the moment Danielle stepped from the van, Callie engulfed her in a big hug.

"Are you all right?" Callie whispered, dropping her gaze to Danielle's stomach.

"I'm fine." And since Callie seemed to be waiting for more, Danielle whispered, "I haven't told him yet. If I tell him, it'll be after Luke's rescue."

"If?" Callie questioned.

She didn't explain further because Colin walked over to her and put his hand on Danielle's shoulder to get her moving inside. Jerry Ortiz was there, along with six others. Since she'd seen three of them at the estate, Danielle narrowed down which one had to be Rusty. He was no doubt the blond-haired young man working at the computer.

Was this Boyd's mole?

"We've got the metal detector ready," Callie let her know. "And I've sent someone for the video game, peanut butter and a change of clothes for both Colin and you. Everything should be here within the hour."

Good. That should get them back to the estate with plenty of time to spare. Danielle checked her watch—they'd only been gone about twenty minutes.

"What if Boyd puts eavesdropping devices in the guesthouse while we're gone?" Danielle asked. "Do we need any extra equipment to detect them?"

Colin shook his head. "Hopefully, Bobby will be able to detect anything with the equipment he already has—because I doubt we can sneak in something like that, and I don't want anyone to have to risk bringing us equipment through the tunnels."

He was right. And they didn't want to do anything to upset Boyd. They'd just have to watch their conversation to make sure they didn't say anything about Bobby's presence—if Bobby could make it back. It was entirely possible that Boyd would figure out the young man had been there and send Bobby running back to the lab.

Colin took the phone from her hand. "I'd better hang on to this just in case Boyd or Luke calls," he commented. He, too, glanced at Rusty. "While I'm here Jerry wants me to go over some of the details of the helicopter and the money transfer, but I'll come and get you the minute the supplies arrive." He lowered his voice to a whisper. "Why don't you ask Callie about Rusty?"

Maybe Colin had come to the same conclusion, that the man had been a little too calm under fire. "I'll ask her about Bobby, Dylan and Jerry, too."

Colin shook his head but then shrugged. "I don't know about Bobby, but Tom Ryan vouched for Dylan, and I trust Tom. He wasn't so praiseworthy of Jerry, though."

"So, be careful around him," she warned. But didn't move. Neither did Colin. And for a moment, she thought he was going to put one of those husbandly pecks on her cheek. It would have been totally inappropriate, but for some reason, she braced herself for it anyway.

It didn't happen.

Colin tore his gaze from hers and followed Jerry toward the back of the lab. Callie motioned for her to go into her office, and once they were inside, Danielle shut the door so they'd have some privacy when she asked about Rusty.

Callie's desk was littered with photos and reports, including pictures of possible escape routes around the estate. Hopefully, there were photos of *all* escape routes, especially considering Boyd's latest threat.

"Boyd said if we didn't do this errand, he'd take Luke and run," Danielle explained, sinking down into the chair across from Callie's desk.

"I figured there was a chance of that. He's got to be getting desperate by now. Don't worry, the FBI and the local sheriff will do their best to keep the tunnels locked down," Callie assured her, but they both knew that was nearly impossible.

If Boyd truly wanted to get out with Luke, he just might succeed.

"I need to ask you about Rusty. And Bobby," Danielle started. "Any chance either of them could be feeding info to Boyd?"

That improved Callie's posture. Her shoulders went back. "Why? Do you have any proof they can't be trusted?" Her voice took on a cool, detached edge. A boss defending her people.

"No proof. Not even anything circumstantial. But someone is giving Boyd information, and Colin and I need to know who's doing that."

"So do I." Callie's shoulders relaxed a bit. "Rusty's fairly new here, but neither Bobby nor he has given me any reason to distrust them. No red flags in their background checks, either, but I'll run them again."

"Thanks."

Callie rummaged in a small fridge behind her and came up with two bottles of orange juice. "So, how have you handled being in such close quarters with Colin?"

Danielle opened her mouth to lie and say everything was fine, but the lie would stick in her throat. "I kissed him."

Her friend had the decency not to laugh or say something about that being a stupid thing to do. But Callie's left eyebrow rose a fraction.

"It meant nothing." Well, nothing other than the fact he could still get her hotter than fire. "The issues that ended our marriage are still there."

"Well, minus the whole fertility thing," Callie reminded her. And now she smiled.

"Colin and I will be divorced in less than two days," Danielle reminded her right back.

"It's not over until it's over."

"It's over," Danielle assured her and wondered if that was the biggest lie of all.

The emotion and feelings weren't over, but she couldn't go through more waiting and watching for Colin to be hurt on the dangerous assignments he seemed to thrive on. She wanted stability. A home for her unborn child. And right now, Colin didn't seem interested in becoming a traditional father in a traditional family.

"What about that *if* you used earlier?" Callie questioned. "Please tell me you're not thinking about keeping this a secret from him."

Danielle groaned softly. "I know I shouldn't even consider it, but this is where my old baggage comes into play. My mother forced my dad into marriage because she was pregnant with me. My father hated her for it. And I don't want Colin to feel the same way about me."

Callie leaned closer and met her eye to eye. "You have to let Colin decide for himself if he'll feel trapped. And for that to happen, you have to tell him."

Callie was right, but Danielle didn't know how she could make him understand that she had no expectations about his role in all of this. Colin was a problem solver. The kind to jump headfirst into a difficult situation, and she didn't want him to make a hasty decision that he couldn't live with.

Just so she wouldn't have to continue this conversation, Danielle picked up one of the photos from Callie's desk. Not of the estate or the kidnapping crime scene. It was the picture of a man with dark brown hair and brooding brown eyes.

"That's Ben Parrish," Callie supplied. "The missing FBI agent that everyone's looking for. He's also a close friend," she added with heavy emotion in her voice.

"The one with the pregnant wife," Danielle mumbled.

Callie nodded and rubbed her fatigue-weary eyes. "We're not even close to finding him. There's no physical evidence, other than a single piece of fabric and some broken tree branches taken from his last known location."

And those things could be signs of a struggle. Or perhaps even an indication he'd been killed. His wife had no doubt already come to that horrible conclusion.

Danielle stared at the photo and thought of Colin. Of how she would feel if he were missing and maybe even dead. Tears filled her eyes before she could stop them, and she silently cursed her overly hormonal reaction. This had to stop. She couldn't continue to let her feelings for him bounce around.

Callie handed her a tissue and would have likely launched into a Q&A about the tears. However, the knock at the door stopped that from happening. The door opened, and Danielle expected to see Colin. But it wasn't him. However, she did recognize the tall, dark-haired man from photos she'd seen in the newspapers.

This was Elliot Hennessey, the attorney for the late crime boss, Vincent Del Gardo. Since it was Del Gardo's money that Boyd was searching for, Danielle was suddenly very interested in why Elliot was at the crime lab.

Did he have anything to do with Boyd and the kidnapping?

"Mr. Hennessey," Callie said, getting to her feet. "I understand you were here yesterday looking for me?"

"Yes. You were out."

"And you refused to leave a message or tell anyone the reason for your visit. So, what can I do for you?" Though it wasn't a warm offer from Callie.

He glanced at Danielle first. "I have something for you." He handed Callie a thick padded envelope. "Under the terms of Mr. Del Gardo's will, I'm to deliver that to you. Your people have already scanned it, to make sure it's not a bomb or anything." Elliot turned to walk away.

"Wait." Callie looked at the envelope. "What's this all about?"

"When you read it, I think you'll know. If you have

questions, give me a call." And with that vague answer, Elliot left.

Danielle peered outside the door to make sure the man wasn't hanging around. He wasn't. However, he did stop when Jerry said something to him. She couldn't hear what, but she wasn't pleased to see that Rusty joined in on the conversation, as well.

"Open it," Danielle insisted when Callie just stared at it. "It might have something to do with Boyd and the kidnapping."

She doubted it. Boyd and Del Gardo were on opposite sides since Boyd was working for Del Gardo's rival, Nicky Wayne. However, that didn't mean the two men hadn't collaborated on a crime, especially one that might be worth so much money.

Callie opened the envelope and silently read the first page. After several moments, she dropped back down into her chair, and the color drained from her face. With her hand trembling, she passed the paper to Danielle.

Oh, mercy. Danielle wasn't sure she wanted to know what had caused her friend to have that kind of reaction.

It was a letter, and according to the signature, it was from Vincent Del Gardo himself. Not a document with legal terms. This letter was personal.

"'Callie, years ago, I met your mother, Brenda,'" Danielle read aloud, "'and we had an affair.'" Danielle stopped. "Whoa. Did you know about this?"

Callie shook her head. "Keep reading."

Danielle did. Del Gardo went on to explain he'd been married at the time of the affair, and that's why Callie's mom and he had kept it secret. And then Danielle got to the next part, and she understood the reason her friend had gone pale. "Vincent Del Gardo is your biological father?"

Callie didn't answer. She downed the juice as if it were hard liquor, and she was probably wishing that it was.

"Your mother never mentioned this before she died?" Danielle asked.

"Not a word." Callie's hands were shaking as she took out the rest of the items in the envelope.

Then, this was indeed a bombshell for Callie.

Danielle kept reading. "Del Gardo says that he's always loved you and that's the reason he bought the estate in Kenner City. So he'd be near you." Even though these were the words of a former crime boss, the next part still touched Danielle. "He said he's sorry you were scared of him, that he only wanted to get to know his daughter."

Callie blinked back tears. "I couldn't figure out why he kept coming around. And yes, I was scared of him."

Danielle reached out and slipped her hand over Callie's. "Of course, you were. You didn't know he was your father."

That hit Danielle like a ton of bricks. How ironic she'd be reading this now, when she had her own doubts about telling Colin that he would soon have a child. Trapping him wouldn't be good, but keeping her pregnancy a secret couldn't happen, either.

Callie brushed the tears from her cheeks. "He might not be telling the truth," she said. She pushed aside the envelope and the other items she'd taken from it and logged on to her computer. "Because he was murdered, Del Gardo's DNA will be on file. Mine, too. All the crime lab employees have DNA profiles in the system because of their background checks."

Callie actually seemed hopeful that this was all some big lie. But Danielle didn't think so. The tone of Del Gardo's letter wasn't that of a liar, but a father who'd desperately wanted to get to know his child.

With the sound of Callie's frantic computer key-strokes clicking through the room, Danielle leaned against the desk. There were other papers in the envelope, and she only hoped they didn't contain unsettling information like the first.

When Callie finished typing, the tears filled her eyes again. "Why wouldn't my mother have told me that Del Gardo was my father? Why did she let me believe a lie all these years?"

Danielle walked around the desk, leaned down and hugged her. "Maybe your mother thought it'd be easier for you this way."

"Easier?" Callie snapped. "And in doing so, she made it a lot harder."

Yes, Danielle could see that. She held Callie until there was a dinging sound on her computer. Callie turned, looked at the screen and shuddered.

Danielle soon saw why.

CALLIE STARED AT THE SCREEN. The DNA comparison was there. Plain as day. Her DNA was a statistical match to Vincent Del Gardo.

The man was her biological father.

"Callie?" Danielle questioned. "Are you okay?"

No. Far from it. But Callie managed a nod. "Could you give me a minute alone?" Callie asked. Even though a minute wasn't nearly enough. She might need a lifetime or two to come to terms with this. God. How could this be happening? She'd devoted most of her adult life to solving crimes, yet her father was a criminal.

Danielle brushed a kiss on her forehead and thankfully walked out, easing the door shut. Callie tried not to cry. She failed. And the tears began to stream down her cheeks. As soon as she wiped them away, more came. Somehow, and fast, she needed to come to terms with this because she didn't have time for an emotional meltdown.

She forced herself to look at what remained in the envelope and prayed it wasn't another bombshell. She'd already had her quota for the day. But she soon realized it was a bombshell of a different variety.

It was another letter from Del Gardo. From her father, she amended. "'I've put money in an offshore account for you,'" she read aloud.

Callie instantly got a bad feeling about this.

"'I didn't want to risk putting this information about the account in my will,'" Del Gardo continued to say, "'so I had parts of the offshore account number put on three medals that were sent to three different people.'"

"The medals," Callie mumbled, recalling the mysterious medals that Tom and Ben had received from Julie Grainger. And she continued to read the letter, the words seemingly echoing through the room. "'The first is the St. Raphael, the patron saint of nightmares, because I hope to never be the cause of another one of your nightmares. The second is the St. Christopher, the patron saint of travelers, so you'll be safe no matter where life takes you. Finally, there's the St. Joan of Arc medal, the patron saint of imprisonment. That represents a prison of my own making. A prison that prevented me from knowing my own daughter.'"

She had to read the last line three times for it to sink in. It sounded as if he loved her.

Maybe he had.

More tears threatened, but Callie choked them back and forced herself to keep reading. "'Each of those medals contains a series of numbers. Put them all together, and you have the offshore account that I left for you.'"

An offshore account and a covert way of hiding the account numbers. Del Gardo was probably accustomed to doing business this way, but Callie hated all this subterfuge.

She stared at the papers that had changed her life. Money, medals and paternity. None of that mattered right now. Freeing Luke was the only thing she wanted on her mind. She wouldn't even bother her husband with this now. It could wait. Besides, she wasn't even sure she wanted her father's money.

Callie grabbed the envelope, shoved the papers back inside and crammed it into her desk drawer. There was no good reason to tell anyone right now about her father and what he'd left her.

DANIELLE LEANED AGAINST Callie's office door and waited. The minutes crawled by, and Danielle was about to knock, to ask Callie if she was okay, but she heard the footsteps. Colin and Jerry were walking straight toward her. Colin had changed his clothes and now wore black jeans and a black shirt. He had his badge clipped to his belt.

Colin handed her a leather overnight bag. "This is a change of clothes for you. But you should probably dress here, because Boyd might not let us take the extra items onto the grounds."

True. She took the bag from him.

Colin looked at Danielle, and then at Callie's closed office door. "What's wrong? Why are you out here?"

Danielle thankfully didn't have to answer because the door opened, and there was Callie. Both Jerry and Colin looked at her and then at Danielle. It was obvious that Callie had been crying, and both men would want explanations.

"I just got some tough personal news," Callie volunteered, "but it's nothing I can't handle."

Danielle studied her friend's somber face and hoped that was true.

"Does this have anything to do with Elliot Hennessey's visit?" Colin asked.

Callie nodded, and Danielle wondered how much she would tell him, especially in front of Jerry.

Colin mumbled some profanity. "I wish I'd known Elliot's visit would upset you, and I would have stayed put while he talked to you. I know him. I've had some long interrogations with one of his clients. During those, he always seemed, well, reasonable. Guess I had the wrong opinion of him."

"He was just the messenger." Callie looked at Jerry. "Could you excuse us for a minute?"

Jerry mumbled, "Sure," and walked away. Maybe because Danielle was suspicious of everything, she thought he seemed a little angry at being dismissed from a private conversation.

Callie then turned to Danielle. "Why don't you go ahead and change your clothes? I want to talk to Colin about the plans for the helicopter and ransom money."

"You're sure?" Danielle asked. "I can wait."

"I'm sure." Callie gave her a reassuring pat on the arm. That was Danielle's cue to get moving. Besides, she didn't want to hang around much longer. Best to get back to the estate so she'd be near Luke in case he needed her.

Danielle went to the bathroom just up the hall. It was unisex and small but thankfully the door locked. She went inside and started to strip down. Colin's old clothes were there, in a folded pile on the floor. Danielle decided to do the same with hers.

She took the clean clothes from the bag and had a moment of panic. There was a loose beige Bohemian style skirt. The stretchy waist was no problem for her slight baby bump. Ditto for the underwear, though her breasts practically fell out of the bra. She panicked when it came to the top. It was dark purple and stretchy, as well, but it clung to her far more than her business suit.

Danielle tried to look in the mirror. No easy task, since it wasn't full-length. And finally she just gave up. If Colin noticed the bump, then that would open up the conversation they needed to have anyway.

She quickly folded her old clothes and stooped down to put them next to Colin's. The glint of metal caught her eye, and she saw the ring sticking out from his back pocket.

His wedding ring.

Strange. *Why would it be there?* She picked it up and headed back to Callie's office.

Colin was still with her, talking about the helicopter arrangements. Thankfully, he didn't seem to notice her slight belly bulge.

But Danielle did notice something.

Rusty was hovering near the water cooler. Only a few

yards from Callie's office. He had his attention fastened to a paper in his hand, but because she was already in a suspicious mood, she had to wonder if he was trying to discreetly listen in on the conversation.

When Danielle walked past him, Rusty looked up. Nodded in greeting. And turned his attention back to whatever he was reading.

"We might have an audience," Danielle whispered to Colin.

Colin stepped out of Callie's office and glanced out at Rusty. "How long has he been there?" And he didn't exactly whisper it.

"I don't know."

Colin stared at the man, and when Rusty noticed them, he quietly walked away.

"We didn't say anything about Boyd or Luke," Colin muttered.

Good. Because Rusty might be on the up-and-up, but she didn't want to take any chances. "Is Callie okay?"

"I think so. She told me that Del Gardo's her father." Colin cursed, shook his head. "That won't be an easy pill to swallow. She also said there was something she might need my help with. Something about an offshore account and some religious medals. She'll give me the details just as soon as Luke is free."

Danielle nodded. And maybe it wouldn't be long before Luke was indeed free. "What about the other items Boyd wanted? Do we have everything we need to take back to the estate?"

"We have all but the video game. The nearest store was out, but the clerk remembered selling one to a kid who lives about a mile from here. Dylan called the family, and they're going to let us have the game. All we have to do is pick it up."

Colin's cell phone rang, and he glanced at the screen and answered it. "Boyd," Colin said. He checked his watch and put the phone on speaker. "Is everything okay?"

"I guess you could say that. I locked the kid in his room so I could search the guesthouse. I didn't find any badges in the guesthouse. That's good."

Danielle pressed her hand to her chest to steady her breathing. This was the news she'd wanted to hear. It meant Bobby was safe. Now, if she could only decide if Colin and she were safe from him. A glance at Callie confirmed that the woman would be making those background checks soon.

"The arrangements for the helicopter and money are final," Colin explained. "In fact, if you want to move up the time for Luke's release—"

"No. I want to spend a few hours with the metal detector first. In fact, I want to spend some time *now*."

"Now?" Colin repeated.

"Now," Boyd confirmed. "I'm giving you and the doc thirty minutes to get back up here. If not, I'll delay Luke's release until tonight. Better hurry." And he hung up.

Colin cursed and latched on to Danielle's arm. They raced toward the van.

Chapter Eight

He was out of breath by the time he made it to the curve on the mountain road. Dead Man's Curve, the locals called it. The name suited it because one wrong jerk of the steering wheel, and a car would plunge right down the mountain.

With luck, that might happen today.

Running, he got into place behind one of the massive outcroppings of rocks that littered the road. He got his rifle ready.

And he waited.

It shouldn't be long. Mere minutes.

"Medals," he mumbled. He smiled just thinking about them.

Specifically, medals that would lead to an offshore account, and thanks to the bug in Callie's office, he'd learned all about it. There'd be tons of money in the account. He had no doubts about that. Vincent Del Gardo had cash to burn and instead of hiding it in the Vaughn estate, maybe he'd put it in that account instead.

For his illegitimate daughter, Callie.

That was touching, but Callie didn't need her late

daddy's cash. *He* did. The last turn at the blackjack table had cost him a fortune. A fortune he didn't have and one he'd have to pay back before the end of the week.

Or else.

This time, that *or else* would almost certainly be his own murder. He wouldn't die because of this sickness, this obsession he had with blackjack. Any shrink worth his salt would say that the gambling was a disease, beyond his control. But the men that he owed money to would only laugh at the idea. They wouldn't care. They'd kill him if he couldn't pay.

That's why the medals were a godsend.

All he had to do was find them. Three people had them. He'd heard Callie tell Colin that she might need his help with the medals and the offshore account—so she'd be able to get the money she didn't even need.

Or deserve.

Vincent Del Gardo had likely gotten all that cash from years and years of illegal deals, years of robbing people at places like blackjack tables, and that meant the money was ripe for the taking. He could use it to save his own life, and that was certainly a better use for it than anything Callie might do with it. Hell, she'd probably just donate it to a charity or something anyway.

So, he had to get his hands on the medals. But first, there was something he had to nip in the bud.

He had to stop Colin Forester and Danielle Connolly.

THIS HAD TO END. Somehow, Colin had to get control of the situation with Boyd.

But how?

He couldn't push too hard or risk upsetting Luke,

but he also couldn't let a man like Boyd continue to call the shots.

Colin stopped at the house to grab the video game. Thankfully, the boy's mother was waiting on the porch for him so he practically snatched it from her hands and thanked her as he ran back to the van. The detour had cost them about ten minutes, but a half hour was plenty of time to do this errand and then make it back. Still, he didn't want to be late. God knew how Boyd would react to that.

"If Boyd's trying to make us crazy," Danielle commented, "then he's doing a good job of it."

Yeah. He was. But the trick was for Danielle and him to stay calm. Boyd might be feeding on the panic that he was creating by issuing orders, only to change them. And maybe there was some logic to this seeming madness. Boyd no doubt wanted them off-kilter so he could ensure that he was the one who stayed in control.

Danielle put the video game into the equipment bag with the other items Boyd had requested. She also retrieved her personal cell phone from her purse that she'd left in the van the day before, and then she checked her watch. "Three and a half hours until the helicopter and the exchange. We'll just have to do as Boyd says until then."

Colin mumbled an agreement and took the road leading to the estate. He didn't object to kowtowing to Boyd during that time, but he kept getting a bad feeling that all of Boyd's ploys had a deeper, more sinister intent. Had all of this been a ruse just to get them away from the guesthouse? And if so, then what had Boyd hoped to accomplish?

Because he didn't want to risk making the call from the guesthouse, he grabbed his personal cell that he'd left in the van and called directory assistance to get Elliot Hennessey's number. Colin called the man, but it went straight to voice mail. It wouldn't be wise to leave a message, especially since he didn't want Elliot trying to call him back. So, Colin would have to try again later.

A sound alerted him. Danielle dropped something into one of the cup holders. It landed with a metallic ping.

His wedding ring.

"It was in the pocket of the pants you left in the bathroom at the crime unit. I wasn't sure what would happen to the clothes, so I decided to...well, get it for you."

"Oh." That was all he said for several moments. "And your rings are on a chain around your neck." He didn't actually say it, but the "Why?" was there.

She didn't respond to that unspoken "Why?" Nor did she pick up on the previous conversation about Boyd. The silence between them became awkward, and Danielle merely looked away and used the moment to shove her cell phone in the pocket of her skirt.

Colin considered an explanation, but when he mentally went through it, he decided it best that he stay quiet, as well. It'd be a bear to explain to Danielle that he'd removed the ring the day before when he'd noticed she wasn't wearing hers. An explanation like that would only make him sound petty.

He fished the ring out of the cup holder and shoved it into his front jeans pocket. Colin didn't look to see what her reaction was to that. He didn't care. He was keeping his ring, even if he never wore it again.

There was a sharp bend in the road, and Colin eased off the accelerator so he could make the turn. He was halfway into it when he heard the loud pop. Before he had time to register what was happening, the steering wheel jerked to the left.

Straight toward the flimsy looking guardrail.

"The tire blew out," Colin told Danielle. Luckily, she was wearing her seat belt, but she also caught on to the armrest and the console.

Colin grabbed the steering wheel with both hands and used every bit of his strength to keep it away from the guardrail. He didn't want to bump it even a little because beyond that was the steep drop down the mountain. There was little chance they'd survive a fall.

There was another loud popping sound.

And with that sound, the adrenaline roared through Colin. Because he knew. This wasn't an ordinary blowout.

Someone had shot out the tires.

"Oh, God," Danielle mumbled.

The van jerked violently to the left again. Someone had shot out a back tire, and that someone was obviously trying to kill them. If Colin didn't do something immediately, the person would succeed.

Colin wrenched the steering wheel toward the right, and he pumped the brakes. But he essentially had no control. The steering wheel felt cemented in place, and they were headed for that guardrail.

Beside him, Danielle arched her back, trying to brace herself for an impact, but there was no way to brace for this.

Colin pinpointed all that adrenaline into one last attempt. He groaned from the strain of his muscles, and he gave the brakes one last pump.

The van skidded to a stop, the front bumper slamming into the guardrail.

Danielle gasped. Colin held his breath.

And with his heart pounding like a war drum, he glanced down. The front left tire was off the road and literally hanging in midair.

"Get out," he told Danielle, though it was risky. After all, someone had shot the tires, and that someone might still be out there.

Waiting to finish the job.

Danielle grabbed the equipment bag that held the supplies, unbuckled her seat belt and threw open the door. The van rocked, threatening to plunge down the mountain.

"Just go," Colin insisted. And he unhooked his own seat belt so he could try to scramble out after Danielle.

She glanced at him, and he saw the terror in her eyes. There wasn't time to reassure her. There wasn't time for anything. One gust of wind could kill them.

"Now!" he shouted.

With the equipment bag in her hand, she plunged out. The van wobbled. As Colin had expected. Without Danielle's weight on the passenger side, the vehicle was off balance.

And about to fall.

He dove across the seat, scrambled out, and the moment his feet landed on the ground, he caught on to Danielle's arm and got her away from the van. It wasn't a second too soon. The van tipped to the side, and it broke through what was left of the damaged guardrail.

It plummeted over the side, bashing against the rocks before it crashed onto a narrow ledge below.

"We could have been killed," Danielle whispered.

Yeah. And it might not be over.

Colin drew his gun and dragged her to the other side

of the road so that the mountain itself would give them some measure of protection. He looked around, but didn't see a gunman.

That didn't mean he wasn't there.

The mountain wasn't a smooth surface but instead was littered with rock outcroppings and crevasses. Someone could be using those to hide.

But who?

Was this the work of the mole?

Or was Boyd behind this?

He could have asked his boss, Nicky Wayne, to send someone in to finish them off. But why would Boyd want them dead?

Colin fired glances all around. And listened. The only sounds he heard were their racing breaths and the wind.

"How far to the estate?" Danielle asked, looking down at her watch.

"Not far. A half mile at the most." He did a time check, too. They still had a little over fifteen minutes before Boyd's deadline was up, but they needed to get moving. He doubted Boyd would care that they'd nearly died. And Colin didn't want the man to use their being late as an excuse to do anything stupid.

Colin positioned Danielle to his side, and they started walking. They didn't get far.

A bullet slammed into the rocks just above their heads.

Colin pushed Danielle behind those rocks, just as another shot came at them. It landed close to where the first shot had landed and sent an angry spray of sharp fragments raining down on them.

Another shot.

Then another.

Each one allowed Colin to pinpoint the direction of the shooter. The person was using a long-range rifle and was ahead of them, higher up the mountain. And in the direction of the estate.

"The gunman might be using the tunnels," Colin heard Danielle say.

Possibly. After all, the tunnels weren't exactly a secret. Everyone in Kenner City no doubt knew about them, including a mole. But Boyd also knew. And Bobby. Colin hated to suspect the young man without cause, but it was obvious that someone wanted them dead.

The shots continued, and Colin knew he had to do something. They couldn't just lie there and hope they continued to be lucky. He levered himself up slightly so he could do another visual check.

There.

He saw it.

A glint of metal coming from another rock outcropping just up the road.

Colin couldn't see the gunman. The person was wearing a dark gray raincoat, and the hood and the shadows concealed the person's face.

The gunman popped off three more shots in a row, causing more rock fragments to pelt them. With Danielle face down on the ground, Colin crawled over her so that he was hovering above her back. This way, he could try to protect her. She probably wouldn't appreciate the fact that he was risking his life to save her, but he didn't care. He was an FBI agent and had been trained to deal with situations like this.

Except he'd never envisioned a situation where he'd have to protect Danielle.

Colin waited for the next round of shots. Like before, there were three more. And he knew he had to act now. He levered himself up again.

Took aim.

And fired.

The blast was deafening and echoed through the mountain.

Colin waited, breath held, and he kept his attention fastened to the area where he'd seen that glint of metal. The seconds ticked off in his head, and just when he was ready to fire a second shot, the hooded gunman dropped out of sight. Like a gopher going into a hole.

Oh, yes. The person had definitely used the tunnels.

"He's gone," Colin relayed to Danielle.

She practically went limp and then tried to get up. But he stopped her. He also kept watch around them. He didn't want the gunman using another tunnel to get closer to them so he could have a better shot.

"We have to get back to the estate," Danielle reminded him.

Yes. But they weren't going to blindly do that without taking precautions. Colin waited several more minutes. Still no sign of the gunman. So, he stood. Waited some more. But no shots came. He helped Danielle to her feet but kept her sandwiched between the mountain and him so that she wouldn't be in the direct line of fine.

Well, unless the guy managed to backtrack.

"Let's go," Colin instructed. He hooked the equipment bag over his shoulder and got them moving.

They started up the mountain, not using the road, but

the narrow easement. Danielle was wearing flat beige shoes that obviously weren't made for walking up mountains. She wobbled on the uneven surface, and he caught on to her arm to steady her.

"We need to hurry," she reminded him. And despite her unsure footing, she fell into a quick pace. Not a run, exactly. But it wasn't a leisurely pace, either.

He checked his watch. This was going to be close. Too close. But Colin wasn't about to call Boyd to give him a heads-up as to what'd happened. What if Boyd was the shooter?

Danielle was out of breath when they reached the top, and he prayed she didn't have another of those dizzy spells. If she was even slightly light-headed, she certainly didn't show any signs of it.

Colin put his gun in the back waist of his pants so that Boyd wouldn't see it, and Danielle and he made a beeline for the front gates. The gates opened as they approached.

The phone rang, and Colin handed Danielle the equipment bag so he could get the cell from his pocket to answer it.

It was Boyd.

"You're late," the man greeted.

"A minute or two. Someone shot out the tires of the van and nearly sent us over the side of the mountain. Would you happen to know anything about that?"

And Colin didn't bother asking it nicely, either. He was pissed that someone had put Danielle in that kind of danger and even more upset that he hadn't been able to stop it.

"Don't have a clue what you're talking about," Boyd

insisted. "But I did hear the shots. It doesn't appear that either of you are hurt."

Boyd sounded so cavalier that Colin wanted to crawl through the phone and knock some sense into the guy, but he forced himself to stay calm.

"We have the supplies you requested," Colin informed him.

"Yeah, I can see the bag."

Which meant Boyd had to be somewhere at the front of the house. Colin checked the gardens where Boyd had surfaced before, but he didn't see him. Finally, he spotted a flutter in the curtains in one of the front-facing rooms. Too bad Colin didn't have a clean shot because he could end this here and now. No more negotiations with this moron.

"Leave the bag on the front porch," Boyd instructed. "And strip down so I can see if you got a gun while you were in town. Because I could have sworn I heard two sets of shots on the mountain."

Colin ignored that last comment, and they started walking toward the porch. "We're not stripping down. Danielle and I have been through hell and back to get you these supplies. Well, we got them, and I'm a little tired of you using this situation to get your jollies at having us strip."

It was a gamble. Because it could enrage Boyd, but if that happened, Colin would deal with it. After all, Boyd needed them if he had any hopes of escape.

The seconds crawled by, and finally Boyd laughed. "Jollies? Well, maybe I got some from the doc. She's a knockout, Colin, and that makes you one stupid man for letting the likes of her get away."

Danielle started to say something, but Colin nudged her so she'd stay quiet. He wanted to continue this banter if possible.

"Yeah. I can be stupid when it comes to relationships," Colin admitted. He went up the steps and dropped the equipment bag onto the porch.

"Many thanks," Boyd said, his voice way too cheery considering the gravity of the situation.

"How's Luke?" Colin asked.

"Finishing up his second bowl of oatmeal. The kid eats like a horse."

Good. Colin certainly didn't hear the little boy complaining or anything. He hoped that was a good sign. "Speaking of Luke, his folks will want proof he's okay before they transfer those funds. So, why don't you bring the boy to the window so we can see him?"

"I'll do that. In an hour or two."

Colin shook his head. "But the helicopter is due in less than three hours. No need to cut it close. I wouldn't want any delays in you getting the ransom money." Colin had to speak through clenched teeth to get out that last part.

"Oh, I'm sure I'll get the money. Both the ransom and what I'm looking for here at the estate. And you see, Colin, that's a problem. Because now that I have a metal detector, I need a little more time."

"Time?" Colin snarled.

Hell. No. This couldn't happen.

"Time," Boyd confirmed. "I figure you're not gonna like this, but you'll have to do it anyway. 'Cause I'm not really giving you a choice."

"What do you want now?"

"Call off the helicopter and the money transfer,"

Boyd said. "I don't want either until tomorrow. And, Colin? Do as I say, or the delay will be permanent. You don't want to know just how long I can stay holed up here with Luke Vaughn."

Chapter Nine

Danielle couldn't stop shaking.

It wasn't just her hands. Her entire body was trembling. It was probably a reaction to nearly being killed and then getting Boyd's latest bombshell about the delay. That was more emotion and danger than she'd ever been asked to deal with.

"Come on," Colin said. He grasped her arm to get her moving off the porch and toward the guesthouse.

She wanted to dig in her heels, to stay put and demand that Boyd release Luke immediately, but she knew it wouldn't help the situation.

"What should we do?" she asked Colin.

He glanced over his shoulder at the estate. "I'll ask Dylan and Tom to try to work their way through one of Boyd's barricades so we can get someone into the estate."

She immediately thought of a problem with that. "What about the mole?"

Colin stopped on the other side of a tree just outside the guesthouse and took out his phone. "I won't call them from inside the guesthouse."

"Because you don't trust Bobby?"

"No. I trust him. Dylan said he was a good guy."

She thought about that several moments. "And you think Dylan is right?"

"Who knows? When I was at the lab, I called my office and asked them to do financial checks on Bobby and Rusty Cepeda. Nothing glaring came back. Neither of them have a lot of unexplained cash in their bank accounts." He glanced back up at the house. "My main concern right now is Boyd. He may have managed to bug the guesthouse, and Bobby's equipment might not detect it."

God, Danielle hadn't even thought of that. If it was true, they basically had no privacy.

The only silver lining in this was that they still should be able to listen in on Boyd's calls if they kept the volume down on the monitoring equipment. Not that the man would say anything to incriminate his mole, but at least they could hear Luke and make sure he was doing okay.

She waited as Colin called Dylan and gave him an update of what had just happened. "No, we weren't hurt, no thanks to the gunman," Colin said. "I want that area searched for footprints, shell casings, anything that will help us fry this SOB."

Dylan apparently promised he would look for those things because Colin issued a "Good" and proceeded with Boyd's latest demand. Or rather his withdrawal of his demands. "It could be that he's still looking for the Del Gardo money inside the estate," Colin concluded. "But I think it's time for us to give Boyd a push."

She listened as Colin requested another check of the tunnel. He kept the call short, under a minute, probably so that Boyd wouldn't be suspicious if he was still watching them, and then Colin ended the call.

"Dylan will check the tunnels," he relayed. "But there's a problem. Apparently when Del Gardo built those tunnels, he installed blast-proof doors on the entryway that would lead directly to the estate. If Dylan has to use explosives to get through one of the doors, then Boyd will almost certainly hear it."

And then he might set off some explosives of his own. After all, he'd admitted to booby-trapping them.

"What about the tunnel from the guesthouse?" she asked. "How did Dylan and the others get through that door to us?"

Colin shook his head. "There wasn't a door on that one. Only the ones that lead directly to the estate. Dylan's been working on getting through one particular tunnel at the back of the house. That door isn't as thick as the others. Still, it might take a while to get through it without alerting Boyd."

So, this might be another dead end, and it could be a deadly search for Dylan.

Colin slipped his phone back into his pocket, checked around them and then led her back inside the guesthouse. The place looked exactly as it had when they'd left.

Except there was no sign of Bobby.

Colin locked the door and looked around. "I don't think Boyd left anything," he said aloud, though they both knew he could have. But it was a cue to Bobby to let the man know they'd returned.

She heard the movement then from the closet, and a moment later the door opened. Bobby was there, at the entrance to the tunnel. "I've set up my equipment down here at the bottom of the stairs," he whispered. "Just in case Boyd makes another unplanned visit."

"What about the explosives?" she whispered back.

"I won't go deeper into the tunnels. And if Boyd says anything or makes a call, I'll let you know."

It couldn't be comfortable down there, but Bobby was right to want to stay out of sight. Boyd wouldn't hesitate to kill him or all of them if he found the young CSI there. And this also worked for Colin and her. Since they couldn't be positive that Bobby was the mole, this kept him out of earshot as long as Colin and she whispered the conversations they wanted to keep private.

Bobby shut the closet door, leaving them in the suddenly quiet room. Danielle didn't like the quiet because it made her think about what had just happened. She didn't want to think about any of it because she kept going back to the images of the van dangling on the side of the mountain.

Colin stepped away from her and went to the sink. He wet some paper towels and came back toward her. At first, she had no idea what he was doing, but then he wiped some mud from her face and hands.

"Thank you," she mumbled.

He put his finger beneath her chin, lifted it and looked at her. Correction: he examined her. And that made her wonder if she had some injury that she was too numb to feel.

"Still dizzy?" he asked. He tossed the soiled paper towels onto the counter.

She shook her head. That was another silver living. Her pregnancy symptoms hadn't interfered with her ability to run and get away from those bullets that had come at them nonstop. The running itself wasn't bad—she'd already discussed exercise with her obstetrician—but she doubted her doctor would approve of the danger and the stress that came with it.

Obviously, neither did Colin.

The examination was apparently over, and judging from his expression, he had moved on to the guilt phase. And he would feel guilty, no doubt about it, even though he'd risked his life to protect her and his unborn child, who he didn't even know existed.

Danielle sighed. The timing was off. Everything about this was off. But Colin needed to know that she was pregnant. Wishing that she had rehearsed it, she opened her mouth to tell him. However, she didn't manage to say a single word.

Colin kissed her.

Hard.

With a groan rumbling deep within his chest, he hauled her to him and kissed her as if this would be the last kiss he'd ever give or receive. In some ways it was punishing. So rough. With all the emotion of the moment. He poured everything into that brutal kiss.

But then it changed. He changed. The grip he had on her arm softened. So did his mouth. He eased her to him, into his arms, so that he was embracing her. He kissed her cheek. Then, her forehead. Before landing another of those emotional kisses onto her lips.

"I'm sorry," he whispered.

Yes, this was the guilt playing out, and it reminded her of the other times he'd no doubt had to dodge bullets while on the job. He carried two scars on his body for the times when dodging hadn't been possible.

Those scars had tormented her.

Until today, she hadn't been able to understand the toll the danger could take on a person. She'd only been able to see it from her point of view, and in the past, she'd reacted out of fear of losing him—while he had been dealing with the strain that she had now experienced firsthand.

"You saved my life," she reminded him. In the back of her mind, she considered that Boyd might be hearing this intimate conversation, but she didn't care.

"You shouldn't have been out there in the first place," Colin mumbled. He groaned, stepped back and scrubbed his hand over his face.

He probably would have added more about that, but his phone rang. "It's Boyd," he said, glancing at the screen. He answered it, put it on speaker and headed for the desk where he'd left his notes.

"Put the doc on the phone," Boyd insisted.

That immediately alarmed her. "Is something wrong with Luke?" She hurried toward Colin and the desk so she'd be able to hear Boyd better.

"Nothing's wrong. The kid just wants to talk to you."

There was a shuffle of movement on the other end of the line, and a moment later she heard Luke. "Thank you for the video game."

Despite the horrible situation, Danielle smiled. Unlike the other times she'd spoken to Luke, this time he was clearly happy. "You're welcome. Have you opened it already?"

"Yep, and it's in the PlayStation, ready for me to start. You got any good hints like you did last time?"

Danielle thought of the various levels and the obstacles he might face. But there was one real obstacle that she needed to work into the conversation. With Boyd's decision to delay the exchange, there was no telling how all of this would play out. She needed to prepare Luke for the worst.

"There aren't any rivers in this game," she said, keeping her voice calm. She hoped. She didn't want Boyd to suspect anything. "But there are some dangers. You know what danger means, right?"

"It's like when things aren't safe. Like playing with matches and stuff like that."

"You're right. Well, in the game there might be some levels where the explorer isn't safe. Maybe there's a mad lion or something out there, and you want to get your explorer away from him." And she hoped she wasn't scaring or confusing him. "Anyway, if that happens, have your explorer hide."

"Hide?" Luke questioned. "But won't that be like cheating?"

"No. It'd be the smart thing to do." She paused. "Do you understand?"

Luke didn't answer right away, which hopefully meant he was thinking about it. "Sure. I guess. But maybe he won't have to hide."

"Maybe not."

He paused again. "I really like the game, but I want to see my dad. When can I see him, Dr. Connolly?"

"Soon. Agent Forester and I are working on it. And we'll tell your dad that you're okay, that you're ready to start Safari Explorer Two."

"Yeah. He'll like that." Luke sounded happy again. "Tell him I'm brushin' my teeth, and I'm sleeping in my sleeping bag in the basement. It's dark down here, but Mr. Boyd puts on the lights for me so I won't be scared."

"That's enough," Boyd interrupted, obviously snatching the phone. Unlike the happy Luke, he sounded concerned. And probably was. After all, Luke had just told them where they were spending the nights. That info might come in handy if Dylan did find a way in through the tunnels.

"What you trying to do?" Boyd challenged. "Pump the kid for information?"

"Not at all. We were just talking about his new video game and what he wanted me to say to his father."

"Right. Well, not to worry. We won't be staying in the basement tonight. In fact, there's no telling where I'll have the kid in this big ol' house."

Yes, no telling, and that was the problem. Still, she was betting that Boyd would stay close to the basement and tunnels while he looked for that money. For now, however, she needed to make sure her conversation with Luke hadn't left Boyd riled.

"Luke seems to like using the sleeping bag," Danielle remarked.

"Who cares what he likes," Boyd snarled.

"You should. Remember, the happier Luke is, the easier he'll make things for you. Maybe you can pretend that using his sleeping bag is a game. Like camping. You could even give him his own flashlight to make sure he doesn't get scared of the dark."

"I'll do that," he said in a tone that indicated he had no intentions of carrying it out.

"Don't hang up, Boyd," Colin insisted. "We need to talk about this helicopter situation. There's a chance of bad weather tomorrow, and I want to bring in the chopper tonight. That should give you plenty of time to use the metal detector."

"Bad weather, huh? I hadn't heard about that."

Neither had Danielle, and she wondered if it was true. Maybe Colin was bluffing to get the man to move.

"Look," Boyd said a moment later, "my boss wants this money. Heck, it's his cash in a way since Del Gardo was always stealing customers and such. Anyway, my boss won't be happy if I waltz out of here with nothing."

"But you'll have plenty of something. You'll have the ransom. Certainly your boss won't care whether the fifty million comes from Del Gardo or Griffin Vaughn."

"Maybe." And for the first time, it sounded as if Boyd was actually giving that idea some thought.

"Why don't you call your boss and see what he has to say?" Colin persisted. "Tell him that things are getting uncomfortable with Luke, that you're worried the FBI might try to storm the place."

"You wouldn't," Boyd snapped.

"Not unless we thought Luke was in imminent danger. If that happened, then we wouldn't have a choice. You, on the other hand, have choices. My advice? Convince your boss to take the fifty million that the Vaughns are willing to pay, you give us Luke, and then you ride the helicopter out of here tonight to the destination of your choice."

"Not tonight."

Colin didn't question that, and Danielle sat there with her breath held, waiting to see where Boyd would go with this.

"Not tonight," Boyd repeated. "But tomorrow for sure."

Colin huffed. "You promised noon today. So, why should I believe you'll go through with it tomorrow?"

"Because I will." Gone was his usual snarky tone. The man was serious, and even though she hated to believe anything a monster like Boyd would say, this was the first time she had any real hope that the release would actually happen.

Boyd hung up, and Colin and she stood there. "This doesn't get easier," Colin mumbled.

"No, but I think you made some headway there. I really think he'll let Luke go tomorrow."

Colin made a sound to indicate he wasn't so sure.

There were footsteps in the direction of the closet, and the door flew open. Bobby stuck out his head. "Boyd's calling his boss, Nicky Wayne."

That sent Colin running for the closet, and Danielle was right behind them. They went down some steep steps and into the tunnel. There were two halogen lights illuminating the area, and Bobby led them to the equipment that he had sitting on the floor. It was obvious he'd been using the equipment bag as a seat.

"Forester might have a point, Nicky," Boyd said. "Maybe it's time to cut our losses and get the hell out of here."

Silence, because they couldn't hear Nicky Wayne's side of the conversation. The only thing they could do was wait and pray.

"All right," Boyd finally said. "Tomorrow at noon I'm out of here. When I get to the pickup point, I'll give you the account number for the ransom money, and then you can get me to the place we discussed. I figure I'll need to be out of the country for a long while."

Danielle wanted to cheer. Obviously, Colin did, too, because he hooked his arm around her and gave her a hug and a peck on the cheek. Hardly the hot, sexy lip-lock they'd experienced earlier, but it soothed her as nothing else could have.

And that wasn't good.

Once this was over, she really did need to take the time to sort out her feelings for Colin.

Boyd ended the call, and Colin and she were about to make their way up the steps, but Boyd's phone rang, and they stopped to listen. Danielle started praying again. Hopefully, Nicky Wayne wasn't calling back with second thoughts.

"It's you," Boyd greeted the caller. He hadn't used the caller's name, unlike the conversation he'd had with his boss.

So, who was this?

The caller obviously had a lot to say because Boyd stayed quiet for at least a full minute. "Well, I'm betting it'd be a lot of money. How close are you to making this happen?"

Danielle stooped down, hoping to hear the caller's response, but she couldn't. Maybe this had nothing to do with Luke or the kidnapping.

But she had a sickening feeling that it did.

"Excuse me?" Boyd said, surprise in his voice. He paused, obviously waiting for an answer from the caller. "That's what I thought you said. You gotta be kidding me."

Colin edged closer and stooped down next to her.

"Risks? What risks?" Boyd challenged. "I'm the one taking the risks here. My face is on wanted posters in every

FBI office in this country, and you're sitting back feeding me information while nobody knows you're doing it."

Oh, mercy. The caller had to be the mole. And it couldn't be Bobby because he was there with them. Of course, the call could perhaps be a ploy to throw suspicion off Bobby, but Danielle was beginning to believe the young CSI was innocent.

"Is there any way to trace this?" she mouthed to Bobby. Bobby shook his head.

"When this is said and done," Boyd continued, "you won't have badges trying to hunt you down. So, don't talk to me about risks."

Obviously, he was having a few differences with his mole. Now maybe Boyd would slip and call the person by his name so they'd know who they were dealing with here.

"No way," Boyd said. "You want me to kill Forester and the doc for you? I don't think so."

Danielle pressed her fingers over her lips to suppress a gasp. Despite the shooting incident, this was the first time she'd ever heard anyone say they wanted to kill her.

Colin put his hand over hers. His muscles were hard and tight. As was his expression.

"You want 'em dead, then kill 'em yourself," Boyd challenged the mole. "After I'm out of here, they're all yours."

"'KILL 'EM YOURSELF'?" he repeated. He cursed. "Didn't you hear what I said, Boyd? I already tried to kill them, and you saw where that got me."

"Well, nobody told you to go after them like that."

"I didn't have a choice!" He took a moment to calm himself down. He was literally racing down the side of a mountain in his car, and the last thing he needed was an accident. "Look, Boyd. I need money. Lots of it. And you know that."

"I know you played a few too many blackjack tables when you shouldn't have. That's a nasty habit you got there."

"Yeah, yeah. And watch your words because you damn well know they're listening to you."

Boyd laughed. "I do at that. But a guy's gotta find fun wherever he can. I'm bored with all this waiting and looking."

Damn. Bored? The kidnapping had alerted every agency in the state. The man was a lunatic. This wasn't the time to play mind games, especially with a federal agent listening in. Colin Forester was no dummy, and he could dissect anything Boyd was saying, and even the smallest clue could come back to bite them in the butt.

And that's why this entire conversation was a mistake. He'd gone to Boyd for help, and the only help he was apparently going to get was some of Boyd's smart-mouthed remarks.

"All I need you to do is sneak down to the guesthouse and take them out. They're loose ends as far as I'm concerned because they might have seen me when I was shooting at them," he confessed.

"Really?" Boyd sounded more curious than alarmed.

"Really. And to make matters worse, the head of the crime lab is running background checks on any- and everyone who works in the lab or has visited recently."

"I see where you're going with this. She might find out about all that money you owe…people."

Well, thank God he hadn't said Callie or Nicky

Wayne's names. But Nicky was only part of the problem. He owed others a lot more than he was in debt to Nicky. And he couldn't pay those others off with bits and pieces of information he got while in the line of duty. No.

These men would demand every drop of his blood.

"The interest on the so-called 'loan' has tripled," he told Boyd. "And now I owe nearly ten million dollars. If I don't have that money within four days, I'll be dead."

"Sorry to hear that, but it sounds like a personal problem to me."

"A personal problem?" He didn't bother trying to keep his voice down.

Boyd had obviously forgotten they were on the same side here. But what had he expected from a glorified killer? Boyd was an animal, not capable of thinking of anyone but himself.

Well, now he knew where they stood.

They might be working for the same man, but he wouldn't get any help from Boyd. Hell, even if by some miracle Boyd found Del Gardo's missing money, then there were no guarantees he'd share it as promised.

So, that left the medals.

It'd been a bad mistake to tell Boyd about them. He should have kept it all to himself, but he'd thought that if Boyd knew what was at stake, he'd be willing to take care of Colin and Danielle to ensure there were no witnesses and no one to interfere with his finding the medals.

Now, he had to get all three of the medals before Boyd made any arrangements to do the same.

It hadn't been easy, but he'd managed to plant a bug in the attorney's car when he'd visited the crime lab the day before.

That bug had led him to a gold mine.

So had Elliot's personal e-mail accounts that he'd accessed with Nicky Wayne's help. His part-time boss had a host of "experts" on his payroll, and through one of those experts, he'd learned that Elliot apparently had orders to personally deliver the letter to Callie on this specific day. The anniversary of the date that Del Gardo had learned Callie's mom was pregnant.

How touching.

Of course, Del Gardo had probably wanted to wait until his estate was settled before telling Callie she was his daughter and that he had left her a ton of money in the offshore account. Too bad though he hadn't just given her the account number, but then Del Gardo hadn't been a man who trusted easily. He probably thought all these measures were necessary.

And they were.

Because if they hadn't been in place, he would have already gotten the account number and the cash. He still would get his hands on it, but it would take some doing. At least he knew who the recipients of the medals were: Dylan Acevedo, Ben Parrish and Tom Ryan.

Tom and Dylan's medals would be fairly easy to get. He'd just break into their houses while the two were tied up with searching the tunnels at the back of the Vaughn estate.

But that left the third medal.

Once he found Ben's, he'd have all the numbers so he could drain that offshore account before anyone realized what was happening.

Then, he would walk right into the guesthouse and

kill Colin and Danielle himself. No more loose ends. No one to tie him to the shooting on the mountain. No one to tie him to the medals that would save his life.

Finally, he had a way out.

Chapter Ten

Yawning, Colin forced himself to get up off the sofa. He needed to hit the bathroom before he went back into the tunnel to relieve Bobby.

Well, if you could call it that.

Relieving Bobby meant the young man stayed put in the tunnels where he took a nap. Since he hadn't wanted Danielle down in that tunnel alone with Bobby, it meant Colin was the only one who was doing relief duty.

Of course, Bobby wasn't their number one suspect now that they'd heard the conversation of Boyd talking to the mole. But Colin wasn't taking that call at face value because Boyd could have faked it to throw suspicion off the young man. For that reason, Colin had taken the extra ammunition and weapons while Bobby was sleeping and hidden them in one of the kitchen cabinets. If the lab tech planned to attack them, he would have to do it without a gun.

Half asleep and more than half exhausted, Colin stumbled into the bedroom to make his way to the adjoining bath, but he came to full stop when he saw Danielle.

She was on the bed, face down, no doubt the way

she'd landed after finally agreeing to get some sleep. Her skirt and shirt were both hiked up, exposing a lot of skin. Her midsection. The backs of her thighs. Even a bit of her left butt cheek.

The sun was just rising, and the golden rays spewed through the edges of the blinds and seemed to spotlight her. Not that he needed anything to do that. He would have noticed her without the well-positioned light.

He walked to the bed and eased down her top. He reached to do the same to her skirt, but Danielle moaned, rolled over and peered at him through her squinted left eye. The corner of her mouth lifted, she closed the eye and pulled him onto the bed with her.

Well, not exactly onto the bed.

She pulled him onto her.

Right between her legs.

"Mmm," she mumbled.

He knew that sound. Had heard it frequently. Right before Danielle and he had had some great first-thing-in-the-morning sex. Colin knew for a fact it was one of her favorite ways to wake up. She liked it rough and fast and even though it wouldn't last long, it would leave them both sweaty.

And very satisfied.

"Danielle," he whispered.

He was about to tell her she was dreaming, or something, but she kissed him. Oh, man. Not just any old kiss, either. She used her tongue, and while she was occupying his mouth with his weak spot of foreplay, she wrapped those long legs around his hips and maneuvered him into a great position.

If they'd been about to have sex.

But they weren't.

Colin kept reminding himself of that.

His body wasn't listening. It was reacting as if he were about to get really lucky. She felt so good in his arms. Like old times. Well, almost. She'd apparently put on some weight, and she was curvier in her hips and middle. He liked that.

Colin tried to move off her, he really did, but her legs tightened, and she mumbled something really dirty that she wanted him to do. He wanted to do it to her, too. Hard, rough and fast. But she was caught up in the sleep and their old routine of morning sex.

"Danielle," he tried again.

He levered himself up just a little, just so that mind-blowing body contact with her panties wouldn't weaken resolve that was fading fast. But Danielle only used the space to run her hands between their bodies.

She unzipped him.

And took him from his boxers.

"Danielle!" Colin ground out, though how he could manage speech, he didn't know.

She opened one eye. The left one, again. And he could see her trying to focus, but her hands didn't stop while she did that. She shoved down her panties. Thankfully, she couldn't get them far because he was lying between her legs. But she shoved the front of them down.

Just enough.

For the tip of his erection to slide an inch or two inside her.

Colin cursed. And bit his lip. If he could have hit himself in the head with the lamp, he would have. Anything to cause pain so he'd stop this. More than life, more than his next breath, more than anything, he wanted to be all the way inside her.

The next sound she made wasn't *mmm*. It was more like *huh?*

"Yeah," he said when her eyes fully opened. He didn't have a clue what it meant. Or what he should say. He was still trying to talk his brainless erection out of doing something really stupid.

But highly enjoyable.

Even with his response, she didn't move. Neither did he. They lay there with him as hard as granite and partly inside her.

It got worse.

He actually saw the debate in her eyes, and because her legs were still wrapped around him, he felt her muscles tighten as if she were trying to stop herself from thrusting her hips up. And if she did that, well, sex would happen.

"Yeah?" he repeated, waiting.

"Uh," she said. And her muscles relaxed. Her butt went back down onto the mattress, easing him out of her.

Colin still didn't move. He couldn't.

"Sorry," Danielle added. "You know I'm a hard sleeper."

Yes, he knew all about *hard*.

He fixed his pants, shoving himself back into his boxers, and grimaced at the extreme discomfort. His body was punishing him, and he needed a cold shower—bad.

"Needless to say, I'm out of it." She adjusted her panties and shoved down her skirt.

"Well, that's what getting only a couple of hours of sleep will do to you. You didn't get to sleep until past three, and you're exhausted."

He'd meant it as a wise explanation to what had just happened, but the wisdom went south when her gaze drifted down to his erection. Her body certainly wanted him. Well, her body wanted sex from him anyway. Her mind was probably screaming for her to run the other direction.

Danielle looked away from him, rolled to the side of the bed and got to her feet. "You probably noticed that I gained some weight."

"A little. It looks good on you." Really good. Her breasts were bigger, and she had more curves.

Colin had to tear himself away from the stored images that his male brain was suddenly providing of her breasts. There was nothing wrong with his memory.

Or the rest of him.

"I need to hit the bathroom," he said, and before he could change his mind, or hers, that's where Colin went.

Since his body was burning, he stripped down and got in the shower as fast as he could. The water was ice-cold. Just what he needed, though it might take a decade or two for him to forget the sight of an aroused Danielle lying beneath him. When they were together, he'd taken mornings like that for granted. He knew now that each one had been a gift.

Colin had hardly had time to take a miserable trip down memory lane when there was a knock at the door. "Yeah?" He turned off the shower so he could hear.

"Bobby just came up," Danielle said. "Boyd's on the phone with Nicky Wayne."

"Again?" Boyd had already called his boss three times throughout the night.

Since that could be a bad signal of a million things

he didn't want to consider and because Colin wanted to hear what he could of the conversation, he hurriedly dried off and threw his clothes back on. He grabbed his boots and decided to put them on in the tunnel. Danielle was ahead of him, racing down the steps.

Colin heard Boyd's voice right away. The man sounded as tired as Colin felt. Obviously no one had gotten much sleep.

"No. He claims he doesn't have any of them," Boyd said. "Between you and me, I think he's lying. That's why we gotta act fast."

"Does this call have anything to do with Boyd's not going through with Luke's release?" Colin asked Bobby while he put on his boots.

"No. The opposite. From what I can tell from the other two calls, Nicky wants Boyd to end this hostage situation as soon as possible."

Good. Because Boyd might need some prodding to finish this, and Nicky was probably the best guy to do that.

"You don't already have one of our men in the area?" Boyd asked his boss. Another pause. "Well, we obviously can't send him."

Him. They were almost certainly talking about the mole. Boyd and Nicky Wayne needed something done, and they couldn't send the guy already on their payroll. Why? Maybe because the something that needed to be done would expose the guy as a mole.

"Don't worry. I'll get it, but in the meantime, get somebody down here to deal with our desperate rifle-shooting *friend.*"

Another reference to the mole? If so, Nicky and Boyd no longer trusted him. That was good. Well, unless the mole was about to go renegade and come after Danielle and him again.

"You want me to leak his name to the badges?" Boyd asked. "They'll take care of him."

Colin would love for that to happen. After all, it was most likely the mole who had nearly killed them.

"You're right," Boyd said a moment later. "No leak. If the badges got him, he'd just spill his guts. And we can't have that. God knows what kind of stuff he'd tell them about you."

Even better. They could bring down Nicky Wayne and at least one of his hired guns. Of course, if Boyd did indeed know they were listening in on his conversations, he could be feeding them only what he wanted them to know. And he could be doing that to steer them in the wrong direction.

"Okay. I'll get the ball rolling," Boyd continued, and then he ended the call.

Colin was about to speculate what that conversation might have been about, but his phone rang. It was Boyd. The man was certainly having a busy morning.

"I have one more chore for the doc and you," Boyd greeted when Colin answered.

Colin automatically scowled. "The last *chore* nearly got us killed."

"That wasn't supposed to happen," Boyd said, as if that clarified everything and negated the fact they'd nearly died on that mountain. "Only a few hours until this ends, Colin. But it could be less than that if the doc and you do good on this one last errand."

That didn't ease Colin's suspicions. "What's the chore?"

"Ever heard of Ben Parrish?" Boyd asked.

Well, Colin certainly hadn't expected that name to come up in this conversation. "He's an agent and he's missing. Know anything about that?"

"Not me. But my boss says there might be something at Ben's house that he wants. If he gets it, I'll move up Luke's release."

That grabbed Colin's attention. He'd consider anything to get Luke out of there sooner. "What does your boss want?"

"I can't say, exactly. We don't intend to go broadcasting stuff we need to keep secret, but if Parrish has it, it'll be something that somebody gave him in the last couple of months."

Colin shook his head, not believing this conversation. "Who might have given Parrish this something?"

"I'd rather not say, other than it's connected to Vincent Del Gardo's money."

"You mean the fifty million he hid at the Vaughn estate?"

"Let's just say, he might not have hid it here after all. He might have entrusted it to the care of one Julie Grainger."

That turned his blood cold. "The agent you murdered."

"Now, now. You can't prove that, and besides, that's not exactly what we're talking about here."

Colin didn't want to get into a contest of words about that, but the FBI could prove it. Boyd would be charged with Julie's murder. It was just a matter of time.

"How is this *something* connected to Julie Grainger?" Colin asked.

"It might be something that Julie had and she sent it to Ben. But it wasn't really Julie's to send."

Colin glanced at Danielle, who had folded her arms over her chest and was shaking her head. Oh, yes. This sounded fishy.

"Let me get this straight," Colin started. "You want Dr. Connolly and me to go to Ben Parrish's wife and ask her to give us *something* that was sent to her husband and is connected to a murdered FBI agent and crime boss?"

"That's it. If Parrish got this thing, then it should be at the house. You badges are real good at finding things so look in all the places where someone would want to tuck a little something out of sight."

Colin rolled his eyes and tried to work through all the possibilities. "Is this something a biological weapon that's going to kill us all?"

Boyd laughed. "You got an imagination there, Colin. But my boss isn't into terrorist stuff. He just wants his money, and this *something* is valuable."

Well, if it was an item a Mob boss wanted, Colin didn't like the idea of it being with Ben Parrish's wife. After all, he'd heard the part about Boyd requesting that Nicky send someone down. Colin didn't want a hired gun going after a missing agent's wife.

"Do you actually know what this item is?" Colin questioned.

"I do. But I can't tell you. I can't risk leaks, and there are people who'd really want it if they knew about it. Just look for it, hard, and let me know if you find it. Leave now."

"We don't have a car," Colin reminded him.

"Call one of your badges, one you trust, and have them come out and get you. No coming inside the gates.

The doc and you will meet them at the start of the mountain road."

That part might be reasonable, but another wasn't. "Why does Dr. Connolly need to go with me?"

"I was doing you a favor, Colin. Come on. Do you really want her here at the estate alone?"

No. He didn't even have to think about that. But he did give more thought to this latest chore.

"It's seven o'clock," Boyd reminded him. "One of your badges could be here in fifteen minutes. Find the package that's been delivered and bring it here. And if you do that, Luke Vaughn goes home on time. Guaranteed. Should I wake the kid up and ask if he wants to go home today?"

"No," Colin and Danielle said at once.

Boyd chuckled. "That's what I thought you'd say." He ended the call.

Colin hung up, still wondering what the heck he was going to do. He had to get to Ben's house, of course, to save Luke three more hours with his kidnapper. But the question was, did he trust Danielle to stay put with Bobby?

No.

Even if Bobby wasn't the mole, he was a lab rat, and he probably wouldn't know how to defend Danielle if Boyd came in there with guns blazing.

"I'm going with you?" Danielle asked.

Colin nodded and hoped like the devil he didn't regret this decision. He could be damned if he did or damned if he didn't.

And worse.

He could be taking Danielle right into a death trap.

Chapter Eleven

Danielle tried to ease up on the tight grip she had on
the car's armrest. It wasn't that Dylan was a bad driver.
Nor was he speeding. But he was taking them down
the mountain.

The same mountain where they'd nearly been killed.

She gave up her attempt to lighten her grip and just
closed her eyes when Dylan drove past the section
where the van had plunged over the side.

The sky was a dull gunmetal-gray, and the clouds
were heavy. It would rain, that was for certain, but she
hoped it held off until after Luke's rescue. She didn't
want weather to play a part in this.

"Did anyone find shell casings out here?" Colin asked
Dylan. Colin was sitting in the back, next to her, and he
had his gun drawn and on his lap. He obviously wasn't
any more comfortable with this drive than she was.

"Not yet," Dylan answered. "We'll keep looking."

Good. Because those shell casings could lead them
to the gunman.

And the mole.

It was hard to know whom to trust with someone out

there leaking information and trying to kill them. For her, that distrust extended to everyone except Colin and her old friend, Callie.

Colin didn't have too many names on his people-to-trust list, either, because when he'd called Dylan to arrange for a car to take them to Ben Parrish's house, he'd asked that this visit, search and any information about it be limited to only FBI agents.

No one from the lab.

That meant no Rusty Cepeda in on this search. Or Bobby. This would be restricted to Dylan, Tom, Colin and her. She was a little concerned, however, that Jerry could have overheard Colin's call to Dylan. After all, Dylan and Jerry were in the same office.

But even with that precaution, Danielle knew this visit could turn dangerous. After all, the person who'd shot at them knew how to handle a rifle, and all agents knew how to do that. Probably plenty of the crime lab folks, too. Even though they'd tried to keep this trip hush-hush, Boyd could have informed the mole what was going on.

"Someone broke into my house last night," Dylan volunteered. "It wasn't ransacked, but I could tell someone had been there."

"Was anything taken?" Colin asked.

"Not that I could tell, but it was too clean to be kids or an amateur burglar. Plus, everybody around here knows it's my place, and it takes a lot of nerve to break into an agent's house."

"Yes," Colin agreed. "You think it's related to this search Boyd wants us to do at Ava's?"

"Could be. Maybe Nicky Wayne, Boyd or someone

else thinks I know something about the money. I don't."
But then Dylan lifted his shoulder. "At least I don't
believe I do. Who knows what could be a link to that
money. Investigation notes. Photos. You name it."

"And maybe there isn't a link at all," Danielle
offered. "Maybe this is just Boyd being desperate."

Well, the man certainly was that.

Danielle forced herself to finish eating the peanut
butter sandwich that she'd slapped together while
waiting for Dylan to arrive. She wasn't hungry. Not in
the least. But she had to eat for the sake of her baby.

Dylan drove them through town and to the outskirts,
right at the point where the land turned hilly. He stopped
in front of a brown frame house that had massive glass
windows across the entire front.

There was another vehicle already in the driveway,
and Tom Ryan was waiting on the front lawn. In the
doorway of the house stood an attractive auburn-haired
woman with a large baby bulge. Ava Wright-Parrish, no
doubt. Danielle figured the woman had to be in the last
trimester of her pregnancy.

Danielle finished the last bite of her sandwich before
Dylan, Colin and she got out and made their way to the
others. Colin and Tom shook hands. A closer look at
Ava's face, and Danielle saw the concern and the
fatigue—two things that Danielle was certain were on
her own face. Tom's, too. But then she'd heard him tell
Colin on the phone that Callie and he had spent the
night trying to find a way through those tunnels. Tom
had come straight to Ava's and his jeans and shirt were
speckled with dirt and dust.

Ava offered a weak smile to Danielle during the introductions, and then stood to the side so they could all enter. The house was chilly, the cool air from the air conditioner spilling over them. Either Ava liked the coolness or her pregnancy had caused her to lower the temperature.

"I don't suppose you could be more specific about what you're looking for?" Ava asked.

Colin shook his head. "Boyd was intentionally vague. But he did indicate that whatever it is, it might be connected to Julie Grainger and Vincent Del Gardo."

That caused Ava's blue eyes to widen. With good reason. Julie Grainger had been murdered by the very man who was holding Luke hostage.

"Ava, this something could be Del Gardo's missing fifty million dollars," Danielle added.

"Fifty million?" she questioned. "I thought that was hidden at the Vaughn estate."

"Maybe." Colin answered so quickly that it meant he'd already considered it. "Or maybe Del Gardo just planted false clues to let people believe that. And maybe Nicky Wayne learned the clues were false."

"How?" Ava wanted to know.

Danielle wanted to know the same thing, and she only hoped that didn't mean that Nicky had gotten the information from Ben. Maybe he'd tortured Ben into telling him.

"Why would Del Gardo have hidden the money here?" Ava continued.

Colin shrugged. "Who knows? Maybe he figured no one would look for the money at an agent's house. Maybe he tricked Julie into hiding it for him. But that something might be here. Something big, or Boyd wouldn't have sent us after it, and I'm thinking that fifty million qualifies as something big."

"You're right," Tom agreed. He glanced around the room. "I'll check the attic. Everybody needs to look for loose floorboards, too, because Del Gardo would have needed a lot of space to hide fifty million."

They all started to fan out into various parts of the house. Tom went up the stairs to the attic. Ava went into the master bedroom. Dylan, into the living room.

Since the other agents were searching, Colin and Danielle went into the other room. A nursery, Danielle realized the moment she stepped inside.

Oh, mercy.

Talk about getting hit with a reminder that soon, very soon, she'd have to create a nursery for her own child. Nothing would make her happier, but it also meant first having to deal with Colin and his reaction to becoming a father.

That sleepy incident on the bed had reminded her of old times. It had also left her wanting more. Which she couldn't have. Sex with Colin would no doubt be as great as it always had been, but it would complicate a situation already too complicated. No. It was best to keep sex out of the picture until they'd resolved everything about the baby. And that wasn't going to happen until Luke was safely back with his family.

Even though she really didn't expect to find anything in the nursery, she went to the closet and looked around. Normal stuff. Shopping bags with new baby items. A changing table ready to be assembled.

They looked through the room and tested every part of the floor for loose floorboards. Nothing. Colin started a wall search, and he knocked on each section of the room, listening for the sound to indicate there was a hollow space.

Still nothing.

Danielle and Colin went back into the living room to find Tom doing the same thing. The men lifted the sofa and chairs and looked underneath them. Definitely no money. And the fireplace was clean, as well.

"I might have found something," she heard Dylan call out from the loft. "But it's not money."

That sent everyone hurrying in that direction, including Ava. When they got to the top of the stairs, Dylan was standing in the middle of the room holding an envelope and a single sheet of paper.

His weary eyes went straight to Ava. "I'm sorry," Dylan said.

Ava shook her head and walked past them to get to Dylan. She reached for the envelope and the paper. Only then did Danielle see that it appeared to be a short hand-written letter.

"It's from Julie Grainger," Dylan explained. But that was all he said. He kept his attention fastened to Ava.

The woman's lips moved as she read through the letter, and at the end of it, Ava shrugged. "What does it mean?"

"Look in the envelope," Dylan instructed.

Ava did, but she opened it as if it were fragile and might break. She froze for several moments when she looked at the first picture, and then she frantically rifled through the others.

"Oh, God," Ava said.

She staggered a bit, and Tom caught her. He caught the paper and envelope, as well. He read the message and looked at the same photos that had caused Ava's reaction. His gaze flew to Dylan's.

"What's going on?" Tom demanded.

"I don't know." Dylan turned to Colin. "The message is from Julie to Ben, and it's her handwriting. I recognize it. The message says, 'I know who you really are.'"

Tom passed the pictures to Colin, and after one glance Danielle knew the reason for Ava's reaction.

There were three pictures, all taken from long range as if the photographer were spying on the people being photographed. Ben Parrish was in all the pictures. Danielle recognized him from the photo she'd seen on Callie's desk. But Ben wasn't alone. He was with Boyd in two of the shots, and in the other one, he was with Nicky Wayne himself.

"It's some kind of mix-up," Tom concluded. He forced Ava to sit down.

She did sit, but she didn't look as if she believed him about this being a mix-up. "Why would Ben be in those pictures?" She looked at Tom first. Then, Dylan.

None of the men apparently had an answer for her.

Tears sprang to her eyes. "Julie obviously thought Ben was a corrupt agent."

Tom stooped down and met her eye to eye. "Julie could have been wrong. All we know at this point is that Ben is missing. That's it. We don't know why, and we certainly don't know that he's working for Nicky Wayne."

Ava wiped away the tears, but Danielle figured more would follow. The woman stood, and she tried to look stronger than she probably felt. She lifted her head high and snagged Colin's gaze. "Do you think this is what Boyd wanted?"

Colin shrugged. "Maybe."

Those photos possibly incriminated Ben, but it also pointed the finger at Boyd, too. What kind of connection had he had with Ben? And maybe Boyd didn't want his connection to the agent to become public knowledge.

"I'm betting Ben met with Boyd and Nicky so he could get answers about Julie's murder," Tom concluded. "And someone, maybe one of Nicky's own men, took those photos to make Ben look like an agent on the take."

Of course, what Tom didn't add was that Ben might also be dead. Danielle hated to even think it, but here was Ava, pregnant and worried, and Ben was nowhere to be found. If he had dealings with the Wayne family, one of them might have murdered the agent.

Ava blinked back more tears and tipped her head to the copier in the loft office. "Why don't you copy everything and take it to Boyd. Since he's in the pictures, he obviously knows he met with Ben."

With that, Dylan took the items to the copy machine in the home office and began to copy them. While he was doing that, Tom put his arm around Ava and led her back down the stairs. "I'll call Callie," Tom said. "She can come out and stay with you."

Ava was already shaking her head before Tom had finished. "No. She's too busy to babysit me. It's more important for her to concentrate on rescuing Luke. Or finding Ben."

Dylan finished the copies and put them into an envelope. He handed it to Colin. The men just stared at each other.

"Ben, Tom and I were all close," Dylan explained. He cursed under his breath. "This'll hit Ava hard."

"You think it's true?" Danielle asked. "Is Ben Parrish really a dirty agent?"

"I think the Wayne family framed him." But Dylan didn't sound totally convinced.

Neither was Danielle, and she had to consider this from a different angle. What if Ben was the mole? What if he still had access to communications equipment? He could possibly be feeding info to the Wayne family.

Colin tucked the envelope under his arm. "Let's get this back to Boyd."

"Of course." Because the sooner they did that, the sooner Luke might get to go free.

Ava and Tom were in the living room when the rest of them made it back down the stairs. Tom was trying to comfort her, but Danielle figured that wasn't possible.

"Come on," Dylan said to her and Colin, "I'll get you back up to the estate."

"Go ahead," Ava insisted when everyone looked at her. "I know you need to get back to work. I'll be fine. I promise." And to make sure she got her point across, Ava caught on to both Tom and Dylan's arms and led them to the door.

Tom waited until Ava gave a firm nod before he started toward his car. And Colin, Dylan and Danielle went to the other vehicle. Danielle reached for the door handle.

And then stopped.

She glanced back at the thick trees behind Ava's house, and she saw something.

Colin stopped, too, and looked at her. "What's wrong?" he asked Danielle, and he followed her gaze.

She took a few steps closer and tried to pick through the branches and see what was there.

A car.

"You need to check on Ava," she told Colin.

Dylan tossed the envelope with the pictures and letter onto the car seat and raced back toward the house. Danielle and Colin were right behind him.

"What's going on?" Tom asked.

Danielle didn't answer. She ran. Ahead of her, Colin threw open the front door, and he drew his gun. But Danielle was already on the steps before she saw what was going on.

Her heart went to her knees.

Because Jerry Ortiz drew his gun, too.

The man shoved Ava in front of him. Like a human shield. And Jerry put his gun to her head.

Chapter Twelve

A dozen questions went through Colin's mind, and none of them were good.

An agent's wife had been taken hostage by another agent, and Colin could only guess why. Was Jerry after the *something* that Boyd had sent them after?

And was Jerry the mole?

Colin tightened his grip on his gun and braced himself for whatever was about to happen. Because if Jerry was the mole, he was the man who'd tried to murder Danielle and him. And now, he had a pregnant Ava at gunpoint.

"Put down your gun," Colin told Jerry.

Behind him, Colin heard Dylan and Tom draw their weapons, as well. Either the show of force would cause Jerry to surrender, or it would send him over the edge.

He looked out of the corner of his eye. Danielle was too close. Practically right in front of one of those massive windows. If Jerry started shooting, she could be hurt by a stray bullet.

"Back up, Danielle," Colin mumbled to her. "Go to the car."

Whether or not she would listen was anyone's guess, and it surprised him when she did as he'd instructed. Tom moved, too, and Colin heard him making his way around the house. Hopefully, to the back. They needed to cut off any escape routes.

"Jerry," Colin said, keeping his voice calm. "Think this through. Think about what you're doing."

Jerry's eyes were wild, and the sweat had popped out all over his face. He certainly looked like he was about to implode. Colin didn't mind taking the guy out, but he couldn't do that until he had Ava out of harm's way.

"I need money, or they'll kill me," Jerry admitted. "So this is how things have to work. All of you will step back and give me a few minutes alone with Ava. She'll tell me what I need to know."

Ava shook her head. "I don't know what you want." She wasn't crying, but Colin could see that she was trembling, and she had her left hand clutched protectively over her pregnant belly.

"Sure you do," Jerry insisted. "Julie Grainger sent it to Ben."

"You mean the photos?" Ava questioned.

"No!" Jerry growled. "Not the letter and the pictures. You damn well know what I'm looking for."

Since Jerry was obviously getting more agitated, Colin interrupted whatever Ava had been about to say. "Jerry, you're scaring her, and that's not good for the baby. You really don't want to hurt a pregnant woman. Not Ava. You know her. You've worked with her. She's a good woman, and she doesn't deserve to be treated like this."

"Well, I don't deserve it, either." The sweat slipped

into his eyes, and he blinked hard, probably because it was stinging. "I have a disease. I'm sick. And if I don't get that money, they'll kill me."

"Who'll kill you?" With his gun ready and aimed, Colin stepped inside, slowly, and maneuvered himself to the right so that Dylan could do the same.

"It doesn't matter who wants me dead," Jerry insisted. "The only thing that matters is the money."

"No. The only thing that matters is Ava's safety. Let her go, and we'll deal with this the right way. We'll figure out how to stop the people who want you dead."

And the best way to do that was with Jerry behind bars.

Jerry pushed the gun harder against Ava's head. "You're the ones threatening Ava's safety. I won't kill her, not unless you make me. I just want to talk to her. Now get out and close the door."

Jerry's hand was shaking, and it was clear to Colin that he wouldn't be able to talk the man into surrendering. But Colin didn't give up. He couldn't.

"Look at Ava, Jerry," Colin said, remaining calm. "She's scared. You don't want her like this. Put down the gun, and we'll figure out a way to get you the money you need. Maybe we can take some from the FBI evidence room and create a sting operation for the people who want to kill you."

That wouldn't happen, but Colin wanted Jerry to start thinking like an agent and not a hostage taker.

Colin saw the door ease open in the kitchen. With Jerry's position, he wasn't able to spot Tom tiptoeing inside the house. Tom quietly made his way toward the man.

"Well?" Colin prompted Jerry. He needed to talk to cover the sound of Tom's footsteps. "What do you say?

Should we all go back to town and work this out? Think about it, Jerry. You need to get these people threatening you off the streets. It's what we do as FBI agents. We stop bad guys from hurting others."

But Jerry only shook his head. "Get out now!" he yelled at the top of his lungs. The veins in his head were bulging, and the sweat was even worse. He kept blinking as he held the gun firmly against Ava's head.

"All right, we'll get out," Colin lied. "We'll give you a few minutes alone with Ava."

Ava's eyes widened, and he saw the terror. She didn't want to be left alone with this monster. Colin wanted to reassure her that all would be well, but he couldn't.

Because it might not be.

Dylan eased back toward the doorway. Colin did, too. Tom continued to make his way across the kitchen. A few more feet, and Tom would have a shot at Jerry. Maybe. If they could get Ava out of the way.

"Why don't you have Ava sit down?" Colin suggested to Jerry.

Ava stared at Colin, and she seemed to be examining his face to determine what was really going on. After all, she was the wife of an agent, and she likely knew they wouldn't just leave her there.

Without taking her eyes off Colin, Ava opened her mouth and moaned. A sound of pain. And she clutched her stomach. "Oh, God," she wailed. "I'm going into labor."

Her voice was certainly convincing enough, but because Colin could see her face, he knew this was a ploy. Smart woman.

And Jerry reacted.

He eased up just a little on the grip he had on her, and Ava slid down as if she were about to sit on the floor.

Everything happened at warp speed after that.

Tom bolted from the kitchen. Jerry turned toward him and aimed his gun. But Tom didn't give the man a chance to get off a shot. Tom fired, just as he'd been trained to do, and two bullets slammed into Jerry's chest.

Jerry dropped to the floor.

Ava rushed toward Colin, and just in case Jerry wasn't finished, Colin moved Ava behind him. Danielle hurried back to the house, latched on to the woman's arm and pulled her in the direction of the car.

"Call an ambulance," Colin told Danielle.

With their guns still drawn and ready, all three agents went toward Jerry. The man was bleeding out fast.

Colin kicked Jerry's gun out of the way and stooped down so he could question him. This might be the only chance he got because Jerry probably wouldn't make it.

"Are you working for Nicky Wayne?" Colin asked.

For a moment Colin didn't think Jerry would answer, but he finally nodded. "I had to. Gambling debts." His gaze came to Colin's. "I was a good agent. Once."

"I know you were." But Colin wasn't about to cut him any slack. "Were you feeding Boyd information?"

Another nod.

Then Jerry was definitely the mole.

"Were you working alone or did someone else in the KCCU or FBI help you?"

"Alone," Jerry whispered.

That left one more question that Colin wanted answered. "Did you fire shots at Danielle and me?"

"Yes." He swallowed hard. Shook his head. "I'm

sorry. I didn't mean for things to get this far out of hand. It wasn't personal."

Well, it'd felt damn personal to Colin, especially since Danielle had been right in the line of fire. Those memories would stay with him for a lifetime. And God knew how many nightmares this would create for both of them. He could thank Jerry and his gambling habits for that.

Because Colin was having a hard time hanging on to his temper, he stepped back.

Tom moved closer to continue. "What did you want to get from Ava?"

Jerry opened his mouth but then clutched his chest. He tried to speak but no sound came. There was a rattle in his throat, and the last breath Jerry would ever take rushed out of his body.

"Hell," Tom mumbled.

The others cursed, as well.

Colin put his gun into the back waist of his pants and turned to check on Danielle and Ava. His phone rang, and he groaned when he saw that the call was from Boyd.

"Yeah?" Colin answered.

"Did you find something for me?"

Colin looked at the dead man on the floor. "We found something." In the distance, Colin heard the ambulance.

A sound he didn't want Boyd to hear.

"We're on our way back now," Colin assured him, and he hung up.

"You won't tell Boyd his coworker is dead?" Danielle asked.

"No." Colin glanced at Dylan and Tom. "We need to keep this as quiet as we can. Until after Luke is released."

If Boyd found out that Jerry had been shot and killed, then who knew how the man would react.

Luke could be put in even more danger.

"REMEMBER," Colin warned her in a whisper. "Don't say a word about the shooting when we're in the guesthouse."

Danielle simply nodded.

This was the first time Danielle had ever seen anyone shot and killed. She didn't regret the outcome of that standoff. The man had been willing to hurt or even murder Ava. All so he could pay off his gambling debts. No. She was glad Jerry was dead, but she would never forget those images.

Images that Colin had no doubt seen too many times.

"Are you okay?" Colin asked.

"Yes." He knew that wasn't true. But there was nothing he could do to make things better. Right now, the only thing that mattered was Luke, and that's what she had to focus on so she wouldn't fall apart.

They walked up the hill to the estate. Dylan had dropped them off at the end of the road, and they'd hurried and hoped that the photos and Julie's letter would be enough to get Boyd to go through with Luke's release time. It had to be enough because she was at her breaking point. No doubt Luke was, too. This couldn't go on any longer.

"Stay back," Colin told her. It was starting to drizzle, so he positioned her just beneath the awning and hurried up the steps and dropped the envelope onto the porch. The moment he did that, his phone rang. He answered it and put it on speaker.

"So, what do you have for me?" Boyd asked.

"A letter and photos that seem to implicate Ben Parrish as a dirty agent. *Seem* being the operative word."

And Danielle held her breath, praying that this was what Boyd wanted. Later, Tom and Dylan could sort out Ben's guilt or innocence, but right now, the potentially incriminating photos would have to work.

"Pictures?" Boyd questioned.

"Yeah. Of you, Ben and Nicky Wayne. Any idea who took them?"

"No. But it'll be interesting to find out. What about money? Did you find out anything about Del Gardo's missing cash?"

"Nothing. We went over every inch of Ben Parrish's house, and there was no money."

Boyd didn't say anything, and the moments dragged by. Danielle had thought she would be numb by now, but she was far from it. She could feel every nerve in her body.

"All right, then," Boyd finally answered. "Leave the envelope on the porch and go back to the guesthouse."

"What about Luke?" Colin immediately asked.

"Don't worry. He's fine. He's playing that new video game. And I'll release the kid like I promised." Boyd didn't sound cocky today. Just tired. "That gives you enough time to make sure there are no hitches with the helicopter and the ransom money. And don't you dare think about using weather as an excuse."

"There'll be no hitches of any kind," Colin promised him. He came back down the steps, and they started for the guesthouse.

The moment they were inside, Bobby raced up the steps. "Boyd's on the phone with Nicky Wayne," he whispered.

Colin slammed the door and hurried down into the tunnel. Danielle tried to hurry but realized she wasn't moving very fast. She was still shaken from the shooting, and she was certain that she was about to have one heck of an adrenaline crash.

"No. They didn't get us what we needed," Boyd said to his boss. "Maybe because it wasn't there. If Ava had it, she would have given it up when she saw these pictures. She must hate her husband by now."

Yes. And things would likely get worse for the woman. After all, she was pregnant and her missing husband now had connections to a crime family.

"No. I don't want to send them back to the Parrish house to keep looking, especially since we don't know if our mutual friend was even telling the truth about it being there," Boyd continued. "I want to get out of here. I don't know how much more I can take being holed up in here with everybody just waiting to gun me down."

Danielle had to put her hand over her mouth to stop herself from cheering. But that's exactly what she wanted to do. This was the first time she could see an end to this nightmare.

"Everything's a go with the helicopter and ransom money?" Bobby asked.

"Yes," Colin answered.

Colin pulled Danielle into his arms for a celebratory hug. Of course, it wasn't really over because the FBI would no doubt try to stop Boyd from escaping, but they wouldn't do that until Luke was safe.

"The pictures?" Boyd said to Nicky. "Yeah. That was some surprise that Parrish's wife had them. I got no idea why Parrish saved them. Or who else might have seen them. Still, no matter."

Boyd paused. Cleared his throat. "Well, you know where I stand when it comes to him. He helped me a lot. If it hadn't been for Ben Parrish, I wouldn't have been able to kill Special Agent Julie Grainger."

Chapter Thirteen

Boyd's admission brought their mini celebration to a grinding halt, and Colin felt Danielle go totally stiff. Bobby froze, as well, and stared at Colin.

Hell.

This was not what they wanted to hear, and it would almost certainly devastate Ava. After everything she'd been through today, she didn't need this news about her husband.

If it was true.

Since Boyd likely knew they were listening, he could be playing mind games with them. Maybe it was a distraction to stop them from focusing on the hostage situation and have them tie up some of the agents and resources to investigate the allegations.

But Colin had to accept that it also might be true, and even though he didn't want resources diverted from this case, he couldn't stand by and pretend he hadn't heard it. Coupled with those pictures and Julie's letter, they were damning words indeed. Had Ben Parrish helped Boyd kill Julie because she'd learned that Ben was working for the Wayne family?

"Call Tom Ryan," Colin instructed Bobby. "Let him know what we just heard. He'll also need a copy of the recording of that conversation."

Bobby nodded, and judging from his somber expression, he knew where this would lead. There'd be an investigation into a dirty agent, and it wouldn't be pretty.

After this hostage situation was over, Colin might be able to lend Tom and Dylan a hand in sorting this all out. But right now, his hands were full.

Colin led Danielle back up the stairs and into the guesthouse. He checked his watch. A few hours to go. That was it—if all went well. But Colin wasn't going to borrow trouble. Boyd had made it clear that he was ready to bring this to an end. Colin certainly was. He wanted both Luke and Danielle far away from Boyd and anyone connected to the Wayne crime family.

He glanced at her to see how she was holding up. Not well, apparently. Danielle had gripped the closet door, her hand was shaking and she looked well beyond exhaustion. She was on her way to a serious crash.

"I don't know how you live with seeing death all the time," she mumbled. She stared at him. "Look at you. You're not even falling apart."

Oh, yes he was. Inside, anyway. It hurt to see her like this, to know that this would be part of her forever, and there was nothing he could do to take it away.

"Now you know why I don't like to talk about my job," he said. He went to her. Scooped her up in his arms and carried her to the bed. He eased her onto the mattress. "Rest until it's time for the exchange."

Danielle opened her mouth to protest, but he pushed his fingers against her lips.

"Rest," he ordered. "I need you to be a hundred percent when Boyd releases Luke because you'll be the one to get the boy away from here and back to his parents."

Colin was betting he would have to go after Boyd once the man surrendered Luke. He couldn't discuss the details with Danielle, not with Boyd perhaps listening, but the plan was to use the GPS on the helicopter and follow it. Boyd would probably head to an airport or maybe even an open area where he'd already arranged to have a getaway vehicle waiting. Colin and the rest of the agents would somehow have to stop Boyd. And as for the money, well, they'd put tracers on it, too, if Boyd somehow managed to transfer it before they caught up with him.

Boyd would fry for this kidnapping and Julie's murder.

Colin started to move away, but Danielle grabbed his hand. "Stay with me," she insisted.

She was still shaking, but her eyelids were already heavy and drifting closed. Hopefully, she would sleep whether she wanted to or not.

He shut the door, climbed onto the bed with her and pulled her into a spoon position so that his front was against her back. It was her favorite sleeping position, and she settled into him, as she always had.

This was familiar ground.

Too familiar. And it brought back memories that he shouldn't be having. After this was all said and done, he needed to take the time to sort out his feelings. For her. For their marriage.

For his life.

Maybe it was those kissing sessions he'd had with her and the near sex earlier that morning, but there seemed to be a renewed intimacy between them. Of course, intimacy had never been their problem. The problem had been getting them on the same page when it came to her fertility treatments and his job. Well, the fertility treatments appeared to be a thing of the past.

That left the job.

He wanted to tell her that he was no longer going to volunteer for the most dangerous assignments available. That wouldn't undo all the arguments and the pain they'd had in the past, but it might be enough of a start that she would rethink the divorce.

He was certainly rethinking it.

Colin was rethinking a lot of things.

The rhythm of Danielle's breathing changed, and he realized she'd fallen asleep. Good. He could thank the exhaustion and the soothing rain that was hitting softly against the windows and roof. But for him, there was nothing soothing about being so close to her. It reminded him they'd done more than spoon while in bed.

Much more.

Once he was certain she was asleep, Colin eased away from her and moved to the head of the bed so he could prop himself against the headboard. He grabbed a pen and some paper from the nightstand and started the notes he'd need to make for the incident report involving Jerry's death.

The paperwork for the shooting would be a bear to complete, and once Luke was free, there'd be paperwork and reports for that, as well. Best to get started rather than gawk at Danielle. Colin forced himself to get busy, and he jotted down times and details so he wouldn't forget them.

But his attention kept going back to Danielle.

How the hell could he possibly want her this much?

She lay on her side, breathing peacefully. However, her left hand was clenched into a fist, so sleep obviously hadn't afforded her the opportunity to relax completely. Still, the tenseness didn't detract from her looks. She was certainly beautiful. He'd thought so the first time he laid eyes on her, and he thought so now.

The fatigue was starting to catch up with him, too, and he scrubbed his hand over his face, hoping that would help. It didn't. But he continued to make notes and then his summary of the incident. He had to include the part about finding the pictures of Ben Parrish with members of a crime family. There was no way to get around that.

His eyelids were suddenly heavy, and Colin closed his eyes for just a minute. He immediately thought of Danielle and knew this would turn into some raunchy fantasy about her. And he was right. That early incident of the near sex had left him primed and ready, and he didn't think a cold shower would help this time.

He felt the movement on the bed and looked down. Danielle was awake, and she was crawling her way to him. At first, he thought it was part of that raunchy fantasy going through his head, but nope, she was coming straight toward him. Maybe so she could resume their spooning position.

But Colin had something else in mind.

Something he was sure he'd regret.

He grabbed her and pulled her into his lap. She landed exactly where he wanted her, with her legs apart and straddling him. Before either one of them could protest or say why this shouldn't be happening, he kissed her.

She had just started to say her usual foreplay *mmm,* but he caught that sound with his mouth.

Danielle didn't resist, which told him they were both going to do something stupid. Fun and satisfying, yes.

But stupid.

The timing was all wrong. Heck, everything about it was wrong. But that only made him want her more. It reminded him of the days when they'd dragged each other to the floor or the most readily available surface, even though they should have been on their way out the door to work.

Danielle and he had made quickies into an art form.

He kissed her hard. Too hard. He always felt rough and clumsy when it came to her. But she never seemed to mind. In fact, she seemed to get off on it, and today was no different. She returned the kiss, and it was just as hot and hungry as the one he was giving her.

This wouldn't last. The fire was already too hot, and he'd been four months without her. He wanted to promise that he'd do better by her next time, but in the back of his mind, he wondered if this was a gift that he wouldn't get again. That nearly caused him to slow down.

Then, she pressed her breasts against him and kissed his neck. Oh, man.

He was a goner.

He shoved down her top, unhooked her bra and nearly died when her breasts spilled out into his hands. Her position was perfect for him to taste her nipples. He remembered that taste, and it went straight to his head. And his groin.

He became hard as a rock.

Danielle noticed. She always did, and she moved

against him, pressing her sex against the hardness of his. After he got his eyes uncrossed, he shoved up her skirt and stripped off her panties.

She did her part. Danielle unzipped him and freed him from his boxers. Colin tried to brace himself for what was coming next, but he couldn't brace himself against the avalanche of sensations and emotions.

With her mouth on his and her fingers wound into his hair, she lowered herself onto him, taking him inside her. She paused, just a moment, and she pulled back from the kiss and looked at him.

She smiled.

And Colin knew there'd be plenty of things about this experience that he would catalog and remember, but that smile would be at the top of his list.

Then, she moved, and the moment was lost. But a new moment began, and Colin caught on to her hips and guided the thrusts that would send them both flying. First, though, they'd both go crazy.

With each thrust, they moved faster. Harder. But they moved together. The friction and the movement brought them closer to the edge. But somehow, the fire just kept building. It kept getting hotter.

Until the primal need was too much for either of them to take.

Danielle came in a flash. She wasn't a screamer. In fact, she hardly made a sound, but he felt her orgasm ripple through her. To every part of her. And it was those ripples and that hazy, satisfied smile of hers that pulled him in right along with her.

Colin kissed that smile to see how it would taste, and he let Danielle take him with her.

WHAT THE HECK HAD SHE DONE?

That was Danielle's first thought, but it was quickly followed by the realization that she didn't regret this, no matter how much she told herself that she should. But she was also aware enough to know that this could complicate things beyond belief. Still, she was going to pull a Scarlett O'Hara and think about this tomorrow, after Luke was safely home with his parents.

And after she'd told Colin about the baby.

If he was still speaking to her after she'd taken so long to tell him, then she'd try to make some sense of what all of this might mean.

Her position on his lap made it so they were right in each other's faces. For sex, that'd been great. But now, it seemed beyond awkward so Danielle eased away and got off the bed. She located her panties on the floor and headed to the bathroom so she could freshen up.

Colin got up, as well, and fixed his clothes. What he didn't do was say a word. Neither did she. Danielle had intended to give him the silent treatment, but she honestly didn't know what to say. This might have been great sex, but it certainly wasn't leading to a reconciliation.

She closed the bathroom door and decided to take a quick shower. It was crazy, but she didn't really want to wash Colin's scent off her.

Definitely crazy.

In a few hours, she'd need to get Luke back to his parents. She'd have to debrief the child and make sure he wasn't experiencing severe mental trauma, as well as have him examined by a doctor for any physical harm. She would also need to talk with the parents and encourage them to make an appointment with a therapist for the whole family, not just Luke. As Colin had said, she would need to be a hundred percent, and she didn't feel anywhere close to that at the moment.

Danielle stripped down, stepped into the shower and quickly washed in case Colin or Bobby needed to use the bathroom. When she dressed and went back into the bedroom, she found Colin sitting in the chair in the corner, and he was making notes again.

He stopped writing. Looked at her. Obviously waiting for her to say something about what had just happened. However, before she could say anything, she heard Bobby calling out to them.

Colin jumped up from the chair and opened the bedroom door. Bobby was already in the living room, and he was carrying the eavesdropping equipment in his hand.

"Sorry to bother you, but you really need to hear this. And I didn't want to waste time with you getting downstairs." Bobby spared them a questioning glance, but he looked away and put the equipment on the coffee table. "Boyd's talking to Nicky Wayne again, and it doesn't sound good."

Both Colin and she walked closer, and it didn't take long, just a couple of seconds, for Danielle to realize that Bobby was right. This didn't sound good. Boyd was obviously agitated.

"No, I'm not calming down," Boyd snapped. "Jerry Ortiz has been shot. And he's dead."

Oh, mercy. He knew.

"How did he find out about Jerry?" Colin asked.

Bobby shook his head. "From what I can determine,

Nicky Wayne told him. I don't know how Nicky found out, though."

Any number of ways. After all, when Colin and she had left the Parrish house, an ambulance had been on the way. That would have alerted people, and in a small town like Kenner City, it was very hard to keep a secret.

"Didn't you hear me?" Boyd continued. "They killed him. No. I'm not doing that."

Whatever Nicky said to Boyd obviously didn't get him to change his mind or calm him down because Boyd ended that call, and within seconds Colin's phone rang.

"Yes, Boyd?" Colin answered, putting the call on speaker.

The first thing Danielle heard wasn't Boyd, but Luke. It sounded as if he was crying. Oh, God. What was going on?

"You failed to mention to me that Jerry Ortiz was killed while you were at Ben Parrish's house," Boyd said to Colin. This certainly wasn't the cocky tone they'd been dealing with over the past two days. Boyd sounded on the verge of a meltdown.

"I didn't know you'd be interested," Colin calmly answered.

"Well, I am. Why'd you kill him?"

"I didn't. Another agent had to shoot him because he had someone from the crime lab at gunpoint."

"Parrish's wife," Boyd spat out.

Luke's sobs got louder.

"I need to speak to Luke," Danielle whispered, tugging at Colin's shirtsleeve. With Boyd's short fuse and obvious agitation, she didn't want Luke's crying to set the man off.

"How's Luke?" Colin calmly asked, though there was nothing calm about his body language. His jaw was so tight she was surprised he could speak.

"The kid's upset because I made him stop playing his video game when I made some calls. All those beeps and noises were driving me crazy."

"He's crying," Colin supplied. "Dr. Connolly is here, and she should talk to him."

"No. No more talking. I want out of here. You've got thirty minutes."

Colin didn't groan out loud, but she saw that silent groan in his expression. "Thirty minutes isn't enough time."

"Well, that's all the time you're getting. No games, Colin. No attempts to gun me down the way you did Jerry. Get the helicopter and the money up here now! Or it'll be Luke who pays the price."

Chapter Fourteen

This was not how Colin wanted things to go down.

Even though Boyd had already hung up, Colin handed the phone to Danielle. "Try to get Boyd to talk to you. While you're doing that, I'll call for the helicopter and money."

She nodded and took the phone. It would take a miracle for her to keep both Boyd and Luke calm, but if anyone could do it, it was Danielle.

While she made the call, Colin used Bobby's cell to phone his office so they could dispatch a secure call to Tom Ryan. The agent answered on the first ring.

"We have a problem," Colin started. "I need the chopper and money ASAP. Boyd learned that Jerry was killed, and he's panicking. I have to get the hostage out of there." He swallowed hard. "Boyd only gave me thirty minutes."

"That's not enough time."

"Yeah. I know. How soon can you make everything happen?"

"An hour. Maybe forty-five minutes if everything falls into place."

"Make everything fall into place, and get some men down here for backup," Colin insisted. Tom sprang into action. Colin heard him tell someone to dispatch the chopper.

"Danielle's on the phone with Boyd now," Colin explained when Tom came back on the line. "I'm hoping she can stabilize the situation with the boy, and then I can get Boyd to accept that we need more time."

But Colin didn't hear Tom's response because it was at that moment that Danielle said something that grabbed his complete attention.

"What do you mean Luke's missing?" she asked Boyd.

"Hold on a sec," Colin told Tom, and he stepped closer so he could hear what was going on.

Danielle put the phone on speaker. "The kid's hiding or something," Boyd snarled. "So help me, God, he'd better come out now, or he'll regret it."

"Luke's probably scared," Danielle said. "He's just a little boy, and he knows something is terribly wrong. He can't help his response."

"Well, he'd better damn well help it. I'm not playing around here—"

"I know," Danielle interrupted. She was trembling, but that didn't come through in her voice. "Just stay calm." She paused, glanced at Colin. "Maybe I can come closer to the estate, maybe onto the porch, and that way I can call out to Luke. He might come to me."

Now, it was Boyd's turn to pause. "You'd do that?"

Hell, no, she wouldn't. Colin started to grab the phone and tell Boyd that Danielle wouldn't be making a trip to the estate, but Tom's voice interrupted him.

"Having Danielle go makes sense," Tom said. He'd

obviously been able to hear the other conversation since it was on speaker.

"It doesn't make sense," Colin snapped, and since he didn't want Boyd to listen in on this argument, he moved to the bedroom and lowered his voice. "Going up to the estate could be beyond dangerous for her."

"Colin, you're thinking like Danielle's husband and not like an agent. Luke could be hurt if Boyd finds him. You just said you had to get the hostage out of there."

"Yeah. But I didn't mean by sending in Danielle."

Tom mumbled some profanity. "You and Danielle have made several trips to the estate, and Boyd hasn't hurt either of you."

It was a lousy argument. One that wouldn't work. Boyd was armed, dangerous and desperate. "She's not going up there. End of discussion. I'll get back on the line with Boyd and make him calm down. Just get me that chopper and the account number for the ransom. And get Dylan or somebody down here now. I want backup I can trust."

"I already have agents and a SWAT team on the way," Tom assured him. "Dylan should be there in less than ten minutes. He was up there trying to clear out a tunnel."

Colin latched right on to that. "Any luck with that?"

"Some. He managed to get one of the barricade doors open on the tunnel that leads to the back of the estate house, but we haven't had a chance to check for explosives. We certainly can't risk sending a SWAT team through there. Don't worry, Colin. We'll sort all of this out and get you some backup."

But he was worrying. Colin hung up and went back into the living room to take the cell phone from Danielle.

But she wasn't there.

Bobby was standing in the room, looking poleaxed, and he pointed to the open door. "She left."

Hell!

Colin raced to the door, but Danielle obviously had a head start. She was already making her way up the steps, and Boyd was there. Standing in the doorway. Waiting for her. Boyd was armed, but didn't aim his gun at her.

For now, anyway.

Colin put his right hand on the gun tucked in the back waist of his pants, and he hurried up the hill. But Boyd stepped from the doorway when he spotted him. Now, Boyd aimed his gun. At Colin.

"Don't come any closer," Boyd yelled. "The doc is the only one I want up here. You just concentrate on getting me that money and helicopter."

Danielle looked back at him and gave him what she probably meant to be a reassuring nod. It didn't work. The only thing that would reassure him at this point was for her to go back into the guesthouse.

"I'll try to find Luke," Danielle said. She cupped her hands around her mouth and called out to the little boy. "It's me, Dr. Connolly. Luke, I need to talk to you."

If the child answered, Colin couldn't hear him, and to make matters worse, the cell phone in his hand rang. From the caller ID, he could see that it was the Kenner County Crime Unit. There sure as hell better not be more bad news because he already had enough.

"Agent Forester," he answered. Even though it was only drizzling, it was heavy enough for him to have to wipe the rain from his face.

"Colin, this is Callie. Tom just called and said Danielle was thinking about going to the estate so she could talk with Boyd."

"It's true. She's already there."

"Oh, God." And Callie repeated that several times. Judging from her tone and choice of refrain, this sounded like a lot more than just concern for a friend. "You have to get her out. *Now.* It's too dangerous for her."

"I know. I'm about to talk to Boyd."

"Do whatever it takes to get her out. Danielle shouldn't be doing this in her condition." Callie stopped and cursed. Other than some static, there was no other sound for several moments. "I'm sorry. I shouldn't have said that."

Everything inside him went still.

"Her condition?" Colin questioned.

Callie didn't answer right away, and even though this conversation had become critical, Colin kept his attention nailed to Danielle and Boyd. She was still calling out Luke's name.

"Danielle wouldn't have wanted you to find out this way," Callie continued. Another long pause. "But she's pregnant."

"Pregnant?"

Danielle was pregnant?

That knocked the breath out of him.

Hell. Everything suddenly started to make sense. Her dizzy spells. The slight weight gain. The *secret* he'd overheard her mention to Callie. He'd known something was wrong, but he'd never suspected this.

Pregnant!

"Colin?" Callie questioned. "Are you still there?"

"Oh, I'm here, all right," he managed to say. "It's my baby?" But he already knew the answer.

It was his.

"Yes," Callie verified. "She's nearly four months. She said it happened just about the time you guys broke up."

No more stillness inside him. It took every ounce of his resolve not to crush the phone in his hand.

How could Danielle have done this to him?

How could she have not told him that he was going to be a father?

How!

Colin groaned and pressed the phone so hard against his ear that he would have a bruise. He didn't care. The pain stopped him from yelling at Danielle. But the desire to yell at her didn't last long.

Danielle stopped calling out Luke's name. Boyd had latched on to her arm.

"No!" Colin shouted, but he couldn't hear the sound of his own voice because of the pounding in his head.

Boyd didn't listen. He didn't even look down at Colin. Danielle did, though.

Her startled gaze connected with Colin's for just a split second before Boyd put the gun to her head and shoved her inside.

DANIELLE HAD KNOWN that Boyd was upset, but she hadn't realized he was desperate. Without Luke, he didn't have a hostage.

Well, not until he'd put that gun to her head.

She had to get out of this. She couldn't panic. Couldn't overreact because she had to think of Luke and her baby. She had to calm Boyd down and get this situation under control.

With the fierce grip he had on her arm, he dragged her toward the massive window in the living room. She couldn't see the guesthouse because of the sloping grounds, but she could still see Colin standing on the front lawn. He seemed oblivious to the rain and was staring at the house. She didn't think it was her imagination that he was furious.

At her, no doubt.

He hadn't wanted her to try to talk to Boyd, and maybe he'd been right about her walking into the lion's den. But she had to do something to help Luke.

Boyd's phone rang. It was clipped to his belt, and he glanced down at it. "It's Colin," he let her know. He flipped it open and said, "Get back to the guesthouse now. We'll talk when the chopper arrives."

Boyd didn't wait for Colin to answer. He hung up, hooked the phone back on his belt and stared out the window with her. Colin was mumbling something. Probably profanity. And then he turned and hurried back to the guesthouse. He wouldn't wait quietly there, she knew. Colin was probably already planning a way to get Luke and her out. She prayed he'd succeed.

"Call out to Luke again," Boyd insisted. "Make the kid come out from wherever he's hiding."

Danielle opened her mouth to do that but then stopped. "Let Luke go."

Boyd moved directly behind her, and she couldn't see his expression. Hopefully, he couldn't see hers, either, because she was certain she looked terrified.

And was.

Her unborn baby was in serious danger, and worse, it was only a matter of time before Colin did something drastic to get her out. He might even storm the place, and that could be disastrous for all of them.

If she could talk Boyd into releasing Luke that might make it easier for her to escape. She wouldn't have to worry about what Boyd might do to Luke if she didn't cooperate. This was the first step to her own freedom.

Besides, she'd gotten Luke into this by suggesting that he hide, which was obviously what he was doing. So, in a sense this was her fault, too. She'd only meant to help him. In case he needed to get away from a dangerous situation. She had no way of knowing that it would be turned against him.

"A child is only going to weigh you down," Danielle said. She cleared her throat to get rid of some of the strain in her voice. "And a boy his size won't make a very good human shield. Think about it."

Boyd apparently did think about it because he stayed quiet. What he didn't do was agree.

"I'll make a better hostage," she pressed. "Besides, the helicopter and money will be here soon. Things will go a lot smoother if you don't have to bother with releasing a three-year-old."

"All right," Boyd finally said. "Call out to him. Tell him to go into the yard and then to the guesthouse."

Danielle nodded and prayed that this would work. "Luke? It's Dr. Connolly. You have to trust me because I'm going to get you back to your dad. So, if you can hear me, come out so I can see you."

There was no response, and then she noticed the intercom on the wall. "I need to use that," she told Boyd.

"This is a big place, and he could be hiding anywhere. He might not be able to hear me from this room."

"Make it quick," he snarled, shoving her toward the intercom.

Danielle pressed the button and got ready to call out Luke's name, but then she heard the sound behind them. Boyd whirled around, dragging her with him.

And there was Luke.

The little blond-haired boy climbed out from the massive stone hearth fireplace and brushed off his jeans and his Spider-Man T-shirt. He certainly didn't look as if he'd been through a horrible ordeal. Well, not until she studied his big brown eyes. There was the fear. And she could tell he'd been crying.

"Hi," Danielle forced herself to say. "Are you okay, Luke?"

He nodded. "I was hiding."

"Yes, I noticed." She glanced back at Boyd. "But you can leave now, so you don't need to hide anymore."

His eyes brightened immediately. "I can really go to my daddy?"

"You can really go," she assured him, even though her words were broken and clipped with emotion.

"Leave through the front door," Boyd instructed. "Go to the guesthouse. And tell them to stay put. Got that?"

"Yup. I tell them to stay put." He ran straight for the door but then stopped and looked back at Danielle. "Are you coming with me, Dr. Connolly?"

"No!" Boyd snarled.

"Not right now," Danielle explained. She forced a smile. "Go ahead. I'll talk to you soon, Luke. Say hi to your dad and mom for me."

"I will." Luke waved at her, opened the door and hurried out.

Boyd was right there to shut the door and lock it. He also took out his phone. He was so close that she could hear the ringing when he made a call.

Colin answered.

"Luke's on his way down to you," Boyd told him.

"What about Dr. Connolly?" Colin immediately asked.

"She's staying with me until the chopper gets here."

Danielle heard Colin's silence and knew what he was thinking. They couldn't trust Boyd, and he might intend to take her on the helicopter. In some ways she would be a preferable hostage to a child. But that also meant he might be more inclined to kill her when she was no longer needed as a human shield.

"I want to talk to her," Colin insisted.

Boyd cursed under his breath and pushed the phone against her ear. "Make it quick."

"Can Boyd hear me?" Colin asked, his voice an angry whisper.

"Probably." Though Boyd had moved several inches away so he could look out the window. "Did Luke make it to you yet?"

"He's almost here. He's just outside the guesthouse."

Thank God. Luke was safe. Now, she could concentrate on her own situation.

Which wasn't looking especially good.

"I'm getting you out of there," Colin insisted, his voice still low but heavy with emotion. "Oh, and Danielle? I know about the baby."

Oh. God.

Colin knew. He knew! How the heck had he found out?

The timing couldn't have been worse. And that explained the anger she heard in his voice. He was furious with her for not telling him.

"I'm sorry," she said, but she was talking to herself because Boyd jerked the phone from her ear and jabbed the end call button.

"Come on." Boyd latched on to her arm and started moving again.

"Where are you taking me?" Danielle asked.

"To a place where I can watch the badges. Especially Colin. Because here's the deal." Boyd jammed the gun against her head. "If he tries to pull a fast one and rescue you, then both of you will die right here, right now. And that includes the baby you're carrying."

Chapter Fifteen

Since he was in earshot of Bobby's eavesdropping equipment, Colin heard the threat that Boyd made to Danielle.

And that includes the baby you're carrying.

Even more, Boyd was expecting an attack of some kind and had no doubt gone to watch the security cameras.

Colin had to get Danielle out of there. But first, he had to deal with the boy who was making a beeline for the guesthouse. The kid looked so little, too little, to have been put through this ordeal.

Colin threw open the door, and Luke came to a skidding halt on the wet grass. The kid didn't trust him. With good reason. After nearly three days with the likes of Boyd Perkins, Colin wouldn't have been in a trusting mood, either.

"It's all right," Colin assured him. "I'm Agent Forester."

Luke nodded. "Dr. Connolly said you're okay."

"I am."

But Colin wondered if that was true.

After all, his own wife hadn't been able to tell him one of the most important things that would ever happen to a couple. Danielle obviously didn't trust him. Still, that was a thought he had to save for later. He needed to get the boy inside and out of the potential line of fire. Danielle had risked her life to make sure Luke was safe, and Colin wasn't going to do anything to cancel out her sacrifice.

Without trying to alarm the boy, Colin gently ushered Luke inside and made a visual check to see if he was all right. Definitely no signs of trauma.

"Are you hurt anywhere?" Colin asked.

Luke shook his head. "But I really don't want to be with Mr. Perkins anymore."

"I know you don't, and you won't have to be. You're safe now." Colin pointed to the sofa where Bobby was sitting with the equipment. "That's Mr. Bobby O'Shea, and he's going to watch you until your daddy gets here."

"My daddy's coming?" The kid sounded so hopeful that it nearly broke Colin's heart.

"Yeah. He's coming." Bobby had already called Luke's father, Griffin Vaughn.

One day, if he got very lucky, he'd be there for his own child when it really mattered. Though he didn't know how any father could endure this.

There were some bumping sounds by the closet door, and several seconds later, Dylan emerged from the stairs. He was out of breath and had probably raced through the tunnel to get to them. Dylan spotted Luke and smiled, but the smile was short-lived.

Dylan whipped his attention to Colin. "How did you get him out?"

"I didn't. Danielle traded places with him."

"And you let her?" Dylan practically shouted.

"No. I didn't let her. She went on her own when I was

talking to Tom." Colin nearly cursed but then remembered the little boy in the room. "Did you know that Danielle's pregnant?"

Dylan shook his head and mumbled the profanity that Colin had bitten off. "Boyd says he'll let her go?"

"Yeah." But they both knew that wasn't worth the breath Boyd had used to make that assurance. No, Boyd would try to take her with him so that the *badges* would back off. And when Boyd was free and away from there, he'd kill her.

But Colin intended to stop that from happening.

"The helicopter is about twenty-five minutes out. If the weather doesn't slow him down," Dylan explained. He handed Colin a piece of paper. "That's the number of the offshore account with the ransom money."

Colin took the paper and shoved it into his pants pocket. He took out his gun and checked the clip. He was loaded up, but he still grabbed two other clips from the kitchen cabinets where he'd hidden them. Colin shoved those into his pocket, as well.

"Where's the SWAT team?" Colin asked Dylan.

"Assembling on the road. They'll be ready in ten, maybe fifteen minutes." Dylan paused and watched Colin position the gun in the waist of his pants. "Why?"

"Because I might need them." He turned to the boy sitting next to Bobby. "Luke, where did Mr. Perkins take you when you were watching the security cameras?"

"You mean the boring pictures of the yard and places like that?"

Colin nodded. To a kid, those would be boring pictures, and who knew how long Boyd had made Luke sit there watching them. But to Colin, he was hoping

those boring pictures would be a distraction, one that
would prevent Boyd from realizing that his plan was
about to fail.

"They're not like TV. They don't show cartoons or
anything, and they're in my dad's little office. Not the
one upstairs where he does work," Luke explained.
"This one is by the kitchen."

It was a lot to ask of a three-year-old to give him
specific directions, but Colin desperately needed them.
"If you go through the back door, where is this room?"

"Well, if you go in the back door, you gotta be careful
'cause it's raining, and the floor might be all slippery.
But you wipe your feet and walk through the kitchen
and go that way." He pointed to his right. "The office is
on that side." And then he pointed to his left. "It's got a
whole bunch of little TVs, but I'm not allowed to touch
'em because they'll break."

"Thanks. Dr. Connolly will really appreciate you
telling me."

"Mr. Perkins locks the door," Luke added.

Of course he did. Boyd wouldn't make any of this easy.

Colin looked at Bobby. "Go ahead and take Luke
through the front tunnel to the road. And call his dad so
he can get out of here."

He wanted that reunion to take place soon, and Colin
didn't want Luke this close to the estate in case something went wrong. The guesthouse had windows, and
bullets could easily eat their way through the glass.

"What do you think you're going to do?" Dylan asked.

"I don't think it. I *will* do it." Colin pointed to the
eavesdropping equipment. "I need you to monitor
that. If something goes wrong inside the estate, call

me. I'll have my cell set to vibrate." And he did just that so that Boyd wouldn't be able to hear the phone if it rang.

Bobby caught on to Luke's hand and helped the boy down the stairs and into the tunnel. Within minutes, maybe less, Luke would be safe.

"What are you planning?" Dylan demanded.

Colin ignored his question. "How do I get to the tunnel that you cleared, the one that leads to the back of the estate?"

Dylan's hands went to his hips. "You mean the tunnel that might have explosives in it?"

"Yeah. That one." Colin got right in his face. "And before you say I'm not going, just think of it this way. What if it were your pregnant wife in there with Boyd?"

A muscle stirred in Dylan's jaw. And he finally nodded. "Go down into the closet tunnel and head right. It'll take you to the road where you'll see a small yellow flag to mark the other tunnel entrance. It leads directly under the estate."

"Thanks." Colin started for the tunnel steps but stopped when he remembered one final detail. "I might need the SWAT for a diversion so have them ready to respond."

"I will." Dylan slapped him on the arm. "Good luck."

Oh, he needed good luck and then some. He had to do everything humanly possible to get to Danielle before the helicopter arrived. Because if Boyd managed to get her off the grounds, Colin knew in his heart he'd never see her alive again.

And with that thought, he barreled down the tunnel steps and started to run.

BOYD FORCED HER INTO A ROOM filled with security monitors. He shut the door, locked it and shoved her into one of the two chairs. The floor was littered with empty bags of chips and other snacks, and there were dirty dishes on the desktops. Boyd had obviously spent some time in here.

"Don't move," he warned Danielle.

She didn't, but she did look around for a possible escape route. Since there were no windows, the only way out was the door, and Boyd was between it and her. Besides, he had his gun, and Danielle knew he wouldn't hesitate to use it on her.

There was no movement on any of the screens, even though they seemed to display every angle of the property. Including the guesthouse. No sign of Luke, which meant he'd already made it inside.

God knew the chaos that was going on in the guesthouse. Colin was no doubt scrambling to come up with a solution to get her out. There was only one problem with that. Boyd wouldn't hesitate to kill Colin, either.

Boyd's phone rang, and while he volleyed nervous glances between the screens and her, he answered it and put it on speaker.

"Boyd, it's me."

Colin. Just the sound of his voice made her feel better, though he did seem out of breath.

"I'm kinda busy here," Boyd barked.

"I know, but I wanted to give you an update. I have the numbers for the ransom account in my hand. And the helicopter should be here any minute. I'll meet you at the chopper to give you the numbers, and you can give me Danielle."

"I don't want you or any other badges near the chopper. I already made that clear."

"Then how is the exchange going to happen?" Not a question exactly. More like a challenge.

"Easy. You'll give me the numbers over the phone, and I'll release the doc."

Boyd was lying, and the icy glance he gave her confirmed that.

He wasn't planning to let her go.

"Did Danielle tell you she's pregnant?" Colin asked.

Boyd shrugged. "It didn't come up in conversation." Though he still had a panicked look in his eyes, that was similar to the same cocky comebacks he'd been giving throughout this hostage situation. "Does that mean some rug rat will be calling you daddy soon?"

"It means that I'll kill you if you hurt her."

The threat caused Boyd to snap to attention. And because she was watching him so closely, she saw the panic go up a notch. For just a second. And then Boyd tried to wrestle it back under control.

"That's not your negotiator's voice, Colin. You having an emotional moment here?"

"I'm not just a negotiator. I'm a federal agent. I know how to kill."

"So do I," Boyd reminded him. "And unlike you, I'm not bothered by a pesky conscience or an oath sworn to a badge."

"But you have no reason to hurt Danielle. We're giving you every demand you've requested."

"Right, no reason. Just don't give me one, okay?"

She heard the sound of the helicopter approaching and knew that time was running out. "May I say something to Colin?" she asked.

Boyd debated it and finally nodded, along with a smile. He knew there was an intimate connection between Colin and her, and if it worked to his advantage, Boyd would exploit it.

"Colin?" she said, leaning in closer to the phone.

"I'm here."

She opened her mouth and rethought the goodbye she'd been about to say. Because she didn't want to make it sound as if she were giving up. She wasn't. *Couldn't* give up. Her precious child's life was at stake, and she had to do whatever was necessary to stay alive.

"I'm sorry I didn't tell you about the baby."

"Oh, this is so touching," Boyd snarled before Colin could respond. "But I'm already tired of this conversation. When the helicopter lands, I'll phone you with final instructions." He hung up and clipped the phone to his belt.

Boyd looked at her. "Don't think for one minute that your pregnancy means anything to me. Because one way or another, I'm getting out of here alive, and if I have to sacrifice somebody to make that happen, that somebody will be you. Got it?"

Since she didn't trust her voice, Danielle settled for a nod.

"Good." Boyd returned the nod. "When we go outside to get on the chopper, you'll need to make it clear to your hubby to back off. Got that?"

She nodded. But Colin wouldn't back off. And he might die trying to save her.

The helicopter came into view, and the sound of the blades whipped through the air. Boyd snatched her arm. Forced her to stand. "It's showtime, Doc."

He unlocked the door and shoved her into the corridor ahead of him. They headed toward the kitchen and the back exit.

His phone rang, and from the corner of her eye, she saw Boyd glance down. Danielle also saw something else. In the kitchen.

Colin.

Somehow, he'd gotten into the house without being seen.

"Get down!" Colin yelled.

She automatically dropped to the floor, protecting her stomach from the fall.

Colin fired.

But Boyd dove to the side. He fired, too. And Danielle watched in horror as the bullet slammed into Colin.

Chapter Sixteen

Even over the deafening noise of the chopper, Colin heard Danielle scream.

He couldn't call out to her, because of the searing pain that robbed him of his voice. He had to clamp his teeth over his bottom lip to keep from groaning.

He scrambled behind a kitchen island. Not easily. But he got out of the immediate line of fire and clamped his left hand over his leg. Boyd's bullet had sliced through the outside of his lower thigh. He didn't think it'd hit the bone but instead had gone clean through. That was the good news.

The bad news was that he was bleeding, bad.

Colin forced aside the pain and tried to pick through the chopper noise so he could hear whatever was happening to Danielle. He'd gotten just a glimpse of her when Boyd had shoved her out of the surveillance room. She appeared to be unharmed, but that might not last. Boyd was on the offensive, and he would kill whoever got in his way.

Colin thought of another hostage situation. The one in Mesa Ridge where the woman had been killed.

He hadn't been able to save her.

He'd failed.

But he couldn't let that failure affect this. He squeezed his eyes shut for just a second and tried to put those fatal images out of his mind.

"Colin?" Boyd shouted.

Two things happened simultaneously. Colin's phone buzzed, and the noise from the helicopter stopped. The pilot had obviously already landed and had turned off the engine. And the call was probably from Dylan. However, Colin couldn't risk answering it. He didn't want Boyd to hear the sound of his voice and use it to pinpoint his exact location.

Colin was going to play dead.

That was his best defense right now, since it might lure Boyd out. After all, the man needed to get to the helicopter and get the account numbers.

"Call out to him," Boyd snarled. No doubt talking to Danielle.

Colin prayed that she would cooperate.

She didn't.

Because a few moments later, Boyd repeated the order, this time in a much sterner voice, and Colin heard Danielle make a sound of pain.

Colin couldn't just lie there and let Boyd hurt her. Trying not to be heard, Colin inched his way to the end of the kitchen island. Hell. He couldn't see them.

"Colin?" Danielle said. Man, her voice was so shaky, and she had to be terrified. He certainly was. Someone like Boyd killed as easily as he breathed, and he had Danielle at gunpoint. "Are you…all right?"

He wished he could assure her that he was. Well, he

was close to being all right anyway. He'd need a doctor soon but not before he took care of this piece of slime who was holding his wife hostage.

"If you can, answer me," Danielle added, no doubt following Boyd's whispered instructions.

Since this angle wasn't working, Colin maneuvered himself to the other end of the kitchen island. He could finally see them, thank God. Boyd was in the corridor, and he had Danielle positioned in front of him.

He had the gun pressed to her head.

Danielle was too pale, and her bottom lip was trembling. She had her left hand clasped protectively over her stomach. The gesture tore at his heart because they both knew if bullets started flying her hand wouldn't be much protection for the baby.

"Colin!" Boyd shouted. "Last chance. Come out or your wife pays the consequences."

It was a bluff. Boyd needed Danielle alive and mobile for now so he could use her as a shield to get to the helicopter. However, after that, well, Colin didn't want to think beyond the moment.

Colin watched Boyd, waiting for the man to move. Once he started for the door, maybe he would turn and put Danielle in front of him. Then, Colin might have a shot.

Might.

Boyd was about five or six inches taller than Danielle so that meant unless Boyd ducked down to completely conceal himself, Colin or another agent would possibly have a clean kill. But not without risks. Because when it came to Danielle, a bullet only five or six inches from her head was too damn close.

Boyd's phone rang, the sound rifling through the

otherwise silent room. Colin used the sound to muffle his own movement, and he maneuvered himself from the island to the edge of the kitchen cabinets.

Another ring.

Then another.

Finally, Boyd answered, and he put the call on speaker.

"Boyd?" the caller said. "This is Special Agent Dylan Accvcdo."

"Where's Colin?" Boyd asked, knowing full well that he was somewhere in the kitchen. Either alive or dead.

"I'm not sure," Dylan responded. "Last I saw him he was taking Luke Vaughn back to his parents."

"Well, he made a detour. My guess is he used the tunnels and somehow got into the house." Boyd paused. "I killed him a few minutes ago."

A sob tore from Danielle, and even though Dylan didn't react, Colin figured the man was probably having plenty of reactions that they couldn't hear. For one thing, he was likely calling for the SWAT team. Colin only prayed that the team did a silent approach. He didn't want to give Boyd any excuse to start shooting.

"You got the account number for my money?" Boyd asked Dylan.

"Yes. I'll give it to you as soon as you've released Dr. Connolly."

"The release will happen when I'm in the chopper. But remember, I want no badges anywhere around. That includes you. When I'm on board, call me with the account number. Once I confirm it, I'll release the doc."

"I'll release all but the last two numbers until Dr. Connolly is free."

"Nice try," Boyd tossed back. "But I keep the doc

until I have the full account number and have verified
that the money doesn't have any tracers on it."

"Then what assurance do I have that you'll really let
her go?" Dylan asked.

"None. Other than my word," Boyd added. "Stay
away from the house because I'm coming out now."

That was Colin's cue to get ready. Boyd put his
phone back in place and hooked his left arm around
Danielle's neck, putting her in a choke hold. He moved
toward the back door, pushing her and keeping her
ahead of him.

Colin used Boyd's steps to muffle the sound of his own
movement. Inch by excruciating inch, he got into place.

And then he waited.

It seemed to take an eternity for Boyd and Danielle to
walk those ten feet or so to the back door. Boyd kept
Danielle in front of him while he unlocked the door. He
didn't open it. Probably wouldn't. Because there was no
way Boyd would want to back his way out onto the porch
and the yard. Instead, he turned to the side and pressed
Danielle right against him with her back to his chest.

Colin didn't have a shot.

Yet.

Boyd peered out into the yard, but he also kept
glancing back into the kitchen. Colin prayed the man
didn't look in his direction because he needed the
element of surprise. And plenty of luck. While he was
praying, Colin added that he hoped Danielle would see
what was happening and dive safely out of the way.

Still sideways, Boyd stepped through the doorway
with Danielle, and he started to turn, so he could place
her in front of him.

Colin got to his feet and ignored the pain in his leg. He took aim. But something must have alerted Boyd because he spun back around. Before Colin could get off a shot, Boyd shoved Danielle in front of him again.

Hell.

He'd failed.

Colin met Danielle's gaze, and in her eyes he saw all the fears and the emotions that were no doubt mirrored in his own.

Boyd, however, smiled. But it wasn't a smile of triumph or even confidence. The man looked ready to snap. With reason. He was standing outside and no doubt realized the possibility of other agents nearby who were ready to descend on him.

"If you shoot me," Boyd warned, "the last thing I'll do is pull the trigger and put a bullet in her. No more wife. No more baby."

And with that warning, Boyd put the gun right to Danielle's temple, and he started across the porch toward the helicopter.

"COLIN," Danielle said under her breath.

She didn't dare shout his name for fear he would take it as a call for help and come rushing after her.

Then Boyd might shoot him again.

God, Colin was already hurt and bleeding, and even though he'd been able to stand, he needed to get to the hospital. Fast. She had to do something to help because the thought of him in pain or dying nearly brought her to her knees.

Danielle tried to dig in her heels, but Boyd dragged her right along with him. The porch spanned the entire width of the house, but it wouldn't be long before he had her in the yard and on that helicopter.

That couldn't happen.

Boyd turned to the side again, probably so he could watch both the back door and the yard. "Keep moving," he snarled.

Out of the corner of her eye, she saw Colin peer out from the door. Boyd apparently did, too, because he immediately turned his gun in that direction and fired.

Danielle yelled for Colin to get down, but she wasn't even sure he heard her over the deafening sound of that shot. Boyd's gun was so close to her ear that the blast pounded through her head.

Colin ducked back out of sight, and Boyd didn't waste any time getting her to move again. He dragged Danielle to the edge of the porch where there was a set of stone and concrete steps. He made it to the first one before Colin darted out again. He didn't fire.

But Boyd did.

The bullet tore through a chunk of the wooden doorframe right next to where Colin had been standing before he ducked back out of sight.

"You want her dead?" Boyd shouted, hauling her down onto the second step. "Because that's what'll happen if you don't back off."

There were only three more steps to go before Boyd would have her in the yard. Danielle knew she had to do something now to stop this.

But what?

Anything was a risk, and she didn't want Colin leaving cover to rush out into what would be a suicide mission. She couldn't lose him. He was too important to her for that. And even though the timing was horrible, Danielle realized something else.

How much she still loved him.

But she might never get a chance to tell him.

Boyd went down another step. And Danielle decided to make her move. Such that it was. It certainly wasn't some grand plan, but she had no weapon, no way to defend herself against this much stronger man. The only thing she had going for her was gravity.

"Colin!" she shouted again, hoping that it would distract Boyd for just a second.

Whether it worked, she didn't know. Danielle didn't look back. Nor did she give herself time to have second thoughts.

She dove to the side of the steps.

And hit the ground. She landed on her right side and shoulder, and the pain shot through her. She ignored it and scrambled away from the steps.

She didn't get far.

Boyd cursed and reached down for her. His hand was mere inches away from latching on to her and using her again as his shield.

"Boyd!" she heard Colin yell out.

Boyd turned. Aimed his gun. At Colin.

And he fired.

Colin fired, too. Two shots. The bullets blasted one right after the other.

Both shots went into Boyd's chest.

But he didn't fall.

Danielle had no idea how he could continue to stand after taking two bullets to the chest. However, he did.

She could only lie there and watch in horror as Boyd re-aimed his gun. Not at Colin.

At her.

Danielle turned to try to brace herself for the impact, but it didn't come. There was another blast. Colin had fired another shot. This one hit Boyd in the head.

The man froze. For mere seconds. But his eyes were blank and lifeless and blood trickled down his face. He tumbled into a limp heap at the bottom of the stairs, his equally lifeless hand landing against her arm.

She struggled to get up from the ground, and she saw the movement all around them. SWAT team members. And Dylan. He was racing across the yard right toward her.

"Colin?" she called out.

But he didn't come. Dylan got to her first. "An ambulance is on the way," he let her know.

"For Colin. He needs a doctor now. He's been shot." She tried to get up again, but Dylan gently held her in place.

"The ambulance is for you, too," Dylan said.

Danielle looked up at him and blinked, not understanding.

"The fall," he said, "it could have hurt your baby."

Chapter Seventeen

"Can you hurry it up?" Colin asked the doctor again.

"Almost done," Dr. Barnwell mumbled, though the craggy-faced MD in the small-town hospital didn't seem to know the meaning of the expression. He'd been "almost done" stitching Colin's leg for a half hour now.

Each of those minutes felt like an eternity.

Colin didn't have a cell phone. He'd lost that in the gun fight with Boyd. Or maybe it'd happened on the ambulance ride or while they'd been rushing him into X-ray to make sure the bullet wasn't still inside him. Either way, he didn't have a way to call anyone and find out how Danielle was.

And Colin hadn't seen her since the shooting.

Two ambulances had arrived at the estate at the same time, within minutes after Colin had fired the last shot, and the medics had whisked Danielle away while they were stabilizing Colin's own injury. But he didn't care about his gunshot wound to the leg. He only cared about seeing her.

Yes, he was mad at her for not telling him about the baby. And he was furious with her for going into the estate so that Boyd could hold her hostage.

But he was more furious with himself.

He only hoped she would talk to him and let him explain why he'd acted like an idiot.

"I have to get out of here," he told the doctor. Maybe if he reworded his urgency, the man would understand.

"Yes. You've made that clear."

Colin scrubbed his hand over his face. "You don't seem to understand. I'm worried about my wife."

"I've already told you she's fine. The nurse gave me a report before I came in here to see you."

Colin knew that, but he had to see for himself. Besides, that was a half hour ago. She might have started bleeding. She might be losing the baby.

And if so, it would be all his fault.

He hadn't been able to kill Boyd before Danielle had been reduced to taking drastic action. That fall from the porch steps could have hurt her and the baby.

Thankfully, the doctor finally stood up and peeled off his latex gloves. "You got about two dozen stitches, but the wound is clean, and I don't think you'll have any problems if you stay off it for a while. I've already given you a shot for the pain, but I'll write you scrips for antibiotics and oral painkillers."

Yeah, yeah. Colin got off the examining table and tried to stand. The pain shot through, but he ignored it and groped for the wheelchair that was next to the bed.

"Hold on," the doctor growled. "You shouldn't be on that leg."

"I need to find my wife."

"Not a chance. You've already been admitted to the hospital, and with your injuries, you have to stay in bed. Hospital rules. I'll find her, and bring her back here to see you. Stay put," the doctor ordered. "I'll also get someone in here to help you change into a hospital gown."

Colin glanced down at his jeans. The medic had cut the denim to expose the wound, and there were blood-stains on both the jeans and his shirt. He was a mess and would likely scare anyone in his path, but even that wouldn't stop him.

"Stay put," the doctor warned, and he headed out the door and disappeared down a corridor.

Colin didn't intend to listen to that order. He reached for the wheelchair, and though the pain watered his eyes, he worked his way into it. To hell with hospital rules. To hell with anything that got in his way.

Since he'd never been in a wheelchair, it took him a few minutes to get the hang of maneuvering it. He bashed into the door, twice, but finally got out into the corridor. There was no sign of any of the agents, or Danielle, but he spotted a pay phone. He made a beeline to it, only to realize he didn't have a wallet or any money.

Cursing, he was about to shout out Danielle's name when he looked up the corridor and saw her walking toward him.

Was she real?

Or was this some hallucination brought on by the painkiller the doctor have given him?

"Please," he mumbled, "let her be real."

He wasn't sure she was until she rushed toward him, and he readied himself to pull her into his arms. But then she stopped. And stared at him.

"Are you speaking to me?" she asked.

The relief was instant. Not only was she real, she also didn't appear to be hurt. But this was only the tip of the iceberg.

"Is the baby all right?" he asked.

"Yes." She nodded along with her response. "They did an ultrasound, and he's fine."

The painkiller might have been making him woozy, but Colin didn't miss that. "He?"

Another nod, and tears sprang to her eyes. "I didn't think they'd be able to tell the sex this soon, but they did. I hope it's okay that I told you. I mean, I should have asked if you wanted to keep it a surprise."

A son.

He was going to have a son.

"I've had enough surprises," he mumbled.

Her lip quivered, the tears misted, and he realized she'd misinterpreted that.

"You're angry," Danielle said. "You have a right to be. I should have told you sooner."

Oh, man. He didn't want to put her through this. "You have a right to be angry, too." Colin caught her hand and eased her closer. "I wasn't a good husband to you. I put the job ahead of you. Ahead of us."

She shook her head. "Because I was making your life hell with those fertility treatments."

He eased her closer still until she was right next to him. "You never made my life hell."

She stopped shaking her head and stared at him.

"Okay, maybe a few times, you did." And because he didn't want her to misinterpret his sick attempt at humor, he pulled her down for a kiss.

It was a simple touching of their lips, but it slammed

through him and dulled the pain far better than any medication could have.

So, he kissed her again.

"Hey, you two, get a room," someone called out. It was Dylan, and he was coming up the hall toward them.

Dylan glanced at both of them. "I'm guessing you're both okay." He tipped his head to her stomach. "And the baby?"

"He's fine," Colin announced. "He, as in a boy. We're having a son." And Colin grinned from ear to ear. In fact, he might never stop grinning.

Danielle smiled, too, and he hoped those tears streaming down her cheeks were of the happy variety.

"Congratulations," Dylan said. "To all three of you." He glanced behind him. "There's someone who wants to see you both. Are you up to having a visitor?"

Dylan stepped to the side so Colin could see Luke. The little boy was at the end of the hall, and he was holding both his mom and dad's hands.

"I'm up to seeing that visitor," Danielle answered.

Colin felt the same way.

Dylan motioned for the boy to come closer, and Luke did. He practically sprinted up the hall, and his little face was beaming with happiness.

"Dr. Connolly and Agent Forester," he said, enunciating Colin's last name. He pointed to the pair who was slowly making their way to join him. "That's my mom and dad. And I get to be with them now again 'cause of you." He pointed first to Danielle and then to Colin. "Daddy said I should thank you, but I thought a hug would be better. Don't you?"

"Much better," Colin agreed.

Luke didn't wait. He managed to maneuver himself around the wheelchair, and he gave Colin a fierce bear hug. He was gentler when it came to Danielle, and he pressed a quick kiss on her cheek. He turned, waved goodbye and hurried back to his parents.

"Thank you," Griffin Vaughn mouthed. His wife did the same. Unlike their son, they were both obviously overcome with emotion.

Colin understood how they felt. Now that he had his own son on the way, he got that whole parent thing, and he knew just how thrilled Luke's parents were to have him safely back with them.

"I need to get back into the office to deal with the paperwork," Dylan said as they watched the Vaughns walk away. "Bobby O'Shea has volunteered to drive you anywhere you need to go, once the doctor has released you, of course. Oh, and you're on medical leave." He pointed to Colin. "Your boss says he doesn't want to see you in the office for at least six weeks."

"Make that two months," Colin supplied. "And no more overtime." He wanted to play catch up on all the things he'd missed in life.

If Danielle would let him, that is.

"Two months," Dylan concurred, the corner of his mouth lifting into a smile. "Good job, both of you. You rescued the hostage, took out a Mob hit man, and you're both still in one piece. Well, sort of." He shook hands with Colin and left.

And that left Danielle and him in silence.

She was nibbling on her bottom lip, something he should be doing, so Colin decided to do a major air clearing.

"I'm not mad at you," he said. "In fact, I'm in love with you, Danielle."

"You are?" Her voice was all breath, no sound. She grabbed him hard and kissed him. "Because I'm in love with you, too."

Those words were pure magic, and a miracle Colin thought he might never hear again.

Smiling through the tears, she started to sit in his lap, and Colin braced himself for the pain, but she sat gingerly on the wheelchair arm instead.

"I swear, I'll make things better in our marriage," he promised.

"Things are already better," she insisted. And she was so right.

She moved in for another kiss, but then she stopped. Froze. Her eyes widened. "The divorce." She checked her watch. "It's supposed to be final today."

Danielle jumped up and reached for a cell phone, which obviously wasn't there. Frantically, she looked around, but the only person in the hall was a tall brunette nurse.

"I need to use your cell," Danielle told the nurse. "It's an emergency. I need to call my attorney."

Obviously alarmed, the nurse took a phone from her pocket and handed it to Danielle. She didn't waste any time. With her hand trembling, she pressed in some numbers, and her attorney must have finally answered.

"Stop the divorce," Danielle practically shouted into the phone.

Colin couldn't hear the attorney's response, but he saw Danielle's face. And it wasn't a happy expression. She ended the call, handed the phone back to the nurse and shook her head. The tears started again. "I'm sorry. The judge signed the divorce papers about an hour ago."

Colin rolled the wheelchair to her and moved to the edge of the seat so he could pull her into his arms. It hurt like the devil, but he didn't care.

"We've divorced," Danielle said. She dropped her head onto his shoulder and cried.

"So?" Colin challenged.

"So?" Her head left his shoulder and she stared at him with suddenly accusing eyes.

"So," he repeated, "it just means I ask you to marry me again. And your answer is…?"

Danielle looked at him as if it were a trick question. Then, the smile started to lift the corner of her mouth. "Yes. My answer is yes."

He'd expected to feel relief. And he did. He'd also expected to feel the love. He did. But he'd never felt it this strong and this unconditional.

"We'll have another marriage ceremony," she whispered. Then, her smile widened. "And another honeymoon." She touched her tongue to her lip and winked at him.

"Oh, I love your dirty mind. Actually, I love everything about you. And you," he added. He lifted her up a little so he could kiss her stomach.

And their unborn child.

"There's only one condition," he said. He pulled her back down to him and looked right into her eyes. "This time, it's forever."

"It always has been," Danielle promised him.

And Colin knew that was true.

* * * * *

AN UNEXPECTED CLUE

BY
ELLE JAMES

First published in Great Britain 2010
Harlequin Mills & Boon Limited,
Eton House, 18-24 Paradise Road, Richmond, Surrey TW9 1SR

© Harlequin Books S.A. 2009

Special thanks and acknowledgement are given to Elle James for her
contribution to the Kenner County Crime Unit mini-series.

ISBN: 978 0 263 88270 4

46-1110

Harlequin Mills & Boon policy is to use papers that are natural, renewable
and recyclable products and made from wood grown in sustainable forests.
The logging and manufacturing processes conform to the legal environmental
regulations of the country of origin.

Printed and bound in Spain
by Litografia Rosés S.A., Barcelona

The 2004 Golden Heart winner for Best Paranormal Romance, **Elle James** started writing when her sister issued a Y2K challenge to write a romance novel. She has managed a full-time job, raised three wonderful children and she and her husband even tried their hands at ranching exotic birds (ostriches, emus and rheas) in the Texas Hill Country. Ask her and she'll tell you what it's like to go toe-to-toe with an angry three-hundred-and-fifty-pound bird!

After leaving her successful career in information technology management, Elle is now pursuing her writing full-time. She loves building exciting stories about heroes, heroines, romance and passion. Elle loves to hear from fans.

You can contact her at ellejames@earthlink.net or visit her website at www.ellejames.com.

This book is dedicated to all the authors who contributed to the success of this continuity. As always, it's a pleasure to work with you all. A special thanks to Allison Lyons for her gentle guidance during the editing process.

Chapter One

He lay against the cool concrete floor, facedown, careful to take slow shallow breaths. The more dead he looked, the more likely the guard would venture in to check on him.

Hidden beneath his body, his fingers curled around the smooth metal of the broken bedpost he'd wrested from the corner of the twin-size utility cot.

Ben Parrish knew what they had planned for him, and he had a good idea what they'd do to Ava if he didn't get to her first. For weeks they'd drugged him through the food he ate. For the past two days he'd eaten very little, flushing what he didn't eat down the toilet in the corner of his cell.

He'd planned his escape carefully. Now with his head clearer than it had been in the weeks of his captivity, he'd learned of Nicky Wayne's plan to dispose of him and go after Ava.

Ben's chest tightened. She'd be in her eighth month of pregnancy, in no condition to run from Nick's goons. Bad guys who wouldn't hesitate to kill a pregnant woman over something as seemingly inconsequential as a necklace.

The necklace was the key. His friend Julie Grainger had given him a medal postmortem, sent in the mail before she died. He'd hung it on a chain and given it to his wife, Ava. Embossed on the medal was the image of St. Joan of Arc, the patron saint of imprisonment. For the past weeks, Ben had laughed at the irony. Perhaps Julie's gift had jinxed him, landing him in this hellhole of Nicky's making. That very medal endangered Ava and their unborn child. He wished he'd never seen the damned thing. All it had brought him was grief.

Nicky Wayne had beaten, tortured and drugged him in his effort to locate the millions Vincent Del Gardo had squirreled away in a secret bank account.

In his assignment as an undercover FBI agent, Ben had worked closely with Del Gardo, getting to know him, infiltrating the Del Gardo crime family. Still, he hadn't even known about the money. No amount of beatings by Wayne or his thugs could coerce the location out of him. All this time the account numbers had been inscribed on the backs of three medallions Julie had sent to her friends from her FBI academy days, Ben, Tom Ryan and Dylan Acevedo.

Now that Nicky knew they were the keys to the millions Del Gardo had stashed, he wanted those medals and to get them, he'd do anything, including kill Ava.

Sounds outside his cell alerted him to the approach of his executioners.

Under no circumstances could he fail. If he did, Ava and their unborn child might be the Wayne organization's next victims.

A key scraped in the lock and the door swung open.

"What the—" The man all the other guards called Hammer stepped through the door first, tapping a hand-carved club in his palm.

Another man, Hispanic, as equally bulky as Hammer and intimidating like a nightclub bouncer followed

Hammer inside. Always wearing a suit and tie, he could have fit into any Mexican Mafia crowd, especially with the scar extending from the right side of his top lip, across his cheekbone to his right ear, which was missing a significant portion of the lobe. "Think he did us a favor and croaked?"

"I don't know, Manny, why don't you ask him." Hammer didn't wait for Manny, but nudged Ben's thigh with his foot.

Careful not to show any signs of life, Ben lay still, allowing his eyelids to open only enough to ascertain the positions of the two men.

"Looks like he passed out," Hammer brilliantly deduced.

"I hope he's not dead." Manny pulled a shiny Sig Sauer nine millimeter pistol from his shoulder holster. "Takes all the fun out of killing him."

"Guess the boss wouldn't care how he expires, so long as he's dead. Nicky said he was done with him."

"I'm gonna miss the guy. Torture ain't never been so much fun." Manny snickered.

"Come on, Mr. Wayne wanted this room cleaned out by the end of the day." Hammer tapped the club in his hand. "You want to do the job or me?"

"I'll do it." Manny squatted next to Ben and pressed the gun to Ben's temple. "Bye, bye Benny Boy."

Ben flipped over, grabbed Manny's hand and jerked it up to Hammer.

The gun went off, the sound deafening in the closet-sized room.

At such close range, the bullet slammed into Hammer with the force of a semitruck, knocking him against the wall. His eyes widened in surprise as he dropped the club and slid down the white walls, leaving a smear of bright red blood.

Before Manny could react, Ben leaped to his feet, still gripping the hand holding the gun. Though weak from hunger, he channeled all his hatred and desperation into swinging the broken metal post down on Manny's arm.

The arm snapped, Manny screamed and the Sig Sauer dropped to the floor. Before Manny could react, Ben jerked his arm, sending the bouncer crashing into the concrete brick walls of his prison.

Instead of dropping unconscious to the floor, Manny swung around and roared like a raging bull. He dropped his undamaged shoulder into a football lineman stance and charged at Ben.

Ben waited until the last possible moment, then smashed Manny across the nose with the post.

Blood spurted, blinding Manny. He stumbled and fell, hitting his head for the second time against the wall and finally slid to the floor.

Now.

Ben spun for the door. Hammer would most likely be dead, but Manny might recover enough to sound the alarm. Ben could stay and finish the guy off, but he didn't know how long it would take for others to come looking for the two. He leaped over Manny, grabbed the Sig Sauer and dove for the open doorway. With only seconds to spare, he had to find his way out of his prison before Nicky Wayne called down his entire arsenal of thugs to finish the job Hammer and Manny failed to complete.

Trouble was, Ben had no idea where he was. From eavesdropping on the guards he'd figured he was in one of Wayne's Las Vegas casinos. But the way casinos were built, he could be lost in the maze longer than he had to get clear.

Ben spotted a security camera in the corner of the

hallway. If Wayne's security was worth anything, a contingent of armed goons would be on their way by now.

He had to make it out of the basement. Once he reached the casino level, he could lose himself in the crowd. Ben snorted and almost smiled at the thought. The torn jeans he'd been captured in weeks ago hung on him, a testament to the amount of weight he'd lost in captivity. After his shoulder wound healed, he'd exercised several times a day to keep up his strength. Mixing in with the crowd in the jeans and a faded, ripped black T-shirt, barefoot, he'd draw attention like a homeless man trying to panhandle in a public place. Yeah, he wouldn't last long.

First things first.

Get the hell out of the fortress-like basement.

A red-lettered exit sign shone like a beacon at the end of the hallway. Ben passed the service elevator and ran for the door. Written in bold letters across the door were the words Opening This Door Will Set Off Alarms. Use Only in Case of Fire.

Ben paused. If he used the elevator, security would surely see him and radio the armed guards hovering near the elevators. They'd wait for him to step out, and either kill him on the spot or return him to his cell and dispose of him there. If he took the stairs, he might make it to the next floor before they came after him.

With a deep breath, he shoved the door open.

Alarms blared, ringing in his ears as he took the stairs two at a time to the next level. A window in the door displayed a parking garage. When he pushed the door, it opened three inches and stopped. A chain had been strung across the exit from the outside.

Abandoning the chained door, he raced up the stairs to

the next level. Another garage level, another chain across the door. Desperation spurred him up yet another level.

A door slammed open two floors below and footsteps echoed in the stairwell.

After a quick glance through the small square window into an empty hallway, Ben pushed hard on the door, half expecting it to be locked as well. Instead of meeting resistance, he fell through.

He ran down the deserted hallway, passing another corridor to the right and skidding to a halt at a T-junction.

Male voices carried around to him. "He just came out of the south stairwell to this floor. Come on." Running footsteps pounded toward Ben.

Backtracking, he turned and raced back to another hallway and turned left. As he passed the corner, he reached up and slammed the metal post he still carried into the camera perched near the ceiling. Plastic shattered and the little red light on top blinked out.

Sounds of music, voices and laughter filled his ears. The marking on one of the doors read Backstage.

Ben tested the door handle. Locked.

The next door was marked Stage Closet and it opened. Great. He'd be cornered in a tiny closet, destined to be captured amid brooms, mops and disinfectant cleaners.

The pounding footsteps drove him through the door into a larger closet than he'd imagined, filled with the usual supplies. As he worked his way through the obstacle course of supplies, the closet opened into a larger room filled with stage props, curtains, stepladders, cans of paint and tools. At the opposite end, light filtered around the edges of yet another door.

Ben raced for the door and had his hand on the knob when the original door he'd entered through jerked open.

With no idea what was on the other side of the door, Ben opened it and slipped through, hoping it took the security guards a few minutes to find their way across.

The door led to another hallway, this one filled with women in tight, skimpy costumes, hurrying away from him.

"Do you mind? We're on in two." A heavily made-up woman in a bright blue bustier, sporting a feathery blue hat and equally feathery tail, squeezed by him and ran after others dressed in a similar fashion.

The muffled sound of applause and music made Ben follow. A door stood open halfway down the hallway. Inside were racks and racks of costumes. From more of the skimpy corsets to evening gowns and men's suits.

Ben hid the bloody bedpost behind a box of wigs and rifled through the costumes until he found a conservative black tuxedo in roughly his size. Not until he slipped it on did he realize it was a stripper tux, complete with Velcro seams. Too late to change his mind now.

The security guards had made their way through the prop closet into the hallway and were asking performers if they'd seen a man running through.

Ben jerked his clothes off and slipped into a snowy white shirt and the tuxedo jacket, hoping the women who'd seen him remained occupied on stage until he could figure a way out.

The guards opened doors and slammed them shut in their search down the hallway.

They'd be at the costumes room next.

After grabbing shoes off a shelf and a top hat, Ben ran for the door.

"Move, jerk!" Another wave of performers filled the hall, this time a mix of women in flowing ballroom dresses, interspersed with men in, wouldn't you know it, black tuxedoes.

Guards bumped their way through the throng of performers hurrying toward the stage.

Ben whipped through buttoning his shirt and jacket and slapped the top hat on his head. When the rush of tuxedoed men crowded past the costume room, he slipped through the door and let the wave of dancers pull him along. As long as the guards didn't see his overgrown, shaggy beard, he might get by.

Once the performers arrived at the stage, they adjusted neckties and hems, awaiting their cue and the exit of the feathered dancing girls.

The guards wove through the performers, scanning the crowd for any sign of the boss's escaped prisoner.

With his face averted and his senses on alert, Ben bunched his muscles, ready to take on anyone who stood in the way of him and freedom.

"Are they looking for you?" A woman carrying a powder puff stepped in front of him just as a guard neared.

"Don't know what you're talking about," he grunted, his voice hoarse from lack of use.

She lifted the puff filled with powder and dabbed it on his face at the exact time the guard pushed past him.

"You can get out the side door behind the lighting catwalk, backstage. It leads to another hallway. Take a left and you'll find the loading docks and to the right of that a small employee parking lot." She raised the puff again, ready to douse him with another layer of powder.

Ben grabbed her hand and stared into tired blue eyes. "Who are you?"

"Kitty."

Applause signaled the end of the feathered dancers' performance. Barely-clad women raced off the stage and the music changed tempo. The emcee, dressed in a navy blue tuxedo, announced the next act with a flourishing wave of his hand.

Ben released the woman's wrist and smiled down at her. "Thanks, Kitty."

Her blue eyes sparkled, a blush filling her wan cheeks. "You better go now."

While the ballroom dancers whirled out onto the stage, Ben ducked behind the catwalk and out the back-stage door.

Just as the makeup artist said, he turned left and emerged into a large loading dock area, the huge overhead doors closed for the night. He found an exit door that lead to a set of metal stairs descending into a small parking lot.

Another door farther along the back of the building opened as Ben's feet hit the pavement. Two men in black suits, carrying handguns, stepped out. Ben ducked behind a car and, hunching low, ran the length of the row of cars to the end.

One of the men shouted. A popping sound was immediately followed by the glass in the passenger window next to him exploding, showering him with tiny shards.

His heart hammering in his chest, Ben evaluated his options in two seconds. Stay where he was and face the two guards who could multiply into many more, or take his chances and run across a thirty foot expanse of open pavement to a low brick wall separating the casino he'd just escaped from the one next door.

Ben launched himself out into the parking lot, zigzag-ging left, then right across the open space, then threw himself over the top of the brick wall. The distance to the ground was much farther on the other side. He landed on his side, bumping his sore shoulder. Pain shot through his arm and back, but he picked himself up and ran for the back of the neighboring casino.

What sounded like a herd of security guards pounded across the pavement in the parking lot behind him.

He'd be a sitting duck if he hung around outside too long.

A group of casino employees exited the back of the casino, speaking in Spanish, laughing and joking. One of them stopped at the door and fumbled in his back pocket. He frowned and waved to his buddies, saying he'd dropped his keys in the hall.

The men laughed and stopped, waiting for their *compadre*.

After a quick glance over his shoulder to gauge his pursuers' progress, Ben made his face go slack and staggered over to the casino employees, feigning drunkenness. "Is this the way to get in?"

"Sorry, mister, you have to use the front entrance." One man, with a heavy Hispanic accent stepped in front of him.

Ben lurched forward, bumping into the man. "Don't know if I can make it that far."

About the time their buddy with the missing keys opened the door, Wayne's security team from the next casino cleared the wall, dropping to the pavement.

Ben dove for the man standing in the doorway. The unsuspecting man's eyes widened, his keys dangling from his fingertips.

When Ben barreled into him, both men toppled inside the casino at the exact same time as a bullet pinged against the metal doorframe.

The man cursed and grunted as he hit the ground on his back.

"Sorry, pal." Ben jumped to his feet and ran deeper into the building, weaving his way through the maze of corridors, until he found an open office door.

He pushed through and closed the door locking it from the inside. His escape meant nothing if he didn't at least warn Ava. A single phone call would do for a start until he could find a way to get to her and provide the protection she'd need. Right now he needed a phone to call Ava in Kenner City, Colorado.

Breathing hard, Ben sat behind the desk and punched the buttons on the phone until he got an outside line. First he dialed home.

"Answer, Ava, answer!" After the fifth ring, an answering machine message in a male impersonal tone asked him to leave his phone number and a brief message. He punched the off button and dialed the Kenner County Crime Unit. Maybe she was working late.

He tried to picture her bending over a microscope. He imagined her belly swelled but beautiful, just like her. A surge of longing hit him full force. Knowing that Ava and his unborn child were alive and waiting for him had been the only thing to keep him going during his captivity.

"Kenner County Crime Unit," the dispatcher answered.

"Get me Ava Parrish."

"I'm sorry, she's not in."

Damn! He hung up and dialed the number for his supervisor, Jerry Ortiz, at the Durango office of the Federal Bureau of Investigations. The operator picked up.

Before she could say two words, Ben demanded, "Get me Jerry Ortiz, and hurry."

"But sir—"

"It's an emergency. Just tell him Ben Parrish is calling. Now do it!"

The operator hesitated. "One moment please." The line clicked.

After several moments of silence, Ben tapped his foot.

Had he been cut off? Was the department slipping in his absence? Here he was in a life-and-death situation and he couldn't get in touch with anyone.

The line clicked again. "Ben, this is Tom Ryan. Are you all right, buddy? Where are you? Better yet, where the hell have you been for the past two months?"

"Tom? Why the hell are you answering Ortiz's line? Never mind, I don't have time to go into detail. I need to know where Ava is."

"Look, Ben things aren't good for you here. Since your disappearance, some have it in their heads that you've gone bad, jumping from Del Gardo's organization to join Nicky Wayne's team of thugs and that you were somehow involved in Julie's and Del Gardo's murders."

"Damn it!" Rage shot through his veins. Just when he thought captivity was the worst place he could be, he'd escaped to find out his own team thought he'd joined the other side. Ben inhaled and let out a long, steadying stream of air before he replied in a tight voice. "You know I had nothing to do with Julie's or Del Gardo's murders, Tom. And isn't it enough to tell you that I've been on assignment?"

"I know you cared about Julie as much as Dylan and I did. You couldn't have had anything to do with it. And for a while there, I'd guessed you were on some kind of mission. I just didn't know what. But when you disappeared, rumors had it you ran because you're guilty and involved in the Wayne organization up to your eyeballs. You have to come in and straighten everyone out." Tom delivered his words in a calm, deliberate tone, one he'd used to talk suicidal maniacs off ledges.

"Including you? I thought we were friends. More than friends."

"The evidence is pretty damning."

"What evidence?"

"We found the note and pictures you received from Julie. You know," Tom continued, "the one where she said 'I know who you really are.' That plus the pictures of you with Nicky Wayne has everyone in Kenner City convinced you're one of the bad guys. You need to turn yourself in and straighten out this mess."

After two months, Ben had almost forgotten the package's other contents besides the medal. Now he recalled the note and pictures Julie had sent, her abbreviated message flashing through his memory. Ben stifled a groan. He could understand how easily her words could have been misinterpreted.

But Ben wasn't going to turn himself in, not with so much at stake. "To hell with everyone else. I need to find Ava. Where is she?" So the FBI even thought he was crooked. That hurt. A lot. He guessed he'd been a little too successful at his undercover role. But he had bigger dragons to slay than a mucked up reputation.

"Look, buddy, you need to come back to Kenner City and talk to the powers that be. It's the only way they'll stop painting you as an insider in a crime ring. We're pretty sure Boyd Perkins killed Julie, but there are those who think you might have orchestrated Julie's death and the hit on Del Gardo."

"Why do you only think it? Why not pull Perkins in for questioning?"

"Boyd Perkins died in a standoff before we could get a confession and you haven't been around to confirm or deny anything."

Ben nodded even though Tom couldn't see him. At least one nasty character wouldn't be plaguing the earth anymore. "I'm not coming in until I find Ava. Either you tell me where she is or I'll hang up and find her myself."

"All right, keep your shirt on." Tom sighed into his ear. "Ava took a leave of absence and left town."

Ben's fingers tightened on the phone until he thought for sure the plastic would crack under the pressure. "Where'd she go?"

"After you disappeared, your house became a crime scene, with you a prime suspect. The stress eventually got to Ava and made her go into premature labor. She had to take off or risk delivering too soon. She's at her sister Emily's house in Vegas."

Ben closed his eyes and fought a wave of hunger, fear and relief that threatened to make him nauseous. Ava was in Vegas. Close to him but even closer to Nicky Wayne.

"Ben? Is there anything I can do to help?"

"Yes, I need money, identification and a vehicle I can count on."

"You know I can't give you those things without becoming an accomplice."

"If not for me, then do it for Ava and my child. I won't let Nicky get his filthy hands on her." Not after all the pain and agony he'd inflicted on Ben.

A long pause stretched the silence between them, then Tom sighed. "I'll have someone out there within two hours. How will I be able to contact you?"

Voices echoed in the hall outside the locked office door. Someone tested the handle.

Ben ducked low in case they broke the door down or used a key. "You still have the same cell number?" he whispered into the phone.

"Yes."

"I'll contact you."

"I really wish you'd turn yourself in, man."

"I can't. Ava's in danger. I'll fill you in when I'm sure she's all right."

"If this is the way you want to play it, I'll get the money and the car to you within the next few hours."

Ben didn't risk a response. Instead, he set the phone back in its cradle and waited for Wayne's people to break down the door or move on. He had to find a way to Emily's house and get there before Nicky Wayne found Ava.

Chapter Two

Ava paced the length of her sister Emily's living room, staring out at the tops of the Las Vegas high-rise casinos in the distance. Neon lights lit the night sky like Christmas on steroids, yet the bright colors and blare of traffic did nothing to lift Ava's spirits.

Emily perched on the arm of her bomber-jacket-brown leather couch, a crease marring her elegant brow. "I wish you'd sit and take a load off your feet. You're making me tired just watching you."

With a wobbling about-face, Ava made another pass across the room. "I shouldn't have taken time off. I'm not used to inactivity."

"Maybe not, but you'd better rest while you can. After that baby comes, you won't get a decent night's sleep."

Ava ran a hand over her swollen belly, trying to imagine holding the baby in her arms at last. With another month stretching before her like a slow-motion film, she couldn't stand the thought of spending it twiddling her thumbs or crocheting baby booties. *Sorry kid, I'm not that maternal.* "I should have stayed in Kenner City."

"Coulda, shoulda, woulda, good grief, sis. You couldn't stay in your house and you know it." Emily was the older sister, and she had a blunt way of telling it like it was, no holding back, no skirting the issue. "If Ben hadn't run off like the criminal he is, you wouldn't be here moaning about nothing to do. You'd be painting the baby room and picking out infant furniture together. That is, assuming Ben isn't guilty like they say he is."

"Much as I'm sure you'd like him to be guilty and out of my life, Ben didn't kill Julie Grainger." She was absolutely certain of that. What she wasn't so certain of was his affiliation with the Wayne organization and the hit on Vincent Del Gardo. Hadn't he reported to Jerry Ortiz all this time? And Jerry had been a dirty agent. Did that make Ben a dirty agent? Guilt by association? Jerry had died trying his best to kill Ava for the medal she had in her possession. "Ben, Tom, Julie and Dylan were close friends. He wouldn't have killed her."

"Maybe so, but what do you really know about Ben? He could be up to his neck in crime with Nicky Wayne. There's the note from Julie and the pictures of him with the Wayne organization. The evidence is pretty strong against him." Emily leaned forward. "He's lied to you in so many ways, I don't see how you can defend him now."

Ava didn't have a comeback. Ben *had* lied and hidden things from her from the get-go. And she'd chosen to believe in him anyway. Call it love, call it blind faith. Call it stupidity. Now she was eight months pregnant, Ben was missing, possibly dead and Ava faced a life of raising their baby alone. Her baby would never know her father.

Damn you, Ben! Tears welled in her eyes as she pictured her daughter at five or six years old asking about her father. What would she tell her? *Your father was an FBI agent who defected to one of the most notorious crime organizations of the century. Live with that, why don't you?*

"No." Ava clenched her fist, refusing to believe what others were so quick to grasp on to. "Ben didn't kill Julie, nor did he have her killed by Boyd Perkins. And I just can't believe he's guilty of going bad and working for Nicky Wayne like Ortiz did." He just couldn't be a member of the Wayne organization. So what if Julie's cryptic note and pictures alluded to a more nefarious life. The note could have meant something else entirely.

All of the evidence so far was supposition and conjecture. As a member of the Kenner County Crime Unit, Ava wouldn't convict him on circumstantial evidence that could be explained away with one interview with the suspect. Even when the evidence had cut her to the core.

Ben hadn't told her about his activities. Seeing pictures of him with the Wayne organization had been devastating. It was as though he had led an entirely different life than the one he'd had with her. Seeing her husband in those pictures reminded her that she didn't really know him. The strain of that realization more than his potential part in Del Gardo's and Julie's deaths had caused her to go into early labor.

Other than lying to her, the worst crime Ben had committed against Ava was leaving her and their baby. A tear breached the corner of her eye and trickled down her cheek.

"Oh, sweetie, I'm sorry. I shouldn't let that son of a gun make me mad." Emily hurried across the floor and wrapped Ava in a hug, smoothing her long red hair down her back. "He'll come home, you wait. He'll come home and explain everything to you."

Ava let her sister hold her, taking comfort in the arms around her. Despite her doubts about Ben and his role in the organized crime world, she missed him lying beside her in their bed. She missed waking up next to him in the morning. She missed sharing the joyous moments of carrying his child, and she hated that he was missing all the changes, as well.

More tears threatened to fall, but Ava gritted her teeth and willed them to dry. She swallowed several times before she could speak. "We'll be fine. Don't worry about us."

"But I *am* worried. It's not like you to be so down."

"I'm sorry, it's just hard having your home searched over and over for any scrap of evidence leading to the whereabouts of a husband accused of being in a crime organization and responsible for a murder." She pushed away from her sister and shoved a hand through her hair. "Everyone at work has been super nice about it all. They talk about the baby to my face, although I know they're talking about the case behind my back." Another wave of emotion blocked Ava's throat, forcing more tears from her eyes.

Emily reached out to brush the moisture from Ava's cheek, smiling at her with that gentle, it'll-be-all-right look she'd given her as a child with a skinned knee. "But they do talk behind your back and that's what bothers you?"

Ava raised a hand. "No, they're just trying not to stress me. They care what happens to me and my baby. They're my friends and it's their job to find the truth." She turned back to the windows and stared out at the brightness lighting the sky above the Strip. "I just wish I knew the truth," she whispered, swiping at another errant tear. She forced a strained smile to the corners of her mouth and squared her shoulders. "I shouldn't let it bother me."

"Shouldn't let it bother you? How could it not? The bastard—*man*—is the father of your child." Emily hugged her from behind.

"Yeah." Ava stepped away from Emily and dried the tears from her eyes. "I don't know what's wrong with me. I'm not normally this weepy." She couldn't give in to raging hormones. Her baby needed a mother who was strong and determined to see her through life without a father. "I guess I'm just tired from my walk."

"You shouldn't have gone so far. Two miles is a bit much when you're as far along as you are."

"And as big as I am, is what you meant to say, isn't it?" Ava grinned. "Go ahead, your turn to tease me. I did enough when you were pregnant with your two."

Emily's mouth twisted. "It's funny how they drive you nuts and you look forward to having a spare minute without them, but then you miss them so much you can hardly stand it when they're gone."

"When is Drew bringing the boys back from his mother's?" Ava asked. Drew was Emily's ex-husband.

"Day after tomorrow." Emily gathered her keys and purse. "I'd have taken them myself if Theresa hadn't quit the day before we were supposed to leave."

"They couldn't find another blackjack dealer to fill in?"

"I wish. I miss my boys when they're gone." Emily sighed. "I'll be home by two-thirty. I'll have my cell phone on vibrate. If you need me, leave a message. I'll check it every fifteen minutes."

"Don't worry. It isn't as if the baby's due yet."

"You never know. Babies have a way of coming when you least expect, and you were having premature contractions just a week ago."

"I haven't had one since I've been here."

"Don't take any chances, sweetie." Emily kissed her on the cheek and opened the front door. "And don't open the door for anyone but me."

"I'll be fine." Ava shooed her outside and held the door. "You're such a worrywart."

"I'm just a concerned sister. Now go lie down."

"Yes, Mother." Ava smiled and waved as Emily drove off. Then she turned and trudged back into the house, her body tired, her mind churning up old memories of her and Ben, a constant reminder of what she'd lost.

Ever since he'd disappeared, Ava had called herself every kind of fool. She'd fallen into the same trap as her mother.

Falling in love with a bad boy was always a mistake. They never stuck around for the duration. Her own father had been a sexy devil with dark hair and green eyes. Emily took after their father. Ava resembled their red-haired mother, but she got their father's green eyes instead of their mother's pale blue.

Her mother had been lured into believing her father had mended his gambling ways and finally settled down to raise their children. He'd promised to love, honor and cherish her until death. In her father's case, until he could no longer fight the addiction. Gambling.

When he'd disappeared, he'd left her mother heart-broken and destitute with two small daughters to raise by herself.

She'd gone to work at a casino using skills her husband had taught her and working her way up to card dealer in less than two years. The hours were terrible, but the money put food on their table. She traded babysitting with another mother working the day shift. They'd struggled. And they wouldn't have had to if their father had lived up to his promises.

Ava swore she'd never marry anyone remotely connected to gambling. She'd never marry a liar or a man who didn't honor his promises. Ha! Eating your own words didn't taste so great. She'd committed sins against every one of her promises to herself.

Her feet hurt and the small of her back ached, testimony to walking too long that day. She'd have to relax or risk going into labor early. The doctor had warned her about overdoing it during her last month. The baby needed the last few weeks of pregnancy to fine-tune its developing organs.

Ava switched off the lights, intent on going to bed. Instead, she eased her body into the lounge chair. She should put on her nightgown and climb into the four-poster in the guest bedroom, but she wouldn't be any more comfortable lying down as reclining. The baby already weighed heavily on her internal organs. She couldn't imagine getting any bigger.

As she flipped through the channels, she came across an oldie and would have skipped right past it, but she hesitated when *An Affair to Remember* blinked onto the screen. Before long, she was bawling her eyes out. With tears streaming down her face, she finally shut off the television and lay staring up at the ceiling until her eyes burned and she blinked. Once, twice… *Give it up, girl.* She closed her eyes.

A little girl in a flowing white nightgown ran through the dirty backstreets of Vegas crying out for her daddy. Ava ran after her, her heart breaking for the child. Soon she couldn't distinguish between herself and the child and she was crying out but not for her daddy.

Ben! She ran toward a tall, dark-eyed man with dirty brown hair and a stubbled beard that darkened his face. The more she ran, the farther away he drifted. Breathing so hard her sides hurt, she staggered to a halt, holding her hand out to the man who was now nothing more than a shadowy image.

How long she slept she had no idea. A minute, an hour,

it didn't matter. The noise that woke her did matter, however.

She struggled to consciousness, sure she'd heard a door open somewhere or the sound of metal clattering. A glance at the clock reflected nine. Hell, she hadn't been asleep for more than thirty minutes. Had Emily forgotten something?

Ava rocked forward in the chair and stood. Yet another reason to sleep in a lounge chair, easy in and semi-easy out.

She walked to the front door and pressed her eye to the peephole. The front porch light shone down on the lighted porch, darkness lay beyond the square of concrete.

"See? No Emily, no salesman, no bogeyman and no Ben." When she said his name out loud, she closed her eyes, her desperation morphing to anger as an image of him appeared in her thoughts. She held out a hand to him, but he didn't take it. Why? *Why did you leave us? One day your daughter will be out there alone, crying for her daddy. Sadly, I'll be all alone, too.*

The image of Ben stood in stoic silence.

Don't you have anything to say for yourself? You've ruined our lives, do you hear me?

His image faded.

Ava's anger faded, replaced by sorrow. She reached out to keep him from disappearing, to keep him by her side, but her hand touched the cool wood panels of the front door. All her life she'd dodged love, afraid to commit for fear of being deserted. She couldn't become her mother, wouldn't let her child mourn the lack of a father. She wouldn't let him disappear again, damn it!

She opened her eyes to the solid wooden door standing between her and an unknown future. She'd make it on her own, if she had to. And she'd love her child enough for two parents.

When she turned back to the living room, the man of her dreams and nightmares stood in front of her, dressed in a crumpled tuxedo, the shirt unbuttoned at the neck, the tie gone, a ragged beard covering his chin and more handsome than any man had a right to be.

Ava's vision blurred at the edges. "Ben?"

"Ava." The deep timbre of his voice filled her senses, dispelling her dream state in that one word.

Gray turned to black as Ava's knees buckled and she sank to the floor.

HE HADN'T MEANT to scare her, but he couldn't come through the front door without possibly alerting the neighbors. When he'd climbed over the privacy fence, he'd tripped over the trash cans on the other side, making enough noise to disturb someone's dog. Between barking and trash cans rattling, he thought for sure Ava and Emily would be calling the police. He'd hurried to the Florida room on the back deck where he found the screen door unlocked and the sliding door into the house equally unsecured.

Had Nicky Wayne already been here?

Was Ben too late? Panic had seized him and he charged into the house. That's when he'd seen her standing by the front door, her back to him, her long auburn hair hanging down over her shoulders in loose waves. To be this close after so long, he stopped and stared, his heart lodged in his throat.

Then she'd turned, her face losing all color, her beautiful green eyes widening in shock.

When her eyes rolled backward, Ben lunged for her, catching her before she hit the floor.

He struggled to steady her, his body weak from lack of nourishment and the long jog across town. But he cushioned her fall with his own body. For the second time that night, his shoulder took the brunt of the impact, pain shooting through him in waves.

He didn't care. Ava was there in his arms and she'd grown even more beautiful since the last time he'd seen her. The color returned to her pale cheeks, infusing the porcelain whiteness with the faint blush of a rose.

"Ben?" Her auburn lashes fluttered upward and emerald eyes stared up into his. "Am I still dreaming?"

"No, sweetheart, it's really me." His chest filled with such an aching sweetness, he thought he would explode. All those weeks in captivity, he'd dreamed of her, of when they'd met, when they'd first made love, and when he'd finally hold her in his arms again. She was the reason he'd survived.

Her hand lifted to her hair, pushing it out of her eyes. "Ben? How…what…where…you've been gone so long, I thought I'd imagined you." She stared around as if the rest of the room had finally come into focus. "Why are we sitting on the floor?"

A chuckle escaped his lips. "It's where we landed."

She stared at their tangle of legs. "Did I—?"

Ben's chest tightened and he turned her to face him, sitting squarely in his lap. "Yes, you dropped like a rock."

Her dark, coppery brows knitted and she struggled to stand. "I haven't done that since…"

"Since you were in your first trimester?" He held her steady until she managed to get to her feet and then he stood up behind her. He wanted to laugh out loud at the joy of being with her, but knew that she wouldn't be as amused, probably thinking she looked huge.

In truth, she hadn't changed much, other than the roundness of her belly. If anything, her pregnancy made her even more beautiful.

All Ben wanted was to hold her in his arms and make up for all the weeks they'd been apart.

When she turned to face him, he knew folding her into his embrace wasn't an immediate possibility.

Her green eyes darkened and she crossed her arms beneath her breasts, resting them on her protruding baby bump. "Where have you been?"

He could go into a long discussion about what had happened to him in the past weeks, but he didn't have clearance to discuss his mission until he talked to his supervisor, Jerry Ortiz.

The important thing was to get Ava to safety. Nicky Wayne had connections and it wouldn't be long before he discovered her whereabouts, if he hadn't already. "I'll answer all your questions later. Right now, we have to get out of here." He hooked her arm with his hand.

Ava jerked free of his hold, her feet planted firmly in her sister's Berber carpet. "I'm not going anywhere until I know what the hell happened to you and why you disappeared off the face of the earth."

The sound of a car door slamming outside made his pulse jump. Ben raced to the front windows and inched the wooden blinds away from the frame. A woman walked up the drive of the neighboring house and entered.

"Expecting someone?" Ava stood behind him, her frown deeper than before.

"Yes. That's why we need to leave here immediately." He grasped her shoulders and stared down into her eyes. "You're in danger."

Her gaze went to where his hands gripped her. "As I see it, the only person I'm in danger of is you." She looked up at him, her face stony cold. "Let go of me."

Hurt tugged at his chest, making it hard to breathe. Ben

didn't have time to explain what had happened. He just needed to get her the hell out of there. "Look, we don't have much time. They'll be here any moment. Get your purse and keys. We have to go, now."

Her brows rose on her forehead. "I'm not going anywhere with you until you tell me what's going on and where you've been."

"I was held captive by Nicky Wayne. I escaped. Now he's after you and me. The end. Can we go now?" He reached for her arm again, anxiety mounting. Any minute Nicky's thugs could storm through the door and...

She stepped back, that stubborn look he'd always found amusing pinching her lips together into a tight line. "And you're just now getting loose? I'm supposed to believe you?" She snorted. "Everyone else must be right. You have gone to work for the Wayne organization. I should have known it."

"Ava. I wouldn't lie to you about this. The stakes are too high." He couldn't help glancing at her belly and she noticed his glance, her hand coming up to rest on the swell. "Wayne was drugging me. I was in too much of a fog to know until I got sick and couldn't hold down the food he'd drugged me with."

"What about Julie? Were you responsible for her murder?"

"Are you crazy? I loved Julie like a sister. I would never have hurt her."

The hard line of her jaw softened briefly before it hardened again. "I'm sorry. I can't do this." She turned away from him and walked into the kitchen.

"Do what?" He followed, his ears straining for any sound out of the ordinary. Once in the kitchen, he reached for a loaf of bread and fumbled with the tie, his hunger threatening to overwhelm his other survival skills.

Ava grabbed keys from the counter and her purse. "I can't fall back into your plans that easily. I don't know who to trust anymore."

Ben set the loaf of bread aside, all thoughts of food taking second place to what Ava said. "You have to trust me on this one, Ava. Your life and the life of our child depend on it."

"*My* child, Ben. I'm not the one who disappeared. I'm not the one wanted for murder. I'm the one carrying this baby. Alone. *My* baby. I'm the one who will be raising it alone if you decide to disappear again." She looped her bag over her shoulder. "I can't do it. I can't be your yo-yo, springing back every time you decide to take off."

Anger and frustration swelled in Ben. "I didn't *take* off. I was *captured*. I'm not running out on you or the child. I'm here to help keep you two alive. Nicky Wayne is coming for you."

"Why? Why would Nicky Wayne want me? I've done nothing to threaten him."

"You have something he wants."

"What?" Ava's eyes widened, both hands going to her protruding belly, her head swaying side to side. "Not my baby."

Ben frowned. He hadn't wanted to scare her, but, damn it, she had to cooperate. "No, he doesn't want your baby. He wants that necklace I gave you with the medal of St. Joan of Arc on it."

"Well, he can't have it."

"Why? What's happened to the medal?"

"I don't know. I don't have it."

"What?" He grabbed her shoulders. "Where is it?"

She looked away, her gaze darting to the corner of the room. "I don't remember."

She did, but she wasn't telling him.

"Look at me, Ava." He held her, his fingers digging into her arms, the soft scent of spring flowers twisting around his starved senses, making him dizzy. Forcing himself to focus on the seriousness of the situation, Ben stared into Ava's eyes, willing her to understand. "This is not the secret to keep, Ava."

"For the second time, let go of me." Her jaw tightened and she matched him stare for stare until he dropped his hold. Immediately, she stepped out of reach, pulling her purse in front of her like a shield. "I'm not a puppet you can string along for your own purposes, to pick up when you feel like it and drop when you're bored."

God, he was losing her. Ben's knees shook. What did he expect? After so many weeks gone and his previous connection to Del Gardo's organization, did he think she'd trust him, fall into his arms and be the loving wife he'd left?

Hell, yes! He'd been through enough under Wayne's treatment, he certainly didn't want more abuse by his own wife. Anger made his muscles stiffen. "You're coming with me."

"Like hell." She stomped toward the door.

"Where do you think you're going?"

"Out." She blew through the door, practically running in her own pregnant waddle.

"Where are Emily and the boys?" Ben asked.

"Emily's at work. The boys are at their grandparents." Ava didn't slow until she reached the car.

"Don't you care that they could be in danger as well?"

"I would if I believed you."

If he wasn't so intent on saving her sorry butt, he'd laugh at the comical picture she made. Pregnant and angry, she was still the most beautiful, sexy, frustrating woman he'd ever met. Ben had his job cut out for him. He ran after her, and tried to grab the keys from her fingers. "You're not driving."

"Oh, yes I am." As if to prove him wrong, she eased behind the wheel of her Honda Civic and plunged the key into the ignition.

Ben hit the unlock button on her door before she could close it and jerked the back door open.

Ava had the car in gear and was rolling backward out of the driveway when Ben flung himself into the backseat.

She slammed on the brakes, dumping Ben onto the floorboard, his legs hanging out of the compact car.

"Get out," she said, her voice tight and angry.

Why did she have to be so stubborn? "I'm going with you. You need protection."

"The only person I need protection from is you, Ben Parrish."

Chapter Three

Still seething, Ava hit the accelerator and shot down the quiet residential street. She didn't know where she was going. Originally, all she'd wanted was to get away from Ben. With him in the backseat, that wasn't likely to happen.

She could abandon the car, but then she'd be on foot. After having walked two miles earlier that day, she wasn't sure she was up to another hike. The muscles across her abdomen tightened, reminding her that she needed to be calm. Under no circumstances was she to stress herself or her baby. The fetus needed another good month of gestation to ensure a healthy delivery.

Calm? Who was she kidding? Her disappearing-act husband, who'd rather lie than tell her the truth, was picking himself up off the back floorboard. Combine that with the fact that she might be the target of a deranged mobster and the minor detail that she really didn't know where the hell she was going, pretty much summed up the stink-hole her life had become. Which reminded her— next step, she'd call Emily and give her a heads-up, just in case Ben was telling the truth and they really were in danger. Calm? Ava stopped short of laughing out loud. She took a corner too fast just as Ben sat up. Centrifugal force did what Ava had hoped, throwing the man across the backseat.

Served him right. After all this time, who did he think he was, waltzing in demanding she just get up and leave with him? How many times had she asked him to trust her and tell her the truth? How many lies had he shoved down her throat? Why should she trust him now? She'd become much more independent and had been without him for this long, she could go the rest of her life without Ben Parrish.

In the back of her mind, she couldn't help the small niggle of joy chinking away at her resolve. Ben was alive. She squelched that joy before it took root and made her forget all the times he'd looked her in the eyes and chosen not to confide in her or tell her the truth about what he was doing. She didn't even know this man who'd been her husband. All the weeks she'd stood up for him while he'd been gone, she'd wondered if she was just one big fool. All the nights she'd cried herself to sleep, worrying about his sorry carcass.

"Where are we going?" Ben pushed himself upright on the backseat and strapped on his seat belt.

"Since *you* weren't invited, *we* aren't going anywhere. *I* on the other hand, am going wherever the hell I please." To prove it, she stomped on the accelerator, shooting through a yellow light.

Ben leaned forward, his breath stirring the hairs on the back of Ava's neck. "Do you think it wise to drive like a maniac in your condition?"

"Do you think it wise to disappear for weeks and then show up unannounced, demanding that I leave with you immediately?" Ava skidded around another corner, just to get Ben and his warm breath off the back of her neck.

It was doing crazy things to her libido, something she thought impossible at this late stage of pregnancy. Oh, but that heat she felt had nothing to do with outside temps. Damn the man! He'd always had that effect on her. One look, one breath and he had her body tied in exquisite knots.

Ben gripped the back of her seat with both hands. "Okay, okay, I'm sorry, but I was in kind of a rush. What with gunmen chasing me and escaping from the prison from hell, I must have lost all my manners." Ben inhaled and let out a slow steady breath. "If you'll head back to Kenner City, I'd like to check in with Tom and the KCCU and straighten out this mess."

"I'm not going anywhere with you, Ben Parrish. As far as I'm concerned, you're one of the bad guys, and I've had enough stress, enough lies…enough!" Ava slammed on the brakes, skidding to a stop in front of a sixteen-show movie theater. She didn't want to drive around town with him breathing down the back of her neck for the rest of the night. All her sleepiness had vanished, she might as well stay up and watch a movie. What the heck! Ava shifted into park and turned back to her husband. "Got any money?"

"Not a dime. I told you, I just escaped from Wayne's organization. I have nothing."

"Good." She grabbed her purse and eased out from behind the wheel. Finally, she had a way of ditching the bastard. With putting distance between her and Ben her main goal, Ava stalked toward the theater, her version of stalking being more akin to an angry shuffle. How foolish she must look, and fat and pregnant. Not that she cared what Ben Parrish thought of her now. He'd run out on her and left her holding the bag, answering the questions, living the lie, facing raising a child alone.

A tear slipped from the corner of her eye as she slapped money on the counter in front of a ticket agent.

"Which movie?"

"I don't care. Surprise me." What was one more surprise in this crazy night?

The kid behind the counter gave her a strange look and pushed a ticket and her change through the window. "Enjoy the movie, ma'am. Theater number seven."

Ben had followed her to the ticket window, but Ava didn't dare look around. If she did, she might fall into his deep dark eyes and cave right there in front of the pimple-faced ticket clerk. She needed time away from him to think. To collect her thoughts and figure out what she should do about her marriage to a man she'd thought she loved. A man she wasn't sure she could trust anymore. The hurt of the past few weeks was too fresh, too deep to forget in a moment. Not that she wanted to forget.

"Ava, don't go in. You know I can't follow you."

"That's your problem. You're so resourceful, you figure it out." Not that she wanted him to, not yet. She really needed time out of his overwhelming presence. When he didn't move out of her way, she ducked around him and headed for the ticket taker.

"At least lend me your phone. I have no way of contacting the unit to let them know where I am."

She hesitated. Should she do anything to make his life easier? If she granted this one request, would she cave altogether and fall back into his arms like the naïve child she'd been? Ava fished in her purse for her cell phone and tossed it to him. She made the mistake of looking at him then.

Ben gave her a sad smile as he deftly caught the cell phone in one hand. He did look tired and thin, his face haggard and long overdue for a shave.

Ava fought the urge to throw herself into his arms. She'd missed him so much. "I want it back." Was she talking about the cell phone or their relationship? She didn't even know.

"Don't worry, sweetheart. You can trust me."

Her shoulders stiffened. "I'm not so sure." She'd heard her father ask her mother to trust him so many times. All lip service. Ava turned and handed her ticket to the teenager wearing a theater uniform and she made her way to theater seven. Not until she settled in her seat did she remember she hadn't called Emily. Ava would wait fifteen minutes and make her way back to the lobby and a pay phone.

FATIGUE DRAGGED AT BEN and the smell of popcorn nearly brought him to his knees. With nothing to eat and no money to enter the theater, Ben leaned against the wall inside the lobby, half hidden by a giant pot filled with a ten-foot tall, fake ficus tree, feeling completely exhausted and thoroughly sucker punched. Yet he kept a vigilant eye on the door, waiting for signs of any of Nicky Wayne's goons. Not that he'd know all of them. They could be as thick as rats in a sewer on the streets of Vegas as far as Ben knew. That man walking in now, with the black polo shirt and black trousers could be one of Nicky's men.

Ben straightened, automatically reaching for the Sig Sauer in his waistband before he remembered he'd left it in Ava's car in case the theater had metal detectors at the entrance. It hadn't, making Ben more certain he should have carried the gun with him.

A trim young woman joined the man, hooking her arm through his elbow and smiling up at him.

Okay, so maybe he was just being paranoid. Ben

rolled his head around, attempting to loosen the stiff muscles in his neck.

Damn the woman! If she'd just come with him when he asked, he wouldn't be standing in the lobby of this theater worrying about every person walking through the door. Ava didn't know what was good for herself or their baby. And Ben did? He laughed out loud, the sound more a hoarse croak. His wife had managed just fine without him, a sobering thought.

He stared down at the phone, his vision blurring. Now what was Tom's number? Lack of food made his brain slower than normal as he punched in the number and hit Send.

"Ava?" Tom's voice came across the speaker.

"No, it's Ben."

"Oh, thank goodness. I have a man on the way over to Emily's with a rental car and some cash."

"Can you call him and tell him to meet me at…" Ben looked up at the theater and gave Tom the address.

"Hold on just a moment while I pass the information." The line went completely silent for a minute. During which time, the aroma of popcorn had Ben in a near-faint. He couldn't give up now. Hunger, plus the added anxiety of Ava being in the theater, in a public place where any one of Nicky Wayne's people could get to her, had his stomach knotting painfully. He stepped out of the theater lobby into the warm, Las Vegas night air.

"Ben?" Tom's voice broke through his gloom and doom thoughts.

Ben couldn't answer right away as he struggled to stand upright.

"You doing okay, buddy?" Tom's tone sharpened.

"I'm okay." Ben didn't feel okay.

"My guy should be pulling up in front of the theater about now. He was just around the corner when you called."

Ben sagged against the wall. "Thank God."

"You want me to come to Vegas?" Tom asked.

"No. I have to get Ava out of here. She's not safe."

"What's going on?"

"I'll call and let you know as soon as I get the situation in hand here." As soon as he got Ava in hand. That would be the day. "By the way, where's Ortiz? Why did I get you instead of him?"

"Ben, Ortiz is dead."

"Damn, Tom, what happened?"

"It's a long story, Ben. When you get here, we need to talk. Maybe you can help us figure that one out."

Ben's breath caught in his throat and held, while he tried to wrap his tired brain around that piece of news. He'd reported to Ortiz throughout his undercover mission with Del Gardo. Had Nicky Wayne figured out that Ortiz had sent Ben into the Del Gardo crime organization and killed him for knowing too much? And how much did Tom and Dylan know about his undercover assignment? At this point, did he tell Tom what he'd been doing? No. He needed to be there in person to tell Tom what he'd been working on and why. Anyone could intercept a cell phone call. "Yeah, we need to talk in private."

"And Ben, Boyd Perkins is dead. We're pretty sure he's the one who actually killed Julie."

Ben's chest tightened as an image of Julie's body lying on the hard ground rose in his mind. "Why? Did you find out why he killed her?"

"We think he wanted the medals. Julie had them until she stuffed them in the mail to each of us."

"I should have been there earlier. I knew she was getting in too deep with the Del Gardo family."

"Don't blame yourself, Ben. It won't bring her back."

No, it wouldn't. Julie's death had been a terrible blow to Ben, Tom and Dylan. They'd gone through the FBI academy together. They had been inseparable. Now one was gone.

"Boyd wanted those medals," Tom continued. "Someone stole mine and Dylan's from the criminal lab. Yours is the only one they haven't managed to steal."

And Ava had it somewhere, making her a flaming red flag in front of the raging bull of Nicky Wayne's crime organization. "Nicky knows that Del Gardo's bank account numbers are inscribed on the backs of all of the medals Julie gave us. Whoever can put them together will have Del Gardo's fortune."

"Yeah. My bet is that whoever has mine and Dylan's is probably pretty anxious to get his hands on the one you had."

Ben pounded his fist against the bricks on the outer wall of the theater. "Damn. My best bet is that Nicky Wayne has the other two by now."

A nondescript sedan pulled in front of the theater. "I have to go. The car just arrived."

"Ben, be careful. Nicky has people everywhere. You're not safe as long as you're in Las Vegas."

Ben had thought of that. Going back to the KCCU might not be such a great idea, either, if everyone still thought he was guilty. All he knew was that Nicky would be very focused on getting his hands on that medal and the inscription on the back.

With a quick scan at the occupants of the lobby, Ben prayed Ava would be all right by herself. Then he stepped to the curb to retrieve the car and cash Tom had promised. He'd only be gone from the theater for a moment. Nothing could happen in that short a time.

AVA TOOK A SEAT in the middle of a practically empty auditorium and stared up at the advertisements for soda and popcorn flashing across the wide screen without really seeing any of it. Other than two couples sucking face in the highest corners of the room, she had the place pretty much to herself. Just what she needed, an empty cavern to think in.

But she couldn't think. Ben was on the other side of the walls, alive and anxious about her. A sob rose in her throat and threatened to cut off her air. How could she turn her back on him now? He'd been gone so long she'd given up on him and presumed him dead or completely corrupt. Either way she'd gone through all five stages of the grieving process: denial, anger, bargaining, depression and finally acceptance. She couldn't do it again. It had taken a huge toll on her health the first time.

For all she knew, he was still involved in one of the crime families. If not Del Gardo then it was Nicky Wayne. He could be lying about being held captive by Wayne. Working for Nicky Wayne made more sense considering he'd come back for the necklace. Ava had known about the bank account numbers. Jerry Ortiz had tried to get hers. She'd thought he and Boyd Perkins were the only ones after them. After Ortiz's death, Ava had hidden the medal in a safe location.

If Ben was telling the truth, for once, and only came back to get the necklace but he still didn't plan on sticking around, she'd be back at stage one. Ava swallowed the sob, her vision blurring.

Through the wash of tears filming her eyes, she saw

another couple walk into the theater, a woman holding the arm of man dressed in a black polo shirt and slacks.

That should be her and Ben. Instead he was outside unable to get in because he had no money. Powerful guilt urged her to get up and go check on him. He'd looked pretty thin and hungry. What if he hadn't been lying? What if he'd really been held against his will by Nicky Wayne?

Ava lurched to her feet and moved to the end of the aisle. She'd just check on him and make sure he wasn't passed out on the floor from lack of food.

The couple stood at the end of her aisle, blocking Ava's path.

"Excuse me," she said.

"Are you Ava Parrish?" the woman asked, her back to the movie screen, her face shadowed.

Ava frowned, the hairs on the back of her neck rising to attention. "No," she answered, instinct warning her that the couple wasn't quite right. "Do you mind, I need to use the facilities." She tried to push her way around the couple, but the man stood firm and the woman closed the gap between her and the backs of the stadium seats.

The man's hand came away from the woman's arm, revealing the cold hard barrel of a gun.

All the air left Ava's lungs and she staggered backward, her legs bumping into the arms of the seats behind her. Her hand rose to protect her baby. "What do you want?"

"Come with us quietly and we won't hurt you…or your baby," the woman said, in a low whisper.

It didn't matter. The couples in the corners were too into themselves to notice what was going on in the rest of the theater.

Ava had two choices, go with the evil couple and look for a way to ditch them, or scream and possibly take a bullet to the belly. Hindsight being twenty-twenty, Ava now saw the benefit of staying with Ben. This wouldn't have happened had he been in the theater with her. Or better still, she wouldn't have put her baby in danger if she'd just gone with Ben like he'd asked—no, demanded.

With the barrel of a gun pointed at her unborn child, Ava had no other choice. "Please, don't shoot. I'll go with you."

Chapter Four

The FBI agent Tom sent delivered the car and cash and left in a yellow taxi, no questions asked. Which was just as well. Ben didn't have time to spare. Ava sat alone in the theater, exposed to who knew what. Ben parked the car in the movie theater lot, then Ben peeled a twenty off the wad of bills the agent had given him. His mouth watered at the thought of the popcorn he could buy. But, first things first. He had to get to Ava and ensure she was all right.

At the ticket counter, he paid for a ticket to theater seven and hurried past the concession stands, his stomach rumbling angrily.

Once he stepped into the darkened theater, he stopped and waited for his sight to adjust to the dim lighting. The metal clank of a door surprised him, the sound coming from near the front of the cavernous room. Who would be leaving before the movie even started?

Ben's heartbeat ratcheted into high gear. Had Ava skipped out the back door to avoid him? He scanned the empty seats noting two couples kissing high in the back corners. The rest of the theater was empty.

"Damn," he muttered beneath his breath and jogged across the darkened theater to the exit door. If the door closing had been Ava leaving, she couldn't have gotten far. Not in her condition.

In order to keep from scaring her, he eased the door open. With her so close to her delivery date, he didn't want to add so much stress that she went into premature labor. When Ben peered out onto the nearly deserted employees' parking lot, he didn't see anyone moving about.

Now a little more than worried, he ran to the nearest corner, stopped and peered around the edge.

In the dim glow of a parking lot light, the dark silhouette of a huddle of people made Ben's blood run cold. What looked like the man and woman he'd seen enter the theater flanked Ava and hurried her toward the cars parked near the front of the building.

No! Ben fought the urge to race after them, his mind grappling with his best options to rescue Ava without her coming to harm in the process. He ducked behind a row of cars and, keeping his head lowered to window-level, he moved as quickly and quietly as he could. When he was within one car length from the others, he paused, looking for his opportunity.

"Is this the fastest you can go?" the woman asked, jerking Ava's arm.

"You try carrying a thirty-pound bowling ball in front of you," Ava retorted, yanking her arm out of the woman's grip.

"Where'd you park the damned car?" the man barked.

"That's it, three cars down."

Ben hunkered low and ducked behind the cars, moving another three cars over before he slipped between the vehicles and waited in the shadows for the two to make their second mistake. The first had been to mess with Ava.

The electronic beep of a car lock and the blink of taillights pinpointed the vehicle they were headed for. The man opened the back door. "Get in."

"No." Ava pulled back, her feet planting on the pavement.

"Don't piss me off, lady." He pointed his gun at her belly. "Get in the damned car."

Ava hesitated only another second, then quietly bent and slid onto the seat. The man and the woman stood outside the car, their backs to Ben.

That's when Ben made his move. He hunched and charged across the open space between the lines of parked cars and barreled into the woman. On impact she crashed into the man, causing the gun in his hand to fly through the air, landing a yard away from where they lay sprawled on the pavement.

Ben crawled over the man and woman, reaching for the gun. "Get out of the car, Ava! Now!" When he thought he had the weapon in his grip, a large hand grabbed his ankle and yanked him back.

Behind him, the woman was climbing to her feet.

Ava swung the car door open, slamming it into the woman's backside, sending her flying yet again. She landed on top of the man, hitting him square in the chest.

Air whooshed from his lungs and his grip on Ben's ankle loosened.

Ben scooted out of reach, grabbed the gun and rolled to his feet all in one movement.

When the woman got to her feet for the second time, she reached beneath her blazer.

"I wouldn't, if you value your life," Ben growled.

Her hand stalled in midair. "You wouldn't shoot a woman, would you?"

"No, but I'd sure as hell shoot a criminal." He held the pistol level with the woman's chest and nodded. "Ease the weapon out of your jacket with two fingers and toss it behind you. If you even twitch an eyelid, I'll shoot."

The woman's lips pressed into a thin line, her eyes narrowing as if she were trying to gauge the sincerity of Ben's promise to shoot. Her hand reached inside the jacket and she hesitated.

When she jerked it out, Ben pulled the trigger on his own weapon, hitting the woman in the shoulder, spinning her around and slamming her into the car next to her. Her weapon dropped to the ground and skidded under the car. She slid to the pavement, holding her shoulder and cursing like a sailor.

The man scrambled across the pavement toward the fallen gun. He reached beneath the car, stretching as far as he could.

Ben leaned over the man and pressed the gun to his head. "Don't."

The car door opened on the other side and a hand reached beneath the car retrieving the gun. Ava slid out and stood, walking around to the end of the car. "Looking for this?" She held the gun in her hand, her finger on the trigger.

"Good, God, Ava. Put that thing down before you shoot yourself."

"I know how to handle a gun." She pointed it at the man's chest. "Want me to demonstrate? Anyone who'd threaten an unborn child deserves a little pain."

The man glared at her.

"That won't be necessary." Ben nodded toward the car. "Anything in there we can use to tie these two up?"

Ava stared at the man on the ground, for a long moment refusing to lower her weapon, her eyes blazing. Then her hand dropped to her side. "Yeah, the duct tape they'd planned to use on me." She hurried back to the car and returned with a roll of thick gray tape.

Ben jerked his head toward the woman. "Start by securing her good hand to the car and taping her feet together." He looked at the woman. "You hurt her in any way and I won't aim for a shoulder this time."

She glared at him. "I'll kill you. You just wait."

"Yeah, yeah. If Wayne doesn't do it for me. You two bungled an easy job. You can't even kidnap an eight-months' pregnant woman without screwing it up. You think you'll last long in his organization at that rate?" Ben snorted. "If I were you, I'd head out of town and keep going until you run out of road. Even then, I'd keep an eye on my back."

After she had the woman's good wrist firmly secured to the handle of a car, Ava squatted down and almost toppled over.

"Wait." Ben moved around the man, still pointing the gun at him. "Here, you hold this. If he so much as sneezes, kill him."

He passed the gun to Ava and took the roll of tape. He quickly wrapped the woman's ankles and reached for the man's hands, yanking them behind his back. "If you ever point a gun at my wife or my baby again, I'll kill you," he said as he pulled the tape tight enough the man would be hurting. After he'd secured his feet and laid a strip of tape on the thugs' mouths, he flung the roll of duct tape across the parking lot.

"Ready?" He hooked Ava's arm and walked her to his rental car.

"I can't leave my car here."

"You can't take it. They know what it looks like. You're not safe in it." He sucked in a deep breath and let it out. "Please, Ava, get in the car."

"No." She pulled out of his grip and marched across to her car.

Ben followed her. "Where are you going?"

"It's none of your business." She climbed in and would have shut the door if Ben hadn't grabbed it and held it open.

"Maybe you don't get it." He leaned close enough to get right in her face. "Your life is in danger."

"So, I'll be careful." Tears hovered on the edges of her eyelids as she jammed the key into the ignition and started the car.

The tears ate at Ben's empty gut, twisting in it like a knife. "You can't go alone. At least let me come with you."

"I need time to think." She rested her forehead on the steering wheel. "Time without you in it."

Although she whispered, Ben heard every word. Her rejection hurt. More than he ever thought it would. His hand fell away from the door and he stepped back, his heart like a dead weight in his chest.

Ava shoved the shift into reverse, and slammed her foot to the floor. As she pulled out of the parking space, her tires squealed.

Ben stared after her in numb silence. After all the weeks he'd spent dreaming of his homecoming, he didn't expect this. And it caused him more pain than all the wounds he'd received during Nicky Wayne's torture sessions.

Before Ava cleared the theater parking lot, Ben came back to his senses with a jolt. He couldn't let her get away. He had no idea where she'd go or when Wayne's organization might strike again.

He ran to the rental car, climbed in and raced after Ava's disappearing taillights. At the rate she was going, she'd kill herself if Wayne didn't get her first.

AVA HATED that Ben had been right. She'd thought his warnings about the Wayne organization were all part of his ploy to get her back to Kenner City and the medal he wanted so badly.

The couple in the movie theater had taken her completely by surprise. But were they really part of the Wayne organization, or were they just a couple of crooks, looking to rob her or kidnap her for ransom?

Ava snorted. Like she had any money to steal. And who would pay a ransom to get her back?

She liked to think Ben would, but after the way she'd treated him…

Her chest tightened at the thought of him being held captive for the past couple months. What kind of torture had he endured? Was she being fair to push him away?

Her fists clenched around the steering wheel. She couldn't fall for his lies. She'd be as bad as her mother, believing her father would come back any day. For years, she'd held on to the hope, like her mother did, that her father would return. But after so long, she'd finally come to the realization that men didn't stay. They made big promises, but didn't deliver. Or at least, the two most important men in Ava's life hadn't delivered. Both times she'd given her love unconditionally, risking her heart.

Both times she'd been disappointed. She'd be damned if her baby went through that.

She could understand why her mother had welcomed her father back each time. He was so charming, endearing and handsome, how could a woman resist?

If she'd been smart, she'd have recognized the same traits in Ben up front, before she'd fallen for him. But she'd been as bad as a besotted schoolgirl with her first crush. Willing to believe she could actually have that fairy-tale happily-ever-after end to her story.

Hadn't her mother proven that wasn't the case?

And her sister Emily had suffered through a divorce, also proving the same.

Was it fate for Ava to fall into the same trap?

With nowhere else to go, Ava headed back to her sister's house. Maybe she'd pack her bags and head for a hotel. Or she could keep driving until she made it to California. She'd always wanted to visit San Francisco and never seemed to have time to get away from the Kenner County Crime Unit. With a month to go before the baby was due and out of work, by doctor's orders, she had plenty of time now.

Yeah, like she'd drive across the state eight months pregnant with no plan, no place to stay and no desire to be alone.

She sat at a stoplight, her foot resting on the brake, thinking she should take the easy route, give in and let Ben take care of her…

The light turned green, her foot fell hard to the accelerator and she shot forward. What was she thinking? Had she become her mother?

When she turned onto the suburban street her sister lived on, she coasted into the driveway and switched the engine off. Tired beyond belief, she could barely stand the thought of packing and leaving. Maybe she'd just go in, take a shower and climb into bed. Tomorrow was another day. Her troubles could wait.

Ava pulled the keys from the ignition, hooked her purse strap over her shoulder and dragged herself out of the compact car, wishing she had bought one a little higher off the ground.

When she reached out to insert her key in the doorknob, her knuckles bumped the door and it swung open.

The hairs on the back of Ava's neck stood on end and she clapped a hand over her mouth to keep from screaming. Instead, she called out softly, "Emily?" She waited for a response, listening for sounds of movement inside the house.

When silence met her call, she pushed the door wider and peered into the dark interior. The house had been a refuge to her when she'd arrived several days ago. Now it stood silent and ominous.

She reached inside, switched on the hall light and gasped.

The view from her position just inside the entryway, revealed overturned bookcases and books littering the floor. Slashed couch cushions spilled stuffing over the carpet. The tasteful curtains gracing the floor-to-ceiling windows of the living room lay in shredded heaps.

A sob rose from Ava's throat.

Emily. Where was Emily? She wasn't due home for another few hours, but what if she'd come home early?

Ava ran into the house and searched room after room, witnessing the same devastation throughout the house. Everything was ruined, including the bedding and mattresses on all the beds. Even in the boys' room, their favorite Spider-Man sheets had been ripped beyond repair.

Standing in their room, Ava couldn't hold back. Tears flowed and her body shook with silent sobs. "Why?"

When a hand clutched her elbow, she screamed and tried to run. But the hand holding her tugged her closer.

"Please! Don't hurt my baby!" She swung around and pounded her fists against her assailant's chest, the tears spilling down her cheeks, blinding her.

"Ava, it's me." Ben grabbed her wrists and held them against his chest with one hand. Then he pulled her into his arms. "You're okay. I won't let anything happen to you or our baby. Shhh. It's okay."

She rested her head against him, her hands fisting in the fabric of his shirt. "How can you say it's okay? Look what they've done to my sister's home." More tears soaked into his shirt.

"Things can be replaced. People can't." His voice stroked her like a gentle hand, soothing her, bringing her heartbeat closer to normal. "Let me keep you safe until this is all over."

For a moment she dreamed of what it would be like to be back with Ben the way they once were, laughing, living together and loving. A real fairy tale.

"I can't." She pushed away from him, her vision blurred, hair sticking to her damp cheeks. "I can't be with you. I won't become my mother. Don't you see? It's happening all over again." She tried to pull free of his grip, but he held on, and she no longer had the strength.

"I don't know what you're talking about. *What's* happening again?" He smoothed the hair behind her ear and brushed his thumb across her wet skin. "Look, just come with me tonight. I'll watch over you and keep you safe."

Numb and exhausted beyond reason, Ava let him lead her toward the door, but when they reached the living room, her heels dug into the carpet as she looked around at what Emily and her family had to come home to. Her heart squeezed in her chest. "What about Emily's house? Her boys will be devastated."

"I'll call and let her know what to expect. When we report the circumstances of the break-in the police should provide some assistance and protection. If she's anything like you, your sister is a strong woman. She'll handle it."

"But she shouldn't have to." Ava broke away from him. She had to clean up the mess. "I can't let her come home to this." Ava pulled loose of Ben's grip and bent over to lift a pillow from the floor.

Ben caught her wrist before she could. "Leave it, Ava. This is a crime scene. You of all people should know that. If you move anything, you destroy evidence."

The truth of what he was saying sank in and she straightened.

"We need to leave in case whoever did this decides to come back." Ben placed a hand on the small of her back and guided her toward the door.

Ava's eyes widened and her gaze met his. "You think they'll come back?"

His mouth formed a grim line. "As long as you're here, they will."

She inhaled a deep breath. "They ruined my sister's house because of me, didn't they?"

Ben frowned. "No. They ruined her house because of Nicky Wayne's greed. You are not at fault in this situation."

"But if I stay, they might come back and maybe hurt Emily and the boys." That sick feeling she used to get during morning sickness returned. "We can't let them hurt my family."

"The best thing we can do for them is leave."

Ava's jaw hardened. "Then let's go." She led the way to the front door.

Before she reached it, Ben stepped in front of her. "Let me." When she opened her mouth to protest, he pressed a finger to her lips.

The warmth made her wish for more than his finger touching her lips.

"I'm trained at this kind of thing." He positioned her around the corner from the door and pointed a finger at her. "Stay."

She crossed her arms over her belly. "I'm not a dog, you know."

Ben smiled, the effect nearly knocking her off her feet. "I know. But I also know how hardheaded you can be. Please stay?"

Her brow furrowed for a second, then she shrugged. "Fine. But make it fast. I want to talk to my sister."

"Yes, ma'am." He popped a salute and ducked around the corner.

Ava held her breath, straining to listen. She couldn't even hear his footsteps as he moved through the house.

The front door opened quietly, the only reason she knew was because of the soft swish of the weather stripping skimming the threshold.

What felt like her entire lifetime had passed before Ben stuck his head back around the corner, scaring ten years off her life.

Ava stifled a scream, her heart thrashing against her ribs. "If you want me to drop this kid soon, keep it up." She pushed past him. "I take it the coast is clear."

"Yes. But let me go out first." He hurried in front of her, his head jerking from left to right as he exited the house. He stayed positioned in front of her until he reached his rental car parked behind hers.

"I'm not leaving my car." Ava stood beside her car.

"We've been over this. They can trace your car. If you take it, you're a rolling target. They might even have a tracking device on it." He opened the passenger door to the rental sedan. "Please, we shouldn't stand out in the open for too long."

Ava's gaze panned the quiet street. Before she'd been in the house, she couldn't have imagined anyone doing anything more criminal in this neighborhood than letting their dog wander into the yard next door. That whole peaceful facade had been shaken, destroyed along with everything her sister owned.

"Okay." Ava slid into the car. "But I want to see my sister. I can't tell her what happened over the phone."

"It's too dangerous."

With one of her feet still on the pavement, Ava pushed the car door wider. "If you don't take me, I'll take my own car."

"Okay, okay." He shut the door, rounded the hood and folded his long length behind the steering wheel. "Where is she?"

"At work at the casino."

Ben groaned.

"What?" Ava gave him a cross look. "Do you have a problem with that?"

"Nothing." He twisted the key in the ignition with more force than was necessary, the engine leaping to life. "Only that a casino is about the last place on earth I ever wanted to go to again. Other than that, nothing."

"Good, because I want to see my sister." Ava leaned back in the seat, her back aching and more tears pooling in her eyes. When would the terror stop?

Chapter Five

"This is too dangerous." Ben spun on his heel in a three-hundred-sixty-degree turn, staring hard at all the cars in the parking lot outside the Lucky Eight Ball Casino where Ava's sister, Emily, worked as a blackjack dealer. The skin on the back of his neck tingled.

He didn't like it. Too many people moved in and out of the casinos and this one was no different. "We should be on our way back to Kenner City. Let the police handle informing your sister of the break-in."

"I won't leave until my sister knows what's happened to her place. Besides, how would she feel if she came home to her house the way it is and me missing?"

Ben blocked her exit from the car. "You could call her."

Her eyes narrowed. "No." The woman could be hard-headed when she wanted.

With a sigh, Ben held out a hand.

Ava stared at if for a moment then slid her fingers into his, as though accepting any help from him went against the grain. He had an uphill battle to win this woman's trust again.

Despite being eight months pregnant, she still felt as light as a child. "The police shouldn't be the ones to break it to her."

"Look, you're in imminent danger. What part of danger don't you understand?"

Ava rolled her eyes. "Then let's get in, get out and on the road."

As he walked toward the entrance, Ben shielded Ava as much as he could with his body, his senses alert for any sign of trouble.

Once inside, Ava stepped ahead of him, leading him through the maze of slot machines, table games and gamblers carrying buckets of tokens or plastic cards tallying their winnings.

When they arrived at the blackjack tables, Ava's sister glanced up, her eyes widening when she saw Ben. With the ease of a professional dealer, used to keeping her cool, Emily continued through the hand.

Ava and Ben stood with their backs to the slot machines and waited. Ben's toe tapped silently against the commercial-grade carpet, his glance panning the floor. He wished he was wearing his blue jeans and cowboy boots instead of the pilfered stripper's tux and borrowed shoes. He garnered more than one stare from passing men and women, which he ignored, more intent on spotting potential trouble than explaining his unusual attire.

The table won the hand and Emily collected the winnings. "My apologies, but I need to take a short break," she said to the customers seated at her table. "I'll be right back." Emily locked her chips in the table drawer and stepped out of the curve of the counter, jerking her head slightly for Ava and Ben to follow.

Ben hadn't had time enough with Emily to win over Ava's only living family member before he was kidnapped and imprisoned. He and Ava had been to Vegas but once since their wedding and his undercover assignment had precluded him from family get-togethers.

When they were in the hallway leading to the restrooms, Emily stopped, her arm going around Ava. "When did *he* show up?" Emily glared across at Ben.

"A couple hours ago." Ava placed her hand on Emily's arm. "I'm leaving town."

"No way." Emily shot a fierce look at Ben, her gaze softened when it returned to Ava. "You just got here. You haven't even seen the boys."

Ava swallowed hard and looked down at her belly. "Nicky Wayne's organization is after me."

Emily's jaw dropped. "You're kidding, right?" Wayne had a reputation in Vegas. Anyone with any idea of the inner workings of the city knew this. Emily was no exception. "Why would Nicky be after you?"

"He wants a necklace Ben gave me," Ava said, picking at the fabric of her maternity top.

Emily glared at Ben once more. "Just one more reason for you to be on my black list."

Ben gritted his teeth, too concerned over Ava's safety to get in a pissing contest with her sister, knowing any argument would cause Ava more stress than she already had to deal with. "She's not safe in Vegas."

Emily's brows rose. "And she's any safer with you? Last I heard you were knee-deep in the Del Gardo family business. Maybe even switched camp to Wayne's."

He didn't know what he could say. Until he got the go-ahead from FBI headquarters, he couldn't share details of the assignment he'd had with the Del Gardo family. "I can't go into that here."

"I know that makes me feel a whole lot better about you taking off to who knows where with my sister." Emily pulled Ava close to her side. "I won't let you hurt her anymore."

Ava might be big around the middle but the shadows under her eyes and the hollows in her cheeks made her appear like a lost waif, tired and vulnerable.

Ben's chest tightened. "I never meant to hurt her."

Ava's head came up. "Now's not the time to discuss this." She turned to her sister and gripped her hands. "I came by because Wayne's men have been in your house."

Emily gasped. "My house? When?"

"Just a little while ago."

Her sister held her away and scanned her from head to foot. "Did they hurt you?"

"No, I wasn't there at the time." Her quick glance at Ben warned him not to mention the incident at the theater. No use worrying her sister further.

Emily hugged her to her chest. "Oh, thank God."

Ava peeled her arms loose and stood her away from her. "I'm sorry, Em, but they trashed your house. Completely."

"I don't care. As long as no one was hurt. We have insurance. Things can be replaced. People can't."

A hint of smile quirked the corners of Ava's lips. "I seem to be hearing an echo," she muttered without looking at Ben.

Her faint smile warmed him more than he cared to admit.

"The point I'm trying to make," Ava continued, "is that we left it as is. You need to call the police and report the break-in. They could dust for prints and maybe catch whoever did it."

Emily snorted. "Like they'd throw Nicky or his men in the slammer? Not a chance. But I will call the police if only to satisfy the insurance company." Her brows drew together. "Where will you go?"

"Back to Kenner City. I have friends there who can

help me." Ava held her sister's hands. "I'm sorry I brought this on you." Tears welled in Ava's eyes, knocking a hole in Ben's gut.

If he could, he'd bear all her pain gladly. Anything to keep her from crying. He'd never been able to ignore her tears. He touched her elbow. "It's not your fault. It's Nicky's. Come on, we need to leave."

Emily held tight to Ava's hands, her gaze shooting to Ben. "You hurt my sister and I'll kill you, do you understand?"

Ben nodded. He felt that way about anyone who tried to hurt this woman. He reached out to Ava. "Ready?"

She shook her head, refusing his hand. "I need to use the ladies' room." Her mouth twisted into a frown. "I don't have much of a choice lately."

Blood rushed through his heart and his breathing quickened. After he'd let his guard down at the theater, he didn't trust even the gray-haired retired ladies. Ben took a step toward the ladies' restroom.

Ava moved in front of him and laid a hand on his chest. "Oh, no. You are not going in there. Emily will go with me. You can stand outside the door and scare away all the grandmas."

Ava grabbed Emily's hand and hustled her toward the restroom, leaving Ben standing in the hallway, his brows turned down in a fierce frown.

Ben didn't like her being out of sight for even a minute. In Vegas, anything could happen.

"WANT ME TO SNEAK you out the back?" Emily said as soon as the door swung closed behind them. She scanned the room. "Uh, on second thoughts, maybe not. I don't think there is a back door to this restroom."

With a weak smile, Ava squeezed her sister's arm. "No, I'm all right. I really did have to go to the bathroom."

Emily shook her head and laughed. "You're right. I think I went every five minutes in the last month of my pregnancies."

Ava held her sister's hands. "I really am sorry about your house. The boys will be beside themselves when they see the damage to their rooms."

"They trashed the boys' rooms, too?" Emily rolled her eyes. "Nothing like a gangster to pop a child's balloon." She patted Ava's hand and turned her toward the stalls. "Go on. Take care of business and don't worry about me and the boys. I'll be sure to get it cleaned up before they come home."

Inside the stall, Ava relieved herself, glad she'd taken the time. The weight of the baby had squished her bladder down to the size of a sheet of paper. No wonder she couldn't last more than a couple hours.

"I'm worried about you, Ava," Emily's voice echoed against the tiles.

"Don't be. I can take care of myself."

"I know you can. Mom raised us to be independent and all, but she couldn't guard our hearts against love. That particular four-letter word can be tricky."

Ava completed her business and exited the stall to wash her hands. With her back to her sister, she asked, "What do you mean?"

"We know how to make a living and support ourselves and any children that might come along, but do we know what love really is?" Emily stared over her shoulder, her gaze capturing Ava's in the mirror.

Did she? She'd thought she loved Ben. But love was a give-and-take effort where truth and honesty were paramount. "I'm not falling for Ben's lies again, if that's what you're worried about. I'm not some besotted fool anymore." Ava grabbed a paper towel and dried her hands before turning back to Emily. "After seeing what happened to your house, I'm not taking any chances with this baby." She wouldn't tell her the part about what had happened in the parking lot of the theater. That had her more scared than anything. What if Ben hadn't followed her into the theater and found the couple ushering her into a car? A cold, clammy chill washed over her. "Don't worry. I won't let love blind me like it did Mom."

"Mom had her faults, too. You were young, so young that you didn't see everything." Emily's eyes filled with unshed tears. "If Ben's really on the up-and-up, you'll have to make up your own mind whether or not your relationship will work."

"I'm not thinking about a relationship right now. I'm focused on this baby. Anything besides delivering a healthy child can wait."

"Don't let it wait too long." Emily tore off a paper towel and dabbed at a tear escaping from the corner of her eye. She wadded the paper and tossed it in the trash. "Um, Ava, did I tell you I found Dad?"

Ava's heart skipped a beat and she forgot to breathe. Then she sucked in a deep breath and leaned against the cool granite countertop, her knees shaking. "No, you didn't."

Emily nodded. "I did."

Ava's fingers clenched around her damp paper towel. "Why didn't you tell me earlier? Why now?"

"I didn't know how to break it to you. I know how you feel about him."

"That son of a bitch ran out on us." Ava tossed the wad into the trash, heat rising in her cheeks with the anger she'd never been able to let go of. "What man leaves his children behind? Certainly not a father."

Emily laid a hand on Ava's arm. "You didn't hear the whole story. I know how to get hold of him if you want to talk. If it makes a difference, he's sorry."

"Sorry?" Resentment bubbled up in Ava's throat, burning like her frequent attacks of heartburn. "Sorry? You know, I don't want to talk about it. He left us and never looked back. In my book, he's nothing but a lowlife. He wanted nothing to do with us and the feeling is mutual with me."

Emily stared at her sister for a long time. "If you ever change your mind and want to talk to him, I have his number."

"Keep it." Ava stomped past her sister, headed for the door.

"Everybody makes mistakes." Emily reached out and captured her sister's hand. "Don't let pride get in the way of your happiness."

Ava stared at the door, refusing to meet Emily's eyes. "Some mistakes are unforgivable."

"And some people have reasons for what they do, if you take the time to learn. Not that I'm forgiving Parrish for what he's put you through. Not yet, anyway. The jury's still out on him." Emily's hand slid down to Ava's and she squeezed her fingers. "Take care of yourself, sweetie. You're the only sibling I have. And I want a shot at holding my niece."

Ava looked up, her gaze connecting with Emily's. "I love you, sis. I'm sorry about your house."

Her sister's shoulders rose and fell. "It doesn't matter. Just get through this and be happy."

The swinging door slammed open and Ben stood there, his face tense, his lips pressed into a grim line. "We have to go. Now."

Ava's heart slammed against her ribs, and the baby kicked at the jolt of adrenaline screaming through her veins.

Ben grabbed her elbow and hurried her from the restroom, pausing for only a moment in the hall to turn toward Emily. "Is there a back way out of here?"

"Yes. Follow me." Emily ducked around them and strode for a door marked Employees Only. She slipped the employee key card attached to a lanyard from beneath her shirt and swiped it through the lock mechanism. When it beeped green, she shoved the door open. "This way."

The corridor led into the back administrative area. Emily passed dark offices and continued on to the exit that led to employee parking. She pulled her keys from a pocket in her trousers and handed them to Ben. "Take my car."

Ava snatched the keys from Ben's hand and shoved them back at Emily. "No way. You need your car."

Emily hid her hands behind her back. "I won't take no for an answer. You can't go back out the front, and I'll bet that's where you parked, right?"

Ben nodded, peeling the keys from Ava's hands. "She's right. If we want to get out of here fast, we have to take her car. Don't worry. I'll get it back to her." Ben dug the keys to the rental car out of his pocket and handed them to Emily, describing the car and where it was parked. "Call the police about your house, but don't go home for a couple days." Ben's eyes narrowed. "Wayne isn't above using family as leverage."

Ava's skin turned cold. "Maybe you should come with us."

"I can't. I need to get to my boys and make sure they're safe."

Sick at heart, Ava hugged her sister. "I love you, and I'll miss you. And I'm so sorry about bringing this on you and the boys."

"I love you, too. And don't be sorry. This isn't your fault. The boys and I will be fine. You just worry about yourself and that baby." She set Ava away from her and moved out of the doorway. "Now get out while you can."

"Thanks." Ben nodded toward Emily, then pushed through the door, dragging Ava through behind him.

"Be careful!" Emily called out after her.

Be careful? Ava almost laughed, but squelched the urge, afraid the laughter would come out as sobs.

BEN DROVE TO THE BACK of the parking lot and out onto a side street leading away from the strip.

"Did you see some of Nicky Wayne's men inside?"

"I couldn't be sure, but a man approached one of the security guards with a photograph. I didn't want to take any chances."

Ava nodded quietly, her face unreadable in the shadows. "Do you think my sister will be okay?"

"As long as she stays low and out of Wayne's way." Ben opened the cell phone the agent had given him and fumbled to enter Tom Ryan's number.

"Give me that before you cause a wreck." She snatched the device from his fingers and entered the number he gave her. After the first ring, she handed it to him.

"This is Ryan."

Tom's voice calmed Ben's racing heart. "Tom. It's Ben."

"Did you find her?"

With a glance at Ava, he answered, "Got her and we're on the road."

"Headed this way?"

"Yeah."

"The FBI and the KCCU will have a ton of questions for you."

Ben didn't respond.

"You *are* turning yourself in, aren't you?" Tom asked.

"Haven't decided."

"Ben, you really should. The more you run, the worse it looks for you."

"I know." Ben negotiated a turn, shifting the cell phone to his other ear. "Tom, something isn't right and I'm not coming in until I've figured it out."

"Don't take too long. I'm not sure how long I can keep helping you."

"Speaking of help, I need another favor."

Tom snorted. "Exactly." He sighed, but continued. "Name it."

"Get a trusted agent out to the Lucky Eight Ball Casino in the next hour to escort Ava's sister, Emily Allen, wherever she needs to go to stay away from Nicky Wayne."

"Think he'll try to use Ava's sister as leverage to get what he wants?"

"I don't want to wait around to find out."

"I'm on it."

Before Ben could hit the off button, Tom caught his attention with, "Ben."

"Yeah, Tom."

"For what it's worth, you me and Dylan are still friends. You can count on us."

A knot lodged in Ben's throat. "I know."

Julie had been one of their friends, too.

Chapter Six

Ben hung up and tossed the cell phone into a cup holder.

An image of Julie's lifeless body remained engraved in his memory. Their little group had been close friends, like siblings. Losing her was like losing the sister he'd never had.

He'd thought finding her body had been the ultimate blow, but when people started looking at him as a prime suspect in her murder, Ben had been even more determined to find the man responsible for her death.

Only his quest had been put on hold while he'd been held hostage and tortured by Nicky Wayne.

Ben wound through the city streets and turned southeast on Highway 95 headed away from Vegas. Wayne would probably have people watching the airport and all the major roads leading out of town. Ava sat on the seat beside him in Emily's silver minivan, her hands clasped tightly together over her belly, her gaze darting to the side mirror, checking to see if they were being followed.

He hated that she was involved in this mess and wished he could hide her somewhere safe until it was all over. Not that she'd let him. At least getting her back to Kenner City might make it easier for him to protect her. Someplace where she was surrounded by her friends in the KCCU. A smaller town where strangers were easily recognized. Strangers like thugs sent by Nicky.

Ben's hands tightened on the steering wheel. If he hadn't caught the couple outside the theater when he had, no telling what Nicky would have done to Ava and the baby.

His chest hurt with the range of emotions swirling around. Anger, fear, worry, amazement and love. From the very first time he'd met Ava he'd known she would be his Achilles' heel. When he'd taken the job with the FBI, he'd known affairs could be nothing more than brief encounters, never anything long-term. At the time it suited him fine. Relationships never worked. Until he'd met an amazing woman.

Ava had changed that belief, making him want more than a fling. More than a romp in the sheets. No, he wanted to spend the rest of his life with her, raising their baby and maybe a couple more. He'd dared to dream about growing old with her.

His jaw tightened.

Fool.

That's what he was. By taking her as his wife, he'd placed her in harm's way. He had numerous enemies, each of whom wouldn't hesitate to use a woman or a child as collateral. He'd be better off leaving her and denying any claim to the child. Maybe then, Nicky would leave her alone.

Ben knew better. A relentless adversary, Nicky Wayne would stop at nothing, destroy everything Ben held dear, or even hinted at holding dear, until he got what he wanted.

Ben opened his mouth to ask Ava where she'd left the necklace, but when he turned toward her, he couldn't.

Her chin dipped toward her chest, her auburn lashes brushing the tops of her cheeks. She'd fallen asleep sitting up.

They'd been on the road for almost an hour and a half, the Vegas skyline was a distant glow in his rearview mirror. Porch lights blinked farther and farther apart as they left the sprawling city behind and slipped into the desert.

Nearing three in the morning, he couldn't keep driving. Not when Ava needed sleep and he needed food. The gnawing in his belly had long since numbed, but he needed something to keep his body functioning or he'd be of no use as protection for the woman he'd risked everything to protect. As he passed the Arizona state line, he started looking for a place to stop. One hundred miles didn't seem nearly far enough away from Nicky Wayne and his network of mercenaries and loyal followers, but Ben had to get sleep and food.

He had zigzagged through the streets of Vegas on his way out of town, checking for signs of being followed. For the past hour, not a single set of headlights had dogged his tail. This late at night, few cars were on the road. For the most part, they were tractor trailer rigs.

So far, he and Ava had eluded the Wayne crime machine. For how long, he had no clue.

He stopped at a gas station to fill up the tank. The next leg of the journey would have few filling stations and he didn't want to get caught in the middle of the desert with an empty tank and a heavily pregnant woman. Unfortunately, he still wore the borrowed tux. He'd be memorable to anyone who saw him. Not to mention the eight-months pregnant woman who was hard to miss.

"Why are we stopping?" Ava sat up in the front seat, blinking the sleep from her eyes.

"We need gas and food."

She reached for the door handle. "I'll go in while you fill up."

"No." Ben shook his head. "Stay in the car."

"Don't be silly." She stared around at the deserted parking lot and the lone clerk behind the window. "You're too noticeable in that getup." She nodded at his attire, gaping open where the Velcro ceased to stick.

She'd voiced only what he'd been thinking, but that didn't make him feel any better about her leaving his side for even a second. "I don't like you going in alone."

"I'll just run in and grab food for the trip and come right out. Besides, what could hurt me inside when I have you out here?"

Ben's gut told him that a lot could hurt her, but he couldn't name a thing at that moment, his mind was too fuzzy from sleep and hunger. He slid out of the van. "Okay, but don't take too long."

Ava grabbed her purse, climbed out of her seat and toddled to the convenience store, her hand pressed to the small of her back. Even pregnant, she was beautiful.

Ben's chest ached with the amount of love he felt for this woman. He plugged the gas nozzle into the tank. As he pumped gas, he kept a close eye on Ava moving about the store, aware of every sound, every vehicle passing on the primarily deserted streets.

INSIDE, Ava hurried down the aisles, grabbing tuna, canned sausages and crackers. She stopped at the glass fronted refrigerator and loaded her arms with milk and orange juice. Her stomach rumbled, reminding her that she hadn't eaten much for dinner with her sister earlier. With the baby taking up more and more space, she couldn't eat much without immediately feeling full.

After dumping the items on the counter, she backtracked to a rack of T-shirts and shorts. Although she'd enjoyed Ben's discomfort in the tux, he couldn't stay in them throughout their trip across the desert and not draw attention. She selected two large black shirts with the Vegas skyline silk-screened across the front and added a Vegas baseball cap to the pile on the counter.

The young man scanned the tags of all the items, one by one while Ava peered through the window at Ben topping off the tank.

He'd lost so much weight since the last time she'd seen him and the dark circles beneath his eyes only made him appear more dangerous and exciting. A thrill of a memory stirred the deep ache of longing she'd experienced during his absence. Too many nights she'd lain awake wishing he'd walk back into her life, take her into his arms and make everything all right again. But two months had passed. Two long months for doubt to creep in and more memories of how she'd felt when her father left for long stretches.

Ava inhaled and breathed out slowly, reminding herself she wasn't an adrenaline junky and she didn't enjoy being around a man who left her for months and then just reappeared expecting to pick up where they'd left off. The situation reeked of the relationship her mother and father had before her father finally disappeared forever.

She thumbed the wad of paper in her pocket her sister had given her before she'd passed through the exit of the casino. Without looking at it, she knew it contained their father's phone number. The man who'd left his wife and two small daughters alone. Abandoning the ones he was supposed to love while he chased after his latest pot of gambling gold.

Ava didn't plan on being the woman left behind. She'd rather do the leaving, or better yet, just not get involved again.

"Will that be all?" The clerk's voice broke into her musings, yanking her back to the convenience store and the plastic bags filled with food, drinks and clothes.

"Yes." She slid her credit card across the counter and waited for him to process it.

Ben stood beside the van, his gaze pinned on her.

Ava's body twitched in places she'd thought long dormant since the baby had made her look and feel like the Goodyear Blimp.

Ben's shaggy dark blond hair brushed the tops of his shoulder and his chocolate-brown eyes warmed her insides to boiling.

"Sign here." The clerk handed her a pen and the credit card printout.

Somehow, she managed to scribble her name on the dotted line, her hand shaking.

When she finished, she handed the man the paper, dropping the pen from her nerveless fingers.

The man frowned. "Hey lady, are you all right?" He glanced out at Ben. "I mean, you're not in some kind of trouble are you?"

Ava fought the urge to laugh hysterically. She was eight months pregnant and racing off through the desert in the middle of the night with a man she'd thought dead for the past two months. "Oh, no, of course not. I'm just fine." The last word caught on a sob. If she wanted, she could tell the clerk she was in trouble and have the police fish her out of this entire situation. Maybe even throw Ben in jail.

He'd been reluctant to call the police. Why? Was he afraid of the law as well as Nicky Wayne?

Ava pressed a hand to her belly. Ben was the father of her baby. Surely he'd never place her or the baby in danger. Would he? Fathers didn't do that.

Then again, her own experience with fathers hadn't given her much faith in the role or the male population.

"Are you sure?" the clerk asked.

Deep down in her gut, she knew Ben wouldn't harm her or their child.

But if she gathered her bags and left the store, she'd be walking directly back into uncertainty with the man she'd promised to love until death. Or until he left her and destroyed her trust or that of their child. Ava might be better able to weather that storm, but no child should have to suffer the rejection of her father. Especially if her father was a criminal.

She glanced up at the clerk. No. Everything wasn't all right. Her husband lied to her, skipped out on her then returned. For how long? Long enough for her child to grow up and eventually be heartbroken?

She could see the same pattern emerging as her mother's doomed marriage. She refused to let her child suffer the same heartache as she had with her on-again, off-again father.

The sooner she left him the better.

Ava opened her mouth. "No, I—"

A hand reached over her shoulder, setting a cup of coffee, a razor, shaving cream and a pair of sweatpants on the counter with a fifty dollar bill.

Ava jumped, bumping into the man standing so closely behind her, she could smell the residual gasoline on his hands. She didn't have to turn to know it was Ben. Every sensory nerve in her body recognized his presence.

"How much do I owe you?" Ben asked the young man behind the counter.

The clerk stared at him for a long moment, then rung up the items and handed Ben the change.

Ben laid a hand on Ava's shoulder. "Ready?"

Guilt heated her face. "Y-yes, I am." Refusing to meet the clerk's eyes, she gathered a bag of groceries.

Ben collected the other and the coffee, following her through the store to the door.

"Ma'am," the clerk called out. "You forgot your credit card."

Ava turned to go back but bumped into Ben, his face set in stern, forbidding lines.

"You used your credit card?" he asked in a voice only Ava could hear, his back to the clerk.

"Yes." Ava frowned. "So what?"

"You can be traced by your credit card."

"That would take more time than we'll be in this Podunk town," Ava hissed. She ducked around him and retrieved her card, smiling her thanks.

The clerk didn't let go immediately. "I can call the police if you want, Ms. Parrish," he whispered to her.

Ava struggled with the urge to glance at Ben to gauge whether or not he'd heard the young man's words. Instead she tugged the card from the clerk's hand and gave him what she hoped was a reassuring smile. "That won't be necessary. This man is my husband." Then she turned and walked out of the store.

Ben followed, a scowl cutting deep lines in his forehead. When they arrived in front of the minivan, he asked, "What did the guy say?"

"Just to be careful." Ava gripped the door handle and pulled. It was locked.

For a long moment, keys in hand, Ben stared at her until the skin on her neck twitched. When she couldn't stand it a second longer, she raised her brows and gave him a pointed look. "Are we going to hit the road again, or did you decide to stay the night at this station?"

His eyes narrowed for a moment, then he shrugged. He tapped his thumb to the remote, a mechanical click snicked in the doors of the minivan. "Get in, we need to get away from the bright lights."

"Bossy, aren't we?" Ava slid the side door open and deposited the bags on the floor of the vehicle.

"It's not good to be exposed for too long." Ben stood behind her, shielding her from the road, hovering like an overprotective mother hen with her chick.

His nearness sparked too much fire in her blood. Ava jerked open the passenger door, anything to get away from his broad, muscular shoulders. "We're not in Vegas, for heaven's sake." She hiked herself up into the passenger seat and buckled her belt. "So, chill." She slammed the door in his face, severing the too-close connection between them.

Ben slid the side door closed, rounded the van and climbed in beside her. With the key in the ignition, he paused, casting a glance her way. "You don't understand. Nicky Wayne plays for keeps. He will find us, and when he does, it won't be a cakewalk." Then he twisted the key, firing up the cylinders in the engine.

His tone, more than the words, set the fine hairs at the base of Ava's neck at attention. "Fine. I'll keep that in mind." She shoved a package of beef jerky at him. "Eat something. You're too thin. You're making me feel even fatter than I am."

She couldn't help the sarcasm and she didn't want him to think she was softening toward him. If she intended to maintain a hold on her sanity, she had to maintain her distance from the man and look for the first opportunity to ditch him and move on by herself.

Ben pulled out onto the street, headed east, moving slowly through the town until he found what Ava could only describe as a hole-in-the-wall motel. A faded neon vacancy sign blinked in dingy red. The single-story, wood-framed motel was the type that had seen its heyday maybe fifty years ago.

Ben parked the minivan at the back of the structure, where it couldn't be seen from the highway. Once parked, he glared at her. "Stay put while I get a room." He disappeared around the corner of the building.

Ava sat in the dark, smoothing a hand over her belly. It wasn't until Ben disappeared that it struck Ava that he'd said room, not rooms. Her heart thumped against her chest and her breathing caught and lodged in her throat. Surely he didn't expect to share a room with her.

Sharing a room with Ben was a bad idea. Especially the way her body reacted in his presence. For some reason, her libido didn't understand desertion or lies. It only knew what it wanted and what it wanted was Ben—tall, dark, dangerous and sexy as the devil.

How was she supposed to resist him if he stayed glued to her side at all times? Any breathing woman would be tempted beyond redemption by the man, even an eight-months pregnant one who resembled a Beluga whale. What she looked like on the outside didn't change the way her insides churned. The way she wanted to reach out and touch the man who'd disappeared for two months without a word and could do it again.

When Ben returned, he carried not one, but two sets of metal keys. He opened the passenger door and held out a hand for Ava as she climbed down.

Ava let out the breath she'd been holding, relief making her somewhat giddy. She took the hand and stepped out onto the uneven pavement of the ancient parking lot. "Which room do I get?"

"We're staying in the same room."

"But you have two sets of keys."

Ben grinned and held up the first set. "This is the one I paid for. Cash." He pocketed that set of keys and held up the second set. "This is the one I borrowed when the clerk was talking to his girlfriend on his cell phone." A smile twitched on the corners of his lips. "We're staying in this one."

Ava's gut knotted. No. She couldn't stay in the same room with Ben. She prayed that at the very least the room had two double beds.

"Come on." He gathered the bags of food and clothing and led the way around the side of the building to the last room on the end farthest away from the office and the highway. The rear of the parking lot led out to a side street, yet another avenue of escape, should the need arise.

Ava's analytical mind noted all the details of the area. As a member of the Kenner County Crime Unit, her job was to recognize the importance of even the most minute detail. Especially when investigating murder cases.

When he flung the door open, all the air whooshed out of Ava's lungs. The small room contained one double bed, with a vinyl chair crammed into the corner on one side and an old-fashioned nightstand with spindled legs on the other side.

"No." Ava backed up.

A hand at the small of her back stopped her retreat. "You need sleep and food."

"I'm not sleeping with you." Inwardly, she cursed her breathy voice.

His hand at the small of her back dropped. "Fine. I'll take the chair, you can have the bed." He hustled her through and closed and locked the door behind them.

Ava stared at the bed, her pulse hammering against her

eardrums, a full-scale panic attack making her breathing come in erratic pants.

"I'm not going to pounce on you, if that's what you're afraid of." Ben stepped around her and dropped the bags on a dresser whose surface had buckled where wet cups had made water rings in the cheap veneer. "You should get something to eat. I'm for a shower." He gathered the sweat pants, T-shirt and shaving gear and headed for the shower, pausing at the door to the bathroom. "Don't open the door for anyone."

"You think Nicky will find us here?" Her brows rose as she took in the room in a motel that was so far off the radar screen for just about anyone.

"Are you willing to take a chance?" He nodded, his gaze pinned on her swollen belly, his meaning implied.

The baby chose that moment to kick hard. Ava's hand rose to calm her. "No."

Ben nodded, leaving the bathroom door open a crack.

Ava rummaged through the bags, knowing she should eat something, but her appetite was tied up in the knot of tension squeezing her insides. The tension stemmed from her nearness to the man in the other room.

The squeak of the water faucet turning made Ava jump. The spray pattering against the plastic shower curtain had her skin quivering. She rubbed her hands on her arms, willing her senses to dull just enough she wasn't a complete basket case by the time Ben emerged from the shower.

With her back firmly to the open bathroom door, Ava chose a bag of peanuts and a small carton of milk from the bags. When she perched on the edge of the bed, all bets were off. No matter how hard she tried, she couldn't stop her gaze from straying to the wedge of light in the open bathroom door.

Thank goodness Ben had already ducked behind the shower curtain, but the dark silhouette of his body behind the thin white curtain stimulated Ava's imagination.

She popped a peanut into her mouth, savoring the salty-sweet flavor of the honey-roasted nuts. *Concentrate on eating, not on the water running down his body.*

Ava moaned softly, remembering the many times they'd shared a shower, rubbing soap over each other and how she'd laughed when he'd gotten to her ticklish places. So carefree, so in love.

So naive.

Deliberately turning her back to the bathroom, she tossed another peanut into her mouth, washing it down with a swallow from the carton of milk. If she couldn't rein in her emotions and memories, this promised to be a long night. She had to get away from Ben. He was too much temptation for any red-blooded woman to resist. And she'd tasted his particular charm and knew exactly what she'd been missing.

She also knew that men like him didn't stay for the duration. Her child deserved better. She deserved to grow up surrounded by the love of a parent who'd never profess to love her and then leave her without ever coming back.

No, she had to stand firm against her own wants and desires.

The shower faucet squeaked and the water shut off.

Good. Her turn in the shower. Convinced she could handle anything Ben Parrish had to throw at her, she stood and set the half-finished carton of milk on the dresser, gathered the second T-shirt and turned toward the bathroom.

Ben had pushed aside the shower curtain and was in the process of reaching for a towel. Rivulets of water ran down his chest, over his taut abs and lower to the thatch of dark hair at the juncture of his thighs. His manhood jutted out, hard and straight.

Ava's heart stopped and for a moment she couldn't breathe.

Ben's gaze captured hers and he winked.

Damn him! Ava swung away, pressing a hand to her heated cheek. Damn her! Why did ignoring him have to be so hard? Back to her original theory: this was going to be a very long night.

Chapter Seven

Ben's groin tightened when he caught Ava staring at him through the crack in the doorway. Throughout his shower, he recalled the many times he'd stood with her, both covered in soap suds, his fingers tracing the lines of her beautiful body. She'd just barely had a baby bump when he'd been kidnapped. He'd found her body utterly sexy, pregnant and all.

That's how he'd remembered her during his captivity. The change in her had been a minor shock, all of his protective instincts leaping into overdrive. This was his woman, the one he'd chosen to spend the rest of his life with—the woman he'd sworn to love, honor and cherish until death. He'd gotten the love part right, but his job had made him skimp on the honor and cherish. He couldn't blame her for pushing him away. For all she knew, he was part of a crime family.

Knowing he'd been at fault in their relationship didn't lessen the pain of her rejections. As quickly as the desire flared in her eyes, she'd spun away, refusing to acknowledge their physical connection.

The big muscle in his chest squeezed hard, making him hurt all over. He knew he hadn't given her much reason to trust him before he left. Because he'd worked closely with crime boss Vincent Del Gardo, anyone would suspect him of foul play. Ben had succeeded at his undercover role a little too well. He'd hoped that Ava could see beneath the surface and recognize he'd never betray his fellow agents. At least she wasn't one of the many who still believed he was the one to kill Julie or to have her killed by another. Ava knew how much he cared about Julie, Tom and Dylan. For all intents and purposes, they were siblings, if not by blood, then by shared experiences.

Ben ran a hand over his smooth chin. Long, shaggy hair couldn't be helped until he could get to a barber or a pair of scissors. But clean and shaved, he almost felt normal, ready to face anything. His stomach grumbled, reminding him he hadn't eaten except for the bite of jerky he'd had in the minivan a few minutes ago. He slid his legs into the sweatpants and pulled them up over his hips. Tossing the towel across his shoulders, he strode from the bathroom into the tiny motel bedroom.

With a T-shirt clutched to her chest, Ava sidled around him, refusing to look at him as she ducked into the bathroom and shut the door.

So that was how she wanted it—in the same room, but nowhere close enough to talk out their problems. Ben had his work cut out for him. But right now he was too hungry and tired to fight. His skin and nerve endings twitched, reminding him he'd only recently gotten off whatever drug Wayne had used to spike his food. Food free of drugs would help combat weakness, but only time would take care of the residual effects of the drugs.

He unearthed a package of miniature powdered doughnuts, a smile lifting the corners of his lips. His favorite.

That Ava had remembered touched him, giving him

hope in this seemingly hopeless situation. He downed all six doughnuts, polished off the package of beef jerky and a pint-size carton of milk before his stomach clenched, rebelling at the onslaught of junk food after two full days of fasting. What he wouldn't give for a thick, juicy steak and a baked potato. Maybe when he got back to Kenner City.

Which reminded him. The cops there probably considered him a fugitive. If they suspected him of involvement in Julie's murder, they'd have a warrant out for his arrest, or at least have him tagged for heavy surveillance, making it difficult for him to further investigate the murder or keep Ava safe.

He flipped open the cell phone Tom Ryan had sent to him via the agent in Vegas and dialed Tom's number. Ben winced when he noted the time on the clock radio beside the bed. In the early hours of the morning, Tom would be sound asleep.

"Yeah," Tom's groggy voice confirmed.

"Tom, it's Ben. Are you awake?"

"I am now. Where are you?"

"On our way home." Ben didn't trust cell phone signals and didn't give out more information than necessary. "Is someone going to arrest me if I show up in Kenner City?"

"Yeah. The city police have had an A.P.B. issued for your arrest since you disappeared. You really should turn yourself in, otherwise they'll think you're guilty."

"No can do. Nicky Wayne's already made a couple attempts to get to Ava. If I turn myself in, Ava's a sitting duck."

"We'll take care of her."

"And would you let anyone else take care of her if we were talking about Callie?"

Silence on the other end stretched for a few long moments. "Okay, I see your point. But it won't be easy eluding the law for long."

"I know."

"Man, let me and Dylan help. You can't go this alone."

"I can't drag you into this," Ben said, knowing that he and his friends would do anything for each other, including breaking the law. "If you assist me or help me any further, you could be arrested for aiding and abetting. I need you two to continue your search for Julie's murderer and be there for backup in case I run into difficulties protecting Ava."

"Gotcha. So what's your plan?"

"I don't know, and I wouldn't tell you if I did."

"I know, can't have too many people able to pinpoint your location."

"Nicky's everywhere. You can't trust anyone."

"You can trust me and Dylan. Just say the word and we're with you, buddy."

"Thanks. In the meantime, I'm probably going to disappear until this blows over."

"With Ava?"

Ben glanced toward the closed bathroom door. "Yeah."

"Are you sure that's a wise move in her condition?"

"Frankly, it scares the hell out of me."

"What if something happens and Ava goes into labor? Have you ever delivered a baby?"

"Once, when I was a street cop in Denver. But I swore then I didn't want to have to do that again."

"Yeah, and this one's yours. Not to mention, she's had premature labor pains. You could be setting yourselves up for a whole lot of trouble disappearing with her now."

"I know, but I can't be certain who she's safe with. If I don't get her away from everyone, I won't be certain she'll be safe."

"And Ava is okay with this plan?"

Hell no. She'd probably pitch a fit and have to be dragged kicking and screaming. She thought she was headed for Kenner City, but since the attacks at the theater, her sister's house and the threat at the casino, Ava wasn't safe anywhere. Except one place where Ben could see the enemy coming from a long way away.

The little cabin in the desert far from Kenner City where he'd holed up several times while working the Del Gardo undercover assignment. No one would think to look for them there.

Now all he had to do was convince Ava to go along with his plan. The thought of Nicky Wayne getting his hands on Ava made Ben's blood run cold. And if all else failed, he'd resort to plan B and just take her there, to hell with convincing.

Ava emerged from the bathroom wearing an oversized black Vegas T-Shirt that hung down past her knees. Her belly filled out the volume, stretching the material over the baby. She held her other clothing in her hands, her gaze darting from the bed to him and back to fix on the bed, her bottom lip caught between her teeth.

"I'll sleep in the chair, if it makes you feel better," he offered, regretting the words as soon as he said them.

She nodded, laying her pile of belongings on the nightstand. Then without a word, she climbed into the bed, pulled the sheets up to her chin and turned her back to him.

Ben sighed. He had the feeling Plan B might be his only option.

AVA LAY FOR A LONG TIME, her heart beating too fast to allow her to get any sleep. The baby, sensing her distress, kicked hard against her ribs.

She pressed a calming hand to her belly, smoothing

over the jersey knit and patting the baby. If only she could calm herself as easily. Sleep appeared to be an impossibility with Ben in the same room. When he'd stepped out of the bathroom in nothing but the sweats, Ava's body jerked to attention and stayed there.

Slimmer than before he disappeared, he had a new scar on his shoulder and other recent scars she didn't recognize. Which led to a question she didn't dare ask for fear of her reaction to the only answer she knew she'd receive. Had Nicky tortured him while he'd been held captive?

Ava fought the urge to go to Ben and smooth her hand over the new welts. She couldn't let herself fall for the man again. She'd rather her baby didn't know her father, especially if he had no intention of sticking around. The disappointment would make her miserable, just like it had made the little girl Ava had been.

Lying on her side, she clutched the sheet around her, refusing to respond to her body's urge to go to Ben. To douse her surging feelings, she thought of the nightmare her life had become since his disappearance. The police had made a crime scene out of her home, asking her questions she didn't have the answers to, making her feel like the criminal when the only crime she'd committed was loving Ben.

The light on the nightstand blinked out and the crackle of Ben's weight sinking into cheap vinyl made Ava's heart skip a beat.

Her jaw tightened. As soon as Ben fell asleep, she'd find a way out of here, get back to Kenner City and pick up where she'd left off in the investigation of Julie's murder.

Somewhere between planning her escape and wishing everything back to the way it was before Ben's disappearance, fatigue claimed Ava and she slipped into the darkness of sleep.

"Mommy? Where did Daddy go?"

Ava glanced down at the golden-haired child with chocolate eyes just like her father. *"I don't know, darling. Want to come sit with me?"*

"No. He promised he'd show me how to fish. When will he be back?"

A solid lump choked Ava's throat. She didn't know when he'd be back. He hadn't even told her when he'd left, slipping into the night while she and her daughter slept.

"I'm going to find Daddy." The little girl ran out the front door before Ava could catch up with her.

Panic seized her as she ran through the house, her feet dragging as if mired in sludge. *"No, baby, don't go!"* she yelled.

When she reached the door, her daughter was but a speck on the horizon, the darkness swallowing her in shadows.

Her little girl's voice echoed in the gulf between them. *"Daddy!"*

Unable to see her, unable to reach her before she completely disappeared, Ava dropped to her knees, her body shaking with sobs. *"Don't leave me, baby. Don't leave me."*

Warm, solid arms encircled her and pulled her against an even warmer wall of muscle. *"Shhh, baby, don't cry. Everything will be all right."*

She wanted to believe the stranger so badly, she snuggled back into his embrace and let him hold her, a pitiful voice she didn't recognize as her own, softly whispering, *"Help me."*

"I'll do the best I can."

Ava awoke in the darkness. A heavy weight rested on her hip, holding her securely in the bed. As the scent of soap, shaving cream and male penetrated the fog of sleep, her eyes widened.

Ben lay in the bed behind her, spooning her backside against his length, his arm draped over her hip, his fingers brushing her thigh.

For a moment, Ava snuggled closer, letting herself believe her life could once again be perfect. The life she'd thought she'd had with Ben at her side, a baby on the way, a job she loved, living the perfect dream in Kenner City. But like the dream she'd just experienced, life wasn't always fair, people didn't always stay and someone usually got hurt.

Still, the warmth of his arms around her, the strength of his body cocooning her, protecting her couldn't be denied. She could easily fall back into the lie they'd lived as husband and wife, waiting for him to return from who knew where. Never knowing whether he worked for the good guys or the bad guys. Never knowing if he'd even come home to her.

Ava's emotions shot from blissful fantasy to heart-pounding panic in mere seconds. The urge to run raced through her body like a freight train racing down a mountainside, completely out of control. Careful to avoid waking Ben, she slid his arm off her hip and rolled off the side of the bed onto her feet—no simple task for a woman nearing the end of her pregnancy.

A quick glance at the man in the bed reassured her that he was in deep REM and might stay that way while she proceeded with her own plan.

Gathering her clothing, she slipped into the bathroom, used the facility and dressed in the dark. When she emerged, Ben had rolled to his other side, his back to her, gently snoring.

Her heart lurched into overdrive as she scanned the top of the dresser for the keys to the minivan. At first she couldn't find them. She dug beneath the white shirt and tux jacket, then moved the trousers. There beneath the pile of clothing were the key fob and key to her sister's minivan. Ava let out the breath she'd been holding and, careful not to jingle, she palmed the keys, clutching them tightly.

She shot another furtive glance toward the man in the bed.

Ben's chest rose and fell in a steady, completely relaxed rhythm. He had to be exhausted from the events of the past twenty-four hours. Ava was, and she hadn't been captured and possibly tortured as Ben claimed. For a moment she faltered. Throughout the past two months, she'd dreamed of Ben returning to her, him holding her in his arms and telling her everything would be okay. The longer he'd been missing, the more she'd realized how much she'd come to rely on his strength and support.

She should have known better. For so many years she'd sworn she'd never be like her mother, yet here she was in love with a drifter. Her mother had fallen into the very same trap. Her love for the man she'd married causing nothing but trouble for herself and her children.

Ava's fingers tightened on the keys. She had to be stronger than her mother for the sake of her child. Her daughter would never know the heartache of losing a father.

She'd never know her father. The only way for that to happen would be if Ava kept her distance from Ben altogether.

Ava gathered her shoes and purse and slipped to the door, hoping beyond hope that unbolting the lock wouldn't wake Ben.

As she gently twisted the dead bolt, a great welling of emotion rose up in her chest, threatening her resolve.

What if she was wrong? What if Ben could be a better father than her own? What if her actions deprived her child of the love Ava had craved throughout her childhood?

Her hand hovered over the doorknob, indecision making her entire body shake.

Then she remembered her mother standing at the window, a smile lifting her lips, only to turn down on the corners when the car she'd thought was her husband's drove by without stopping. Ava remembered the days when she and Emily sat on the curb while vehicles filled with happy families passed—mother, father and children all laughing and smiling. The longing those scenes invoked nearly knocked her to her knees.

Ava's hand closed around the knob and she twisted it. The door opened without making a sound. To Ava, her noiseless departure was a sign that she'd done the right thing. Leaving Ben now would save significant heartache later.

Cool night air caressed her fevered cheeks as she eased the door closed behind her. When she turned and faced the semi-deserted parking lot, her pulse raced.

How she'd sneaked out of the room without waking Ben, she didn't know, but if she didn't hurry, he'd wake and discover her missing before she made it to the car.

Ava hustled around the corner of the building, pressing the button on the remote lock.

Not until she'd climbed in, buckled up and pulled into the backstreet behind the motel did she let out the breath she'd been holding. She'd made it!

A SOFT METALLIC CLICK penetrated Ben's awareness, shoving aside the heavy shroud of exhaustion. When he rolled over in the bed, the empty space beside him jerked him the rest of the way to consciousness.

"Ava!" He shoved the tangle of sheets aside and leaped from the bed, his head spinning as soon as he stood upright—residual effects of the drugs. He checked the bathroom. No Ava. A quick glance around the room made him stop and force himself to breathe. Her clothes and purse were gone, along with the keys to the minivan.

Barefoot and dressed only in the sweats he'd slept in, he ran out the unlocked door turning toward the end of the building where he'd parked the car. Even before he rounded the corner, he knew what he'd find.

Nothing.

The minivan and Ava were gone.

"Damn!"

Without wasting time, he jogged back to the room, dressed in the Vegas T-shirt and borrowed shoes. Back out on the street, he scanned nearby cars for an older model.

Two streets over, he found a 1967 Mustang parked on the street. The red paint had long since turned powdery but the tires were fairly new.

Ben searched the surrounding area for something large and hard. He found a large gray rock. Removing his T-shirt, he wrapped the rock in it and then smashed the back window of the antique sports car, a twinge of regret filling him for damaging such a sweet ride. But windows could be replaced. Ava couldn't.

Within seconds, he had the engine running. He shifted the car into Drive and peeled out onto the road. Lights blinked on the porch of the house where he'd been. It wouldn't be long before the police received the report of a stolen car.

Adrenaline crashing through his veins, Ben slammed his foot to the accelerator and sped out of town, headed for Colorado. If he was lucky, he'd catch up with Ava before she got there—if he didn't get pulled over for speeding, and if the police didn't arrest him for stealing the car. As he left the lights of the little town of Kingman behind, he glanced down at the gas gauge. It appeared to be full. Good. At least he didn't have to stop for gas any time soon. It might be enough to get him all the way to Kenner City. As he settled back against the old vinyl seats, he wondered if the mess he was in could get any worse.

Yeah. Nicky could reach Ava before he did.

Fifty miles from town, the little red Mustang chugged, coughed and died.

What the hell? Ben let it drift to a stop on the side of the road, cursing his luck. He checked his cell phone. No reception. He got out, looked under the hood, jiggled wires but the car still wouldn't start. The engine turned over, but the engine didn't engage. Ben tapped the gas gauge, after fifty miles it should show a lot less than full.

He smacked a hand to his forehead, climbed out of the car and rounded to the back where he twisted off the gas cap and bounced the car. Gasoline didn't slosh around the insides as it would if the tank was full. A broken gas gauge and an empty tank. Great.

Ben looked up the highway and back behind him. No headlights, which on the one hand was good. No headlights meant none of Nicky Wayne's thugs close on his tail. On the other hand, with another hour before sunrise, he couldn't expect much traffic. With limited choices, he set off on foot, walking as fast as he could toward Colorado, praying a trucker would pass by soon and give him a lift.

Chapter Eight

When Ava arrived in Kenner City, her stomach rumbled and her bladder screamed for release. With the baby turning cartwheels inside her belly, she'd been in considerable pain for the past thirty minutes. Yet, she kept moving until she reached the Kenner County Crime Unit. She figured that if she made it there, she'd be surrounded by the people who cared about her. They'd make sure she didn't fall victim to Nicky Wayne's evil machinations.

When she climbed from the van, her knees buckled, a sharp pain shooting down her sciatic nerve. The pain triggered a Braxton Hicks contraction, tightening the muscles across her belly. She clung to the door for a moment, focusing on her breathing. When the pain receded, she flexed her calf muscles, reminding them how to work after being stuck in a car for the past seven hours.

Guilt gnawed at her insides the entire way, churning the acids eating a hole in her stomach. She'd only stopped briefly to put gas in the tank and use the bathroom, preferring to reach her destination as soon as possible. She swayed on her way through the front door. For the first time since she'd left Ben she thought about her sugar levels. If she was hungry and affected by the lack of nutrients, her baby was suffering as well. Maybe stopping here first wasn't such a good idea.

Ava turned, with the intention of exiting to find something to feed her weakening body. The sudden change in direction made her head spin. She placed a hand on the wall to steady herself, afraid that if she took another step, she might fall flat on her face.

"Ava!" Callie MacBride's voice echoed off the clean white walls behind her. "I thought you were in Vegas."

Ava spun back around again, this time her vision blurred and she staggered. "I was…" She reached for the steadying wall only to find air. Her body tilted.

"Whoa, there." Callie raced up to Ava and slid an arm around her waist. "You look a little shaky. Let's get you to a chair." She inched Ava through the door. "Miguel, Bart, give me a hand here."

Fellow forensic scientist Miguel Acevedo and KCCU's techno geek Bart Fleming rushed to Ava, practically lifting her off her feet.

"This really isn't necessary. I can walk." Heat filled Ava's cheeks, chasing out the cool clammy chill of a moment ago.

"No, you can't. You're staggering like a drunk on a binge," Callie chastised.

The men deposited her onto a padded office chair and held onto her until certain she wasn't going to slide out of it.

"I'm okay," Ava said, brushing them aside.

Callie crossed her arms over her chest and frowned down at Ava. "Then why did you almost pass out on the floor back there?"

Ava squirmed. "Probably because I haven't eaten in at least twelve hours."

"Mig—"

"I know. Get her something to eat." Miguel disappeared toward the employee break room.

"Why are you here and not in Vegas?"

"Please, can I get some food in me before you begin the inquisition?" The last thing she wanted was to talk about Ben's miraculous reappearance. She hadn't thought about what she'd say when she got here, only that at the KCCU she felt safe and surrounded by people she could trust.

"Miguel!" Callie yelled.

"Right here. You don't have to yell." Miguel carried a cellophane-wrapped sandwich and a bottle of orange juice.

"Where'd you get that?" Callie asked.

"Your desk." Miguel grinned. "It was your lunch."

Ava held up her hands. "No way. I'm not taking your lunch."

Callie's light blue eyes narrowed and she planted fists on slim hips. "Look. Who's the boss around here, anyway?" Her fierce look softened. "You're the pregnant one. Besides, I could stand to lose a pound or two."

"Yeah, right." Ava snorted. "This from stick lady, while blimp mamma gets the sandwich. No." She pushed to her feet, swayed and sat down hard.

Her boss held out her hand. "Sandwich, please."

Miguel slapped the sandwich in her hand like a surgical nurse and popped a salute. "Yes, ma'am."

"I really am okay." Ava's voice didn't sound convincing even to her own ears and tears sprang to her eyes. "I'm just tired."

Callie pulled up a chair beside her, unwrapped the sandwich and handed it to Ava. "Make me happy and eat this thing."

Ava reached for the offering, a sob rising in her throat. "It's just been a long night."

"Eat, then you can tell us all about it."

Given the opportunity to delay the inevitable, Ava ate the sandwich, choking it down with swallows from the bottle of orange juice. With the sandwich half-consumed, she leaned back in the chair. "I'm always hungry, but I can't eat more than a handful."

"The baby's taking up all the room. Not much longer, is it?"

"No." Her eyes filled again. "Oh, shoot. Why am I such a crybaby?"

"Comes with the territory." Callie patted her shoulder and then straightened. "Okay, spill. Why are you back from Vegas? What happened out there?"

Fortified by the food she'd eaten and the juice supplying the necessary electrolytes to her bloodstream, Ava brushed the tears from her face and met Callie's frank gaze. "Nicky Wayne is after me."

Callie's eyes widened. "Nicky Wayne of the Las Vegas Mafia?"

Ava swallowed and nodded. "That's the one."

Miguel whistled. "I'm impressed. What did you do to warrant his attention?"

"He's after a necklace Ben gave me before he disappeared." Why she refrained from telling the others of Ben's reappearance, she couldn't say, but for now, she didn't want them to know. They'd find out soon enough. Maybe then she'd be prepared to answer the barrage of questions they were sure to hit her with. Just the thought of him stranded in Kingman filled her with an extra dose of guilt. More tears threatened and Ava closed her eyes, refusing to let them fall. She'd cried enough over that man to last a lifetime. She had to be strong and think of the future for her and her baby.

Callie clasped Ava's hands in hers and squatted down beside her. "What's so important about the necklace, sweetie?"

Ava blinked the moisture out of her eyes. "It has the medal with the St. Joan of Arc on it. One of the medals Julie gave to Ben, Tom and Dylan. Apparently Nicky Wayne found out that the numbers engraved into the backs of the medals are bank account numbers that lead to the fortune Vincent Del Gardo stashed in a Cayman Island bank."

"Where is it now?"

"I don't have it on me," she said carefully, refusing to lie to the woman she respected most. The box containing the medal was hidden somewhere safe, hopefully where no one would have known to search for it. "It's been months since I've seen it." Another half truth.

Callie's hand rested on her arm, her beautiful face creased in a frown. "You have to get it and give it to the police. It's the only way to get Wayne off your back."

"I thought of that, that's why I came back. To get that medal." She hadn't made up her mind whether or not she'd hand it over to the police. First, she had to retrieve it without anyone knowing.

She'd also returned to Kenner City more determined than ever to solve the case of who killed Julie Grainger. Ben wouldn't have killed his friend or set up the hit on Vincent Del Gardo. Ava believed that, even if she didn't trust any of the other lies he'd told her. Ava believed justice must be served to those who deserved it, and Julie's murderer might still be out there, ready to strike again. Ava had the added incentive of Ben, back from his disappearance, alive and desperate to save her. He remained the prime suspect in the Grainger and Del Gardo murder cases and he'd be either in jail or on the run until the real criminal was caught.

No matter her distrust of the man, Ava couldn't let Ben pay for a crime he didn't commit. No time like the present to get started unraveling the mystery.

Revived by the sandwich and juice, Ava pushed herself up from the chair. "What's the latest on the Grainger murder?"

AFTER BEN TRAVELED five miles on foot in the dark, a sympathetic trucker needing a companion to keep him awake while driving stopped and offered him a lift. The price? An ear to lean on for the long trek across the desert to Gallup, New Mexico. There, they rolled into a truck stop and parted ways—the trucker continuing on to Albuquerque, Ben turning north to the Four Corners region of Colorado, Utah, Arizona and New Mexico. More specifically Kenner City, Colorado.

At the truck stop, Ben found a trucker headed north passing through Kenner City as soon as he filled his tanks with diesel. Ben figured he was about two hours behind Ava by now. The best he could hope for was that Nicky Wayne hadn't figured out where they were headed right away. With the number of hired thugs on his payroll, he probably sent people on every route to cover all the bases.

Ben stepped inside the convenience store for a cup of coffee and a biscuit to tide him over until he got to Kenner City. While paying for his purchases, he noted a dark SUV pulling up to a gas pump between the building and the truck he planned to ride in. When two men stepped out of the vehicle, Ben's blood screeched to a halt in his veins.

Both wore dark suits and sunglasses. Suits in the New

Mexico heat didn't make sense. The bigger guy had the dark hair and swarthy skin of someone of Latino heritage. When he turned toward the store, Ben could see the white bandage taped across his nose and the sling his arm hung in.

Manny.

Blood thundered against Ben's ears, his first instinct to charge outside and finish off the man. Manny and Hammer had been his tormentors, torturers and nemeses for the past two months. As far as Ben knew, Hammer died when hit by the bullet from Manny's gun and, if Ben knew Manny, he'd be out for revenge. Dirty, painful revenge and he wouldn't care how he got it. Using an innocent pregnant woman would appeal to his sense of sadism.

Ben pointed at the pocketknife beneath the glass counter. "How much?"

The grizzled old man behind the counter lifted the knife from the box and read the sticker. "Nineteen-ninety-nine."

"I'll take it." Ben grabbed a baseball cap from a stand near the counter and slapped two twenties on the counter. "Keep the change." He plunked the cap on his head, tucked the knife in his pocket, collected his coffee and biscuit and casually left through the door on the opposite side of the building from Wayne's men.

He circled around the building and waited for his chance. When the men entered the store together, Ben slipped the knife from his pocket and approached the car as though just passing. When he reached the side away from the store, he dropped low and jabbed the knife into both driver's side tires.

The air horn honk of a tractor trailer rig alerted him to the trucker waiting for him. Perfect timing. Ben climbed up into the truck, keeping his back to the convenience store. As the truck slowly pulled away from the pumps and out onto the highway, Ben stared into the large side mirror. Manny and his sidekick had just left the store. By the time they noticed the flat tires, Ben and the trucker would be well on their way out of Gallup, New Mexico.

"Friends of yours?" the trucker asked.

Ben sat back in his seat. "Let's just say I owed them."

"Remind me never to let you borrow anything."

"You're safe. You've never broken one of my ribs or slashed me with knives."

The trucker nodded. "Nope. And I won't. I like my tires the way they are, thank you very much." He grinned and launched into a story about a time he'd gotten into a fight in a barroom in Texas.

Ben opened his coffee and sipped the scalding liquid, on edge with worry after Ava. About his second sip, a fast moving sedan appeared in the passenger side mirror.

Oh, no. Ben set the cup in a cup holder on the dash. "We may have company."

The trucker glanced in his mirror, his lips pressing into a line. "Might be nothin.'"

"Yeah, but I wouldn't bet on it. Maybe you should let me out here. I don't want to get you involved."

The trucker snorted. "Haven't had this much fun in a long time. You stay right where you are."

"These guys are a part of a Mafia organization out of Vegas. They don't mess around, they come prepared to do some damage."

"So do I." With one hand guiding the large black steering wheel, the trucker reached beneath his seat and pulled out a sawed-off shotgun. "There are more shells in that box on the floor."

A grin spread across Ben's face. "Remind me not to flip off truckers ever again."

The man nodded, his face serious. "No, that's never a good idea."

"Do you mind?" Ben reached for the gun.

"How do I know you're not one of them?"

"You don't. All you have is my word. I'm Special Agent Ben Parrish, with the FBI."

The trucker's brows rose. "Got any credentials to go with that?"

"No." He explained the kidnapping and subsequent escape. "But then all you still have to go on is my word."

"Sounds good enough for me. I'm Earl Cutter, retired marine." The trucker glanced again in the mirror. "You were right. We've got company." He shoved the shotgun at Ben and swerved out into the middle of the highway, forcing the vehicle behind them to swerve to the right around the truck. The maneuver gave Ben the clear shot he needed.

As the target came in view, Ben had only enough time to verify the man driving as the one he'd seen with Manny at the service station. Manny emerged from the passenger window, his pistol drawn and cocked over the top of the car.

The truck driver swerved to the right, slamming into the side of the vehicle, knocking them onto the shoulder. Manny, struggling to hold on, fired. The bullet went high, completely missing the truck. Manny slid down into the car.

The driver gunned the engine, rocketing ahead of the tractor trailer rig. Manny climbed into the backseat.

"Slow down!" Ben shouted.

The truck driver slammed on his brakes, the scream of metal on metal filling the air.

Ben opened the passenger side door and leaned out, balancing the shotgun in the open window, aiming it at the car in front of them now slowing.

Ben waited until the car was in range, then taking aim, he shot at the back windshield. Glass shattered, spraying across the road and inside the car.

Manny returned fire, his bullet blasting through the windshield into the passenger seat.

Still hanging out the door, Ben fired again, this time aiming for the driver.

The driver jerked, the car swerving to the left, crossing into the path of oncoming headlights. A horn blared. Manny flew across the backseat, his weapon knocked from his grip. As quickly as the car swerved to the left, it swung back to the right. Too quickly. The tires dropped off the edge of the shoulder, the car ran off the road into the ditch, flipping on its side and rolling to a metal-crunching stop on all four tires.

"Holy smokes!" As the truck driver passed the wreckage, he slowed, craning his neck to see down into the ditch.

Ben swung his door shut, leaning out the window to watch for signs of movement.

A dark head emerged from the shattered back windshield, blood dripping from a gash over his eye. Manny. And he had his gun in hand.

"Go! Go! Go!" Ben yelled.

Earl shifted into low, and gunned the accelerator, but the big truck lumbered along, slowly gaining speed.

Manny climbed over the trunk and dropped to the ground, aiming at the retreating truck. He fired, the bullets pounding into the passenger door.

Ben ducked low, shoving more shells into the shotgun, slamming the bolt home. When he sat up, he swung around and aimed the gun out the window behind him. By then, the truck had gained enough speed, Manny had all but disappeared.

Ben dropped back into his seat, laying the shotgun across his lap. "I'm sorry about your truck, Earl."

Earl shook his head. "Don't be. I haven't had this much excitement since…well…since Vietnam. I can't wait to tell the wife."

"If she's like my wife, she won't be too thrilled to know you've been shot at." Or at least he thought Ava wouldn't be thrilled he'd been shot at. However, the way she'd run out on him earlier, maybe she wished he'd disappear again and never come back.

His jaw tightened. *Sorry, Ava. I'm not going to disappear again. I'm here for the long haul.*

Chapter Nine

Ava borrowed Callie's car instead of using Emily's minivan to run two errands. First she wanted to collect the box of keepsakes she'd stashed away in the cabin in the woods where she and Ben had holed up when they'd gotten lost in a rainstorm on their first date. The cabin was also where they'd spent their honeymoon.

After the long drive from Las Vegas, she didn't look forward to another thirty-minute ride out to the cabin in the mountains, followed by thirty minutes back. But she had to retrieve the box she'd put away when she'd been certain Ben was never coming home again. With him back in the picture, everything changed.

The cabin was along a narrow dirt road leading high up on a mountain. The FBI had combed over every inch of the cabin in their search for Ben or evidence of his defection, but they hadn't found her secret stash, nor had she volunteered the location. If they wanted information, they had to find it for themselves. And if they didn't find anything, their loss.

She drove carefully over the dirt road, regretting having to take Callie's car over what amounted to not much more than a rutted track. When she reached the little wooden cabin, she turned the vehicle around, facing the road, before climbing out.

Ava stood for several moments in front of the cabin, her heart caught in her throat, ready tears filling her eyes. Everything about this place reminded her of the time spent in Ben's arms. The time she'd allowed herself to fall in love with the FBI agent. She'd been so head over heels, she hadn't stopped to really dig and get answers to all the questions she had about him and his connection to Vincent Del Gardo or the crime families of the Four Corners area of the country. She'd trusted him.

"Damn you, Ben Parrish!" The tears tipped over the edges of her eyelids and spilled down her cheeks. "Oh, shoot, I'm not going to cry again." She scrubbed at the moisture on her face and strode forward, determined to get in and get out, without dredging up another single memory of her husband.

As soon as she stepped through the door, she knew what a lost cause that was. Every inch of the place had a memory of Ben in it. Hurrying across the floor, she entered the bedroom and struggled to shove aside the heavy bed she and Ben had shared. Beneath one of the posts was a loose board, tacked in place with a single rusty nail. She knew because she'd placed it there to keep anyone from assuming the board was anything other than flooring.

Ava hurried to the storage cabinet in the kitchen and retrieved a screw driver and a hammer. When she returned to the bedroom, she lowered herself to the floor. A month ago when she'd visited the cabin, getting up and down hadn't been nearly as difficult. The baby had gained an additional four pounds, a pound a week. The weight itself wasn't the problem, the bulk of her belly made lowering and raising herself from the floor more complex.

Once on the ground, she leaned over sideways to pry the floorboard loose, working around her baby bump. The wood must have swelled around the nail; it didn't come up easily. One final whack with the hammer and the nail popped loose.

Her heart banging against her chest, Ava pried the slat up and reached into the gap between floor joists. Her fingers encountered spiderwebs and dust and she cringed. She didn't remember the box being too terribly far down in the narrow gap, but she couldn't see it. Had someone found it after all? Nicky Wayne wouldn't be after her if he'd found the box with the medal inside.

She scrambled to her feet and headed back to the kitchen for the flashlight in the cabinet, praying the batteries were good. When she returned, she shined the light down into the gap between the boards. The brushed metal finish of the fireproof box she'd shoved down there a month ago reflected the light. Ava leaned down to retrieve the box wedged between the floor joists.

The baby chose that moment to kick hard against her insides. Ava gasped and dropped the box back to the dirt beneath the house, only this time, farther away.

"Great." It was hard enough to grab the box in the first place, now she'd need to lie flat on her tummy to reach it. And lying flat on her tummy was out of the question.

Ava lay on her side and stuck her arm down into the hole stretching as best she could. Her fingers brushed against the box. "Almost there."

She tapped the corner and nudged it toward her with the tip of her finger. "Am I getting closer?" She shined the light on the box. Yup. It was definitely a little closer. And something else reflected light. A shiny silver metal gadget lay in the dirt farther back from where she'd stashed the box.

Ava nudged the box closer and finally got her fingers around the box's edges, lifting it up and out of the hole. No amount of stretching would put her close enough to retrieve the other object. She'd have to find something to move it closer. After setting the box on the floor, she pushed to her feet for yet another trip back to the kitchen for the broom. Why she hadn't thought of it earlier, she didn't know.

When she returned she flipped the broom upside down and tapped the metal gadget closer to her with the wooden handle. Once it lay directly below her, she laid on the floor and snagged the device with her hand. By the time she had the box and what she now determined was a digital recording device, she knew she had to leave. She'd been in one place too long. No need to give Nicky Wayne time to find her. She still had one more stop to make before heading back to Callie and Tom's place. She pocketed the recorder and set the box on the car's passenger seat and climbed in. Her back hurt and her belly felt too tight, but she'd gotten what she came for and a bonus. She couldn't wait to give it over to Bart Fleming at the lab. He'd know what to do with the digital recorder.

The drive back to the main road took less time than the drive up the mountain. If she hit a few more ruts than the first time, she counted it down to the scary fact that she had the box with the one thing Nicky Wayne wanted most. Now all she had to do was retrieve the key, a change of clothing and shoes from her house and she'd be set.

The road home was bittersweet. Since Ben had disappeared, the house hadn't seemed like home.

She couldn't stay out at her house alone because it set her up as an easy target for Wayne's men. They'd probably look there first. But she had to go to the house to retrieve the key to the box. The other option was to break the box open.

With a glance at the box on the seat next to her, she knew she couldn't destroy it without a great deal of effort. The box was built strong enough to survive a fire. Short of running it over with the car and destroying everything inside, she'd be hard-pressed to open it without the key.

Knowing the St. Joan of Arc medal lay inside the box made her anxious to open it and look at the numbers on the back. She'd known the numbers were key to something, but she'd assumed Jerry Ortiz and Boyd Perkins were the only two people who were looking for them.

Now that the big crime boss, Nicky Wayne, had his sights set on the medal, the danger was magnified. The last time she'd seen the necklace, she'd tucked it away with other mementos into the box, locked it and left it in the cabin she and Ben had camped out in for their honeymoon so long ago.

She'd been so hurt by his disappearance, she'd preferred to set all her memories aside, out of view. But she'd held on to the key, maybe in the slim hope Ben would one day return. When she could stand the separation no more, she'd thrown the key into the bushes off the back deck of their home in a fit of anger. About that time she'd given up on Ben ever coming home to her and the baby. Had the key washed away in a rainstorm? What were the chances she'd find it?

Up until the point she locked her mementos away, she'd worn the necklace day and night, praying to St. Joan of Arc that Ben hadn't been lying when he'd promised to love her. For months after their marriage, she'd worried that he'd only married her because she carried his child. When he had shown no signs of wanting to leave, she'd slipped into the world of a happy wife and soon-to-be mother, thinking her life could not be better—perfect job, perfect home and perfect husband.

Then Ben had disappeared from the local Ute Reservation while on an organized manhunt for Sherman Watts, a man wanted for the attempted murder of Aspen Meadows. Somehow Ben had been injured during the search. When the rescue workers went in to find him, he'd disappeared. No sign of Ben other than an area of disturbed ground, as if a struggle had taken place there. Otherwise, no leads, nothing for two months. Two months of agony, depression and second-guessing the supposedly perfect life she'd built in her mind.

Ava's hand slid over the mound of her belly. Two months had given her time to think, to put her life and her baby's life in perspective. Special agents like Ben usually didn't marry, and for good reasons. They couldn't commit. They were adrenaline junkies who lived for their jobs. If she hadn't gotten pregnant, he'd never have asked her to marry him. Of that, she was thoroughly convinced.

Basically, her marriage ended when Ben disappeared. Now she needed to get on with her life and find that damned key so she could take the necklace to the police.

The drive up to the house had reawakened bittersweet memories of better times. Ava parked in front of the structure, turned off the car and sat for a long moment, staring up at the building that had once been her home.

The rough cedar and stone exterior blended with the rugged Colorado landscape, an extension to the natural beauty of the surroundings. She remembered how excited she'd been when Ben first brought her up here. Then she'd been filled with happy dreams and hopes for a future together with Ben and their baby.

When her hands began to hurt, she looked down at where they gripped the steering wheel, the knuckles white. She jerked them loose and flapped her hands until the blood circulated to the tips. Dwelling on the past wouldn't get her through the next few days. *Get a grip, Ava.* Steeling her hormonally unbalanced emotions, she pushed the door open and climbed out of the car, her back straining with the effort. Four more weeks of this, just four more weeks and she'd have her body back and a baby to hold in her arms.

Ava climbed the steps and entered the two-story house, her chest tight, her eyes burning with unshed tears. The house was beautiful, even in disarray from the numerous searches performed by the local police and FBI. Perched on the ridge of a hill, the floor to ceiling windows in the living area looked out over miles of rugged Colorado terrain. Pine trees, aspens and scrub brush clung to the rocky slopes, reaching into clear blue skies. Every time she stood at the windows, Ava drank in the majesty of the landscape and thanked God she lived in Colorado. She'd been many other places, but Colorado called to her like no other place on earth.

For now, she had to be content to enter and leave quickly. She'd promised Callie she wouldn't linger. She'd already been gone too long, having detoured to the cabin. She hadn't told Callie about the side trip. As it was, her boss and friend hadn't wanted her to come here by herself. It was too dangerous, Callie had argued. What with Wayne after her.

Ava had insisted on coming home alone, reassuring Callie that she was way ahead of any of Wayne's thugs. A few minutes inside her old home wouldn't put her or her baby at risk.

As she moved through the bedroom, collecting clothes and shoes, she hurried past the king-size bed she'd shared with Ben for the few short months of their idyllic marriage. She could still feel the warmth of his arms around her as they'd lain in bed earlier that morning. A sob rose up to choke her.

Quickly, before she lost her composure, she tossed toiletries, underwear, shoes, blouses and maternity slacks in a bag.

When she had enough for a couple of days, she set the bag by the front door and crossed to the back of the house and out onto the deck. She and Ben had spent hours sipping cold drinks and planning the future on this deck, the view equally spectacular here as at the front of the house.

Why did everything have to change? Why couldn't they have continued with the life she'd come to love?

Why was she standing there, wishing for a dream that wouldn't have come true no matter whether Ben had stayed or left? It wasn't in his nature to stay put for long.

Ava descended the steps off the back deck and moved into the brush. They'd left the landscape more or less natural, which translated to overgrown with scrub. Prickly cedar branches lashed out at her arms and briars tugged at her trouser legs. She pushed through, searching carefully for the shiny silver chain and key she'd chucked weeks ago.

Squatting close to the ground, intent on her search, Ava could almost forget the looming danger. Sun glinted off something shiny and she ducked beneath a branch to get a closer look. As she reached out to lift a dirty silver chain into her palm, footsteps clattered on the deck above. She snatched her hand back, leaving the key where it lay in the dirt.

"Callie sent me out to check on you," a male voice called out from above her.

Ava screamed and dropped to her hands and knees behind a bush.

Tom Ryan leaped from the deck and pushed his way through the brush. "I'm sorry, Ava. I didn't mean to scare the baby out of you. Callie got worried when you weren't back in an hour and wanted me to come out and check on you." He extended a hand to her and pulled her to her feet. "Are you all right?" His gaze traveled from her face to her belly.

"I'm okay. You just scared a year off my life, that's all."

"What are you doing crawling in the bushes anyway? Callie said you came out for some clothes and that you'd be back soon and would be staying with us for a few days."

"That's what I was doing, I just wanted a breath of fresh air," Ava lied, her face heating with the effort.

Tom's lips twisted. "Yeah, and I'm the tooth fairy." He crossed his arms over his chest. "Ben called and said you'd ditched him in Kingman. The guy's having a hell of a time making his way up to Kenner City without his own transportation."

Ava looked away, guilt clawing at her conscience. She refused to respond to Tom's questioning glance and pushed past him to mount the steps of the deck. "I should get my clothes and head back to town."

Tom caught her elbow as she passed him, halting her progress up the steps. "Ben didn't leave you because he wanted to. You know that, don't you?"

She shrugged without looking up. "Sure."

"I can't imagine how you feel with all that's happened. All I know is that Ben's a good guy, if you give him a chance."

Anger bubbled up inside. Deep resentment clambered to cut loose, bitterness that originated a lot longer back than when Ben disappeared. Ava jerked her arm free of Tom's grip. "What do you know about good guys? You weren't the one left alone for two months with a storm of accusations pounding you from all sides. You weren't the one worrying every day about whether he was alive or dead. You weren't the one who died a thousand deaths when you thought he was never coming back. What do you know about how I feel?"

She stomped up the steps as best an eight-months pregnant woman could without looking completely ridiculous. Not that she cared how she looked. So what if Ben made his way back. His return was all the more reason for her to gather what she needed and get the hell out of there.

Tom followed her through the living room and darted in front of her to grab the heavy bag of her personal items. "I'm sorry. I didn't mean to upset you. I just know Ben, and he really loves you."

"Save it for someone who likes being abandoned." She stepped around him and marched out the front door.

Before she reached the stairs leading off the front porch to the driveway, a shot rang out across the hilltop. Wood splinters rained down over her head.

"Get down!" Tom leaped in front of her, blocking her body with his, gun drawn.

Ava ducked behind a thick post and squatted low. Not that the post covered her entire body, but she had nowhere else to go. The front door stood open but too far for her to make it there without exposing herself or her baby to gunfire.

Another shot rang out; Tom's cowboy hat whipped off his head, clattering to the wood planks of the porch. He dropped to his knee and fired off three shots in the direction from which the bullets originated.

Crouched in an awkward fetal position, Ava gasped when blood dripped onto the decking. Her gaze rose to Tom's face. A bright red streak marred his left temple, blood oozing from a jagged line. "Oh, my God, Tom, you're hurt!" She reached up to touch his face.

"It's nothing, just a flesh wound." His gaze remained

fixed on the dense brush along the drive leading up to the cabin. "Stay down."

Ava wrapped her arms around her baby and cursed silently. This was her fault. Tom was shot protecting her. If she could give the shooter the damned necklace, maybe none of this would be happening. Maybe the shooter would take the key and the box and leave them the hell alone. If only she'd picked up the key when she'd had the chance. Her gaze darted to the door. Dare she go back out in the brush and look for it?

Before she could make a move, Tom spoke. "I'm going to fire into the brush. Can you move fast enough to get inside the house and lock the doors?"

Move fast? Eight months pregnant? Was he kidding? Ava's jaw tightened and her muscles bunched beneath her. "Fire away."

Tom unloaded his clip into the brush.

Ava lurched to her feet and ran for the front door, ducking behind the heavy wood paneling. She slammed it closed, her fingers hovering over the dead bolt. Should she lock it with Tom out there? Could she take the time to run out the back and find that damned key?

She peered out a side window.

Tom had disappeared. A brief flicker of the light brown jacket Tom wore flashed between the trees along the edge of the drive.

Ava's breath caught in her chest. Was he nuts? Tom was headed straight for the shooter.

She watched in morbid fascination, only catching glimpses of Tom until she lost him altogether.

No other shots broke the silence of the hilltop for several long minutes. Ava craned her neck, straining to find Tom among the trees and brush.

Her heart hammered against her ears and she had to remind herself to breathe. At last, Tom appeared around the curve of pavement, walking up the middle of the driveway.

Ava threw open the door and almost ran out on the deck, but stopped herself before leaving the house. What if the shooter circled back and started firing at them again?

As Tom mounted the steps, he shook his head. "He got away in a car parked farther down the hill."

Air escaped Ava's lungs in a long steadying breath. "At least he's gone."

"For now." Tom's glance narrowed. "Let's get you back to my house. You're too isolated out here."

"If it's all right with you, I'd rather get back to the lab."

"From what Callie tells me, you've been up all night. Shouldn't you get a little rest?"

"There's a couch in the lounge at work. I'll lie down there if I feel the need."

Tom tipped his head to the side. "I don't know…Callie will likely string me up."

"I can't sleep right now. I'm too wound up."

Tom held the car door for her as she eased herself behind the wheel. "I can understand that. It's not every day you're shot at."

At the rate she was going, it might be. Ava buckled her seat belt below her belly.

"I'll follow you into town. Go straight to the lab."

Ava saluted. "Yes, sir."

Tom gave her a grim smile. "And be careful." He shut her door and climbed into his car.

Ava turned around and headed down the hill to the highway. Despite the doctor's orders to stop working, it appeared as though the Kenner County Crime Unit lab was the safest place for her and her baby. She might as well camp out there. Maybe she could dig up enough evidence to completely clear Ben of Julie's murder. Then the police and feds would withdraw the warrant for his arrest and he'd be free of his life in Kenner City. He could leave on his next assignment. The sooner Ben left, the sooner Ava could start the grieving process all over again and the less likely her child would know her father. Better not to know the man than to be disappointed by him.

"THANKS, EARL. I owe you." Ben waved as the truck driver shifted into drive and pulled out of the gas station a block away from the Kenner County Crime Unit lab, close to the edge of town.

Ben ducked behind a line of bushes and glanced in both directions. No signs of cops or special agents. If he could get inside the lab without anyone seeing him, it would be a minor miracle. Getting Ava to listen to him would take an act of God.

A dark gray Lexus pulled past him.

The redhead driving looked familiar. Ava! Ben almost ran out into the street until he noticed a black SUV following the Lexus. He recognized his friend Tom Ryan as the driver.

The Lexus and SUV turned into the parking lot of the three-story office building where the crime lab took up the entire third floor. A wave of relief washed over Ben. She'd made it here apparently unharmed, and, if he wasn't mistaken, Tom Ryan, the driver of the SUV, was watching out for her.

Another car passed and continued down the street past the crime lab. Ben ducked his head low and sauntered across the street as if he belonged in Kenner City and didn't have a warrant out for his arrest.

On the opposite side of the road, he moved from shadow

to shadow, keeping close to bushes and large tree trunks on the way to the lab. Nicky's men would be in town already, no telling where.

He reached the building in time to see the back of Ava's head as she entered the front door. Tom sat in his SUV, a cell phone pressed to his ear.

Keeping close to the building and in the shadows, Ben moved closer. When he was as near as could be to the SUV, he set off across the paved parking area and knocked lightly on the window.

Tom's eyes widened and he popped the lock button, letting Ben climb into the passenger seat. He said something into the phone and clicked the off button.

"Ben!" He reached across and gripped Ben's hand, pulling him over the top of the console to wrap him in a clumsy bear hug that felt a little stilted even to Ben. "You don't know how glad I am to see you."

Despite the wary embrace, warmth filled Ben's chest. He'd missed his friends from the bureau. Tom was like a brother and mentor to him. During the long trying days in Nicky Wayne's hellhole, he'd tried to think what Tom would have done in the same situation. He sat back in his seat, moisture clouding his vision at the overwhelming surge of emotion flooding his heart. "Can we go somewhere a little less open?"

"Sure." Tom shifted into drive and pulled out of the parking lot onto the road. "Where to?"

"My place."

Tom shot a quick glance at Ben. "Are you sure?"

"Yeah. I could use a change of clothes." Ben glanced down at the Vegas T-shirt, the sloppy sweatpants and the shoes that didn't belong to him. What he wouldn't give for a pair of jeans and cowboy boots.

"I don't know if that's a good idea."

Ben turned to Tom. "Why?"

"The police do a drive-by once or twice a day, hoping you'll return. And if that's not bad enough, Ava and I just came from out there." Tom's hands gripped the wheel with enough force his knuckles turned white. "Someone shot at us."

"By us do you mean you and Ava?"

"Ava, at first." Tom held up a hand when Ben opened his mouth. "Don't worry, she's okay, he missed her."

Ben ran his hand through his hair, standing it on end. "Thank God."

"Yeah, but he wasn't shooting as a warning. He got me." Tom turned his face around enough for Ben to see the line of dried blood on his temple and smeared across his left cheek.

"Damn, Tom, have you seen a doctor?"

Tom shook his head. "Just a flesh wound. Besides, I was more concerned about getting Ava back to town. She was shaken up pretty bad. I don't think she feels safe anywhere but in the lab."

"Damn!" Ben pounded his fist against the arm rest and stared straight ahead. "I'll kill Nicky Wayne if he hurts one hair on her head."

"Problem is that he's got people hiding in the bushes, literally. It's not safe to go to your house."

"I have to get clothes and shoes that fit. I'll make it quick. In and out."

Tom sighed and turned onto the highway leading north of town toward the house Ben and Ava had shared as husband and wife.

Coming home should have felt good, a happy occasion to be celebrated with his wife. Instead, Ava thought he was part of the very crime organization that had tortured and imprisoned him for the past two months. He'd laugh at the irony, if it didn't hurt so much.

"What happened to you in Vegas? People thought you might have joined Wayne's crime organization out there." Tom kept his face pointed forward, but the seriousness of his voice made Ben look twice at him.

"So everyone was convinced I went over to Wayne?" Ben snorted. "In a way I guess I did. Nicky Wayne held me in the basement of his casino. Caged and drugged like an animal."

"Damn." Tom glanced his way, his brow furrowed. "We shouldn't have doubted you, but the evidence was pretty damning. If we'd only known what had happened, you know we'd have come after you. But you didn't give us much to go on. For a long time there, we really thought we were losing you to Del Gardo."

"Yeah, well, it's over." The flesh wounds would mend before the scars on his soul. Caged like an animal, harassed, beaten, tortured, Ben had somehow survived, and he'd die before he ever let anyone capture him again.

"So are you going to tell me what happened between you and Del Gardo?"

"I can't, yet. I need clearance from above in the Bureau."

"I'll see what I can do to arrange a meeting with George." Tom nodded. "And until Nicky gets that last medal, or we manage to kill his entire army of mercenaries, we're in for a long fight."

"More reason for me to get Ava out of here. I couldn't live with myself if something happened to her because I gave her that damned medal. I can't believe such a little piece of jewelry could be such a pain in the butt."

"You didn't know. It's not your fault."

"Yeah. And you think she'd forgive me if she lost the baby?" Ben stared across the console at Tom. "I wouldn't forgive myself."

Tom shook his head. "Don't borrow trouble, Ben. She's going to be fine and so is the baby."

Ben wished he could be so certain. Having spent time with some of Wayne's hired thugs, he knew what they were up against. These guys played rough. "Ava can't stay in the lab forever. I can't be there for her, not while I have a warrant out for my arrest."

"No, but you could turn yourself in and see if they'll let you out on bail."

"No." Ben shook his head. "I can't risk being locked up in jail while Nicky's men run rampant in Kenner City. Ava doesn't stand a chance."

"Thanks. It's not like she'd be out there alone."

Ben looked out the passenger window without seeing the beauty of the Rockies. "I ask you again, if it were Callie in this situation, would you rely on anyone other than yourself to look after her?"

Tom drove on, his jaw tightening. "No."

"I need to get Ava out of here, hide her, anything. She won't be safe unless Nicky Wayne can't find her."

Chapter Ten

The muscles across her abdomen tightened in a long excruciating clench. Ava bent over the microscope she'd been standing behind for the past fifteen minutes.

"I saw that." Callie hurried over to where she stood. "You're coming with me, and I won't take no for an answer."

Ava forced a smile past the pain. "It's just Braxton Hicks contractions. No biggee."

"I don't care. I won't have you going into labor on my watch, not when the baby isn't supposed to be here for another four weeks. Let the others handle the tests. They'll be back from lunch any time." She hooked Ava's elbow with one hand and circled the other around her back, edging her toward the lounge. "At least take a load off your feet. It can't be good for the baby or for you to be so worn out you can't think."

Ava dug her heels into the linoleum tiles and pulled free of Callie. "We have to completely clear Ben of Julie's murder."

"Look, Ava, Boyd Perkins killed Julie. The evidence points to him," Callie said quietly.

"I know, but some people still think Ben was involved somehow. We have to clear him."

"We'll have Bart working on the digital recorder you found as soon as he returns from lunch. Let him do his magic. Maybe it's the key to clearing Ben."

Ava palmed the digital recorder safely in her pocket. It had to hold the evidence needed to clear Ben of conspiracy with Del Gardo and Nicky Wayne.

Callie clasped Ava's face between her palms and made her look her in the eyes. "Ava, I know Ben's back."

Ava stared hard into Callie's light blue eyes. "I don't know what you're talking about," she said, her voice weak.

"Tom told me Ben's back from wherever he disappeared to for the past two months. I understand your determination to clear him of the charges, but you have to let the rest of us handle it. You're in no condition."

"I'm not sick, I'm pregnant!" Ava stepped away and stomped her foot. She realized the gesture was childish and wished she hadn't as soon as another Braxton Hicks contraction seized her belly and pulled tight. Ava sucked in a breath and held it until the pain eased.

Callie pointed down the hallway. "In the lounge. Now."

"I'm okay. Really," Ava protested, her voice a little breathier than a moment before the contraction hit. She let Callie drag her toward the lounge, too tired to fight and knowing she'd be foolish if she didn't heed her body's warnings. "Okay, okay. I'll rest for a few minutes. But then I'm going back to work."

"You're not even supposed to be in the office. You're on medical leave. If something happens to you or the baby, our liability insurance carrier will flip." Callie aimed her toward the couch against the far wall of the lounge. "Sit. Better yet, lie down."

Ava turned to Callie. "Please don't make me leave. I'll

go nuts with nothing to do. And I *have* to clear Ben of any suspicion."

Callie glared at her. "You don't have to do anything but sit," she said, her voice softening. "You have to think about the baby. Ben's a big boy, he can take care of himself. Besides, technically, you shouldn't even be working the case. You're too close to one of the suspects. A prosecuting attorney would cry conflict of interest faster than you could get from here to the door."

"Thanks." Ava frowned at Callie. "I know Ben can take care of himself, but his disappearance, the note and photos point to him. And though he was gone for two months, I know it wasn't because he's guilty. Julie was like a sister to him. He loved her and would never have hurt her. However, I can't vouch for the Del Gardo murder." But she wouldn't believe Ben was a cold-blooded killer.

Callie perched on the seat beside her. "You know that and I know that, but we have to find the evidence to prove it."

"Exactly." Ava pushed to the edge of the seat and prepared to stand. "Which is why I need to get back to work."

Callie laid a hand on her shoulder and stopped her from getting off the couch. "Not yet, you don't."

A door opened down the hall and voices filled the hallway.

"There you go. The cavalry have arrived." Callie smiled, her relief almost comical. "Let the rest of the crew sift through what we've found so far. You just relax." She patted Ava's hand and stood.

"Where is she?" Fellow teammate Olivia Perez burst into the lounge, followed by her fiancé, Jacob Webster. Both forensic scientists were fit, tall, slender and made a striking couple.

Miguel, the lab's forensic crime scene investigator and Bart, the computer guru, brought up the rear.

"Ava! We heard you were back." The normally shy Olivia leaned over and gave her a tight hug, her medium-length brown hair brushing against Ava's face. "What happened? Are you okay? How's the baby?"

Quietly reserved, Jacob stood back and smiled down at her. "Hi, Ava. It's good to see you."

Olivia's barrage of questions, being surrounded by all her teammates and the sudden overwhelming outpouring of love from the people who meant the most to her made a lump rise up and lodge in Ava's throat. She swallowed hard, fighting back the quick surge of tears in her eyes.

"I'm fine," she managed in a gravelly whisper. She felt like she'd come home and these people were her family.

"Give the girl some room." Callie waved everyone back.

"Miguel said you had trouble in Vegas." Olivia, being closest, stroked her hand. "What's this about Nicky Wayne going after you?"

"Yeah." Ava forced a laugh that came out more of a sob. "Nothing like almost being kidnapped and having your sister's house ransacked."

Jacob frowned. "Dear Lord, how'd you get away?"

"Yeah, how?" Special Agent Dylan Acevedo, FBI and one of Ben's close friends spoke from the doorway, his blue eyes intent on her face. "Was it Ben? Did he help?"

Olivia's gaze shot from Dylan back to Ava. "Is Ben alive?"

Ava didn't know what to say. Should she lie and cover for her husband? Ben had a warrant out for his arrest. Dylan claimed to be his friend, but would their friendship be enough to keep Dylan from turning Ben in to the authorities as his job demanded? One look at all the faces of her friends and she knew she couldn't outright lie to them. "Yes, Ben's alive."

The entire room exploded in questions, everyone talking at once.

"Where is he?" Miguel asked.

Olivia squeezed Ava's hand. "Is he okay?"

Dylan stepped into the room. "Did he come back with you?"

"Is he really involved in the Vegas Mafia?" Bart wanted to know.

One question bled into the next. The noise level rose until Ava's blood pounded in her ears and her heart raced behind her ribs. "He's okay as far as I could tell. I don't know where he is, now. No, I don't think he's part of the Mafia. No! I don't know where he is!" Ava pushed to her feet, teetering off balance with the added thirty pounds she'd gained with the baby. "I'm going to work."

She pushed through the crowd on her way to the lab.

Olivia held her arm to steady her. "Oh, honey, you shouldn't work in your condition."

"Someone has to find out the whole truth behind Vincent Del Gardo's and Julie Grainger's deaths."

"We've all been working on it, Ava," Jacob said.

"I know, but right now people want to point fingers at Ben as an accomplice. If we don't find out the truth, an innocent man will pay for a crime he didn't commit."

Miguel nodded. "We know. And you know how long it takes to go through all the evidence."

"Understood." Ava's brows dipped downward. "But Ben may not have time on his side."

Bart's gaze captured hers. "What if we prove Ben was involved in the killing? What if we find out that he was part of the Del Gardo family and maybe even the Wayne organization like it's being rumored?"

Miguel elbowed him in the stomach. "Shut up, man."

Ava's breath caught in her throat and it took a long moment before she could force words past her vocal chords. She pushed her shoulders back and matched Bart, stare for stare. "He didn't kill Julie, nor was he a part of her murder." She couldn't vouch for his involvement in organized crime or Del Gardo's death, but she knew in her heart that Ben Parrish did not have any part in killing Julie Grainger.

Tension sizzled like mist on a power line, the silence stretching taut.

Too mentally exhausted to deal with people anymore, Ava straightened her aching back, dug in her pocket and shoved the digital recorder at Bart Fleming. "Check this out. I think it might be Ben's." As she laid it in Bart's hand, she hesitated. What if it was the evidence pointing to Ben's guilt?

She had to believe in him, had to trust that what he'd told her was the truth. Ava let go of the device. "Now, if you'll excuse me, I'll get started." She left the room and hurried to the lab, her composure slipping with every step. Once she entered the cool interior of the crime lab, the tears spilled from the corners of her eyes.

She brushed them aside and bit her lip to stop it from trembling. Crying wouldn't solve anything. Only cold hard facts could resolve this case.

Ava sat at the stool behind her microscope, until her vision cleared and she could see the outline of the fiber found on Julie's body.

A few minutes passed and Callie joined her, pulling out a tray filled with bits and pieces of evidence found in the vicinity of Julie's body. Without a word, she went to work.

Olivia and Jacob filed into the lab and went to work on the various pieces of equipment stationed throughout the open room, each showing their support by getting down to the task of sifting through the evidence. Miguel and Bart opened the door to the lab, blocking Dylan's entrance. "Sorry, but you'll have to come back later. Ava's not up to answering any more questions today."

Dylan shot a glance across the room toward Ava as though he wanted to slug Miguel and march across the room to demand more information.

Ava's heart thudded in her chest and she held her breath. Then Dylan nodded, spun on his heel and left, flipping his cell phone open as he walked away.

TOM STASHED THE CAR in the bushes and played lookout while Ben had gone through his house twice, rage bubbling beneath the surface. How could the police and FBI think he'd had anything whatsoever to do with Julie's death? He loved Julie like he loved Tom and Dylan. They'd gone through the academy together, forging bonds of friendship through their shared adversity. Bonds that could only be broken by death.

Wanting a little privacy, Ben had asked Tom to wait outside.

Tom stood in the shadows of the deck, watching for any signs of the earlier sniper or the police making a routine drive-by.

At least Tom believed Ben couldn't have been involved in Julie's death, even if he was still hesitant on Ben's affiliation with the crime families of Del Gardo and Wayne.

He should be grateful for that. The irony of the entire situation wasn't lost on Ben. All this time his unit and the people of Kenner City thought he'd gone dirty and joined Wayne in his aspirations to become the king of Vegas. When in fact, Ben had been imprisoned in Wayne's basement. Given the circumstances and his covert actions within the Del Gardo organization, he couldn't blame them. He just wanted it all to be over so that he could get his life back on track with Ava. If he could convince her to let him.

Tom's cell phone chirped, the sound somehow jarring in the natural surroundings outside of Kenner City.

While Tom talked quietly, Ben changed into jeans and boots, cinching his belt tight to keep the denim from falling off his hips. He'd probably lost twenty pounds during his captivity. Once he'd dressed, he stuffed a change of clothing and toiletries into a large duffel bag. Next, he scrounged through the kitchen cabinets, grabbing canned foods, a can opener and anything edible that didn't have to be refrigerated. He rummaged in the hall closet for a sleeping bag, stuffing it in on top of everything else.

Tom entered the kitchen. "Dylan's on his way out. He'll be here in five minutes."

Ben's eyes narrowed. Had Tom ratted him out? He'd never expect that from Tom or Dylan, but still...

His friend raised a hand. "Don't worry, he's not going to turn you in. But he'll probably try to talk you into coming back to the unit with us."

"I can't. They'll kill for that necklace. I won't let anything happen to Ava if I can help it."

"I think you're making a mistake."

"If you're going to gang up on me, expect a fight."

Tom grinned. "If I remember correctly, you were always the one to beat at the academy."

"And don't you forget it." The heaviness weighing on Ben lightened a little at the teasing from his friend.

"Wouldn't it be nice to go back to those days?" A smile tilted Tom's lips.

Ben almost smiled at the good memories, then his jaw tightened. "Yeah, Julie would still be alive."

Tom nodded and turned toward the windows as a truck rounded the bend in the drive and pulled to a stop in the bushes near the house.

Dylan emerged from the scrub brush and stalked toward the house, his face set in grim lines.

Tom chuckled. "Get ready for that fight we were talking about."

Dylan entered through the open door, his gaze going to Tom. "Where is he?"

Ben stepped out of the shadows. "Dylan."

Not as tall as Tom, but just as intimidating, Dylan Acevedo's blue eyes pinned Ben with a glare. "Where the hell have you been?"

Ben's lips twisted. "Good to see you, too."

Dylan's fists clenched and he stalked across the room. "You know I should kick your ass for scaring all of us like that. You know that?" He stopped in front of Ben, glaring like a bull in the ring. Then he pulled Ben into his arms, hugging him hard, pounding his back with enough force to break bones.

"Careful there. Those ribs aren't fully mended." Ben laughed, pushing Dylan away. His smile died, his eyes burning. "You two don't know how good it is to be back."

"Tell us about it. What with Julie dead and you gone, too…" Dylan shoved a hand through his coal-black hair and blinked suspiciously. "Glad you're back."

"Thanks."

The men stood staring at each other for a long moment until Ben reached down to lift the duffel bag he'd been packing.

Dylan beat him to it, hefting the bag. "What have you got in here? Bricks?"

"Supplies. Wayne's already got men on the ground here.

I can't stay. I have to get Ava out of here as well or she'll be his next target."

Tom told Dylan about the attack earlier.

"Damn. That would explain why she blew up at the lab." Dylan dug his thumbs into his belt loops and rocked back on his heels. "Only way to stop this craziness is to get rid of Nicky."

Ben shook his head. "That'll be tough. He's surrounded by bodyguards everywhere he goes."

"Maybe so." Dylan's lips quirked upward. "But I got word from my contacts in Vegas, he's on his way out here."

Ben's brows rose and then narrowed. "He must really want that money bad. What I wouldn't give to be the one to take him down."

"We need a plan to capture Nicky," Tom said.

Ben nodded. "He wants that medal."

"Where is it?" Dylan's brows rose.

"I gave it to Ava before I was kidnapped. She says she doesn't know where it is, but I think she's lying."

A chuckled rumbled in Tom's chest. "Ava? Lie?"

"Go figure." Ben grinned. "She'll take some convincing before she 'remembers' where it is and hands it over." He just hoped she didn't hold on to it so long she put herself any more at risk than she already was.

The lines deepened on Tom's forehead. "That might have been what she was looking for when she was out here earlier."

"Why do you think?" Ben asked.

"She was out back on her hands and knees in the brush."

Ben's heart banged against his chest. "Where?"

"Off the back deck."

The three men moved as one, each racing for the back door.

Ben ran out on the deck and down the steps, his gaze panning the acres of brush stretching out before him. "Do you remember about where she was when you saw her?"

Tom stood at the top of the stairs and pointed. "Somewhere around the base of that juniper."

Ben and Dylan spread out about four feet apart and moved slowly forward, scanning the ground with each step they took.

"Are we getting close?" Ben called out.

"Yeah, right around where you're standing."

Both men dropped to their haunches and looked beneath the brush.

"I've found something!" Dylan called out.

Ben hurried over to the other man, hope pulsing through his veins. Finding the necklace was the most important key to getting Nicky Wayne off Ava's back.

"I see something shiny." Dylan, on his hands and knees in the dirt, reached beneath the sage and pulled something out and held it up. "Recognize this?"

Instead of the medallion Ben expected, Dylan held up a silver chain with a key at the end. Ben straightened. "Are you sure this is where she was?" He looked to Tom on the deck above him.

"Positive."

Could the key unlock whatever she might have stored the medal in? "I have no idea what this goes to."

"It's got to go to something. Let's look through the house and see if it fits anything."

Ben climbed the stairs and hurried inside. Nothing in the kitchen required a key to unlock it except the back door. He moved on to the living room. Again, no locks. When he entered the bedroom, he found a lock box in the top of the closet. The key didn't fit. Under the bed, he found one of his rifle cases with a lock on it. The key didn't fit there, either. A thorough search of every nook and cranny inside the house and outbuildings revealed nothing that the key fit.

"We'll have to get Ava to tell us what it goes to. For now, we need to get going," Tom said.

Ben snorted softly. "Good luck. She still thinks I left of my own volition."

Dylan's gaze narrowed. "You have to admit your actions since Julie's death haven't been stellar. You've played the disappearing act on more than one occasion."

Dylan's jab had a lot to do with how Ben had called in Julie's death on 9-1-1. He'd gotten a text to meet Julie out in the desert. When he'd gotten there, she was already dead. The pain and anger of finding her hit him square in the chest all over again, as fresh as if it occurred yesterday. Ben immediately realized the text had been a setup. Still deep undercover, Ben couldn't be caught answering a text from an FBI agent. It would have blown his cover. He left and called 9-1-1 anonymously.

Unfortunately, the police and FBI had recognized his voice. Every time he'd gone out to do Del Gardo's business, he'd been performing his part as an undercover agent, infiltrating the Del Gardo machine. He couldn't just announce where he was going as he left. His friends in the FBI would have recognized that if he'd been at liberty to tell them of his assignment. Until he spoke with George Stacy, he wasn't sure he could reveal what he'd been up to. And he couldn't meet with George until he was absolutely certain Ava would be safe.

Ben straightened, his jaw firming. "I had reasons."

Tom grabbed his arm and swung him around. "Then share them."

He wanted to more than anything. But he didn't know

how much he could say until he had the clearance to. Nicky Wayne didn't know he wasn't working for Del Gardo. He hadn't confessed to anything other than working for Vincent. He shrugged Tom's hand off his arm. "I can't until I'm debriefed."

"Then deal with the repercussions." Dylan dropped the duffel bag and stalked off toward his vehicle.

Tom walked toward the door and paused in the door-frame. "Unfortunately, Dylan's right. If you can't tell everyone what you've been up to, they're not going to trust you. You'll eventually be hauled in, no matter what we do."

And they were risking their careers in the FBI by even meeting with him now. The anger seeped out of Ben's body, replaced by a knot in his gut. "I understand. When the time is right, I'll tell you everything. Until then, all you can do is trust me."

Tom stared into his eyes and then nodded. "That's getting harder and harder, considering all the circumstances. But you've been my friend for a long time, therefore I trust you. Don't make me regret it. We still need to have a long talk. A lot has happened since you've been gone."

"And we will talk, as soon as I know Ava will be safe." Ben nodded toward the door. "You and Dylan need to go before you're caught with me."

Tom stared at the duffel bag. "Can I give you a lift somewhere?"

Ben figured if Ava had been crawling around in the bushes looking for the key she'd be back to collect it. "No, thank you. I'll find my own way around. You can't afford to be seen with me." After he stashed the duffel bag, he planned to take his motorcycle back into town to check on her.

"It might already be too late."

"I'm sorry. If I go down, I don't want you in the middle of it."

"What about Ava?" Tom asked.

"She's not safe in Kenner City. Not with Nicky Wayne after her."

"She's not going to leave willingly."

"I know." Ben pushed a hand through his shaggy hair. "But I won't risk Nicky Wayne getting his filthy hands on her."

"Good point." Tom grinned. "Good luck. You've got your work cut out for you convincing her to go anywhere with you. She's a pretty determined lady."

Ben's lips twisted. "I know."

Chapter Eleven

Ava rubbed the center of her back, easing the pain and tension that had built up over the past two hours of being on her feet. While combing through the evidence gathered where Julie was found for the hundredth time, her mind had drifted to the key she'd left in the bushes at the house. She had to get to it and open the box containing the St. Joan of Arc medal. Then she could give it to the police and this whole Nicky Wayne thing would end.

Why she didn't just let someone else handle it, she wasn't certain. The risks were too high for her to go back to her house. Especially by herself. What she needed was an armed escort and a giant-sized bulletproof vest to protect her and the baby.

Bart had spent two hours trying to break into the digital recorder. It had some kind of password protecting the device from tampering and he hadn't come up with the right combination to unlock the contents. What was on it? Why was it in the hidey hole in the cabin. As far as Ava knew, she and Ben were the only ones who knew about the loose floorboard in the house.

Too tired to think clearly, Ava decided to pack it in. But first, she had to get out to the house and retrieve the key.

Maybe if she was careful and sneaked out of town without anyone knowing, she'd be all right. She'd left the box containing the necklace in a large handbag on the back floorboard of Callie's car. She thumbed the keys in her pocket. The keys she hadn't given back when she'd returned to the KCCU.

Guilt gnawed at her gut. She'd seen the doubts about Ben's innocence in the eyes of her teammates. Oh, they cared about her, but not having been around Ben much, they didn't know him like she did and they didn't have any reason to trust him. She hadn't missed the expressions of pity on their faces when they thought she wasn't looking.

She had to find that key, get that necklace and get it back to Ben. What he did with it would prove whether or not he was on the right side of the law.

Her chest hurt, the heartache a physical pain to be endured until this was all over. How could she expect the rest of the KCCU to believe in Ben when she's refused to believe him?

When Callie wasn't looking, Ava slipped past her office and out the door. She took the stairs, easing down the three flights to avoid running into anyone in the elevator. By the time she reached the bottom, her knees hurt, her back ached and another Braxton Hicks cramp stretched across her abdomen.

Great, all she needed was to go into labor while being chased by Nicky Wayne's thugs. She paused in the stairwell to catch her breath and let the pain pass. She wasn't much use as a detective or anything else in the condition she was. Who could miss a woman the size of a barn running around the small town?

Darkness was settling in, long shadows spilling over the parking lot. Ava poked her head out a side door and scanned the few cars still parked in front of the building. No signs of anyone sitting in them and the streets were empty. The KCCU office building stood at the edge of town. Unless someone was coming specifically to this building or headed to one of the outlying homes in the area, a person had no business being this far out.

With the coast clear and no one raising the alarm that the pregnant woman was missing, she had her opportunity to escape, and she took it.

Half walking, half running, she hurried as fast as her limited waddle let her, punching the unlock button on the remote.

As soon as she slid behind the steering wheel, she hit the lock button on the armrest. Not until the locks clicked did she feel anywhere near safe. Then she laughed, shakily at first.

All this scary nonsense for a walk to the car in Kenner City.

After the shootout at her home earlier, she hesitated with the key in the ignition. Was she just plain crazy? Would a shooter be waiting for her out there?

How else would she get the key?

Her hand twisted the key in the ignition and the car's engine revved to life.

If she felt at all apprehensive when she got to the house, she'd turn right around and come back to town. She wouldn't stop to collect the key, she wouldn't get out.

With her alternate plan in mind, she drove the couple miles out into the Colorado mountains, intent on settling the matter of the medal once and for all. Tomorrow she'd hand the medal over to Ben. He would be in town by then and hopping mad that she left him stranded in Kingman.

On the drive out of town, Ava glanced in the rearview mirror to see a man on a motorcycle following her. Could it be one of Nicky's men? She pressed harder on the accelerator and before long, the motorcycle disappeared. Ava sucked in a calming breath. She was getting paranoid. Ava wondered whether or not Ben had already made it to Kenner City. And if so, would he try to contact her?

She certainly hoped not. Being with him opened up all the old insecurities and wounds she'd worked hard to push aside.

The devil on her shoulder wished Ben would ride into Kenner City and rescue her from Wayne and her own doubts. But how likely was that to happen? Especially when Ben Parrish was wanted in connection with the murder of Julie Grainger and possibly the hit on Del Gardo. Plus they'd want to question him about his nefarious association to the Del Gardo crime family.

Why did Ava care about clearing Ben's name? She should just ignore the man and everything about him and get on with life. But would she want her child to bear the burden of being the spawn of a criminal? What if Ben wasn't a criminal at all? Children could be cruel in their taunts and name-calling. Did she want her child to go through that?

No.

The turn-off sneaked up on her and she had to slam on her brakes at the last minute, overshooting her mark.

She shifted into Reverse and backed up enough to make the turn onto the quarter-mile drive up to the house perched on the hilltop.

Darkness was settling in, cloaking the mountains in inky black. Stars blinked to life, providing some illumination in the moonless sky.

The house stood silent, no lights shown cheerily from the windows. Even the birds quieted with nightfall. The clear sky allowed the heat of the day to dissipate quickly, chilling the air.

Ava pulled up in the drive and sat for a moment with

her engine running, her gaze panning sinister shadows on the edge of the clearing surrounding the house. If someone was out there, she wouldn't see them. Not without night vision goggles.

Should she turn around and head back to town, give up on getting the key and accept the hospitality and protection of Tom and Callie?

She shut off her engine and rolled her window down enough to listen for sounds of movement. The scent of juniper, pine and decaying leaves drifted in to wrap around her senses. How could such a peaceful place be the setting for an ambush?

She stared at the house, wishing she could drive around to the back where she could jump out, run into the bushes, grab the key and chain and get right back in the car.

She'd parked as close to the house as she could get. Her only other course of action was to get out. If she found a flashlight in the car, she would, otherwise she'd take it as a sign that she shouldn't be here and head back to town.

Ava bent sideways and fished beneath the seat, hoping Callie kept a flashlight handy in case she had a breakdown. She didn't find one there, so she leaned across the console and dug in the glove box, breathing a sigh when her hand closed around the cylindrical casing of a metal flashlight. Okay, well that settled whether or not she'd get out of the car.

Flashlight in hand, she pushed herself out of the seat and stood in the dark, listening. She wouldn't use the flashlight until she absolutely had to. It would allow her to see, but would also make her a highly visible target in the thickening darkness.

Taking cautious steps around the side of the house, she emerged in the back, below the deck steps. She'd found the chain not far from here. Her finger rested on the switch.

A twig snapped close by.

Her heart pounded like a snare drum, whisking blood through her veins, rocketing her pulse into high speed. Ava ducked between bushes and dropped to her knees. A branch gouged her kneecaps and she bit down hard on her lip to keep from crying out.

For at least two minutes, she knelt in the dark, with only the sound of her breathing and blood banging against her eardrums to fill her thoughts.

Ava let loose the breath she'd been holding and switched on the light, angling the beam at the ground near the base of the bushes. Probably a rabbit or a possum.

She edged along the ground, keeping the light low. When she came to the place she could have sworn she'd found the chain and key the first time, the ground was empty but for leaves and sticks.

"Looking for this?" A deep voice spoke directly behind her.

Ava swallowed her scream, immediately recognizing the deep timbre as none other than Ben Parrish.

She sat back on her butt and shined her light up at him, at once irritated and relieved to see the sharp angles of his face, the dark blond, shaggy hair hanging down and the deep brown eyes. "How the hell did you get here?"

He held up a hand to shield his eyes from the glare of her flashlight. "I have my ways." He held the silver chain and key up to the light. "Does this belong to you?"

Her gaze shot from the chain to him and back. "Maybe."

"If it doesn't, you wouldn't care if I tossed it, would you?" He cocked his arm and prepared to throw.

Ava struggled to her feet. "No, don't!" She grabbed his wrist. "Don't."

He stared down into her eyes. His own eyes deep,

mysterious pools of darkness. "Why shouldn't I?" He stood so close, she could feel the warmth of his body in the cool night air.

"You've probably already guessed." She pushed her shoulders back, tilting her head up to look at him. "It's the key to the box where I stored the medal." She reached out to take it from him. "Give it to me."

His hand jerked out of her reach, a grin spreading across his face. "Give me one good reason I should after you left me stranded in Kingston."

She stretched high, determined to get the key, her belly bumping against Ben's hip. Her uterus contracted and she forgot about the key, instead clutching her abdomen.

Ben's grin froze, his hands reaching out to steady Ava. "Darlin', are you all right?"

"Yeah. This baby is already so big, I can't imagine getting any bigger." When the pain subsided, she grabbed for the chain and yanked it from his hand. "Got it!" She smiled up at him in triumph. "And I'm sorry for leaving you."

"Honey, I'd have given the key to you, had I known you wanted it so much." He stared down into her eyes. "Apology accepted, but don't do it again."

"Deal," Ava said.

"Now, where is the medal?" Ben said, his voice deep and dangerous.

The liquid heat of his tone melted every nerve ending in her body, setting her on fire. Suddenly her knees were weak, her belly flip-flopping and her head spinning. "I'll tell you when I'm good and ready. But right now I need to sit down." She reached out to lean on a tree, missed and would have toppled over if Ben hadn't been holding her arms.

"Let me help." He bent and scooped her up in his arms, carrying her up the steps into the house as if she weighed nothing.

"Are you sure it's safe to be here?" She glanced around, her head more than a little dizzy, not so much from the effects of being pregnant as from the effects of Ben's hands on her body.

"It'll have to do for the moment." He laid her on the couch in the living room and sat down on the coffee table, still too close for Ava to catch her breath. "I wouldn't recommend us staying here for long."

Ava pushed her hair out of her face, her gaze avoiding his. "No kidding. Did you see the bullet holes in the columns out front?"

"Yeah." His lips pressed into a straight line. "Which reinforces my position. We can't stay here."

"I suppose not." She sighed, running her hands over the brown leather of the couch. "Do you remember when we bought this couch?"

A smile tipped the corners of his mouth upward. "Yeah. You wanted the red one."

"Burgundy," she corrected. "And you insisted on brown."

He nodded.

"You were right." She glanced around the rest of the room. "The brown suited the room better. But I wasn't going to tell you that."

"Why tell me now?"

She shrugged. "The color of the couch doesn't seem that important now."

"No." He held out his hand. "We need to leave."

"Callie's probably frantic, wondering where her car is. I'd better get back to town."

"No." He held her hand tightly. "It's dark. We don't

know who might be on the road watching for us. We wouldn't see them until too late."

Ava frowned. "I made it here just fine."

"Luck." He took her hand and half lifted, half dragged her off the cushion. "That doesn't mean they won't be watching for you on the way back."

"I have to get back to Callie's. That's where I'm staying." She tugged against his handhold, but he didn't release her.

"Not anymore."

"And where do you suggest we stay?"

"Tonight we're camping out."

"Camping out?" she squeaked. "Excuse me? Pregnant woman here." She waved at her enormous girth. "Hard ground and bugs don't work for me."

Ben studied her for a long moment a frown marring his forehead. Then the frown disappeared. "You're right."

A little disappointed he didn't try harder to convince her to stay with him, Ava moved toward the front door. "Glad you can see reason."

"Wait here." Ben disappeared and ran up the stairs to the loft. Sounds of closet doors opening and closing rumbled against the high ceiling.

What was he doing? Whatever. Ava needed to be heading back to town. "I'll be in the car. If you want a ride back to town, you better hurry."

"Don't you ever do as you're told?" Ben stood at the top of the stairs carrying a large bag.

"We'd better hurry. Callie and Tom will be beside themselves wondering where I am."

"We need to talk about that. You can't keep running off without an armed escort."

"You make *me* sound the like the criminal." Her voice

trailed off. She realized her mistake as soon as she'd said the words. Ben would think she meant he was the criminal needing the armed guards.

Ben's jaw tightened so hard, Ava could see it twitch in the limited lighting of the strategically placed night-lights throughout the house.

"I'm sorry, Ben." Ava laid a hand on his arm. "But it's hard to believe in someone when they don't tell you the whole truth."

"I couldn't."

"And still can't?"

His silence answered.

"With the supposed good guys turning bad, and shooting at you, a person begins to suspect everyone."

Ben grabbed her arm. "What do you mean good guys turning bad? Did someone shoot at you besides today?"

Ava tilted her head. "Didn't Tom tell you about Jerry Ortiz?"

"Only that he's dead."

She snorted. "Yeah. He tried to kill me."

"You're kidding, right?"

"No, I'm not."

Ben's fists clenched. "Tom didn't get around to that particular detail. Why didn't you tell me earlier?"

"You really don't know?" Ava's brows rose into her hairline. "Seems FBI Special Agent Ortiz was a mole for the Wayne organization. He came after me."

"Ortiz?" Ben shook his head from side to side, trying to grasp the full impact of her words. "Ortiz was a mole. Tom didn't tell me about that either." He'd been so intent on saving Ava he hadn't slowed down long enough to get the full scope of everything that happened during his absence.

"Yeah. I thought you would have known. If you were working with Nicky Wayne you would have known." Her eyes widened. "You really weren't working for him, were you?"

"I told you, Wayne captured me and held me prisoner for two months of hell." Ben sat in a leather chair and rested his head in his hands. "Ortiz was the one who gave me the orders to infiltrate Del Gardo's crime family."

"He did what?" Ava sat back down on the couch, her legs suddenly too weak to hold her upright.

"It's all beginning to make sense now." Ben spoke as if he were alone in the room and talking to himself. "That son of a bitch had me spying for him. He set me up. And Boyd Perkins was working for Nicky. No wonder he seemed to know what was going down before it happened." Ben drew in a deep breath, the ache in his chest over Julie's death stabbing him anew—the pain fresh and burning a hole in his gut.

He stared across at Ava, without really seeing her wavy red hair and green eyes. Instead he saw Julie lying at his feet, pale and unmoving. "I was going to warn Julie to back off her pursuit of Del Gardo so that she wouldn't blow my cover. I told Ortiz what I was going to do." Ben leaped from his chair and marched across the floor, his fists clenching and unclenching. "He must have told Boyd and Boyd got to Julie first. Ortiz lied to me and he sold out on the bureau. If either Boyd or Ortiz were still alive, I'd kill them."

Ava leveraged herself off the couch and went to Ben. "It should make you feel better knowing that both Boyd and Ortiz got what they deserved."

Ben gripped her arms so hard, Ava knew she'd have bruises the next day. "And Ortiz tried to hurt you. Damn it, I should have been here." Ben stared at her, his gaze passing over her from head to toe.

"It's okay. He didn't get to me. I'm okay. The baby's fine. Ortiz paid with his life."

"Saves me the pleasure of killing him." The vicious glint in Ben's brown eyes made Ava shiver.

"Could you loosen up a bit? You're hurting me."

Ben let go as if he'd been burned and stared at her arms where dark bruises were already appearing on her smooth white skin. "I'm sorry."

"Don't worry." Ava rubbed her hands over her arms. "So that's what you were doing all this time? Working undercover for the FBI with Del Gardo?"

"I thought so." Ben laughed, the sound empty and without humor. "Seems Ortiz was using me to bring Del Gardo down." Ben slammed his fist into a rough cedar column. "The bastard. And he tried to kill you and our baby." Ben stared at her, his face a study in anguish.

For all the times Ava tossed and turned in bed at night questioning her judgment about the man she'd married, he'd been doing his job as an undercover agent. The look of betrayal on his face couldn't be faked.

"Ortiz was after me for the same reason Nicky Wayne is after me now." She inhaled and let it out slowly, then reached for a chair to lean on, suddenly too tired to stand. "He wanted that medal." She stared across at Ben. "We have to get that thing and put it somewhere safe. Give it to someone who can unravel Del Gardo's code."

"Wayne probably has the other two medals. Until he has all three, the code can't be broken."

"Then maybe we need to destroy the last one. That way Nicky Wayne will never get his hands on that money."

"You don't know Nicky." Ben spoke quietly, his tone flat

and emotionless. "He doesn't like to be thwarted. He takes it personally and seeks his own revenge." Ben gathered the bag he'd dropped on the floor when he'd learned of Ortiz's betrayal. "Come on, we have to leave before Nicky finds us."

Chapter Twelve

Ava stood outside the tent, hugging her arms in the cool mountain air, her teeth chattering, her body shaking. "Are you absolutely sure we can't make it back to Kenner City tonight? It's only a couple miles. Really fast by car."

"And a car is extremely visible on the road." Ben wanted to wrap her in his arms and chase away the cold and fear, but Ava wasn't ready for that. She had a long way to go before trusting him again. Owning up to his undercover mission had helped in breaking down the barriers. Time would take care of the rest. He hoped.

She heaved a sigh and pressed closer for warmth. "Can't blame a pregnant lady for trying to convince you."

"It's not safe. Nicky's men could be hiding out along the road, ready to take you out or hijack your car." He lifted the binoculars he'd taken from the house and stared across the valley to the next hilltop where their house stood. "Not to mention staying with Tom and Callie puts them at risk too." He tossed the binoculars inside the open door of the tent. What good did it do to stare at the house? They couldn't stay there. Not with Nicky and his men on their tails.

"I don't want Callie and Tom to be hurt and they weren't upset when I called about our extended use of Callie's car." Ava's lips pressed together. She sighed and another shiver shook her from head to toe. "Just don't make me climb another hill. I'm not up to it."

"Sorry about that. I couldn't get out on the main roads and Callie's car could only go so far on the dirt road." Ben wanted to assure her that she'd be safe out in the woods far from the house, but he wasn't certain this idea was any better than staying in town. At least out in the woods, he'd hear anyone approaching them well before they attacked. He'd double-checked the Sig Sauer he'd taken from Manny back at the casino. That and a full box of ammo didn't make him feel any less exposed. "You can have the air mattress. I'll sleep on the ground."

He held the door flap open for Ava and cringed as she eased her body down onto the queen-size air mattress they'd kept at the house for excess surprise visitors when the guest bedroom wasn't enough. Somehow, this wasn't what he pictured for his wife when he'd first learned of her pregnancy. Once he'd gotten used to the idea, he'd envisioned picking out paint colors for the baby's room, not picking which tree to burrow under out in the woods with the temperature dropping like a rock in a pond.

The more he saw her suffer, the more he determined to make it right by her even if he had to kill Nicky Wayne with his bare hands.

Once inside the tent, Ava pulled the sleeping bag up to her chin, the light from a mini flashlight all there was to see by.

"Got any more of those canned peaches?" she asked.

"Sure do." He pealed the lid back on the can and handed it to her with a fork.

Ava pushed to a sitting position, crossing her legs akimbo, the mattress rocking with every movement. Once stable she reached for the can and fork. "I'll be glad when I'm eating for one again."

Ben smiled at her. "You barely eat enough for one now."

"That's what you think. I eat more often."

He poked a hole in the bottoms of the three cans they'd emptied for their dinner. Using a ball of twine he'd scavenged at the house before they left, he tied the cans together with ten feet of string between each.

"What are you doing?" Ava's fork paused on its way to her mouth, a juicy peach slice dripping into the can. Her lips were slick with peach syrup and shining in the dim lighting.

It took every ounce of control for Ben to look back down at the string, when he wanted more than anything to kiss the juice from her lips. His groin tightened. He'd never seen a more sensuous woman than Ava sitting cross-legged in a tent, a can of peaches clutched in her hand. When he finally answered her question, his voice came out a little more abrupt than he'd intended, bordering on angry. "Creating an alarm system."

"You don't have to bite my head off. If we'd gone back to town, you could have gone your way, and I would have gone mine." She stuck the peach between her teeth and licked the drops off her lips. "You want the rest? I'm full."

"You just opened it."

"I can't help that my stomach only has room for so much these days." She gripped her belly and looked down at it. "Not very sexy, is it?" Her lips twisted.

Ben bit hard on his tongue. She really didn't have a clue as to how sexy she was, with the lush fullness of her breasts and the way her wavy red hair tumbled about her shoulders. Ben counted himself fortunate that Ava didn't know how much he wanted to take her there, big belly and all.

He took the can and downed the rest of the peaches,

drinking the remaining syrup. He'd have to ration the rest of the food he'd grabbed from the house. Tomorrow they'd be on the move to the safest place he knew.

They just had to make it through tonight.

He jammed the tip of a pocketknife into the bottom of the can and strung the twine through the hole. When he was done, he crawled out of the tent.

"Wait." Ava's small fingers gripped his arm in a firm hold. "Where are you going?"

He patted her hand. "To set the alarm. I'll be right back."

As he moved away from the tent, his eyes slowly adjusted to the darkness. He'd chosen a copse of trees and brush near the top of the ridge across from the house. If anyone wanted to find them, they'd have to climb up the ridge in the dark. If they made it that far. Once he set the cans in place, he'd have a rudimentary early warning system.

He loaded the cans with loose rocks and set them up straight, the line pulled tautly between each, just high enough off the ground to snag a foot.

The snare took nearly fifteen minutes for him to set in place, the entire time he spent worrying about Ava alone in the tent. He could see the copse of trees near the top of the ridge, but not the tent tucked into the forest bower. By the time he completed his chore, he trotted up the hill, his heart racing in anticipation of seeing Ava again.

When he entered the tent, she fell into his arms, her baby bump bouncing against his hip. "I thought you'd never get back," she said, her voice and body shaking.

"Shhh…" He stroked her hair, the sweet smell of peaches invading his senses. He ran his hands over her back and down to her waist. "I'm here. We'll be fine. Shhh…"

"I want to go home."

He tipped her face up and stared down into wet green eyes, marveling at how sad they looked in the shadows. "Remember when I promised I'd take you on your first campout?"

"Yeah, you said *after* the baby came."

"So, it's been pushed up a bit. Let's enjoy it." He waved toward the tree brachcs where twinkling starlight filtered through the leaves. "Could we have picked a nicer evening?"

"It could be warmer," she grumbled, snuggling closer to him. "And don't think I'm coming on to you, so much as I'm trying to avoid hypothermia. There's a difference, you know."

"I'll take it." He'd take anything just to hold Ava in his arms, even if only for the night. How he'd dreamed of the time they could be together. The excruciating weeks he'd been held captive made the pleasure of her company that much more intense.

"A campout, huh?" She scrubbed her hands over her eyes and turned her face to the sky. "I pictured roasting marshmallows somewhere in Estes Park, not camping across the way from our house. A perfectly good house with a nice soft bed."

Ben thought of what had once been their home, visions of Ava lying naked among the sheets on their four-poster bed. His body quickened, his hardness rubbing against the denim of his fly. He laid back on the mattress, taking her with him, holding her in the crook of his shoulder. "This isn't so bad."

"At least there are no mosquitoes." She snuggled closer, her belly fitting into his side, her breath warming his chest through the thin cotton of his shirt.

His hand slid up and down her arm, smoothing away chill bumps. "Are you warm enough?"

"Ummmm."

"I take it that's a yes."

"Ummmm." She nestled as close as she could, her hand tentatively sliding across his tight abdomen. "I'm going to regret this in the morning, but I'm cold and I can't get warm enough."

"Regret what?"

When her hand slid beneath the tail of his blue chambray shirt, his breath caught in his throat and lodged there.

"Don't think this means we're getting back together. The jury's still out on that." Her hand slid higher until her fingertips found one of his nipples.

Dear, sweet heaven. His blood pounded through his veins, shooting south to that uncomfortable bulge in his jeans. He shifted his hips to alleviate the tightness, but it didn't help. His own fingers slipped beneath her arm and down over her waist. The taut skin stretched over her belly was as smooth and soft as the finest silk.

She shifted beneath him. "I feel like we have a basketball between us. I'm sure that inspires great desire in a man, huh?"

"You have no idea how incredibly sexy it is to feel you beside me, the baby nudging against me. It's a part of you, a part of us." He turned on his side and lifted himself up on his elbow, staring down into her eyes in the dim light shining through the door of the tent. "Your body is doing something miraculous. It's an incredible turn-on."

She flicked the buttons loose on his shirt, one at a time until it hung open. Once his chest was bared, she leaned forward and bit gently on one of his nipples. "You're lying."

"You think so?" He thumbed her sultry red hair out of

her face, tucking it behind her ear. "Let me show you just how sexy I think you are."

Her eyes widened, and she captured her bottom lip between her teeth. "I don't know if that's such a good idea."

His brow furrowed. "Then don't start something you can't finish." His hand dropped to his side. He didn't touch her, fearing if he did he couldn't stop, whether she wanted him to or not.

Her teeth worked her bottom lip, her brows tugging downward as she stared at his naked chest. "I'm not starting anything."

"Aren't you?"

Ben almost chuckled when her hand reached out to touch his midsection, as if she couldn't stop herself. The warmth of her fingertips, threading through the hairs on his chest were almost his undoing. He captured her wrist in his hand. "You're starting something."

She sucked in a breath and let it out, her gaze finally meeting his. "So I am. What are you going to do about it?"

That's all he needed. His lips captured hers, slanting over her mouth, claiming her as he'd wanted to for so long.

She fell back against the air mattress, her lips parting on a gasp.

Ben took that opportunity to dive in, slipping his tongue past her teeth to twist and taste hers until they were both gasping for air.

His hands smoothed her hair back from her face, the silky red waves, spreading across the mattress, starlight glinting off the coppery strands.

Ben's heart swelled behind his ribs until he thought it would explode in his chest. He'd wanted her in his arms for so long, living through the horror of his imprisonment only to be here at last. He kissed her lips, his mouth skimming across her cheekbone to the delicate curve of her ear. From there he worked his way down, licking and nibbling a path along the slender column of her neck to the hollow at the base of her throat.

Her pulse thrummed a fast, erratic beat beneath her skin and she moaned. "Oh, please."

"Please what?" he murmured his mouth hovering over her swollen breast.

Beneath the thin layer of her blouse and the lace of her bra, her nipple puckered into a tight peak. "Please," she repeated, her hands tugging at the hem of her top.

With the deliberate slowness of one determined to savor every bite of an extremely delicious chocolate soufflé, Ben slid the shirt up over the mound of her belly. Her pale skin shone in the starlight, glowing a deep shadowy blue.

Her hand caught his halfway up. "Maybe this isn't such a good idea."

"Why?" He released his hold on the shirt, his hand cradling the baby in her womb.

"Because I'm so fat!" She tried to push the blouse down to cover her enormous belly.

"Don't." His hand stilled hers and he laid his lips against her soft skin, reveling in the beauty of what was happening to her body. "Can you hear me in there?" he called out softly.

Ava laughed, her belly shaking. "Yes, she can."

His gaze captured hers. "She? It's a girl? Are you sure?"

Her smile spread wider. "Yes. The sonogram techs and the doctor all think it's a girl. No dangly parts to be found."

A girl. He had a daughter. "I hope she has red hair like her mother." His hand circled her belly again and he pressed a kiss to his baby. Then he captured the hem of her blouse and pushed it up over her breasts. "Do you think she will mind if her mom and dad…you know." He tugged until the blouse came up and over Ava's head. Her breasts were even more beautiful, their fullness enhanced by her pregnancy.

"I hope not." She reached beneath her back and flicked her bra open, her breasts spilling into his palm.

God, it had been a long time since she'd felt anything but fat and pregnant. She'd allow herself this one night with Ben. Just this one. Not that she could resist him even if she wanted to. Tomorrow was soon enough to put distance between them.

Ben kissed her hardened nipple, rolling the nub between his teeth.

Waves of desire rolled over her body, pulsing through her veins to that warm, wet place between her legs. Ava moaned, her channel clenching in anticipation of more to come.

A large rough hand skimmed over the tautly stretched skin of her belly, slipping beneath the elastic band of her maternity pants and down to the thatch of hair at the juncture of her thighs.

Was this really happening? After all the months of fear for his life, anger because he'd left her and finally acceptance that he'd never come back. In a brief moment of clarity, she questioned her own ability to blow off all of that and let him have his way with her. Her cravings for love and sex overpowered her intelligence. She opened her mouth to tell him to stop.

But his fingers slid between her folds and thumbed that little sliver of desire, the center point of highly sensitive nerves she'd almost forgotten existed in her pregnant state.

He strummed her senses, his strokes at first gentle, soft, swirling lower to collect her creamy moisture. A master at his craft, Ben used every weapon in his arsenal. He let go of her nipple and pressed soft, feathery kisses across her abdomen, easing his way down her body. He hooked the elastic waistband and dragged the pants off her legs, tossing them into the corner of the tent. Then he settled between her legs, draping her thighs over his shoulders.

Just the position had Ava wet and ready for anything he wanted to do to her.

And Ben didn't disappoint. His tongue delved in, teasing and flicking her to new heights.

Her heels dug into the mattress, her bottom rising up to meet his every stroke. When she catapulted over the edge of reason and sanity, her world exploded in a burst of ecstasy she hadn't remembered existed. "Oh, Ben!" she shouted.

Immediately, Ben climbed up the mattress to lie beside her. "Are you all right?" He smoothed damp hair from her forehead, pressing his lips to hers.

"No." Her head tossed from left to right. "Yes. Oh, wow. How do you do that?" She collapsed back against the air mattress, her breathing ragged, her body a jumbled mass of tightly strung nerves, wanting more.

Ben chuckled and nipped her earlobe, the stiffness of his denim jeans a blatant reminder that he was still wearing clothing and she wasn't.

She reached for the metal button on his jeans and flicked it open.

His hand stayed hers. "Do you think it's a good idea to go farther?"

"Oh, yes." Her fingers gripped the metal tab and pulled the zipper down.

He sprang free of the denim into her palm.

Her hand wrapped around him, contemplating the length and heaviness of him before she made her move. In long steady strokes, she eased her hand up and down his length.

Ben's body tightened, his hips moving to the rhythm of her hands.

His eyes closed, his jaw tightening, his body went rigid and he pulled free of her hand. He eased her onto her side away from him. Cupping her hips, he pulled her against him, his erection pressing into her core from behind.

Ava welcomed him, guiding him into her slick channel.

In slow, steady strokes, he eased in and out of her, careful not to injure her or the baby.

Ava's fingers dug into the sleeping bag as her body reached a second climax.

Ben's movements ground to a halt as his body stiffened, his fingers digging into her hips, his member throbbing inside her.

Ava drifted back to the ground, the tent, the scents of pinion pine and cool mountain air. Tears slipped from the corners of her eyes.

Ben gathered her against him and kissed her softly at the base of her neck. "We should dress before we sleep."

Limp as a rag doll, Ava let Ben pull her clothes over her.

Exhaustion from the eventful day and the magic of their lovemaking tugged at Ava's eyelids.

When they were both dressed again, Ben spooned Ava's backside into the curve of his body and pulled the edges of the sleeping bag up around them.

As Ava drifted to sleep, the rich, low sound of Ben's voice rumbled against her. "I love you, Ava."

Yeah, but for how long? A single tear slipped from the corner of Ava's eye.

BEN LAY AWAKE, long into the night, listening to the sound of Ava breathing. He didn't dare go to sleep. Too much remained at stake. As far as Nicky was concerned, Ava had something he wanted and he wouldn't stop until he got it.

Ben's arms tightened around Ava, his love for this woman almost debilitating in its intensity. How could he get her out of this mess?

The scarier question was, when would Nicky make his next move?

Chapter Thirteen

"Ava, wake up." A deep voice penetrated the shroud of sleep, snapping Ava awake.

She pushed herself upright. "What? What's wrong?"

"We may need to leave here. Something's not right." Ben crouched in the doorway of the tent, staring out at the sky.

The moon must have risen, as the soft glow of starlight had been replaced by a brighter orange glow.

Ben reached for the binoculars buried beneath the corner of the sleeping bag. Then he left the tent and straightened, cursing.

Ava rubbed the sleep from her eyes and looked again. No, that wasn't moonlight. She crawled on her hands and knees to the door. The sky was filled with a bright haze, the arid scent of smoke drifting across the hilltops.

"Is there a fire?" Ava scrambled to her feet, her pulse racing. Fires in this part of the country could easily escalate, gobbling up acres of dry timber.

"Yeah." Ben stared through the binoculars at the origin of the glow, another curse leaving his lips.

"Let me have those." She reached for the binoculars. A heaviness settled over Ava, filling her chest with a poison as potent as smoke, making it difficult for her to breathe. Before she parted the branches of the low-lying scrub, she knew.

On the opposite hilltop, flames licked at the sky from what had once been their home. Dark, shadowy figures moved at the base, shaking what looked like gasoline cans. More flames rose, eating away at the timbers of the porch.

Ava choked on a sob. "No!" She shoved the binoculars at Ben, pushed the brush aside and would have run down the hillside if Ben hadn't stopped her.

He held her arm in a vice grip. "You can't stop the damage now."

"We have to do something." She turned in his arms and stared up, tears blurring his image. "We can't let them destroy our house."

"The fire department won't be able to get there in time to save much. There's nothing we can do." His face may as well have been granite with no signs of feeling. His stoicism absolutely infuriated Ava.

"We have to do something. It's our home." She ran for the tent and pulled out her handbag. Digging around inside, she unearthed her cell phone.

Before she could flip it open, it rang. The tone and vibration startled her so much she dropped the phone to the ground.

Ben bent to pick it up.

Ava snatched it from him and stared down at a number she didn't recognize. She flipped it open.

"Hi, Mrs. Parrish. This is Nicky Wayne. Let me speak to Ben Parrish," a voice said into her ear.

Ava's eyes widened and she held out the phone to Ben. "It's Nicky Wayne. He wants to speak to you."

Ben took the phone, a knot forming in his gut. The damage Nicky Wayne had inflicted on him and those he cared about most had to stop. "Bastard."

"Like our little campfire, Parrish? We built it just for you."

Ben pressed the binoculars to his eyes and stared down at the flames lighting the area around his house. Was Nicky Wayne really there? He stared at the men standing around silhouetted against the flames. "You're sick, Wayne."

"No, just determined. I get what I want."

"Not this time." Ben zeroed in on one of the men. One wearing a suit, of all things. Ben zoomed in the binoculars to get a closer look. Nicky's face was turned toward him and he was smiling.

"See me down here, Ben?" Nicky waved up at him. "I know where you are. No matter where you go, I'll find you."

Ben pulled the binoculars away and then put them back. It was Nicky and he seemed to know exactly where Ben was. How? "Go back to your casinos, Wayne, and leave us alone."

"Not until you give me what I want."

"I don't know what you're talking about."

"You know exactly what I'm talking about. And if I don't get it, your pretty wife will pay for it with her life. Oh, and it'll be a two-for-one deal, won't it. Seeing as how she's very pregnant with your spawn." His laughter blasted into Ben's ear.

Ben gripped the cell phone so hard he was surprised it didn't shatter into a million pieces.

The laughter died. "I want that medal."

"I don't have it."

"Then you'll get it to me by tomorrow night or I go after her." Nicky pointed at Ben as though he could see him from the distance. "Do you hear me, Parrish?"

"I hear you." Ben's gaze zeroed in on Nicky. If he had a high-powered rifle, he'd shoot the bastard here and now and rid the world of his kind of stink.

The call ended and Nicky waved to his men. As they loaded up in SUVs, Ben punched 9-1-1.

Even if they couldn't stop the fire from completely destroying the house, maybe the police might catch up with Nicky and his men before they disappeared.

After he'd placed the call to 9-1-1 and another to Tom Ryan, he flipped the phone shut and looked around for Ava.

She sat on the ground at the edge of the copse of trees, her arms wrapped around her belly, rocking back and forth.

Ben dropped to the ground beside her and gathered her in his arms. "Tom and Callie are on their way along with the fire department and the police."

"What does it matter?" She stared at the flames eating a hole through the roof of their house and a tear leaked out of the corner of one of her eyes, followed by another and another. "It's gone."

"The house can be rebuilt."

"No!" She pushed against him, using him as leverage to climb to her feet. Once there, she let go and stood away from him. "What we had is gone. The home, the family… all of it was a lie."

Ben's chest squeezed as he got to his feet. "What do you mean?"

"You never wanted to get married. You never wanted children." Tears were falling in earnest down her cheeks. "I've been a fool to think you'd change and settle down. It's not in your nature."

Ben reached for her and she stumbled backward to avoid his hold. Of all the pain he'd endured during his incarceration at Wayne's casino, he'd never felt as much agony as he did when Ava flinched away from him and from a life that included him and their baby. Anger surged, driving him forward. He grabbed her arms and stared down into her face. "What do you know about me? You've barely given me a chance."

"I know your type."

"My type?" He laughed, the sound more like an angry bark. "And what type is that?"

"The type that won't stay, that won't be around for his child to grow up. The type who doesn't care enough about his family to stick around during the hard times."

"Are you out of your mind? Why would you think I'd be like that?"

Her lips clamped together and she stared up at him accusingly.

Then all his actions over the past year tumbled in on him and he could see where she'd accumulated her belief.

He'd been undercover with Del Gardo for so long, he'd barely known where his life with the FBI ended and his life as a member of the Del Gardo crime family started. He'd disappeared from their home for long stretches in order to meet with Del Gardo or one of his bodyguards. He'd met with Ortiz on the side to fill him in, unknowingly setting up Del Gardo for his fall to Nicky Wayne's organization.

He'd wasted his time infiltrating Vincent Del Gardo's inner circle, discovering a lonely old man with a lot of regrets. He should have come clean earlier and maybe Julie and Del Gardo wouldn't be dead. If he'd stayed away from Ava, her life wouldn't be in danger.

He spun to face the house. The home he'd loved and shared with Ava. The only time in his life he'd felt a real sense of belonging and family.

"You're right. It's all been a lie." He never should have gotten involved with Ava. In his line of work, there wasn't room for emotional attachments. His enemies would use those attachments to get to him.

Yet, no matter how wrong he was for Ava, he was the only person he trusted to guard her against Nicky Wayne's attack. The only way he could do that was to get her to take him to the necklace.

Ben turned away from her, gathered the duffel bag and loaded the remaining cans and sleeping bag into it. Turning his back to the blazing fire, he headed for the path leading down the backside of the hill to where he'd hidden Callie's car. "Come on, Tom and Callie will want to see that you are okay."

He waited at the edge of the path, taking her elbow to help her down the hill in the smoky haze.

TOM, Dylan and Callie met Ben and Ava at the bottom of the hill out of line of sight from the police and rescue vehicles speeding by on the highway toward the destroyed house.

Although her tears had dried, Ava's heart weighed heavily. She'd pushed Ben away for the final time as far as she was concerned. As much as she wanted him to fit into her idea of a family life for her and her child, she had been setting them all up for failure.

The life of an FBI agent made sense for Ben. He was born to be a drifter, a man without ties. She'd done him a favor by pushing him away. Now he didn't have to feel guilty when he left.

And her daughter wouldn't have to go through the heartache of losing someone she loved because the man couldn't be tied down, not in his business. Now that she had the key, why didn't she just give him the medal and be done with him? She'd be safe.

Because she knew once he had what he came for she might never see him again. The ache in her chest intensified as she watched Ben shake hands with Tom and Dylan.

"Ben, you have to come back to town with us," Dylan insisted.

"No, it's too dangerous." He glanced at Ava. "Nicky Wayne's determined to get that medal and will kill anyone in the way." Ben pulled the men to the side and gave them the scoop on what Nicky had said and done.

"You have to let the police and the FBI protect you two," Tom said.

"They can't. If Ortiz was bad, who else could be a sleeper for the Wayne crime organization? I won't expose Ava to any more danger than I have to. And if I go back, they'll throw me in jail for murders I didn't commit."

"That's just it. They won't throw you in jail. Ava found the digital recorder you stashed in the cabin in the mountains. Bart was finally able to get past your password— clever, by the way—to the recordings. It was smart on your part to record your orders from Ortiz and your conversations with Nicky Wayne. Using that recorder, we should be able to prove your innocence and that Jerry Ortiz set you up with Del Gardo."

Ben sucked in a deep breath and squeezed his eyes shut. "Thank you."

While Ben, Dylan and Tom discussed the details of Ben's mission to infiltrate the Del Gardo family, Callie hugged Ava close to her. "Are you doing okay?" She held her away from her and stared hard at her in the darkness.

"Yeah." Ava's gaze followed the bright flashing lights of a fire engine wailing by on the road nearby. A sob rose up in her throat and caught. "I'm getting numb to the pain."

"Oh, Ava, sweetie, your house can be rebuilt. You'll see. It'll be better than before."

She shook her head. "I don't think so." She didn't add that she didn't plan on rebuilding. When this was all over, she'd move to Denver, Wichita or Little Rock. It didn't matter as long as she got as far away from Ben, Colorado and the little bit of heaven she'd dreamed up while married to the man.

Callie hugged her again. "You're tired. Why don't you guys come back with us to the house?"

"We can't." Ben moved over to stand next to Ava without putting his arm around her. "We're leaving as soon as we can sneak out of here."

"What?" Tom, Dylan, Callie and Ava all looked at Ben as if he'd lost him mind.

"Where will you go?" Tom asked.

Ben turned to Ava. "We're going to hide out for a couple of days. When Ava tells me where the necklace is, we'll bring it back and either hand it over to the police or give it to Nicky Wayne to get him off our backs."

"You wouldn't give it to Nicky, would you?" Dylan's brows narrowed.

"I'd give it to the devil himself to keep Nicky away from Ava." Ben's mouth hardened into a thin line.

"You can't give it to Nicky." Dylan stepped forward. "With that money, he'll be unstoppable in this half of the country."

Ben didn't back down. "And would losing Ava or the baby be worth the trade-off?"

Dylan glanced from Ava and back to Ben. "I just don't believe you'd give it to him. You'd never give anything to Nicky. Not willingly."

For a moment Ben stared into Dylan's eyes. Then a slow, sad smile curved his lips. "Thanks for believing in me."

His gaze shifted from Dylan to Tom. "I know I've been very secretive lately, but I promise you, it was all part of the mission I was on. I'm still the same Ben you knew in the academy."

Dylan's frown deepened. "You better be. I can still beat the snot out of you."

"In your dreams." Ben grinned and then his lips firmed into a straight line. "If you had doubts about my innocence, why did you come?"

Dylan crossed his arms over his chest, and he gave Ben a long assessing look. Finally he nodded. "Because at the root of it all, you're still my friend and I like to think I'm a good judge of character."

Ben held out his hand. Dylan clasped it and they shook. Man to man. Then Ben yanked him into a hug. "Take care of yourself."

"You're the one who needs a keeper, as much coming and going as you do." Dylan slapped Ben on the back and then pushed him to arm's length. "Really, where are you going?"

"Away from here. Far enough out Nicky wouldn't know where to look for us."

"You sure you don't want us to go with you?"

"No. I think if we just disappear until I can get Ava to cough up the location of the medal that will be sufficient."

"Okay, then be careful." Tom stuck his hand out. "Nicky has his way of finding people who don't want to be found."

Ben shook Tom's hand and hugged his friend. "That's the beauty of where I'm going. I can see people coming for miles. I'll be ready."

"We'll be on the lookout for Nicky." Tom slapped a hand to Ben's shoulder. "You know we're just a phone call away."

"Where we're going, I'd have to send up a smoke signal. No cell towers."

Dylan frowned. "Then maybe you should reconsider."

"No. We need to get away from all the trees we love so much. You can never tell who's hiding behind one." The image of Nicky Wayne pointing toward them across the valley, three hundred yards away, was etched in his mind.

"And Ava's okay with this?" Tom stared across where the women had their heads together talking.

"I haven't told her."

"Somehow, I don't think she's going to go willingly."

"Then let me handle it." Ben glanced at Ava. "In the meantime, take this. I think it's how Wayne traced us." He handed Ava's cell phone to Tom.

"I'll make sure it's disabled."

"Good. And thanks. Did you bring everything I asked for?"

"Sure did. And you're taking my SUV." Tom's lips twisted. "Callie included clean blankets and some canned goods. You didn't ask for much, except the one thing I didn't want to give you. My brand-new Forerunner." He stared across at the gleaming black vehicle catching the moonlight. "Go easy on her, will you?"

"I'll do the best I can." He might need its four-wheel drive capability before this was all over.

"I installed a GPS tracking device on my SUV so that I'll know where you are. Don't worry, I'm the only one who knows about it. And Bart loaned me a pair of satellite phones. You have one in the truck, so no excuses about limited cell tower coverage. If you get in trouble…call."

Ben clapped a hand on Tom's back. "You think of everything."

"We'll do our damnedest to catch up with Nicky before he catches up with you. Check in every once in a while so we can update you on our progress."

"How many people know I have a satellite phone?"

"Me, Callie and Dylan. Bart doesn't know why I asked for it. He just set me up with a pair."

A frown pulled Ben's brows together. "Then I'll keep the calls to a minimum. Emergency only." After Jerry Ortiz's defection to Nicky, he wasn't sure who he trusted in the department other than Tom and Dylan. Ben stared across at his friend for a moment before he turned and strode over to Callie and Ava. "Ready to go?"

"I'll ride with Tom and Callie. My things are in Callie's car." Ava looked across at Ben, her brows raised as if challenging him to disagree.

He fought to keep a steady tone. If he made her think he was demanding she come with him, she'd fight tooth and nail. His best bet was to make her think they were all going to the same place. "And put them at risk? We'll see them soon enough."

Ava's teeth chewed on her bottom lip, then she glanced at Callie and sighed. "I'll ride with Ben." She reached into the car and claimed her heavy bag from the back floorboard, moving it to Tom's SUV.

Tom cleared his throat and hooked Callie's arm. "Then we need to duck out one vehicle at a time to keep from drawing attention to ourselves." He gave Ben a hard, steady look. "Be careful." Then he herded Callie to her car. "Nicky's men won't be expecting to see you in my SUV. That should give you a lead on them." He called over his shoulder. "Coming, Dylan?"

"I'm with you." Dylan nodded at Ben. "See ya soon." He turned and trotted to Callie's car, climbing into the backseat.

When their taillights disappeared through the trees and onto the main road, Ben turned to Ava. "It's just us now."

"For the moment. It only takes a few minutes to get to Tom and Callie's."

Ben sucked in a deep breath and let it out slowly. "We're not going there."

Ava's brows furrowed. "Not going there?" She crossed her arms over her belly. "What do you mean?"

"We're not going there. Nicky is after us in earnest. I want us to get as far away from here as possible until we can decide what our next move will be."

She held up her hands and backed away from him. "No way."

Ben should have anticipated her immediate resistance, but the way she backed away from him hurt. "There's nowhere safe with Wayne's organization after us. We have to use the confusion of all the rescue workers to slide out of town."

"I'm not going with you, Ben. I can't. I'm eight months pregnant. If it's all the same to you, I'll find my own ride to Callie's house." She backed farther away and turned, heading toward the highway, her waddling step slow and unwieldy.

Ben shook his head. He hated to do it, but he saw no other recourse. If she wouldn't come willingly, he'd just have to take her by force.

Ava passed the SUV and was well on her way to the road when Ben caught up with her and scooped her into his arms.

"Put me down!" she hissed, her feet flailing in the air.

"I can't. You're not safe here or anywhere near here."

"I can take care of myself, Ben Parrish."

"I'd rather not take that risk." He opened the passenger door of the SUV and deposited her on the leather seat. Pointing a finger in her face, he said, "Stay."

Ava blinked, a flush of red filling her pale cheeks, her mouth opening and closing before she could utter a word. "I. Am. Not. A. Dog!"

Realizing his mistake, Ben closed the door and ran around to the driver's side, hoping to jump in and drive off before she could get out. Using the remote key fob, he locked the doors.

Every time Ava hit the unlock button, he hit the lock button, stalling while he rounded the hood. He ripped open the driver's door and threw himself inside, grabbing her arm before she could get out of her side. "Woman, be reasonable."

"And you call this being reasonable?" She fought to loosen his grip. When she couldn't overpower his strength she sank her teeth into his hand.

Ben let go. "Ouch! Did you have to go and bite me?"

"Yes!" She leaned into her door handle, but Ben caught her again, hitting the lock button on his side.

With his right hand holding onto her arm, he had to reach beneath the steering column and turn the key with his left hand. The engine roared to life.

"Let me go!" Ava tried peeling his fingers off her arm, but his grip remained firm.

He shifted with his left hand, whipped the SUV around in the dark and headed for the road. Once the vehicle was in motion, he let go of her arm. "Don't think about jumping. You have the baby to consider, remember."

"Jerk!"

Ben paused at the edge of the brush lining the road and waited for a chance to get out without being seen by passing vehicles. He'd purposely kept his headlights off, rather than risk Wayne's men seeing the vehicle before they could get the heck away from their wreck of a home and Kenner City altogether.

When a gap presented itself in the rush of fire engines, EMT vans and police, Ben shot out on the road and drove as fast as he dared with the lights off, headed away from town, away from civilization and hopefully away from Nicky Wayne and his gang of hired mercenaries.

Ava sat in her corner of the front seat, her lips pressed together in a tight line. "Don't think I'm going to let you off light on this one, Ben Parrish."

Chapter Fourteen

Ava must have fallen asleep somewhere along the way. When she came out of her near-coma, her bladder screamed for release. "Stop the car."

"What?" Ben slammed his foot to the brakes, pitching Ava forward.

Her seat belt caught against her shoulders and across her hips, further aggravating her bladder situation. "I said stop the car, not wreck it."

"Why? What's wrong?" He eased up on the brakes, but brought the car to a smooth stop on the side of the road.

"I'm pregnant." She unfastened her seat belt before the car came to a complete stop.

"Are you in pain? Do we need to get you to a doctor?" Ben shifted into park and released his seat belt. "Isn't it too soon for you to go into labor?"

Ava almost laughed, forcing her lips to frown instead. After all, he'd kidnapped her, whisking her away from Kenner City without giving her the choice. What was there to laugh about? "I'm not having the baby, but I am in pain. If I don't find a bush quickly…let's just say, it won't be pretty."

Ben let out a long breath. "Next time just tell me you need to go. You about gave me a heart attack."

"Serves you right for kidnapping me." She pushed the door open and pulled herself out of the car. "Where are we anyway?"

"Another thirty minutes and we'll be there."

Stars shown in the endless sky, like millions of diamonds bejeweling the desert night. "You didn't answer my question."

"It's a surprise." Ben leaned over the console. "Need help or privacy?"

"Both, but since I can't have one without the other, I'll manage on my own. I wouldn't have to manage at all if you'd left me back in Kenner City." With very little in the way of bushes in the desert, Ava stepped to the rear of the SUV and took care of business. Thank goodness the road was deserted and she could see miles into the distance to spot the headlights of anyone who might happen upon them. Too bad there wasn't quite enough starlight to see a car sneaking up on them *without* their headlights on. She kept a wary eye on the road.

When she climbed back in the car, Ben waited until she had her seat belt fastened before he took off.

"I couldn't and wouldn't leave you in Kenner City. Nicky is a mean son of a bitch," he said quietly. "He wouldn't give a damn that you are a woman and pregnant. To him, your condition would only mean more leverage."

Leverage. A cold lump settled in Ava's squashed stomach. She sat quietly, reflecting on what Ben said and attempted to study her surroundings.

"I'm sorry I got you into this mess," Ben said after a while.

"Yeah, so am I. But now that we're in it, how do we get out?"

"We have to get that medal and either give it to Nicky or give it to the FBI."

Ava shot a glance his way. "I don't think giving it to Nicky Wayne is a valid option."

Ben stared straight ahead. "If it means getting him to leave you and the baby alone, I'd give him anything."

Warmth spread through every cold place in Ava's body. But she couldn't let his words sway her to take him back. Ben was a man just like her father—addicted to his job, addicted to the next exciting thing that came along. An adrenaline junky, needing the rush to keep his interest. It wasn't fair of her to saddle him with a child he would resent and eventually leave. "You don't have to stay with me, you know?" Ava said out loud, wishing she could take it back as soon as the words left her mouth.

Ben's foot left the accelerator, slowing the car automatically. "What do you mean I don't have to stay with you?"

"I know you didn't want to get married in the first place and a baby will just slow you down with your job and all."

In the light from the dash, Ben's lips pressed into a hard line. "It might be news to you, but I don't run out on family. My incarceration with Nicky Wayne was completely out of my hands. I couldn't get to you or a telephone to let you know what had happened." He slammed his open palm against the steering wheel. "Damn it, Ava! You can't hold that against me."

Ava turned away at the agony in Ben's voice. She could and she did hold it against him that he'd lied, drifted in and out of her life and would continue to unless she put a stop to it. Cutting the ties now would be easier than leaving her heart and that of her child's open to pain in the future. She'd been without him for two months, gone through the grieving process, she could do it again, but her child wouldn't go through that. Not if she could help it.

Never mind she'd always felt safe and secure when Ben was around. A woman could easily get used to having a man in her life.

Like her mother. Then, when he was gone? Her mother had never gotten over her father's desertion. Never stopped loving him, even after all the years.

Ava risked a glance at Ben. Would she be the same? Would she love him even after he'd been gone for years?

Her chest tightened in answer. Yes. For the few short months they'd been together, she'd known more happiness than she had in her entire life. If she could, would she go back and relive those months without Ben in them?

No. Then why would she deny her child the chance to get to know her father? Because a father's desertion is much worse than a husband's. A child doesn't understand and thinks it was something she did that caused her father to leave.

No! Ava stared out her window at the starlit night. She wouldn't let her daughter go through her young life feeling as though she were the one who drove her father away. Ava would do that up front before the baby came along. That way there would be no misunderstanding as to who was at fault.

First thing she had to do was get Nicky Wayne off their backs. As long as Wayne remained a threat, Ben would stay glued to her side. "If the medal is all you need, I can get it for you."

Ben's brows knit over his eyes. "You remember where it is?"

Butterflies flickered in her gut and she laid a hand on her belly protectively. "I've known where it was all along."

She dug the box out of her bag, opened it with a key and removed the necklace three people had tried to kill her for.

Ben shook his head. "It's too late to go back to Kenner City tonight. You might as well hang on to that until morning."

Ava slipped it around her neck, the medal lying cold against her skin, reminding her that this was the last thing keeping her and Ben together. Tears welled in her eyes, but she refused to let them fall.

BEN PULLED THE CAR around the rear of the cabin, out of sight from the dirt road leading into the place. Devoid of paint, the weathered building had seen better days. From the outside it appeared like an abandoned shack. Inside was little better, but at least the structure was sound.

He only knew of this place because he'd used it when he needed to get away from Del Gardo and Nicky Wayne. When he needed time to think and regroup. He'd come here when he'd learned of Ava's pregnancy. Out in the desert, with nothing but earth and sky all around, he couldn't get lost in distractions or the craziness of his secret life.

He'd come here to work through decisions concerning his duty and his desire. The duty to his job and his superiors and his desire for a life without lies, a life with Ava and his unborn child. Ava was right. He hadn't wanted to marry her when he did. He'd wanted to be free of the secrets when he committed to a woman. To Ava.

But the job hadn't been over and he couldn't come out of his undercover persona until it was and he would never leave Ava pregnant and alone. So he'd committed to her, knowing he couldn't tell her everything about himself. Especially the important stuff, like he wasn't part of a crime family and he wasn't a bad cop on the take.

Ava had accepted him, knowing he held back, knowing

there were things she wouldn't like about what he did. She'd accepted him unquestioningly and what had he done in return? Gotten her in more hot water than any pregnant woman deserved.

He wanted to tell her everything now that his assignment was over. One glance at the dark circles under her eyes spoke of her exhaustion. Now wasn't the time to confess all. Ava needed sleep.

Ben grabbed a flashlight and the satellite phone from the glove box, got out and circled the car, arriving before Ava could get up out of her seat. "Let me help."

She eyed his extended hand like one would eye a live snake. Eventually, she laid her hand in his.

The warmth of her skin on his flushed heat throughout his body, the lonely cabin leading him to thoughts of what they could do to pass the time. Tom could take his time finding Nicky and his thugs. A couple days of forced togetherness might be just what they needed to salvage what was left of their relationship and marriage.

Ava straightened and immediately flinched, her free hand going to her belly. "Ouch."

Fear replaced any thoughts of reconciliation in the forefront of Ben's mind. "Are you all right?" Had bringing Ava out this far been a really bad idea? Suppose she went into premature labor? What then? He had the satellite phone, but how long would it take an ambulance or EMT personnel to come if something went terribly wrong.

"I'm fine. The baby's getting so big that my skin doesn't seem to want to stretch with it." She massaged her side until she could stand straight again. "See? No problem."

Yeah, right. Ben could see through her lie. The tightness around her mouth always gave her away. "Let's get you inside. A nice long rest might help."

Ava smothered a yawn. "A bed does sound good. I don't suppose there's one there? One without bugs or snakes?"

Ben nodded. "One bed coming right up." He flung the door open to the small cabin with its meager amount of furnishings all covered in white sheets and a layer of dust blown in off the desert. "No guarantees on the critters. It's been awhile since I've been here."

Ava entered. "Interesting place you have here."

"In case you're wondering, I used it as a hideout when I worked undercover with Del Gardo."

Ben set the satellite phone and the flashlight on the table, then hurried through the cabin, lifting the sheets to reveal a full-size bed in the corner and a table with two chairs.

Ava sneezed and winced, her hand going to her belly. "Ouch." She sat in one of the two wooden chairs and rested her elbow on the table, chin in hand. "Wake me up when you're done."

Ben pulled clean sheets and a light blanket from an airtight trunk and quickly made the bed. "Hey, sweetheart, come lie down." He took her elbow and helped her up, walking her to the bed.

"I can take care of myself," she said, her voice soft, her attempt to push him away, halfhearted. "Really."

He pressed her back against the mattress and lifted her legs up to slide beneath the sheets. "Better?"

"Mmmmm. Much." She snuggled into the sheet and closed her eyes.

Ben kneaded the muscles along her shoulders, gently massaging the stiffness out of her neck. He worked his way down her back.

"Lower, please," she moaned.

Working his way down her spine, he reached her lower back.

"Oh, God. There." Ava dragged in a deep breath. "You wouldn't think that carrying an extra thirty pounds would be so hard," she mumbled. "But that feels so good."

"I'm sorry I haven't been here for you." He'd wanted to be with her every minute of her pregnancy, to see the changes, to feel the baby and hear its heartbeats. "I've missed a lot."

Her back stiffened and she drew away. "Yes. You have."

"Hopefully that will change once Nicky Wayne is caught and tried." Ben rubbed the small of her back, massaging away the stiffness. "Feel better?"

"Much better." Her breathing evened out within a minute of her head hitting the pillow.

"Poor baby." Ben brushed a stray curl of red hair from her face, tucking it gently behind her delicate earlobe. He bent close, touching his lips to her temple. "Sleep."

He switched the flashlight off and stepped out the front door into the desert night. Exhausted from his escape and subsequent dash across the desert to get to Ava, Ben needed sleep as badly as Ava. With Nicky Wayne on his tail, could he risk a few hours' sleep?

Ben scrubbed a hand over his face. He retrieved the duffel bag from the car and went through the contents one more time, searching for any tracking devices in case Ava's cell phone hadn't been the only one Nicky had followed. He unearthed the Sig Sauer and checked the clip. Almost full. Good. He slammed it back into the handle and stuck it in his belt. He spread the remaining contents of the bag on the table. Not much in the way of food and water for an indefinite stay in the desert, but it would have to do for a day or two until he could figure a way out of this mess and for Tom and Dylan to find Nicky and his thugs.

He grabbed a chair and headed outside. Propping the

chair against the outer wall, Ben sat, staring at the road leading up to the cabin from the main highway. A person would have to know the cabin was here. Strangers didn't just wander off the main road to find this place. Fairly certain Nicky Wayne wouldn't have bugged Tom's SUV and with Ava's cell phone now in Tom's hands, Ben didn't think Wayne would find them easily. Still, he didn't feel that Ava and the baby were safe. The only way to be certain of their security was to eliminate Nicky Wayne altogether.

For the next hour, he sat in the chair, leaning back against the weathered boards of the cabin, watching and listening in the stillness of the night. With no cloud cover to hold in the heat, the temperature dropped to below sixty. Ben shivered, wishing he'd remembered to snatch a jacket from his closet at the house. Now it was too late. Everything he'd owned, everything he'd worked to accumulate was gone.

Thanks to Nicky Wayne and his thugs for setting fire to his house. Anger surged through his veins, warming him for several minutes. The image of the flames from the only home he'd known for a long time burned a place in his memories. Would he and Ava eventually rebuild? Would their marriage survive this final brutal attack? All the time he'd been incarcerated in Nicky's basement, he'd never felt quite as hopeless as he did now.

His home was gone. Ava had rejected him. She didn't want him in her life or in their baby's life. But damn it! That's what had kept him alive when the torture seemed too much to bear. He'd be damned if he let her go without a fight.

The chill night air wore down his defenses. He quit shivering and grew sleepier by the minute. If he wasn't careful, hypothermia would set in. After his head nodded for the tenth time, Ben rose and stepped back in the cabin.

Ava lay on her side, the moonlight streaming through the one window at the back of the cabin bathing her in an ethereal glow. Too tired and cold to worry about upsetting her, Ben lay on the bed beside Ava, gathering her in his arms.

For the first time since Ben's escape from Wayne's casino, Ava didn't push him away or argue. Too deeply asleep, she let him pull her against him, let him spoon her backside against his front. The heat from her body chased away the chill of the night air. Ben fell into a restless sleep filled with fire, bad guys and images of Nicky standing over him with a loaded gun.

His arms and legs were tied to a pole in a shallow pit filled with snakes hissing and twisting around his bound ankles. If he moved at all, the snakes would bite, sending their poison straight into his system. On the ledge above, Nicky Wayne stood with a gun aimed at Ava, demanding the medal. Ben could do nothing to help her.

He struggled to free his hands. "No! Don't hurt her!" he yelled out to Nicky.

The more he struggled, the more the snakes tightened around his legs until the ropes became snakes and they inched up his legs.

If only he could wake from this nightmare. If only he could get to Ava before it was too late.

Ben forced himself up out of the quicksand of his dream. Pale gray light of predawn shone through the window. Ava lay curled into his arms, her breathing slow and regular, one leg sprawled out over his on top of the blanket.

Relief washed over him as he realized the snake pit had been nothing more than a dream. The leg on top of his moved. But not like a leg at all. It slithered sideways.

Adrenaline shot through Ben's blood, bouncing off his nerves, setting his senses on full alert in the amount of time it took for one beat of his heart. Carefully, he lifted his head, ever so slowly, trying not to move his legs even the tiniest bit.

Sprawled across the blanket was a six-foot diamond-back rattlesnake, snuggled among the folds, seeking the warmth of the bodies beneath.

"Ben?" Ava yawned and her body tensed to move.

"Sweetheart, don't move even a muscle."

She grew still, her body tightening next to his. "Why?"

"Just don't move," he commanded softly. Keeping his legs still, he raised his body upward. How to do this without risking Ava getting bit ran through his mind in a million directions.

"When I count to three, jerk your legs up under you." Clutching the edge of the blanket, he counted. "One… two…three!"

Ava jerked her legs up as Ben tossed the blanket over the top of the rattler.

The snake hissed and struck at the blanket then he was buried beneath it, slithering frantically to find his way out.

Ben leaped from the bed, grabbed the blanket's edges together and lifted it like a sack. The heavy weight of the snake bulged at the bottom, swirling and twisting.

"Oh, God." Ava swung her legs over the side of the bed and stood, her hands clutching at her belly, her gaze on the blanket. "Is that a snake?"

"Yes, it is. Will you get the door?" He held the blanket away from her and away from his own body.

"Gladly." She hurried toward the door, her gaze panning the floor every step of the way. "Think there are more where that one came from?"

"Doesn't hurt to be on the safe side." Ben hefted the blanket the short distance across the wood plank floor, the weight of the snake straining his muscles.

Ava reached the door and flung it open, pulling her belly far out of range from the captured snake. "What are you going to do with it?"

"Take care of it." Ben left the building, scanning the area for a stick or shovel or something with which to kill the snake. He refused to give it the opportunity to visit the cabin again. Especially while Ava was there.

Ava stood in the doorway, her hand resting on her swollen belly.

"Go back inside. I don't like you out in the open."

"Why? I can see for miles. We must be out in the middle of absolute nowhere."

Ben nodded, a smile quirking his lips. "Pretty much. Now be a good girl and go inside while I take this snake for a walk."

Ava closed the door.

Ben took the snake around the back of the cabin and kept walking far enough way from the building that once he killed the snake the smell and the scavengers wouldn't bother the people in the house.

He almost hated killing the rattler, but after it had crawled in bed with him and Ava he couldn't trust it not to find its way back inside the cabin and do it all over again.

With no stick or knife nearby, he located a large rock before he flung the snake free of the blanket.

The sidewinder hit the ground with a thud and immediately started slithering away.

Ben lifted the rock high and stalked the snake. As he closed in, the snake slid to a halt and wrapped its body around itself, its head raising high, the rattles on his tail warning his attacker to stand clear.

"Ben!"

With the rock balanced over his head, Ben paused. Was that Ava? He stood still, listening, his gaze on the snake, the snake watching him, his rattle growing angrier by the second.

"Ben!" Ava called out, her voice urgent.

Ben dropped the rock, all intentions of killing the snake gone in a flash. He had to get to Ava.

Chapter Fifteen

Ava stood near the open window at the back of the cabin, her heart racing, her breath caught in her throat. "Ben!"

She ran back to the front of the cabin and peered out the door. A blur of dust rose from the dirt road. Out of the cloud emerged a convoy of dark vehicles, all headed toward the cabin. She didn't know who they were or why they were coming down the road, but her gut told her it wasn't good.

Ava ran to the back window. "Ben! We've got company!"

Ben raced toward her, rounding the side of the building to the only entrance at the front.

Ava flung the door wide, expecting Ben to come inside. When he didn't, she grabbed his arm and tugged. "Get in here. We don't know who those people are."

Ben allowed her to pull him inside, his face grim. "Those are the vehicles from last night. They were nearby while the house burned."

Ava's stomach flipped. "Nicky."

With a nod, Ben cracked open the door and peered out at the vehicles coming to a halt in a phalanx out front.

Ben glanced around the tiny room and ran to the bed, lifting the mattress up on its side. "Get behind this."

"I'm not leaving you out here by yourself."

He propped the mattress and box springs against the headboard and shoved it away from the wall, leaving space for her between the mattress and box springs. Then in a soft, intense voice, he said, "If you love our baby, you'll get behind this, now."

Fear for her baby and the man she loved squeezed hard on her heart. Ben could possibly take care of himself, the baby couldn't.

Car doors opened and slammed closed outside.

Ava jumped.

"Parrish!" Nicky Wayne's voice came through the thin board walls of the cabin.

"That's my cue." Ben tipped Ava's chin up and pressed a hard kiss to her lips.

Ava reached out to grab his arm. "What are you going to do?" Her fingers twisted in the fabric of his shirt. Was this it? Would this be the last time she saw Ben?

"I'm going out there to negotiate."

She dug inside her blouse for the chain lying close to her heart. "Take this."

Ben raised his hand to the St. Joan of Arc medal. "No. You keep it safe for the moment."

"But that's all he wants. The medal. Give it to him and he'll go away."

"That's not how Nicky works." Ben peered out the window again. He handed her his pocketknife. "If I tell you to or if you hear gunshots, scrape the numbers away on the back of the medal. Got that?"

"Damn it, Ben, don't go out there."

"I have to." He bent down and kissed her again, hard on the lips. "I love you, Ava. Now stay between the mattresses and whatever you hear, don't come out."

"No." She held his arm, refusing to let go. "Damn it, Ben Parrish, I love you, too." Tears choked off her words.

Ben's hand covered hers. "Just know that I'd do anything for you and our child." He plucked her fingers from his sleeve and turned her toward the bed. He snatched the satellite phone from the table and shoved it in with her. "Call Tom and find out how far they are from us and how long until they can get here. Now please, for me, be safe."

"But…" When she turned back, he'd already gone through the door, closing it softly behind him.

Ava stepped between the mattresses, the tears flowing in earnest now. She fumbled with the satellite phone, trying to remember the instructions Ben had given her while driving last night.

BEN GRABBED THE PISTOL off the table and stepped out into the glare from the rising sun. The air had already begun to warm. Before long, the cabin would be too hot for Ava to be comfortable without air circulating through it. He didn't know how long she'd last sandwiched between the mattresses. Hopefully, if Nicky had found them, Tom and the cavalry wouldn't be far behind.

"Well, Ben. You're looking well for a man on the run." Nicky Wayne's voice came from one of the shadowy faced silhouettes closing in on him.

"Stay back or Ava will destroy the medal."

Nicky held a hand up and his men stopped. Sun glinted off an arsenal of weapons. Every man had a gun and all of them were trained on Ben.

Comforting. Ben just had to keep Nicky talking long enough for the Kenner City contingent to find them. A sinking feeling filled him, dragging him down. And how long would that be? Tom knew where he'd gone. Would he know that Nicky's people had found him already?

"You were quick to follow," Ben observed.

Nicky laughed. "Handy thing having you unconscious for the first forty-eight hours of your stay with me. You may not know this, but I had a GPS tracking device implanted in your shoulder when my physician stitched you up."

Ben's hand went to his shoulder, the ache of his injury throbbing anew. "Bastard."

"Tsk. Tsk. You know as well as I do that anything goes in this business and loyalty is a consumer commodity, for sale to the highest bidder."

"Like Jerry Ortiz?"

"Precisely." Nicky stepped forward another yard.

"That's close enough," Ben warned.

"What makes you think I won't just shoot you and take what I want from the pretty lady inside?"

"Because you don't know how serious I am about destroying your last link to the Del Gardo fortune."

"You'd destroy something that could make you richer than you'd ever be in the FBI?"

"Unlike Ortiz, I'm not monetarily motivated. The money's not worth it."

Nicky shook his head. "Then you're a fool. Money is everything." He tilted his head to the side. "Isn't that so, Manny?"

The big Mexican who'd been one of the guards in Ben's cell stepped forward, his arm in a sling, a large white bandage across his nose and bruising around his eyes. "*Sí,* Mr. Wayne." Tucked inside his sling was a Sig Sauer similar to the one Ben had stolen from him when he'd run from the casino. The one he held in his hand now. Ironic.

"How's the arm, Manny?" Ben asked.

Hatred glared from Manny's eyes. "Broken, no thanks to you."

Ben's eyes narrowed. "Guess it's better than being dead."

Nicky nodded at the gun in Ben's hand. "Plan on using that?"

Ben's hand didn't waiver from his target—Nicky. "Maybe."

"There's only one of you and a dozen of my men."

Ben pointed the gun at Nicky, his mouth firming into a straight line. "It only takes one well-placed bullet through the head to stop a snake."

"True. But my men have orders to shoot you if anything happens to me. Then what will become of your pretty wife?"

Ben's hands tightened on the grip, sweat popping out on his upper lip. What would happen to Ava if he were killed? He couldn't think about that. He had to trust that Tom would show up in time to help Ava and the baby out of this.

"So what's it going to be? Are you going to leave, or do I have to shoot you?" Ben asked Nicky.

"Seems like you're not the one capable of issuing ultimatums, Mr. Parrish. You killed one of my best men."

Ben snorted. "Hammer was an idiot. You could do better."

"Like you?" Nicky's brows rose. "How about it? Want to come to work for me? I'll pay more than you make at the FBI."

"No thanks."

Nicky's brows dropped low over his eyes, his gaze narrowing. "Then give me the medal and we'll leave."

"What guarantee do I have you'll leave without harming my wife?" Ben demanded.

"Well now." Nicky smiled, no warmth lighting his eyes. "You don't have any guarantees, do you?"

"That's not good enough." Ben raised his voice. "Ava, get ready to destroy it," he shouted.

"I'm ready," she called out, her voice barely audible through the wood door and mattress.

Nicky's smile shifted down a notch. "Let's not get crazy here."

"I'm not the crazy one." Ben's hand remained steady, the gun pointed squarely at Nicky's chest. "You hurt me, Ava destroys the medal."

Nicky's brows rose, a dark gleam in his eyes. "And I destroy Ava and the baby she carries."

Ben's jaw tightened, his heart racing inside his chest while he maintained a cool exterior in the face of his enemy. "The way we see it, you'll do that anyway."

"Probably so. So let us handle this delicately. How do I know you haven't already destroyed the medal?"

"You don't. If you want proof…" Ben nodded at the others gathered around, inching their way closer to Ben. "It's on my terms."

"Name them."

"You. Alone. Inside."

"No way." Nicky shook his head. "How do I know you don't have someone besides your beautiful wife inside? Make it me and two of my men and you have a deal."

"No."

His eyes narrowed. "Me and one of my men."

Ben considered. He might not get another chance to separate Nicky from the rest of his goons. "Okay."

Manny stepped forward. "Boss, let me."

Nicky nodded. "I wouldn't dream of denying you the pleasure."

Ben didn't like it. He didn't want either one of them close to Ava and the baby. But he had to buy time for Tom to get there and bring backup. Had Ava contacted them? Where the hell were they? Surely they would have been able to find Nicky and his small convoy of vehicles by now.

"Leave your weapons here." Ben nodded at the guns in both Nicky's and Manny's hands.

"Sorry. If you're keeping yours, I'm keeping mine." Nicky's hand waved out to the side. "It's only fair. You put yours down and I'll put mine down."

Ben couldn't put his down. It was the only incentive keeping Nicky from killing him and attacking Ava. "Then Manny doesn't go in."

Nicky stood silent for a moment. "Manny, give your gun to Jim." He jerked his head toward the man behind him.

"But—"

"Do it!" Nicky bit out.

Manny awkwardly handed the gun to the other man, wincing when he bumped his arm with the metal barrel. If possible, the frown on his face looked even more furious.

"If you so much as touch Ava, I'll kill you both." Ben's pistol remained pointed at Nicky. "Understood?"

Nicky raised his hands. "I wouldn't dream of touching her. Just give me the medal. That's all I want."

With little else he could do to prolong the wait for help to arrive, Ben led the way back to the cabin, walking backward, one slow, steady step at a time. When he bumped into the front door, he called out, "We're coming in, Ava. Stay back."

"And bring me the medal," Nicky called out.

Ben didn't grace Nicky's shout with a comeback. Ava wouldn't run out and just give him the medal without knowing what was going on.

Reaching behind him with one hand, Ben held his gun pointed at Nicky with the other. He grasped and turned the knob. "I'm coming in, and I'm bringing guests. Stay where I told you."

She didn't answer.

Ben fought the urge to look around for her. He had to keep his eye on Nicky and Manny. Either one of them could jump him and he'd only have time to fire off one round. He'd go for Nicky. If Ben had to die, Nicky wasn't going to stay around to cause any more damage than he already had to so many. He just needed to keep Nicky's attention on himself and keep Manny from getting to Ava.

"How'd you get to Ortiz?" Ben asked.

"Like I said, loyalty can be bought for the right price. I promised to pay off some of the gambling debts he owed me in return for information on Del Gardo." Nicky smiled, his lips curling satanically.

Once inside, Ben kept his back to the mattress leaning against the wall behind him, using his body as a shield to protect Ava and the baby.

Nicky stepped into the small cabin and stared around, blinking in an attempt to adjust his vision to the darkness. "Is this the best you can do for your wife, Parrish?"

Ben refused to respond to the jibe, his attention firmly rooted on Nicky and his every move.

Manny's big body filled the doorway, blocking the sunshine and casting much of the room in the shadow. Ben could make out the white of the mattress, but not much else after standing in the sunshine.

Nicky pointed his weapon at Ben. "Enough with the small talk, where's the medal?"

Ben remained standing between Nicky and the mattress, hoping his body would be enough to stop a bullet, should Nicky decide to pop off a round. He hoped Ava was crouching low. The stuffing in the bed would do little to slow a bullet.

"Show him the medal, Ava," he said.

"Gladly." Ava's voice came from the darkness behind the door. She emerged with the leg of a chair in her hand and smashed it down on Nicky's shooting arm.

Nicky shouted, his weapon falling to the floor. "Stupid bitch!"

When Manny bent to retrieve the fallen weapon, Ben got there first, kicking the gun beneath the small table and chairs. He held his Sig Sauer steady, pointed at Manny's chest. "Don't move or I'll sink a bullet into you just like I did into Hammer."

Nicky spun around and grabbed Ava around the neck, swinging her in front of him. "Drop it, Parrish, or I'll break her neck." He clamped his good arm against her throat and squeezed, lifting her off the ground.

Ava's eyes rounded and her fingers clutched at Nicky's arm.

Ben lunged toward them.

When he did, Manny swung a fist, connecting with Ben's midsection.

Air whooshed out of Ben's lungs and he staggered, unable to catch his breath. He couldn't go down. Ava needed him. With swift determination, he lifted his gun and fired at Manny, clipping him in the shoulder. As close as he stood, the impact sent him backward, slamming him against the wall. He slid down the wood planks, his good hand going to the hole ripped into his flesh to stem the flow of blood.

"Drop the gun, Parrish. Now!"

Ava's feet dangled above the floor, her face turning purple, her belly jutting forward. Hatred raged through Ben, hatred and desolation. He couldn't shoot Nicky without hitting Ava or the baby. If Nicky didn't let go of his hold on her throat, it wouldn't matter. She'd be dead in minutes.

Ben tossed the gun to the floor. "Let her go, Nicky."

Chapter Sixteen

Ava's vision blurred, the arm around her throat choking off any amount of air she tried desperately to drag in. The muscles around her uterus contracted, pulling tight across her belly.

She dug her nails into Nicky's arm in an attempt to ease his hold on her.

When Ben tossed his gun to the floor, Ava knew it was all over, but refused to go down without a fight.

"You'll have to let her go in order to get the medal, Nicky," Ben reasoned. His brows pressed toward his nose and he hovered, ready to rush forward to help her.

Tears sprang from Ava's eyes. Ben had tried to protect her, tried to keep Nicky from getting the information he wanted. But there were just too many bad guys for one lone FBI agent and an eight-month pregnant woman to battle by themselves.

She wanted to tell him help was on the way and not to give up, but she couldn't even breathe, much less push air past her vocal chords.

Thankfully, the arm around her throat eased and Nicky dropped her enough that her feet touched the floor. The arm remained around her neck, tight enough he could easily squeeze it again.

Ava gulped in air, willing her brain to engage and function sufficiently to get her out of this mess. As a member of the Kenner County Crime Unit, she'd been trained in self-defense techniques as a rookie, with an annual refresher course. That and a year of Tai Kwon Do training ought to be worth something. With time precious for herself, Ben and the baby, she had to think fast.

The talent scene from *Miss Congeniality* flashed through her mind and Ava acted on it. She jerked her elbow back hard into Nicky's solar plexus.

He grunted, his arm tightening in reflex.

Before Nicky could lift her off the ground, Ava stomped on his instep as hard as she could.

Nicky Wayne shouted and bent at the middle, enough that Ava could duck beneath his arm and twist out of his grasp.

He grabbed for her, catching her long hair in his fist.

But Ben was on him before he could drag her back to him, slamming a solid punch to Nicky's nose.

Blood spurted out on the floor and Nicky jerked his hand to his face, releasing Ava's hair.

She darted away and rushed across the small room to the gun on the floor.

Ben threw punches and Nicky fought back, blood running down his face and soaking his shirt.

"What's going on in there?" One of Nicky's men called from right outside the door.

As Ava bent to retrieve the gun, the door burst open and one of Nicky's men raced in, carrying a semiautomatic weapon. He blinked, his eyes squinting in the near-dark of the cabin.

Ben threw another punch.

Nicky's head hit the side of the small wooden table with a loud crack and he slumped to the floor.

His chest heaving, Ben swung to face the newest threat filling the doorway.

By the time the latest arrival's vision adjusted and he could focus on the occupants of the cabin, Ava had the gun in her hand and pointed at a struggling Nicky Wayne. "It ends here," she said quietly.

Nicky hauled himself up to a sitting position, his nose broken and bleeding, one eye swelling shut and managed to sneer past his split lip. "Kill her," he said.

"I wouldn't, if I were you," she warned the man in the doorway. "My finger's on this trigger. If you shoot, I squeeze and your boss is dead."

"Kill her, damn it!" Nicky spit blood on the wood floor.

"I don't know, Boss. There are helicopters arriving."

It was then Ava heard the whopping sound of rotary blades slashing the air outside. She fought to keep a smile from forming on her lips. "That would be the police and FBI." She tipped her head to the side and raised her eyebrows. "Are you going to shoot me? I don't think this guy is worth going to prison over, do you?"

Ben grinned. "You don't want to shoot a pregnant woman. No court in any of the fifty states would show you an ounce of mercy."

"Shoot, I tell you!" Nicky raged.

The man in the doorway stared from Nicky to Ava and back. Then he glanced over his shoulder at the helicopters swooping in over the cabin.

Ben seized the opportunity and charged him, knocking the weapon from his hands and sending him back out into the dusty front yard of the cabin. They landed in a puff of sand and dust.

Ava balanced Nicky's pistol in both hands, the heavy metal weighing on her arms.

Nicky's body tensed.

Ava's finger tightened. "Don't do it," she warned him.

When Nicky flung himself toward her, she fired, hitting him in the belly and knocking him backward. Wayne fell flat on his back, bright red staining his shirt. "Bitch," he said, clutching his gut. "Why'd you have to go and shoot me?"

Her heart pounding a hundred miles an hour, Ava stepped out of range of Nicky, Manny or anyone else who might want to grab her. "I warned you." She'd never shot a man before. But she'd do it again in a heartbeat to save herself and the life of her unborn child. "You don't mess with a Parrish."

When the gunshot blasted from inside the cabin, Ben's heart stopped. He threw a last, hard punch at the man he'd straddled, knocking his head back hard enough the man fell unconscious.

What the heck had happened inside the cabin? Why the hell had he left Ava alone for even a minute? Nicky Wayne would stop at nothing to get his revenge. Killing a pregnant woman wouldn't make him lose a minute of sleep.

His heart banging against his chest so hard he couldn't breathe, Ben burst through the doorway, his clothes and hair covered in dust. "Ava?" He blinked in the shadows, the bright sunshine outside having destroyed his night vision. For a moment he couldn't find her. "Ava, are you okay?"

Ava stood on the other side of the cabin, her face pale and both hands holding Nicky Wayne's pistol. She stared at the man lying on the floor. "I shot him."

"Good." Ben stepped over Nicky to reach Ava and wrap his arms around her. "He deserved it."

She stared up at him, her eyes glassy and round. "I shot a man."

He gripped her shoulders and stared down into her eyes. "You had to. If you hadn't he'd have killed you and the baby."

As if just realizing she still held the gun, she shoved it into his hands. "Take this."

He grabbed the gun in one hand and wrapped his other arm around her, pulling her against him and squeezing. "You're going to be all right."

"What about the others?"

"Nicky's men jumped in their vehicles and split as soon as the helicopter showed up."

Outside, the steady whopping sound of the helicopter blades churning the air reassured him like nothing else.

"They'll get away. We can't let them get away."

"Ava, don't worry about them." He tilted her chin, forcing her to stare into his eyes. "Are you sure you're not hurt?"

She nodded, tears trembling on her lashes.

"Then sit here for a moment while I check these guys' wounds."

Ben eased her into the only chair still standing in the building. After making sure she wouldn't fall out of it, he turned to the man who had been his nemesis for so long.

Nicky Wayne lay in a pool of blood, his hand clutching the open wound in his gut. "Help me." He reached his bloody hand toward Ben. He'd gone from being one of the meanest, nastiest and most ruthless of the organized crime bosses to a pitiful man clinging to life on the dirty floor of a desert cabin. He wasn't so tough now.

Ben fought his urge to spit on the man who'd almost killed Ava. Instead he tightened his jaw and said, "Keep applying pressure to that wound. Let me check on Manny."

He turned his back on Nicky and crossed to Manny who was slumped against the wall, his face waxy and white. Ben pressed two fingers to the man's carotid artery. He was dead.

"Ben! Ava!" Tom Ryan burst through the door, carrying a semiautomatic rifle. "Sorry it took us so long. We figured Wayne would find you soon, so we were already airborne when we got the call from Ava." Tom nodded to Ava. "Good job."

"The team is rounding up the rest of Wayne's gang." Dylan crowded in behind Tom. "Everything under control in here?"

"We need medical evacuation for him." Ben grabbed a sheet from the chest and dropped to his knees beside Nicky Wayne, pressing the sheet against the wound in Wayne's gut.

"What about this guy?" Tom pointed his gun at Manny.

"Dead." Ben glanced at Ava. "One of you guys mind taking over here?"

Ava sat with her arms around her belly, staring at the two men covered in blood on the floor. Her face was white. Then her face pinched, her eyes squeezing shut.

Ben hurried to her side, his arm going around her. "Hey, sweetie, are you doing okay?"

"Not so good," she managed to get out, before she clutched at her lower belly and bent into the pain. "I'm having labor pains. It's too early for this baby to come."

Ben's heart stopped and then roared to a start again, pumping blood so fast it banged against his eardrums. "Tom, Dylan. I need that helicopter. Now!" He lifted Ava in his arms and strode for the door.

"Put me down. I can walk."

"Just shut up and let me take care of you." His voice softened. "Please."

Ava smiled up at him and cupped his beard-roughened chin with her palm. "Okay. As long as you promise never to leave me."

"Deal."

Her brow furrowed. "Deal what?"

"I'll never leave you."

She pulled his face closer to hers, her lips within a hair's breadth. "You promise?"

He leaned forward and brushed a kiss to her mouth and pulled back. "I promised until death do us part on the day I said 'I do.'"

Ava's brows wrinkled. "You did, didn't you?"

"Yes, I did, and I keep my word."

The lines on her forehead smoothed. "I guess I didn't believe you."

His arms tightened around her. "Maybe it's time you started believing in me."

"Maybe it is." Ava wrapped her arms around his neck and snuggled closer.

His steps ate the distance between him and the helicopter. The pilot met him halfway.

"How long will it take us to get to Kenner County Hospital?"

"Forty-five minutes tops."

"Let's go." Ben loaded Ava into the backseat of the craft and buckled her belt across her lap. He sat beside her and buckled in, slipping the headset over his ears.

He held Ava's hand and felt pretty much worthless in the face of this crisis. What did he know about delivering babies?

Ava sat beside Ben, concentrating on relaxing, willing the pains to abate and eventually go away. But they kept coming. If they weren't careful, she'd have this baby a month early in the back of a helicopter. With modern technology the way it was, a month early didn't sound so bad. But out in the middle of the desert and even in Kenner City, they didn't have the prenatal equipment necessary to care for a premature infant should it have complications.

Ben's hand squeezed hers reassuringly. As much as she hated to admit it, she needed him. She'd become her mother, relying on a man for emotional support.

After all that had happened, would Ben keep his promise? Would he stay until death parted them—preferably in old age? Really old age.

Ben lifted her hand to his lips and stared down into her eyes, mouthing over the noise of the helicopter engine, "I love you."

Though she couldn't actually hear the words, she could see the warmth in his eyes and feel the strength behind his touch. Ben wasn't her father. Ben was a man of his word. Hadn't he proven it by coming back to her as soon as he could escape Nicky Wayne's prison? Hadn't he proven it by keeping the secret of his assignment to the Del Gardo case? He hadn't even told his tight circle of friends, he was so committed to doing the right thing and staying in his undercover persona until the case was closed.

Warmth filled her chest and spread throughout her body. The spasms attacking her uterus subsided, the pains coming less often.

By the time they landed and the emergency staff wheeled her into the E.R., she was relaxed enough to smile.

Ben loved her and she wouldn't be having the baby until she was good and ready to come out.

"Feeling better?" Ben asked, as he stood beside her bed in the E.R.

"You have no idea."

Epilogue

"Here, let me hold her for a while." Ben slipped a hand under Lola's head and he carefully lifted her from Ava's arms. Only a month old, she was still an enigma to him. How could something so small and helpless scream loud enough to wake the dead in the middle of the night? With a smile, he stared down at his baby daughter, whose green eyes and cap of wavy red curls looked so much like her mother's. He leaned over his little girl and kissed her mother.

Ava smiled, her pale skin rosy with health and happiness. Behind her, tall aspens glowed a brilliant yellow and oaks dropped their red and orange foliage after a warm Indian summer.

Local millionaire Griffin Vaughn and his wife, Sophie, couldn't have picked a better day for the outdoor barbecue. It wouldn't be long before the first snows fell and everyone would retreat indoors for the winter except those who indulged in snowboarding and skiing.

Ben glanced around at the crowd of people gathered together, his heart swelling with his own good fortune. With the conversations on the digital recorder and the additional evidence he'd turned over to the FBI of the orders he'd gotten from Jerry Ortiz, his name had been cleared of all suspicion of working with Nicky Wayne's crime family. He had his beautiful wife Ava at his side and she'd given him his beautiful daughter, Lola, over a month ago. Life couldn't be better.

"Let me see her." Callie Ryan leaned over Lola and cooed to the baby. "She's just beautiful, the spitting image of her mother."

Ava smiled at her boss. "I hear you got good news."

Callie straightened and reached for her husband Tom's hand. "That's right. We're now the owners of the fifty million dollars my father left to me." She stumbled over the word *father* but smiled. "It sounds strange to me to call Vincent Del Gardo my father. I never really got to know him." She sighed. "What's this I hear about you reuniting with your own father?"

Ava glanced up at Ben and he nodded at her. He knew how hard it was for Ava to talk about her father. After hating him all these years for deserting her family, she'd finally made the call with the number her sister had given her.

"That's right. I met with him a week ago." She blinked back the ready tears that plagued her when she spoke of that meeting. "Come to find out, he didn't want to stay away, but he had more than an addiction to gambling. He was also addicted to drugs and he didn't want to bring us down with his bad habits."

Callie's brows drew together. "Then it was a good thing he left you guys. Kind of like my father. He didn't want me involved in his world of organized crime."

Ben stared down at Lola. "That doesn't mean either one of them didn't miss their daughters. I couldn't imagine leaving mine for anything but a life-or-death reason."

"That's what my father told me." Ava hooked her arm through Ben's and tucked Lola's blanket around her. "He watched us grow up from a distance and regrets missing out on knowing us and being a part of our family."

"Is he still addicted to gambling and drugs?" Tom asked, his arm going around Callie's waist.

"He'll never get over the gambling, but he's been drug-free for ten years and he's learned to control his urge to gamble, even if he can never be totally free of it." Ava smiled up at Ben. "I'm just glad I had the opportunity to clear the air and get past all the anger and bitterness I'd been carrying around since I was a child."

Callie nodded. "I wish I'd had that opportunity. Before I knew he was my father, Del Gardo was gone."

"But he must have loved you. He left you a fat bank-roll." Dylan Acevedo joined the conversation. His wife, Aspen, was at his side, carrying their squirming baby boy, Jack.

Callie shrugged. "The FBI couldn't link the money to any particular crime so they ended up giving it to me. The government will take a chunk of it in taxes. But the rest is ours."

"We're going to donate most of it to charities," Tom said.

"Some of it will go to the local schools, both on and off the reservation." Callie smiled. "They could use new buildings and computers."

"They've set up a sizable donation to go to the Sisters of Mercy Hospital where I was treated when I had amnesia." Aspen laid a loud kiss on Jack's chubby cheek. "Isn't that right, Jack?"

The baby giggled and batted at her with his chubby fist.

"This will make the team happy," Callie said with a proud tilt of her chin. "I've set aside money to upgrade the equipment at the lab to help us solve future cases."

Ava clapped her hands. "That's great. That makes me want to get back to work sooner."

"You still have a month on maternity leave, don't you?" Callie asked. "If I were you, I'd enjoy every minute of it with that beautiful baby of yours."

"Oh, I will." Ava hugged Ben close and stared down at her child. "She's been great."

"Sleeping all night already?" Aspen asked.

"Ha!" Ben snorted. "Not our Lola. I think she's got her nights and days mixed up."

Ava slapped at his arm, playfully. "She's nursing, silly. You're just jealous you can't do the feeding."

He was a little, but he stayed up to watch Ava as she breast-fed their baby. The look of love in her eyes for Lola and for him made Ben so glad they were still together he could burst.

"Did you hear that Nicky's trial date has moved up to next month?" Dylan asked.

Ben's warm feelings cooled. "About time. The man needs to spend the rest of his days behind bars."

"With all the charges he's up on, surely something will stick to him long enough to make that last. Let's see," Tom ticked off on his fingers, "kidnapping of a federal agent, orchestrating the hit on Vincent Del Gardo and attempted murder of both Ava and Ben. He should get nice long prison terms."

"Yeah, it's almost too bad he even survived to stand trial, as much heartache as he caused here in Kenner City," Dylan added.

"What heartache are we discussing?" Griffin Vaughn joined the expanding group. "I hope we're not talking shop. This barbecue is to celebrate."

"Hi, Griffin. Thanks for having us all out to your place.

It's been a long time since we've had a get-together with everyone," Ben said. "We should do this more often."

"I'm just glad the weather cooperated." Sophie joined her husband and smiled at the people standing around on the concrete patio. "Luke's having the time of his life, playing with all the babies."

"How's Luke doing?" Ava asked.

"He's doing great. I'm sure glad Danielle and Colin Forester decided to patch things up and stay in Kenner City. Luke's been seeing Danielle for the past few months. His nightmares from the kidnapping are gone and he's back to being a normal little boy."

"That's great." Ava's gaze followed the little boy across the yard. "Luke deserves to be happy."

Sophie grinned up at Vaughn. "He's even happier he gets to be a big brother."

Ava's brows rose. "Are you pregnant?"

"Yes, she is." Vaughn's arm circled her and he patted her flat belly. "The baby is due next spring."

Ben stuck out his hand. "Congratulations."

During a loud round of well-wishing and more congratulations, Emma and Miguel Acevedo joined them.

Miguel nudged Dylan. "What's the big news, brother?"

"Griffin and Sophie are expecting a baby." Dylan clapped a hand on his twin brother's shoulders. "What's up with you guys hiding out in the bushes? Can't you wait to get home to make out? Marriage seems to agree with you two."

Emma blushed. "I didn't know what I was missing."

"So what do you see in the future for this big crazy group of crime fighters?" Dylan asked.

Known for her psychic visions, Emma was still a little shy about offering her input. "I don't know."

"Oh, please, tell us," Ava urged.

With a sigh, Emma closed her eyes and silence reigned. After a few moments, a smile curled her lips and she opened her eyes again. "I see lots of children—*our* children—playing together."

The group laughed as one.

"I don't think you have to be psychic to come to that conclusion," Miguel said. "What with baby Lola and Jack, Sophie expecting and Bree due to pop any minute."

Everyone turned toward a miserably pregnant Bree Martinez, leaning back in a lounge chair, her attentive husband, Patrick, hovering beside her.

Bree, her hair pulled back in the usual thick black ponytail grinned. "Right, pick on the pregnant lady." She winced and pressed a hand to her belly. "I'm just as ready to pop as Patrick is ready to get this over with."

"Yeah, you *think* you're ready." Ben chuckled. "Nothing prepares you for a baby. You just have to jump in with both feet."

"Thanks, I'll remember that advice." Patrick rubbed Bree's back. "In the meantime, I'd just like to see Bree a bit more comfortable."

She grimaced. "My back hurts so much today, I think I'll have to head home early."

"Could it wait for a few minutes?" Tom asked. Then he raised his voice to be heard over all the other conversations around him. "Now that all of us are together, I'd like to say a few words."

Everyone gathered closer.

"First off, thanks to Griffin and Sophie for throwing this barbecue on perhaps the last day of good weather before the cold sets in. Great timing. For those who haven't heard, Griffin, Sophie and their son Luke expect to add to their family in late spring. Congratulations!"

The crowd clapped and added their well-wishes to Tom's.

Ben smiled down at Lola and pulled Ava closer to him. Nothing could be better than a baby in the house. He'd never thought so until Lola had arrived and charmed her way into his heart from day one.

"Now, Ethan asked for a moment of your time." Tom turned to Ethan. "Ethan?"

Ethan cleared his throat and stepped forward. "Joanna got her promotion at the FBI."

Ben turned toward Joanna, sitting in a deck chair on the edge of the group and clapped politely. Joanna was a crack behavioral scientist with the FBI in Kenner City, a great addition to the crime investigation unit. He'd hate to see her transferred out. "Does this mean you'll be leaving us?"

Joanna smiled at Ethan while answering Ben's question. "No. I've asked the Bureau to allow me to base out of Kenner City."

Ethan beamed. "Which brings me to…" He dropped to one knee in front of her and held out a jeweler's ring box with a simple, yet beautiful, marquise diamond ring nestled against the black velvet. "Joanna Rhodes, will you marry me?"

Her eyes widened and she reached out for the ring in the box. "It's beautiful."

Ethan laughed. "That's not an answer. Could you focus on the question, please?"

She smiled and threw her arms around his neck. "Yes! Of course I'll marry you."

Ben glanced across at Ava, noting the glaze of tears in her eyes. The happiness in the air was overwhelming with only one dark cloud on the recent events.

After a round of congratulations, the noise died down

and Ben stepped forward, lifting his glass. "I'd like to take a moment to reflect on our fallen partner, FBI Special Agent Julie Grainger."

Tom and Dylan stepped forward with Ben.

"If not for her foresight to mail us the three medals, circumstances might not have turned out the way they did," Tom said.

Dylan nodded. "If you think about it, she knew us better than we knew ourselves."

"How's that?" Ava asked.

"Each of the medals was of saints with a very specific meaning." Dylan glanced at Tom. "Tom received the St. Christopher, patron saint of travelers, because he could never settle in one place for very long."

Callie hooked her arm through Tom's. "Yeah, the medal brought him good luck."

Tom kissed the tip of her nose. "And enough common sense to recognize a good deal when I stumbled into it. My wandering days are over."

"Glad to hear it." Callie kissed his lips and snuggled into his arms.

"As I was saying before these two got all mushy," Dylan continued, "the medals all meant something. Ben got the St. Joan of Arc, patron saint of prisoners. And what happened to him? He was imprisoned by Nicky Wayne for two months."

"Not just by Nicky but by the bogus assignment Jerry Ortiz had me on. I couldn't tell anyone what I was working on and it almost cost me my friends and my family." Ben's arm tightened around Ava and he stared down at the beautiful baby girl in his arms.

Tom clapped a hand on Dylan's back. "And Dylan, here, got the medal with Rafael the Archangel on it. He's the patron saint against nightmares. I guess because he's such a nightmare, wouldn't you say, Aspen?"

Aspen shifted Jack to her other hip and slid in beside Dylan, smiling up at him. "No, he's a dream come true."

Ava laughed. "Right answer."

"But Dylan was still suffering nightmares from the serial killer case he'd worked before coming to Kenner City. Are the nightmares gone, Dylan?" Tom asked.

Dylan nodded. "Totally."

Ben shook his head slowly. "Julie knew us. It's a tragedy she isn't here to witness the good that's come of her investigation."

Tom raised his glass of wine. "To a true friend and excellent agent, Julie Grainger."

Everyone raised their glasses. "To Julie." Silence followed, and a few tears slipped down cheeks.

Callie stepped forward, brushing a tear from her cheek. "Enough sadness! Julie wouldn't have wanted everyone frowning on a beautiful day of celebration." She lifted her glass high. "I'd like to propose a toast to the Kenner County Crime Unit and its extended family, including our partners in the FBI and the sheriff's department. Let's drink to surviving our first big case and coming out all in one piece—mostly."

Glasses raised and clinked one against the other as everyone congratulated each other on bringing down Nicky Wayne and his organized crime family.

"Excuse me." Bree Martinez's voice rose above the chatter. "Could I get a little help here?"

The entire gathering turned toward her.

"What's wrong?" Callie hurried over to the woman on the lounge chair, who was flanked by her husband, Patrick.

"I need a little help getting up. I have to get to the hospital."

"Is it time?" Ava asked.

"My water broke." Bree smiled then grimaced as a contraction seized her. "Yup, I think it's time."

Ben handed Lola to Ava and cleared a path through the throng. Patrick and Callie eased Bree from her chair and helped her make her way across the patio and through the house to Patrick's car.

Once the couple drove away, Ben collected his family and headed for his own car. As he tucked Lola into her car seat, he kissed her smooth baby cheek and counted his blessings. Then he straightened and took Ava in his arms. "I'm the luckiest man alive."

She leaned into him, standing on her toes to press a kiss to his lips. "Yes, you are."

INTRIGUE...

MILLS & BOON®
HAVE JOINED FORCES WITH THE LEANDER TRUST AND LEANDER CLUB TO HELP TO DEVELOP TOMORROW'S CHAMPIONS

We have produced a stunning calendar for 2011 featuring a host of Olympic and World Champions (as they've never been seen before!). Leander Club is recognised the world over for its extraordinary rowing achievements and is committed to developing its squad of athletes to help underpin future British success at World and Olympic level.

'All my rowing development has come through the support and back-up from Leander. The Club has taken me from a club rower to an Olympic Silver Medallist. Leander has been the driving force behind my progress'

RIC EGINGTON – Captain, Leander Club Olympic Silver, Beijing, 2009 World Champion.

Please send me [ ] calendar(s) @ £8.99 each plus £3.00 P&P (FREE postage and packing on orders of 3 or more calendars despatching to the same address).

I enclose a cheque for £ _____ made payable to Harlequin Mills & Boon Limited.

Name ....

Address ....

.... Post code ....

Email ....

Send this whole page and cheque to:
Leander Calendar Offer
Harlequin Mills & Boon Limited
Eton House, 18-24 Paradise Road, Richmond TW9 1SR

All proceeds from the sale of the 2011 Leander Fundraising Calendar will go towards the Leander Trust (Registered Charity No: 284631) – and help in supporting aspiring athletes to train to their full potential.

2 FREE BOOKS
AND A SURPRISE GIFT

We would like to take this opportunity to thank you for reading this Mills & Boon® book by offering you the chance to take TWO more specially selected books from the Intrigue series absolutely FREE! We're also making this offer to introduce you to the benefits of the Mills & Boon® Book Club™—

- **FREE home delivery**
- **FREE gifts and competitions**
- **FREE monthly Newsletter**
- **Exclusive Mills & Boon Book Club offers**
- **Books available before they're in the shops**

Accepting these FREE books and gift places you under no obligation to buy, you may cancel at any time, even after receiving your free books. Simply complete your details below and return the entire page to the address below. You don't even need a stamp!

YES Please send me 2 free Intrigue books and a surprise gift. I understand that unless you hear from me, I will receive 5 superb new stories every month, including two 2-in-1 books priced at £5.30 each and a single book priced at £3.30, postage and packing free. I am under no obligation to purchase any books and may cancel my subscription at any time. The free books and gift will be mine to keep in any case.

Ms/Mrs/Miss/Mr _____ Initials _____

Surname _____

Address _____

_____ Postcode _____

E-mail _____

Send this whole page to: Mills & Boon Book Club, Free Book Offer, FREEPOST NAT 10298, Richmond, TW9 1BR